The Swiss Family Robinson; or Adventures in a Desert Island

Johann David Wyss

About the Author

Johann David Wyss

Johann David Wyss German pronunciation: [ˈjoːhan ˈdaːfɪt ˈviːs] (May 28, 1743 in Berne - January 11, 1818 in Berne) is a Swiss author, best remembered for his book The Swiss Family Robinson (Der schweizerische Robinson) (1812). It is said that he was inspired by Daniel Defoe's Robinson Crusoe, but wanted to write a story from which his own children would learn, as the father in the story taught important lessons to his children. The Swiss Family Robinson was first published in 1812 and translated into English two years later. It has since become one of the most popular books of all time. The book was edited by his son, Johann Rudolf Wyss, a scholar who wrote the Swiss national anthem. Another son, Johann Emmanuel Wyss, illustrated the book. Unlike his son, Johann David Wyss lived up to the age of 74, dying in 1818. Wyss has been described as an author whose style was "firmly Christian and moral in tone"s.

The Swiss Family Robinson; or Adventures in a Desert Island

The tempest had raged for six days, and on the seventh seemed to increase. The ship had been so far driven from its course, that no one on board knew where we were. Every one was exhausted with fatigue and watching. The shattered vessel began to leak in many places, the oaths of the sailors were changed to prayers, and each thought only how to save his own life. "Children," said I, to my terrified boys, who were clinging round me, "God can save us if he will. To him nothing is impossible; but if he thinks it good to call us to him, let us not murmur; we shall not be separated." My excellent wife dried her tears, and from that moment became more tranquil. We knelt down to pray for the help of our Heavenly Father; and the fervour and emotion of my innocent boys proved to me that even children can pray, and find in prayer consolation and peace.

We rose from our knees strengthened to bear the afflictions that hung over us. Suddenly we heard amid the roaring of the waves the cry of "Land! land!" At that moment the ship [pg 002] struck on a rock; the concussion threw us down. We heard a loud cracking, as if the vessel was parting asunder; we felt that we were aground, and heard the captain cry, in a tone of despair, "We are lost! Launch the boats!"

These words were a dagger to my heart, and the lamentations of my children were louder than ever. I then recollected myself, and said, "Courage, my darlings, we are still, above water, and the land is near. God helps those who trust in him. Remain here, and I will endeavour to save us."

I went on deck, and was instantly thrown down, and wet through by a huge sea; a second followed. I struggled boldly with the waves, and succeeded in keeping myself up, when I saw, with terror, the extent of our wretchedness. The shattered vessel was almost in two; the crew had crowded into the boats, and the last sailor was cutting the rope. I cried out, and prayed them to take us with them; but my voice was drowned in the roar of the tempest, nor could they have returned for us through waves that ran mountains high. All hope from their assistance was lost; but I was consoled by observing that the water did not enter the ship above a certain height. The stern, under which lay the cabin which contained all that was dear to me on earth, was immovably fixed between two rocks. At the same time I observed, towards the south, traces of land, which, though wild and barren, was now the haven of my almost expiring hopes; no longer being able to depend on any human aid. I returned to my family, and endeavoured to appear calm. "Take courage," cried I, "there is yet hope for us; the vessel, in striking between the [pg 003] rocks, is fixed in a position which protects our cabin above the water, and if the wind should settle to-morrow, we may possibly reach the land."

This assurance calmed my children, and as usual, they depended on all I told them; they rejoiced that the heaving of the vessel had ceased, as, while it lasted, they were continually thrown against each other. My wife, more accustomed to read my countenance, discovered my uneasiness; and by a sign, I explained to her that I had lost all hope. I felt great consolation in seeing that she supported our misfortune with truly Christian resignation.

"Let us take some food," said she; "with the body, the mind is strengthened; this must be a night of trial."

Night came, and the tempest continued its fury; tearing away the planks from the devoted vessel with a fearful crashing. It appeared absolutely impossible that the boats could have out-lived the storm.

My wife had prepared some refreshment, of which the children partook with an appetite that we could not feel. The three younger ones retired to their beds, and soon slept soundly. Fritz, the eldest, watched with me. "I have been considering," said he, "how we could save ourselves. If we only had some cork jackets, or bladders, for mamma and my brothers, you and I don't need them, we could then swim to land."

"A good thought," said I, "I will try during the night to contrive some expedient to secure our safety." We found some small empty barrels in the cabin, which we tied two together with our handkerchiefs, leaving a space between for each [pg 004] child; and fastened this new swimming apparatus under their arms. My wife prepared the same for herself. We then collected some knives, string, tinder-box, and such little necessaries as we could put in our pockets; thus, in case the vessel should fall to pieces during the night, we hoped we might be enabled to reach land.

At length Fritz, overcome with fatigue, lay down and slept with his brothers. My wife and I, too anxious to rest, spent that dreadful night in prayer, and in arranging various plans. How gladly we welcomed the light of day, shining through an opening. The wind was subsiding, the sky serene, and I watched the sun rise with renewed hope. I called my wife and children on deck. The younger ones were surprised to find we were alone. They inquired what had become of the sailors, and how we should manage the ship alone.

"Children," said I, "one more powerful than man has protected us till now, and will still extend a saving arm to us, if we do not give way to complaint and despair. Let all hands set to work. Remember that excellent maxim, God helps those who help themselves. Let us all consider what is best to do now."

"Let us leap into the sea," cried Fritz, "and swim to the shore."

"Very well for you," replied Ernest, "who can swim; but we should be all drowned. Would it not be better to construct a raft and go all together?"

"That might do," added I, "if we were strong enough for such a work, and if a raft was not always so dangerous a conveyance. But away, [pg 005] boys, look about you, and seek for anything that may be useful to us."

We all dispersed to different parts of the vessel. For my own part I went to the provision-room, to look after the casks of water and other necessaries of life; my wife visited the live stock and fed them, for they were almost famished; Fritz sought for arms and ammunition; Ernest for the carpenter's tools. Jack had opened the captain's cabin, and was immediately thrown down by two large dogs, who leaped on him so roughly that he cried out as if they were going to devour him. However, hunger had rendered them so docile that they licked his hands, and he soon recovered his feet, seized the largest by the ears, and mounting his back, gravely rode up to me as I was coming from the hold. I could not help laughing; I applauded his courage; but recommended him always to be prudent with animals of that kind, who are often dangerous when hungry.

My little troop began to assemble. Fritz had found two fowling-pieces, some bags of powder and shot, and some balls, in horn flasks. Ernest was loaded with an axe and hammer, a pair of pincers, a large pair of scissors, and an auger showed itself half out of his pocket.

Francis had a large box under his arm, from which he eagerly produced what he called little pointed hooks. His brothers laughed at his prize. "Silence," said I, "the youngest has made the most valuable addition to our stores. These are fish-hooks, and may be more useful for the preservation of our lives than anything the ship contains. However, Fritz and Ernest have not done amiss."

"For my part," said my wife, "I only contribute good news; I have found a cow, an ass, two goats, six sheep, and a sow with young. I have fed them, and hope we may preserve them."

"Very well," said I to my little workmen, "I am satisfied with all but Master Jack, who, instead of anything useful, has contributed two great eaters, who will do us more harm than good."

"They can help us to hunt when we get to land," said Jack.

"Yes," replied I, "but can you devise any means of our getting there?"

"It does not seem at all difficult," said the spirited little fellow; "put us each into a great tub, and let us float to shore. I remember sailing capitally that way on godpapa's great pond at S--."

"A very good idea, Jack; good counsel may sometimes be given even by a child. Be quick, boys, give me the saw and auger, with some nails, we will see what we can do." I remembered seeing some empty casks in the hold. We went down and found them floating. This gave us less difficulty in getting them upon the lower deck, which was but just above the water. They were of strong wood, bound with

7

iron hoops, and exactly suited my purpose; my sons and I therefore began to saw them through the middle. After long labour, we had eight tubs all the same height. We refreshed ourselves with wine and biscuit, which we had found in some of the casks. I then contemplated with delight my little squadron of boats ranged in a line; and was surprised that my wife still continued depressed. She looked mournfully on them. "I can never venture in one of these tubs," said she.

"Wait a little, till my work is finished," replied I, "and you will see it is more to be depended on than this broken vessel."

I sought out a long flexible plank, and arranged eight tubs on it, close to each other, leaving a piece at each end to form a curve upwards, like the keel of a vessel. We then nailed them firmly to the plank, and to each other. We nailed a plank at each side, of the same length as the first, and succeeded in producing a sort of boat, divided into eight compartments, in which it did not appear difficult to make a short voyage, over a calm sea.

But, unluckily, our wonderful vessel proved so heavy, that our united efforts could not move it an inch. I sent Fritz to bring me the jack-screw, and, in the mean time, sawed a thick round pole into pieces; then raising the fore-part of our work by means of the powerful machine, Fritz placed one of these rollers under it.

Ernest was very anxious to know how this small machine could accomplish more than our united strength. I explained to him, as well as I could, the power of the lever of Archimedes, with which he had declared he could move the world, if he had but a point to rest it on; and I promised my son to take the machine to pieces when we were on shore, and explain the mode of operation. I then told them that God, to compensate for the weakness of man, had bestowed on him reason, invention, and skill in workmanship. The result of these had produced a science which, under the name of Mechanics, taught us to increase and extend our limited powers incredibly by the aid of instruments.

Jack remarked that the jack-screw worked very slowly.

[pg 008]
"Better slowly, than not at all," said I. "It is a principle in mechanics, that what is gained in time is lost in power. The jack is not meant to work rapidly, but to raise heavy weights; and the heavier the weight, the slower the operation. But, can you tell me how we can make up for this slowness?"

"Oh, by turning the handle quicker, to be sure!"

"Quite wrong; that would not aid us at all. Patience and Reason are the two fairies, by whose potent help I hope to get our boat afloat."

I quickly proceeded to tie a strong cord to the after-part of it, and the other end to a beam in the ship, which was still firm, leaving it long enough for security; then introducing two more rollers underneath, and working with the jack, we succeeded in launching our bark, which passed into the water with such velocity, that but for our rope it would have gone out to sea. Unfortunately, it leaned so much on one side, that none of the boys would venture into it. I was in despair, when I suddenly remembered it only wanted ballast to keep it in equilibrium. I hastily threw in anything I got hold of that was heavy, and soon had my boat level, and ready for occupation. They now contended who should enter first; but I stopped them, reflecting that these restless children might easily capsize our vessel. I remembered that savage nations made use of an out-rigger, to prevent their canoe oversetting, and this I determined to add to my work. I fixed two portions of a topsail-yard, one over the prow, the other across the stern, in such a manner that they should not be in the way in [pg 009] pushing off our boat from the wreck. I forced the end of each yard into the bunghole of an empty brandy-cask, to keep them steady during our progress.

It was now necessary to clear the way for our departure. I got into the first tub, and managed to get the boat into the cleft in the ship's side, by way of a haven; I then returned, and, with the axe and saw, cut away right and left all that could obstruct our passage. Then we secured some oars, to be ready for our voyage next day.

The day had passed in toil, and we were compelled to spend another night on the wreck, though we knew it might not remain till morning. We took a regular meal, for during the day we had scarcely had time to snatch a morsel of bread and a glass of wine. More composed than on the preceding night, we retired to rest. I took the precaution to fasten the swimming apparatus across the shoulders of my three younger children and my wife, for fear another storm might destroy the vessel, and cast us into the sea. I also advised my wife to put on a sailor's dress, as more convenient for her expected toils and trials. She reluctantly consented, and, after a short absence, appeared in the dress of a youth who had served as a volunteer in the vessel. She felt very timid and awkward in her new dress; but I showed her the advantage of the change, and, at last, she was reconciled, and joined in the laughter of the children at her strange disguise. She then got into her hammock, and we enjoyed a pleasant sleep, to prepare us for new labours.

[pg 010]

CHAPTER II.

At break of day we were awake and ready, and after morning prayer, I addressed my children thus: "We are now, my dear boys, with the help of God, about to attempt our deliverance. Before we go, provide our poor animals with food for some days: we cannot take them with us, but if our voyage succeed, we may return for them. Are you ready? Collect what you wish to carry away, but only things absolutely necessary for our actual wants." I planned that our first cargo should consist of a barrel of powder, three fowling-pieces, three muskets, two pair of pocket pistols, and one pair larger, ball, shot, and lead as much as we could carry, with a bullet-mould; and I wished each of my sons, as well as their mother, should have a complete game-bag, of which there were several in the officers' cabins. We then set apart a box of portable soup, another of biscuit, an iron pot, a fishing-rod, a chest of nails, and one of carpenter's tools, also some sailcloth to make a tent. In fact my boys collected so many things, we were compelled to leave some behind, though I exchanged all the useless ballast for necessaries.

When all was ready, we implored the blessing of God on our undertaking, and prepared to embark in our tubs. At this moment the cocks crowed a sort of reproachful farewell to us; we had forgotten them; I immediately proposed to take our poultry with us, geese, ducks, fowls and pigeons, for, as I observed to my wife, if we could not feed them, they would, at any rate, feed us. [pg 011] We placed our ten hens and two cocks in a covered tub; the rest we set at liberty, hoping the geese and ducks might reach the shore by water, and the pigeons by flight.

We waited a little for my wife, who came loaded with a large bag, which she threw into the tub that contained her youngest son. I concluded it was intended to steady him, or for a seat, and made no observation on it. Here follows the order of our embarkation. In the first division, sat the tender mother, the faithful and pious wife. In the second, our amiable little Francis, six years old, and of a sweet disposition.

In the third, Fritz, our eldest, fourteen or fifteen years old, a curly-headed, clever, intelligent and lively youth.

In the fourth, the powder-cask, with the fowls and the sailcloth.

Our provisions filled the fifth.

In the sixth, our heedless Jack, ten years old, enterprising, bold, and useful.

In the seventh, Ernest, twelve years of age, well-informed and rational, but somewhat selfish and indolent. In the eighth, myself, an anxious father, charged with the important duty of guiding the vessel to save my dear family. Each of us had some useful tools beside us; each held an oar, and had a swimming apparatus at hand, in case we were unfortunately upset. The tide was rising when we left, which I considered might assist my weak endeavours. We turned our out-riggers length-ways, and thus passed from the cleft of the ship into the open sea. We rowed with all our might, to reach the blue land we saw at a distance, but for some time in vain, as the boat kept [pg 012] turning round, and made no progress. At last I contrived to steer it, so that we went straight forward.

As soon as our dogs saw us depart, they leaped into the sea, and followed us; I could not let them get into the boat, for fear they should upset it. I was very sorry, for I hardly expected they would be able to swim to land; but by occasionally resting their forepaws on our out-riggers, they managed to keep up with us. Turk was an English dog, and Flora of a Danish breed.

We proceeded slowly, but safely. The nearer we approached the land, the more dreary and unpromising it appeared. The rocky coast seemed to announce to us nothing but famine and misery. The waves, gently rippling against the shore, were scattered over with barrels, bales, and chests from the wreck. Hoping to secure some good provisions, I called on Fritz for assistance; he held a cord, hammer, and nails, and we managed to seize two hogsheads in passing, and fastening them with cords to our vessel, drew them after us to the shore.

As we approached, the coast seemed to improve. The chain of rock was not entire, and Fritz's hawk eye made out some trees, which he declared were the cocoa-nut tree; Ernest was delighted at the prospect of eating these nuts, so much larger and better than any grown in Europe. I was regretting not having brought the large telescope from the captain's cabin, when Jack produced from his pocket a smaller one, which he offered me with no little pride.

This was a valuable acquisition, as I was now enabled to make the requisite observations, and [pg 013] direct my course. The coast before us had a wild and desert appearance,--it looked better towards the left; but I could not approach that part, for a current which drove us towards the rocky and barren shore. At length we saw, near the mouth of a rivulet, a little creek between the rocks, towards which our geese and ducks made, serving us for guides. This opening formed a little bay of smooth water, just deep enough for our boat. I cautiously entered it, and landed at a place where the coast was about the height of our tubs, and the water deep enough to let us approach. The shore spread inland, forming a gentle declivity of a triangular form, the point lost among the rocks, and the base to the sea.

All that were able leaped on shore in a moment. Even little Francis, who had been laid down in his tub, like a salted herring, tried to crawl out, but was compelled to wait for his mother's assistance. The dogs, who had preceded us in landing, welcomed us in a truly friendly manner, leaping playfully around us; the geese kept up a loud cackling, to which the yellow-billed ducks quacked a powerful bass. This, with the clacking of the liberated fowls, and the chattering of the boys, formed a perfect Babel; mingled with these, were the harsh cries of the penguins and flamingoes, which hovered over our heads, or sat on the points of the rocks. They were in immense numbers, and their notes almost deafened us, especially as they did not accord with the harmony of our civilized fowls. However I rejoiced to see these feathered creatures, already fancying them on my table, if we were obliged to remain in this desert region.

13

Our first care, when we stepped in safety on [pg 014] land, was to kneel down and thank God, to whom we owed our lives; and to resign ourselves wholly to his Fatherly kindness.

We then began to unload our vessel. How rich we thought ourselves with the little we had saved! We sought a convenient place for our tent, under the shade of the rocks. We then inserted a pole into a fissure in the rock; this, resting firmly on another pole fixed in the ground, formed the frame of the tent. The sailcloth was then stretched over it, and fastened down at proper distances, by pegs, to which, for greater security, we added some boxes of provision; we fixed some hooks to the canvas at the opening in front, that we might close the entrance during the night. I sent my sons to seek some moss and withered grass, and spread it in the sun to dry, to form our beds; and while all, even little Francis, were busy with this,

I constructed a sort of cooking-place, at some distance from the tent, near the river which was to supply us with fresh water. It was merely a hearth of flat stones from the bed of the stream, fenced round with some thick branches. I kindled a cheerful fire with some dry twigs, put on the pot, filled with water and some squares of portable soup, and left my wife, with Francis for assistant, to prepare dinner. He took the portable soup for glue, and could not conceive how mamma could make soup, as we had no meat, and there were no butchers' shops here.

Fritz, in the mean time, had loaded our guns. He took one to the side of the river; Ernest declined accompanying him, as the rugged road was not to his taste; he preferred the sea-shore. Jack proceeded to a ridge of rocks on the left, which ran [pg 015] towards the sea, to get some muscles. I went to try and draw the two floating hogsheads on shore, but could not succeed, for our landing-place was too steep to get them up. Whilst I was vainly trying to find a more favourable place, I heard my dear Jack uttering most alarming cries. I seized my hatchet, and ran to his assistance. I found him up to the knees in a shallow pool, with a large lobster holding his leg in its sharp claws. It made off at my approach; but I was determined it should pay for the fright it had given me. Cautiously taking it up, I brought it out, followed by Jack, who, now very triumphant, wished to present it himself to his mother, after watching how I held it. But he had hardly got it into his hands, when it gave him such a violent blow on the cheek with its tail, that he let it fall, and began to cry again. I could not help laughing at him, and, in his rage, he seized a stone, and put an end to his adversary. I was grieved at this, and recommended him never to act in a moment of anger, showing him that he was unjust in being so revengeful; for, if he had been bitten by the lobster, it was plain he would have eaten his foe if he had conquered him. Jack promised to be more discreet and merciful in future, and obtained leave to bear the prize to his mother.

"Mamma," said he, proudly, "a lobster! A lobster, Ernest! Where is Fritz! Take care it does not bite you, Francis!" They all crowded round in astonishment. "Yes," added he, triumphantly, "here is the impertinent claw that seized me; but I repaid the knave,"

"You are a boaster," said I. "You would have got indifferently on with the lobster, if I had not [pg 016] come up; and have you forgotten the slap on the cheek which compelled you to release him? Besides, he only defended himself with his natural arms; but you had to take a great stone. You have no reason to be proud, Jack."

Ernest wished to have the lobster added to the soup to improve it; but his mother, with a spirit of economy, reserved it for another day. I then walked to the spot where Jack's lobster was caught, and, finding it favourable for my purpose, drew my two hogsheads on shore there, and secured them by turning them on end.

On returning, I congratulated Jack on being the first who had been successful in foraging. Ernest remarked, that he had seen some oysters attached to a rock, but

15

could not get at them without wetting his feet, which he did not like.

"Indeed, my delicate gentleman!" said I, laughing, "I must trouble you to return and procure us some. We must all unite in working for the public good, regardless of wet feet. The sun will soon dry us."

"I might as well bring some salt at the same time," said he; "I saw plenty in the fissures of the rock, left by the sea, I should think, papa?"

"Doubtless, Mr. Reasoner," replied I; "where else could it have come from? the fact was so obvious, that you had better have brought a bagful, than delayed to reflect about it. But if you wish to escape insipid soup, be quick and procure some."

He went, and returned with some salt, so mixed with sand and earth, that I should have thrown it away as useless; but my wife dissolved it in fresh water, and, filtering it through a piece of canvas, managed to flavour our soup with it.

[pg 017]
Jack asked why we could not have used sea-water; and I explained to him that the bitter and nauseous taste of sea-water would have spoiled our dinner. My wife stirred the soup with a little stick, and, tasting it, pronounced it very good, but added, "We must wait for Fritz. And how shall we eat our soup without plates or spoons? We cannot possibly raise this large boiling pot to our heads, and drink out of it."

It was too true. We gazed stupified at our pot, and, at last, all burst into laughter at our destitution, and our folly in forgetting such useful necessaries.

"If we only had cocoa-nuts," said Ernest, "we might split them, and make basins and spoons."

"If!" replied I--"but we have none! We might as well wish for a dozen handsome silver spoons at once, if wishes were of any use."

"But," observed he, "we can use oyster-shells."

"A useful thought, Ernest; go directly and get the oysters; and, remember, gentlemen, no complaints, though the spoons are without handles, and you should dip your fingers into the bowl."

Off ran Jack, and was mid-leg in the water before Ernest got to him. He tore down the oysters, and threw them to his idle brother, who filled his handkerchief, taking care to put a large one into his pocket for his own use; and they returned with their spoil.

Fritz had not yet appeared, and his mother was becoming uneasy, when we heard him cheerfully hailing us at a distance. He soon came up, with a feigned air of disappointment, and his hands behind him; but Jack, who had glided round him, [pg 018] cried out, "A sucking pig! a sucking pig!" And he then, with, great pride and satisfaction, produced his booty, which I recognized, from the description of travellers, to be the agouti, common in these regions, a swift animal, which burrows in the earth, and lives on fruits and nuts; its flesh, something like that of the rabbit, has an unpleasant flavour to Europeans.

All were anxious to know the particulars of the chase; but I seriously reproved my

17

son for his little fiction, and warned him never to use the least deceit, even in jest. I then inquired where he had met with the agouti. He told me he had been on the other side of the river, "a very different place to this," continued he. "The shore lies low, and you can have no idea of the number of casks, chests, planks, and all sorts of things the sea has thrown up; shall we go and take possession of them? And to-morrow, father, we ought to make another trip to the vessel, to look after our cattle. We might, at least, bring away the cow. Our biscuit would not be so hard dipped in milk."

"And very much nicer," added the greedy Ernest.

"Then," continued Fritz, "beyond the river there is rich grass for pasturage, and a shady wood. Why should we remain in this barren wilderness?"

"Softly!" replied I, "there is a time for all things. To-morrow, and the day after to-morrow will have their work. But first tell me, did you see anything of our shipmates?"

"Not a trace of man, living or dead, on land or sea; but I saw an animal more like a hog than [pg 019] this, but with feet like a hare; it leaped among the grass, sometimes sitting upright, and rubbing its mouth with its forepaws; sometimes seeking for roots, and gnawing them like a squirrel. If I had not been afraid it would escape me, I would have tried to take it alive, it seemed so very tame."

As we were talking, Jack had been trying, with many grimaces, to force an oyster open with his knife. I laughed at his vain endeavours, and putting some on the fire, showed him them open of themselves. I had no taste for oysters myself; but as they are everywhere accounted a delicacy, I advised my sons to try them. They all at first declined the unattractive repast, except Jack, who, with great courage, closed his eyes, and desperately swallowed one as if it had been medicine. The rest followed his example, and then all agreed with me that oysters were not good. The shells were soon plunged into the pot to bring out some of the good soup; but scalding their fingers, it was who could cry out the loudest. Ernest took his large shell from his pocket, cautiously filled it with a good portion of soup, and set it down to cool, exulting in his own prudence. "You have been very thoughtful, my dear Ernest," said I; "but why are your thoughts always for yourself; so seldom for others? As a punishment for your egotism, that portion must be given to our faithful dogs. We can all dip our shells into the pot, the dogs cannot. Therefore, they shall have your soup, and you must wait, and eat as we do." My reproach struck his heart, and he placed his shell obediently on the ground, which the dogs emptied immediately. [pg 020] We were almost as hungry as they were, and were watching anxiously till the soup began to cool; when we perceived that the dogs were tearing and gnawing Fritz's agouti. The boys all cried out; Fritz was in a fury, took his gun, struck the dogs, called them names, threw stones at them, and would have killed them if I had not held him. He had actually bent his gun with striking them. As soon as he would listen to me, I reproached him seriously for his violence, and represented to him how much he had distressed us, and terrified his mother; that he had spoiled his gun, which might have been so useful to us, and had almost killed the poor animals, who might be more so. "Anger," said I, "leads to every crime. Remember Cain, who killed his brother in a fit of passion." "Oh, father!" said he, in a voice of terror; and, acknowledging his error, he asked pardon, and shed bitter tears.

Soon after our repast the sun set, and the fowls gathered round us, and picked up the scattered crumbs of biscuit. My wife then took out her mysterious bag, and drew from it some handfuls of grain to feed her flock. She showed me also many other seeds of useful vegetables. I praised her prudence, and begged her to be very economical, as these seeds were of great value, and we could bring from the vessel some spoiled biscuit for the fowls.

Our pigeons now flew among the rocks, the cocks and hens perched on the frame of the tent, and the geese and ducks chose to roost in a marsh, covered with bushes, near the sea. We prepared for our rest; we loaded all our arms, then offered up our prayers together, thanking [pg 021] God for his signal mercy to us, and commending ourselves to his care. When the last ray of light departed, we closed our tent, and lay down on our beds, close together. The children had remarked how suddenly the darkness came on, from which I concluded we were not far from the equator; for I explained to them, the more perpendicularly the rays of the sun fall, the less their refraction; and consequently night comes on suddenly when the sun is below the horizon.

Once more I looked out to see if all was quiet, then carefully closing the entrance, I lay down. Warm as the day had been, the night was so cold that we were obliged to crowd together for warmth. The children soon slept, and when I saw their mother in her first peaceful sleep, my own eyes closed, and our first night on the island passed comfortably.

CHAPTER III.

At break of day I was waked by the crowing of the cock. I summoned my wife to council, to consider on the business of the day. We agreed that our first duty was to seek for our shipmates, and to examine the country beyond the river before we came to any decisive resolution.

My wife saw we could not all go on this expedition, and courageously agreed to remain with her three youngest sons, while Fritz, as the eldest and boldest, should accompany me. I begged her to prepare breakfast immediately, which she warned me would be scanty, as no soup was provided. [pg 022] I asked for Jack's lobster; but it was not to be found. Whilst my wife made the fire, and put on the pot, I called the children, and asking Jack for the lobster, he brought it from a crevice in the rock, where he had hidden it from the dogs, he said, who did not despise anything eatable.

"I am glad to see you profit by the misfortunes of others," said I; "and now will you give up that large claw that caught your leg, and which I promised you, to Fritz, as a provision for his journey?" All were anxious to go on this journey, and leaped round me like little kids. But I told them we could not all go. They must remain with their mother, with Flora for a protector. Fritz and I would take Turk; with him and a loaded gun I thought we should inspire respect. I then ordered Fritz to tie up Flora, and get the guns ready.

Fritz blushed, and tried in vain to straighten his crooked gun. I let him go on for some time, and then allowed him to take another; for I saw he was penitent. The dogs, too, snarled, and would not let him approach them. He wept, and begged some biscuit from his mother, declaring he would give up his own breakfast to make his peace with the dogs. He fed them, caressed them, and seemed to ask pardon. The dog is always grateful; Flora soon licked his hands; Turk was more unrelenting, appearing to distrust him. "Give him a claw of the lobster," said Jack; "for I make you a present of the whole for your journey."

"Don't be uneasy about them," said Ernest, "they will certainly meet with cocoa-nuts, as [pg 023] Robinson did, very different food to your wretched lobster.

Think of an almond as big as my head, with a large cup full of rich milk."

"Pray, brother, bring me one, if you find any," said Francis.

We began our preparation; we each took a game-bag and a hatchet. I gave Fritz a pair of pistols in addition to his gun, equipped myself in the same way, and took care to carry biscuit and a flask of fresh water. The lobster proved so hard at breakfast, that the boys did not object to our carrying off the remainder; and, though the flesh is coarse, it is very nutritious.

I proposed before we departed, to have prayers, and my thoughtless Jack began to imitate the sound of church-bells--"Ding, dong! to prayers! to prayers! ding, dong!" I was really angry, and reproved him severely for jesting about sacred things. Then, kneeling down, I prayed God's blessing on our undertaking, and his pardon for us all, especially for him who had now so grievously sinned. Poor Jack came and kneeled by me, weeping and begging for forgiveness from me and from God. I embraced him, and enjoined him and his brothers to obey their mother. I then loaded the guns I left with them, and charged my wife to keep near the boat, their best refuge. We took leave of our friends with many tears, as we did not know what dangers might assail us in an unknown region. But the murmur of the river, which we were now approaching, drowned the sound of their sobs, and we bent our thoughts on our journey.

The bank of the river was so steep, that we could only reach the bed at one little opening, [pg 024] near the sea, where we had procured our water; but here the opposite side was guarded by a ridge of lofty perpendicular rocks. We were obliged to ascend the river to a place where it fell over some rocks, some fragments of which having fallen, made a sort of stepping-stones, which enabled us to cross with some hazard. We made our way, with difficulty, through the high grass, withered by the sun, directing our course towards the sea, in hopes of discovering some traces of the boats, or the crew. We had scarcely gone a hundred yards, when we heard a loud noise and rustling in the grass, which was as tall as we were. We imagined we were pursued by some wild beast, and I was gratified to observe the courage of Fritz, who, instead of running away, calmly turned round and presented his piece. What was our joy when we discovered that the formidable enemy was only our faithful Turk, whom we had forgotten in our distress, and our friends had doubtless dispatched him after us! I applauded my son's presence of mind; a rash act might have deprived us of this valuable friend.

We continued our way: the sea lay to our left; on our right, at a short distance, ran the chain of rocks, which were continued from our landing-place, in a line parallel to the sea; the summits clothed with verdure and various trees. Between the rocks and the sea, several little woods extended, even to the shore, to which we kept as close as possible, vainly looking out on land or sea for any trace of our crew. Fritz proposed to fire his gun, as a signal to them, if they should be near us; but I reminded him that this signal might bring the ravages round us, instead of our friends.

We rested in the shade, near a clear stream, and took
some refreshment.
"We rested in the shade, near a clear stream, and took some refreshment."

[pg 025]
He then inquired why we should search after those persons at all, who so unfeelingly abandoned us on the wreck.

"First," said I, "we must not return evil for evil. Besides, they may assist us, or be in need of our assistance. Above all, remember, they could save nothing but themselves. We have got many useful things which they have as much right to as we."

"But we might be saving the lives of our cattle," said he.

"We should do our duty better by saving the life of a man," answered I; "besides, our cattle have food for some days, and the sea is so calm there is no immediate danger."

We proceeded, and entering a little wood that extended to the sea, we rested in the shade, near a clear stream, and took some refreshment. We were surrounded by unknown birds, more remarkable for brilliant plumage than for the charm of their voice. Fritz thought he saw some monkeys among the leaves, and Turk began to be restless, smelling about, and barking very loud. Fritz was gazing up into the trees, when he fell over a large round substance, which he brought to me, observing that it might be a bird's nest. I thought it more likely to be a cocoa-nut. The fibrous covering had reminded him of the description he had read of the nests of certain birds; but, on breaking the shell, we found it was indeed a cocoa-nut, but quite decayed and uneatable.

Fritz was astonished; where was the sweet milk that Ernest had talked of?

I told him the milk was only in the half-ripe nuts; that it thickened and hardened as the [pg 026] nut ripened, becoming a kernel. This nut had perished from remaining above ground. If it had been in the earth, it would have vegetated, and burst the shell. I advised my son to try if he could not find a perfect nut.

After some search, we found one, and sat down to eat it, keeping our own provision for dinner. The nut was somewhat rancid; but we enjoyed it, and then continued our journey. We were some time before we got through the wood, being frequently obliged to clear a road for ourselves, through the entangled brushwood, with our hatchets. At last we entered the open plain again, and had a clear view before us. The forest still extended about a stone's throw to our right, and Fritz, who was always on the look-out for discoveries, observed a remarkable tree, here and there, which he approached to examine; and he soon called me to see this wonderful tree, with wens growing on the trunk.

On coming up, I was overjoyed to find this tree, of which there were a great number, was the gourd-tree, which bears fruit on the trunk. Fritz asked if these were sponges. I told him to bring me one, and I would explain the mystery.

"There is one," said he, "very like a pumpkin, only harder outside."

"Of this shell," said I, "we can make plates, dishes, basins, and flasks. We call it the gourd-tree."

Fritz leaped for joy. "Now my dear mother will be able to serve her soup properly." I asked him if he knew why the tree bore the fruit on its trunk, or on the thick branches only. He immediately replied, that the smaller branches [pg 027] would not bear the weight of the fruit. He asked me if this fruit was eatable. "Harmless, I believe," said I; "but by no means delicate. Its great value to savage nations consists in the shell, which they use to contain their food, and drink, and even cook in it." Fritz could not comprehend how they could cook in the shell without burning it. I told him the shell was not placed on the fire; but, being filled with cold water, and the fish or meat placed in it, red-hot stones are, by degrees, introduced into the water, till it attains sufficient heat to cook the food, without injuring the vessel. We then set about making our dishes and plates. I showed Fritz a better plan of dividing the gourd than with a knife. I tied a string tightly round the nut, struck it with the handle of my knife till an incision was made, then tightened it till the nut was separated into two equally-sized bowls. Fritz had spoiled his gourd by cutting it irregularly with his knife. I advised him to try and make spoons of it, as it would not do for basins now. I told him I had learnt my plan from books of travels. It is the practice of the savages, who have no knives, to use a sort of string, made from the bark of trees, for this purpose. "But how can they make bottles," said he. "That requires some preparation," replied I. "They tie a bandage round the young gourd near the stalk, so that the part at liberty expands in a round form, and the compressed part remains narrow. They then open the top, and extract the contents by putting in pebbles and shaking it. By this means they have a complete bottle."

We worked on. Fritz completed a dish and some plates, to his great satisfaction, but we considered, [pg 028] that being so frail, we could not carry them with us. We therefore filled them with sand, that the sun might not warp them, and left them to dry, till we returned.

As we went on, Fritz amused himself with cutting spoons from the rind of the gourd, and I tried to do the same with the fragments of the cocoa-nut; but I must confess my performances were inferior to those I had seen in the museum in London, the work of the South Sea islanders. We laughed at our spoons, which would have required mouths from ear to ear to eat with them. Fritz declared that the curve of the rind was the cause of that defect: if the spoons had been smaller, they would have been flat; and you might as well eat soup with an oyster-shell as with a shovel.

While we talked, we did not neglect looking about for our lost companions, but in vain. At last, we arrived at a place where a tongue of land ran to some distance into the sea, on which was an elevated spot, favourable for observation. We attained the summit with great labour, and saw before us a magnificent prospect of land and water; but with all the aid our excellent telescope gave us, we could in no direction discover any trace of man. Nature only appeared in her greatest beauty. The shore enclosed a large bay, which terminated on the other side in a promontory. The gentle rippling of the waves, the varied verdure of the woods, and the multitude of novelties around us, would have filled us with delight, but for the painful recollection of those who, we now were compelled to believe, were buried beneath that glittering water. We did not feel less, however, the mercy of God, who had preserved us, and [pg 029] given us a home, with a prospect of subsistence and safety. We had not yet met with any dangerous animals, nor could we perceive any huts of savages. I remarked to my son that God seemed to have destined us to a solitary life in this rich country, unless some vessel should reach these shores. "And His will be done!" added I; "it must be for the best. Now let us retire to that pretty wood to rest ourselves, and eat our dinner, before we return."

We proceeded towards a pleasant wood of palm-trees; but before reaching it, had to pass through an immense number of reeds, which greatly obstructed our road. We were, moreover, fearful of treading on the deadly serpents who choose such retreats. We made Turk walk before us to give notice, and I cut a long, thick cane as a weapon of defence. I was surprised to see a glutinous juice oozing from the end of the cut cane; I tasted it, and was convinced that we had met with a plantation of sugar-canes. I sucked more of it, and found myself singularly refreshed. I said nothing to Fritz, that he might have the pleasure of making the discovery himself. He was walking a few paces before me, and I called to him to cut himself a cane like mine, which he did, and soon found out the riches it contained. He cried out in ecstasy, "Oh, papa! papa! syrup of sugar-cane! delicious! How delighted will dear mamma, and my brothers be, when I carry some to them!" He went on, sucking pieces of cane so greedily, that I checked him, recommending moderation. He was then content to take some pieces to regale himself as he walked home, loading himself with a huge burden for his mother and brothers. We now [pg 030] entered the wood of palms to eat our dinner, when suddenly a number of monkeys, alarmed by our approach, and the barking of the dog, fled like lightning to the tops of the trees; and then grinned frightfully at us, with loud cries of defiance. As I saw the trees were cocoa-palms, I hoped to obtain, by means of the monkeys, a supply of the nuts in the half-ripe state, when filled with milk. I held Fritz's arm, who was preparing to shoot at them, to his great vexation, as he was irritated against the poor monkeys for their derisive gestures; but I told him, that though no patron of monkeys myself, I could not allow it. We had no right to kill any animal except in defence, or as a means of supporting life. Besides, the monkeys would be of more use to us living than dead, as I would show him. I began to throw stones at the monkeys, not being able, of course, to reach the place of their retreat, and they, in their anger, and in the spirit of imitation, gathered the nuts and hurled them on us in such quantities, that we had some difficulty in escaping from them. We had soon a large stock of cocoa-nuts. Fritz enjoyed the success of the stratagem, and, when the shower subsided, he collected as many as he wished. We then sat down, and tasted some of the milk through the three small holes, which we opened with our knives. We then divided some with our hatchets, and quenched our thirst with the liquor, which has not, however, a very agreeable flavour. We liked best a sort of thick cream which adheres to the shells, from which we scraped it with our spoons, and mixing it with the juice of the sugar-cane, we produced a delicious dish. Turk had the rest of the lobster, which we now despised, with some biscuit.

[pg 031]
We then got up, I tied some nuts together by their stems, and threw them over my shoulder. Fritz took his bundle of canes, and we set out homewards.

CHAPTER IV.

26

Fritz groaned heavily under the weight of his canes as we travelled on, and pitied the poor negroes, who had to carry such heavy burdens of them. He then, in imitation of me, tried to refresh himself by sucking a sugar-cane, but was surprised to find he failed in extracting any of the juice. At last, after some reflection, he said, "Ah! I remember, if there is no opening made for the air, I can get nothing out." I requested him to find a remedy for this.

"I will make an opening," said he, "above the first knot in the cane. If I draw in my breath in sucking, and thus make a vacuum in my mouth, the outer air then forces itself through the hole I have made to fill this vacuum, and carries the juice along with it; and when this division of the cane is emptied, I can proceed to pierce above the next knot. I am only afraid that going on this way we shall have nothing but empty canes to carry to our friends." I told him, that I was more afraid the sun might turn the syrup sour before we got our canes home; therefore we need not spare them.

"Well, at any rate," said he, "I have filled my flask with the milk of the cocoa-nut to regale them."

[pg 032]
I told him I feared another disappointment; for the milk of the cocoa-nut, removed from the shell, spoiled sooner than the sugar-cane juice. I warned him that the

milk, exposed to the sun in his tin flask, was probably become vinegar.

He instantly took the bottle from his shoulder and uncorked it; when the liquor flew out with a report, foaming like champaign.

I congratulated him on his new manufacture, and said, we must beware of intoxication.

"Oh, taste, papa!" said he, "it is delicious, not at all like vinegar, but capital new, sweet, sparkling wine. This will be the best treat, if it remains in this state."

"I fear it will not be so," said I. "This is the first stage of fermentation. When this is over, and the liquor is cleared, it is a sort of wine, or fermented liquor, more or less agreeable, according to the material used. By applying heat, a second, and slower fermentation succeeds, and the liquor becomes vinegar. Then comes on a third stage, which deprives it of its strength, and spoils it. I fear, in this burning climate, you will carry home only vinegar, or something still more offensive. But let us drink each other's health now, but prudently, or we shall soon feel the effects of this potent beverage." Perfectly refreshed, we went on cheerfully to the place where we had left our gourd utensils. We found them quite dry, and hard as bone; we had no difficulty in carrying them in our game-bags. We had scarcely got through the little wood where we had breakfasted, when Turk darted furiously on a troop of monkeys, who were sporting about, and had not perceived him. He immediately seized a female, holding a [pg 033] young one in her arms, which impeded her flight, and had killed and devoured the poor mother before we could reach him. The young one had hidden itself among the long grass, when Fritz arrived; he had run with all his might, losing his hat, bottle, and canes, but could not prevent the murder of the poor mother.

The little monkey no sooner saw him than it leaped upon his shoulders, fastening its paws in his curls, and neither cries, threats, nor shaking could rid him of it. I ran up to him laughing, for I saw the little creature could not hurt him, and tried in vain to disengage it. I told him he must carry it thus. It was evident the sagacious little creature, having lost its mother, had adopted him for a father.

I succeeded, at last, in quietly releasing him, and took the little orphan, which was no bigger than a cat, in my arms, pitying its helplessness. The mother appeared as tall as Fritz.

I was reluctant to add another mouth to the number we had to feed; but Fritz earnestly begged to keep it, offering to divide his share of cocoa-nut milk with it till we had our cows. I consented, on condition that he took care of it, and taught it to be obedient to him.

Turk, in the mean time, was feasting on the remains of the unfortunate mother.

28

Fritz would have driven him off, but I saw we had not food sufficient to satisfy this voracious animal, and we might ourselves be in danger from his appetite.

We left him, therefore, with his prey, the little orphan sitting on the shoulder of his protector, while I carried the canes. Turk soon overtook us, and was received very coldly; we reproached [pg 034] him with his cruelty, but he was quite unconcerned, and continued to walk after Fritz. The little monkey seemed uneasy at the sight of him, and crept into Fritz's bosom, much to his inconvenience. But a thought struck him; he tied the monkey with a cord to Turk's back, leading the dog by another cord, as he was very rebellious at first; but our threats and caresses at last induced him to submit to his burden. We proceeded slowly, and I could not help anticipating the mirth of my little ones, when they saw us approach like a pair of show-men.

I advised Fritz not to correct the dogs for attacking and killing unknown animals. Heaven bestows the dog on man, as well as the horse, for a friend and protector. Fritz thought we were very fortunate, then, in having two such faithful dogs; he only regretted that our horses had died on the passage, and only left us the ass.

"Let us not disdain the ass," said I; "I wish we had him here; he is of a very fine breed, and would be as useful as a horse to us."

In such conversations, we arrived at the banks of our river before we were aware. Flora barked to announce our approach, and Turk answered so loudly, that the terrified little monkey leaped from his back to the shoulder of its protector, and would not come down. Turk ran off to meet his companion, and our dear family soon appeared on the opposite shore, shouting with joy at our happy return. We crossed at the same place as we had done in the morning, and embraced each other. Then began such a noise of exclamations. "A monkey! a real, live monkey! Ah! how delightful! How glad we are! How did you catch him?"

[pg 035]
"He is very ugly," said little Francis, who was almost afraid of him.

"He is prettier than you are," said Jack; "see how he laughs! how I should like to see him eat!"

"If we only had some cocoa-nuts," said Ernest. "Have you found any, and are they good?"

"Have you had any unpleasant adventures?" asked my wife.

It was in vain to attempt replying to so many questions and exclamations.

At length, when we got a little peace, I told them that, though I had brought them all sorts of good things, I had, unfortunately, not met with any of our companions.

"God's will be done!" said my wife; "let us thank Him for saving us, and again bringing us together now. This day has seemed an age. But put down your loads, and let us hear your adventures; we have not been idle, but we are less fatigued than you. Boys, assist your father and brother."

Jack took my gun, Ernest the cocoa-nuts, Francis the gourd-rinds, and my wife the game-bag. Fritz distributed his sugar-canes, and placed the monkey on Turk's back, to the amusement of the children. He begged Ernest to carry his gun, but he complained of being overloaded with the great bowls. His indulgent mother took them from him, and we proceeded to the tent.

Fritz thought Ernest would not have relinquished the bowls, if he had known what they contained, and called out to tell him they were cocoa-nuts.

"Give them to me," cried Ernest. "I will carry them, mamma, and the gun too."

[pg 036]
His mother declined giving them.

"I can throw away these sticks," said he, "and carry the gun in my hand."

"I would advise you not," observed Fritz, "for the sticks are sugar-canes."

"Sugar-canes!" cried they all, surrounding Fritz, who had to give them the history, and teach them the art of sucking the canes.

My wife, who had a proper respect for sugar in her housekeeping, was much pleased with this discovery, and the history of all our acquisitions, which I

30

displayed to her. Nothing gave her so much pleasure as our plates and dishes, which were actual necessaries. We went to our kitchen, and were gratified to see preparations going on for a good supper. My wife had planted a forked stick on each side the hearth; on these rested a long thin wand, on which all sorts of fish were roasting, Francis being intrusted to turn the spit. On the other side was impaled a goose on another spit, and a row of oyster-shells formed the dripping-pan: besides this, the iron pot was on the fire, from which arose the savoury odour of a good soup. Behind the hearth stood one of the hogsheads, opened, and containing the finest Dutch cheeses, enclosed in cases of lead. All this was very tempting to hungry travellers, and very unlike a supper on a desert island. I could not think my family had been idle, when I saw such a result of their labours; I was only sorry they had killed the goose, as I wished to be economical with our poultry.

"Have no uneasiness," said my wife, "this is not from our poultry-yard, it is a wild goose, killed by Ernest."

[pg 037]
"It is a sort of penguin, I believe," said Ernest, "distinguished by the name of booby, and so stupid, that I knocked it down with a stick. It is web-footed, has a long narrow beak, a little curved downwards. I have preserved the head and neck for you to examine; it exactly resembles the penguin of my book of natural history."

I pointed out to him the advantages of study, and was making more inquiries about the form and habits of the bird, when my wife requested me to defer my catechism of natural history.

"Ernest has killed the bird," added she; "I received it; we shall eat it. What more would you have? Let the poor child have the pleasure of examining and tasting the cocoa-nuts."

"Very well," replied I, "Fritz must teach them how to open them; and we must not forget the little monkey, who has lost his mother's milk."

"I have tried him," cried Jack, "and he will eat nothing."

I told them he had not yet learnt to eat, and we must feed him with cocoa-nut milk till we could get something better. Jack generously offered all his share, but Ernest and Francis were anxious to taste the milk themselves.

"But the monkey must live," said Jack, petulantly.

"And so must we all," said mamma. "Supper is ready, and we will reserve the cocoa-nuts for dessert."

We sat down on the ground, and the supper was served on our gourd-rind service, which answered the purpose admirably. My impatient boys had broken the nuts, which they found excellent, and they made themselves spoons of the shell. Jack [pg 038] had taken care the monkey had his share; they dipped the corner of their handkerchiefs in the milk, and let him suck them. They were going to break up some more nuts, after emptying them through the natural holes, but I stopped them, and called for a saw. I carefully divided the nuts with this instrument, and soon provided us each with a neat basin for our soup, to the great comfort of my dear wife, who was gratified by seeing us able to eat like civilized beings. Fritz begged now to enliven the repast by introducing his champaign. I consented; requesting him, however, to taste it himself before he served it. What was his mortification to find it vinegar! But we consoled ourselves by using it as sauce to our goose; a great improvement also to the fish. We had now to hear the history of our supper. Jack and Francis had caught the fish at the edge of the sea. My active wife had performed the most laborious duty, in rolling the hogshead to the place and breaking open the head.

The sun was going down as we finished supper, and, recollecting how rapidly night succeeded, we hastened to our tent, where we found our beds much more comfortable, from the kind attention of the good mother, who had collected a large addition of dried grass. After prayers, we all lay down; the monkey between Jack and Fritz, carefully covered with moss to keep him warm. The fowls went to their roost, as on the previous night, and, after our fatigue, we were all soon in a profound sleep.

We had not slept long, when a great commotion among the dogs and fowls announced the [pg 039] presence of an enemy. My wife, Fritz, and I, each seizing a gun, rushed out.

By the light of the moon, we saw a terrible battle going on: our brave dogs were surrounded by a dozen jackals, three or four were extended dead, but our faithful animals were nearly overpowered by numbers when we arrived. I was glad to find nothing worse than jackals; Fritz and I fired on them; two fell dead, and the others fled slowly, evidently wounded. Turk and Flora pursued and completed the business, and then, like true dogs, devoured their fallen foes, regardless of the bonds of relationship.

All being quiet again, we retired to our beds; Fritz obtaining leave to drag the jackal he had killed towards the tent, to save it from the dogs, and to show to his brothers next morning. This he accomplished with difficulty, for it was as big as a large dog.

We all slept peacefully the remainder of the night, till the crowing of the cock awoke my wife and myself to a consultation on the business of the day.

CHAPTER V.

"Well, my dear," I began, "I feel rather alarmed at all the labours I see before me. A voyage to the vessel is indispensable, if we wish to save our cattle, and many other things that may be useful to us; on the other hand, I should [pg 040] like to have a more secure shelter for ourselves and our property than this tent."

"With patience, order, and perseverance, all may be done," said my good counsellor; "and whatever uneasiness your voyage may give me, I yield to the importance and utility of it. Let it be done to-day; and have no care for the morrow: sufficient unto the day is the evil thereof, as our blessed Lord has said."

It was then agreed that the three youngest children should remain with my wife; and Fritz, the strongest and most active, should accompany me.

I then arose, and woke my children for the important duties of the day. Fritz jumped up the first, and ran for his jackal, which had stiffened in the cold of the night. He placed it on its four legs, at the entrance of the tent, to surprise his brothers; but no sooner did the dogs see it erect, than they flew at it, and would have torn it to pieces, if he had not soothed them and called them off. However, their barking effectually roused the boys, who rushed out to see the cause. Jack issued first with the monkey on his shoulder; but no sooner did the little creature see the jackal, than he sprang into the tent, and hid himself among the moss, till only the tip of his nose was visible. All were astonished to see this large yellow animal standing; Francis thought it was a wolf; Jack said it was only a dead dog, and Ernest, in a pompous tone, pronounced it to be a golden fox.

Fritz laughed at the learned professor, who knew the agouti immediately, and now called a jackal a golden fox!

[pg 041]
"I judged by the peculiar characteristics," said Ernest, examining it carefully.

"Oh! the characteristics!" said Fritz, ironically, "don't you think it may be a golden wolf?"

"Pray don't be so cross, brother," said Ernest, with tears in his eyes, "perhaps you would not have known the name, if papa had not told you."

I reproved Fritz for his ridicule of his brother, and Ernest for so easily taking offence; and, to reconcile all, I told them that the jackal partook of the nature of the wolf, the fox, and the dog. This discussion terminated, I summoned them to prayers, after which we thought of breakfast. We had nothing but biscuit, which was certainly dry and hard. Fritz begged for a little cheese with it; and Ernest, who was never satisfied like other people, took a survey of the unopened hogshead. He soon returned, crying "If we only had a little butter with our biscuit, it would be so good, papa!"

I allowed it would be good, but it was no use thinking of such a thing.

"Let us open the other cask," said he, displaying a piece of butter he had extracted through a small crack on the side.

"Your instinct for good things has been fortunate for us," said I. "Come, boys, who wants bread and butter?"

We began to consider how we should come at the contents of the hogshead, without exposing the perishable matter to the heat of the sun. Finally, I pierced a hole in the lower part of the cask, large enough for us to draw out the butter as we wanted it, by means of a little wooden shovel, which I soon made. We then sat down [pg 042] to breakfast with a cocoa-nut basin filled with good salt Dutch butter. We toasted our biscuit, buttered it hot, and agreed that it was excellent. Our dogs were sleeping by us as we breakfasted; and I remarked that they had bloody marks of the last night's fray, in some deep and dangerous wounds, especially about the neck; my wife instantly dressed the wounds with butter, well washed in cold water; and the poor animals seemed grateful for the ease it gave them. Ernest judiciously remarked, that they ought to have spiked collars, to defend them from any wild beasts they might encounter.

"I will make them collars," said Jack, who never hesitated at anything. I was glad to employ his inventive powers; and, ordering my children, not to leave their mother, during our absence, but to pray to God to bless our undertaking, we began our preparations for the voyage.

While Fritz made ready the boat, I erected a signal-post, with a piece of sailcloth for a flag, to float as long as all was going on well; but if we were wanted, they were to lower the flag, and fire a gun three times, when we would immediately return; for I had informed my dear wife it might be necessary for us to remain on board all night; and she consented to the plan, on my promising to pass the night in our tubs, instead of the vessel. We took nothing but our guns and ammunition; relying on the ship's provisions. Fritz would, however, take the monkey, that he might give it some milk from the cow.

We took a tender leave of each other, and embarked. When we had rowed into the middle of [pg 043] the bay, I perceived a strong current formed by the water of the river which issued at a little distance, which I was glad to take advantage of, to spare our labour. It carried us three parts of our voyage, and we rowed the remainder; and entering the opening in the vessel, we secured our boat firmly, and went on board.

The first care of Fritz was to feed the animals, who were on deck, and who all saluted us after their fashion, rejoiced to see their friends again, as well as to have their wants supplied. We put the young monkey to a goat, which he sucked with extraordinary grimaces, to our infinite amusement. We then took some refreshment ourselves, and Fritz, to my great surprise, proposed that we should begin by adding a sail to our boat. He said the current which helped us to the vessel, could not carry us back, but the wind which blew so strongly against us, and made our rowing so fatiguing, would be of great service, if we had a sail.

I thanked my counsellor for his good advice, and we immediately set to the task. I selected a strong pole for a mast, and a triangular sail, which was fixed to a yard. We made a hole in a plank, to receive the mast, secured the plank on our fourth tub, forming a deck, and then, by aid of a block used to hoist and lower the sails, raised our mast. Finally, two ropes fastened by one end to the yard, and by the other to each extremity of the boat, enabled us to direct the sail at pleasure. Fritz next ornamented the top of the mast with a little red streamer. He then gave our boat the name of the Deliverance, and requested it might henceforward [pg 044] be called the little vessel. To complete its equipment, I contrived a rudder, so that I could direct the boat from either end.

After signalling to our friends that we should not return that night, we spent the rest of the day in emptying the tubs of the stones we had used for ballast, and replacing them with useful things. Powder and shot, nails and tools of all kinds, pieces of cloth; above all, we did not forget knives, forks, spoons, and kitchen utensils, including a roasting-jack. In the captain's cabin we found some services of silver, pewter plates and dishes, and a small chest filled with bottles of choice wines. All these we took, as well as a chest of eatables, intended for the officers' table, portable soup, Westphalian hams, Bologna sausages, &c.; also some bags of maize, wheat, and other seeds, and some potatoes. We collected all the implements of husbandry we could spare room for, and, at the request of Fritz, some hammocks and blankets; two or three handsome guns, and an armful of sabres, swords, and hunting-knives. Lastly, I embarked a barrel of sulphur, all the cord and string I could lay my hands on, and a large roll of sailcloth. The sulphur was intended to produce matches with. Our tubs were loaded to the edge; there was barely room left for us to sit, and it would have been dangerous to attempt our return if the sea had not been so calm.

Night arrived, we exchanged signals, to announce security on sea and land, and, after prayers for the dear islanders, we sought our tubs, not the most luxurious of dormitories, but safer than the ship. Fritz slept soundly; but I could not [pg 045] close my eyes, thinking of the jackals. I was, however, thankful for the protection they had in the dogs.

CHAPTER VI.

As soon as day broke, I mounted on deck, to look through the telescope. I saw my wife looking towards us; and the flag, which denoted their safety, floating in the breeze. Satisfied on this important point, we enjoyed our breakfast of biscuit, ham, and wine, and then turned our thoughts to the means of saving our cattle. Even if we could contrive a raft, we could never get all the animals to remain still on it. We might venture the huge sow in the water, but the rest of the animals we found would not be able to swim to shore. At last Fritz suggested the swimming apparatus. We passed two hours in constructing them. For the cow and ass it was necessary to have an empty cask on each side, well bound in strong sailcloth, fastened by leather thongs over the back and under each animal. For the rest, we merely tied a piece of cork under their bodies; the sow only being unruly, and giving us much trouble. We then fastened a cord to the horns or neck of each animal, with a slip of wood at the end, for a convenient handle. Luckily, the waves had broken away part of the ship, and left the opening wide enough for the passage of our troop. We first launched the ass into the water, by a sudden [pg 046] push; he swam away, after the first plunge, very gracefully. The cow, sheep, and goats, followed quietly after. The sow was furious, and soon broke loose from us all, but fortunately reached the shore long before the rest.

We now embarked, fastening all the slips of wood to the stern of the boat, thus drawing our train after us; and the wind filling our sail, carried us smoothly towards the shore. Fritz exulted in his plan, as we certainly could never have rowed our boat, loaded as we were. I once more took out my telescope, and was remarking that our party on shore seemed making ready for some excursion, when a loud cry from Fritz filled me with terror. "We are lost! we are lost! see, what a monstrous fish!" Though pale with alarm, the bold boy had seized his gun, and, encouraged by my directions, he fired two balls into the head of the monster, as it was preparing to dart on the sheep. It immediately made its escape, leaving a long red track to prove that it was severely wounded.

Being freed from our enemy, I now resumed the rudder, and we lowered the sail and rowed to shore. The animals, as soon as the water became low enough, walked out at their own discretion, after we had relieved them from their swimming girdles. We then secured our boat as before, and landed ourselves, anxiously looking round for our friends.

We had not long to wait, they came joyfully to greet us; and, after our first burst of pleasure, we sat down to tell our adventures in a regular form. My wife was overjoyed to see herself surrounded by these valuable animals; and especially pleased [pg 047] that her son Fritz had suggested so many useful plans. We next proceeded to disembark all our treasures. I noticed that Jack wore a belt of yellow skin, in which were placed a pair of pistols, and inquired where he had got his brigand costume.

"I manufactured it myself," said he; "and this is not all. Look at the dogs!"

The dogs wore each a collar of the same skin as his belt, bristling with long nails, the points outwards--a formidable defence.

"It is my own invention," said he; "only mamma helped me in the sewing."

"But where did you get the leather, the needle and thread?" inquired I.

"Fritz's jackal supplied the skin," said my wife, "and my wonderful bag the rest. There is still more to come from it, only say what you want."

Fritz evidently felt a little vexation at his brother's unceremonious appropriation of the skin of the jackal, which displayed itself in the tone in which he exclaimed, holding his nose, "Keep at a distance, Mr. Skinner, you carry an intolerable smell about with you."

I gave him a gentle hint of his duty in the position of eldest son, and he soon recovered his good humour. However, as the body as well as the skin of the jackal was becoming offensive, they united in dragging it down to the sea, while Jack placed his belt in the sun to dry.

As I saw no preparation for supper, I told Fritz to bring the ham; and, to the astonishment and joy of all, he returned with a fine Westphalian ham, which we had cut into in the morning.

[pg 048]
"I will tell you," said my wife, "why we have no supper prepared; but first, I will make you an omelet;" and she produced from a basket a dozen turtle's eggs.

"You see," said Ernest, "they have all the characteristics of those Robinson Crusoe had in his island. They are white balls, the skin of which resembles moistened parchment."

My wife promised to relate the history of the discovery after supper, and set about preparing her ham and omelet, while Fritz and I proceeded in unloading our cargo, assisted by the useful ass.

Supper was now ready. A tablecloth was laid over the butter-cask, and spread with the plates and spoons from the ship. The ham was in the middle, and the omelet and cheese at each end; and we made a good meal, surrounded by our subjects,-- the dogs, the fowls, the pigeons, the sheep, and the goats, waiting for our notice. The geese and ducks were more independent, remaining in their marsh, where they lived in plenty on the small crabs which abounded there.

After supper, I sent Fritz for a bottle of the captain's Canary wine, and then requested my wife to give us her recital.

CHAPTER VII.

"I will spare you the history of the first day," said my good Elizabeth, "spent in anxiety about you, and attending to the signals; but this morning, being satisfied that all was going right, I [pg 049] sought, before the boys got up, a shady place to rest in, but in vain; I believe this barren shore has not a single tree on it. Then I began to consider on the necessity of searching for a more comfortable spot for our residence; and determined, after a slight repast, to set out with my children across the river, on a journey of discovery. The day before, Jack had busied himself in skinning the jackal with his knife, sharpened on the rock; Ernest declining to assist him in his dirty work, for which I reproved him, sorry that any fastidiousness should deter him from a labour of benefit to society.

"Jack proceeded to clean the skin as well as he was able; then procured from the nail-chest some long flat-headed nails, and inserted them closely through the long pieces of skin he had cut for collars; he then cut some sailcloth, and made a double lining over the heads of the nails; and finished by giving me the delicate office of sewing them together, which I could not but comply with.

"His belt he first stretched on a plank, nailing it down, and exposing it to the sun, lest it should shrink in drying.

"Now for our journey: we took our game-bags and some hunting-knives. The boys carried provisions, and I had a large flask of water. I took a small hatchet, and gave Ernest a carbine, which might be loaded with ball; keeping his light gun for myself. I carefully secured the opening of the tent with the hooks. Turk went before, evidently considering himself our guide; and we crossed the river with some difficulty.

"As we proceeded, I could not help feeling [pg 050] thankful that you had so early taught the boys to use fire-arms properly, as the defence of my youngest boy and myself now depended on the two boys of ten and twelve years of age.

"When we attained the hill you described to us, I was charmed with the smiling prospect, and, for the first time since our shipwreck, ventured to hope for better things. I had remarked a beautiful wood, to which I determined to make our way, for a little shade, and a most painful progress it was, through grass that was higher than the children's heads. As we were struggling through it, we heard a strange rustling sound among the grass, and at the same moment a bird of prodigious size rose, and flew away, before the poor boys could get their guns ready. They were much mortified, and I recommended them always to have their guns in readiness, for the birds would not be likely to wait till they loaded them. Francis thought the bird was so large, it must be an eagle; but Ernest ridiculed the idea, and added that he thought it must be of the bustard tribe. We went forward to the spot from which it had arisen, when suddenly another bird of the same kind, though still larger, sprung up, close to our feet, and was soon soaring above our heads. I could not help laughing to see the look of astonishment and confusion with which the boys looked upwards after it. At last Jack took off his hat, and, making a low bow, said, 'Pray, Mr. Bird, be kind enough to pay us another visit, you will find us very good children!' We found the large nest they had left; it was rudely formed of dry grass, and empty, but some fragments of egg-shells were scattered near, as if the young had [pg 051] been recently hatched; we therefore concluded that they had escaped among the grass.

"Doctor Ernest immediately began a lecture. 'You observe, Francis, these birds could not be eagles, which do not form their nests on the ground. Neither do their young run as soon as they are hatched. These must be of the gallinaceous tribe, an order of birds such as quails, partridges, turkeys, &c.; and, from the sort of feathered moustache which I observed at the corner of the beak, I should pronounce that these were bustards.'

"But we had now reached the little wood, and our learned friend had sufficient

42

employment in scrutinizing, and endeavouring to classify, the immense number of beautiful, unknown birds, which sung and fluttered about us, apparently regardless of our intrusion.

"We found that what we thought a wood was merely a group of a dozen trees, of a height far beyond any I had ever seen; and apparently belonging rather to the air than the earth; the trunks springing from roots which formed a series of supporting arches. Jack climbed one of the arches, and measured the trunk of the tree with a piece of packthread. He found it to be thirty-four feet. I made thirty-two steps round the roots. Between the roots and the lowest branches, it seemed about forty or fifty feet. The branches are thick and strong, and the leaves are of a moderate size, and resemble our walnut-tree. A thick, short, smooth turf clothed the ground beneath and around the detached roots of the trees, and everything combined to render this one of the most delicious spots the mind could conceive.

[pg 052]
"Here we rested, and made our noon-day repast; a clear rivulet ran near us, and offered its agreeable waters for our refreshment. Our dogs soon joined us; but I was astonished to find they did not crave for food, but laid down to sleep at our feet. For myself, so safe and happy did I feel, that I could not but think that if we could contrive a dwelling on the branches of one of these trees, we should be in perfect peace and safety. We set out on our return, taking the road by the sea-shore, in case the waves had cast up anything from the wreck of the vessel. We found a quantity of timber, chests, and casks; but all too heavy to bring. We succeeded in dragging them, as well as we could, out of the reach of the tide; our dogs, in the mean time, fishing for crabs, with which they regaled themselves, much to their own satisfaction and to mine, as I now saw they would be able to provide their own food. As we rested from our rough labour, I saw Flora scratching in the sand, and swallowing something with great relish. Ernest watched, and then said, very quietly, 'They are turtles' eggs.' We drove away the dog, and collected about two dozen, leaving her the rest as a reward for her discovery.

"While we were carefully depositing our spoil in the game-bags, we were astonished at the sight of a sail. Ernest was certain it was papa and Fritz, and though Francis was in dread that it should be the savages who visited Robinson Crusoe's island, coming to eat us up, we were soon enabled to calm his fears. We crossed the river by leaping from stone to stone, and, hastening to the landing-place, [pg 053] arrived to greet you on your happy return."

"And I understand, my dear," said I, "that you have discovered a tree sixty feet high, where you wish we should perch like fowls. But how are we to get up?"

"Oh! you must remember," answered she, "the large lime-tree near our native town, in which was a ball-room. We used to ascend to it by a wooden staircase.

43

Could you not contrive something of the sort in one of these gigantic trees, where we might sleep in peace, fearing neither jackals nor any other terrible nocturnal enemy."

I promised to consider this plan, hoping at least that we might make a commodious and shady dwelling among the roots. To-morrow we were to examine it. We then performed our evening devotions, and retired to rest.

CHAPTER VIII.

"Now, my dear Elizabeth," said I, waking early next morning, "let us talk a little on this grand project of changing our residence; to which there are many objections. First, it seems wise to remain on the spot where Providence has cast us, where we can have at once means of support drawn from the ship, and security from all attacks, protected by the rock, the river, and the sea on all sides."

My wife distrusted the river, which could not [pg 054] protect us from the jackals, and complained of the intolerable heat of this sandy desert, of her distaste for such food as oysters and wild geese; and, lastly, of her agony of mind, when we ventured to the wreck; willingly renouncing all its treasures, and begging we might rest content with the blessings we already had.

"There is some truth in your objections," said I, "and perhaps we may erect a dwelling under the roots of your favourite tree; but among these rocks we must have a storehouse for our goods, and a retreat in case of invasion. I hope, by blowing off some pieces of the rock with powder, to be able to fortify the part next the river, leaving a secret passage known only to ourselves. This would make it impregnable. But before we proceed, we must have a bridge to convey our baggage across the river.

"A bridge," said she, in a tone of vexation; "then when shall we get from here? Why cannot we ford it as usual? The cow and ass could carry our stores."

I explained to her how necessary it was for our ammunition and provision to be conveyed over without risk of wetting, and begged her to manufacture some bags and baskets, and leave the bridge to me and my boys. If we succeeded, it would always be useful; as for fear of danger from lightning or accident, I intended to make a powder-magazine among the rocks.

The important question was now decided. I called up my sons, and communicated our plans to them. They were greatly delighted, though somewhat alarmed, at the formidable project of the bridge; besides, the delay was vexatious; [pg 055] they were all anxious for a removal into the Land of Promise, as they chose to call it.

We read prayers, and then thought of breakfast. The monkey sucked one of the goats, as if it had been its mother. My wife milked the cow, and gave us boiled milk with biscuit for our breakfast; part of which she put in a flask, for us to take on our expedition. We then prepared our boat for a voyage to the vessel, to procure planks and timber for our bridge. I took both Ernest and Fritz, as I foresaw our cargo would be weighty, and require all our hands to bring it to shore.

We rowed vigorously till we got into the current, which soon carried us beyond the bay. We had scarcely reached a little isle at the entrance, when we saw a vast number of gulls and other sea-birds, fluttering with discordant cries over it. I hoisted the sail, and we approached rapidly; and, when near enough, we stepped on shore, and saw that the birds were feasting so eagerly on the remains of a huge fish, that they did not even notice our approach. We might have killed numbers, even with our sticks. This fish was the shark which Fritz had so skilfully shot through the head the night before. He found the marks of his three balls. Ernest drew his ramrod from his gun, and struck so vigorously right and left among the birds, that he killed some, and put the rest to flight. We then hastily cut off some pieces of the skin of the monster, which I thought might be useful, and placed them in our boat. But this was not the only advantage we gained by landing. I perceived an immense quantity of wrecked timber lying on the shore of the island, which would [pg 056] spare us our voyage to the ship. We selected such planks as were fit for our purpose; then, by the aid of our jack-screw and some levers we had brought with us, we extricated the planks from the sand, and floated them; and, binding the spars and yards together with cords, with the planks above them, like a raft, we tied them to the stern of our boat, and hoisted our sail.

Fritz, as we sailed, was drying the shark's skin, which I hoped to convert into files. And Ernest, in his usual reflective manner, observed to me, "What a beautiful arrangement of Providence it is, that the mouth of the shark should be placed in such a position that he is compelled to turn on his back to seize his prey, thus giving it a chance of escape; else, with his excessive voracity, he might depopulate the ocean."

At last, we reached our landing-place, and, securing our boat, and calling out loudly, we soon saw our friends running from the river; each carried a handkerchief filled with some new acquisition, and Francis had over his shoulder a small fishing-net. Jack reached us first, and threw down before us from his handkerchief some fine crawfish. They had each as many, forming a provision for many days.

Francis claimed the merit of the discovery. Jack related, that Francis and he took a walk to find a good place for the bridge.

"Thank you, Mr. Architect," said I; "then you must superintend the workmen. Have you fixed on your place?"

"Yes, yes!" cried he; "only listen. When we got to the river, Francis, who was looking about, [pg 057] called out, 'Jack! Jack! Fritz's jackal is covered with crabs! Come!--come!' I ran to tell mamma, who brought a net that came from the ship, and we caught these in a few minutes, and could have got many more, if you had not come."

I commanded them to put the smaller ones back into the river, reserving only as many as we could eat. I was truly thankful to discover another means of support.

We now landed our timber. I had looked at Jack's site for the bridge, and thought my little architect very happy in his selection; but it was at a great distance from the timber. I recollected the simplicity of the harness the Laplanders used for their reindeer. I tied cords to the horns of the cow--as the strength of this animal is in the head--and then fastened the other ends round the piece of timber we wanted moving. I placed a halter round the neck of the ass, and attached the cords to this. We were thus enabled, by degrees, to remove all our wood to the chosen spot, where the sides of the river were steep, and appeared of equal height.

It was necessary to know the breadth of the river, to select the proper planks; and

Ernest proposed to procure a ball of packthread from his mother, to tie a stone to one end of the string, and throw it across the river, and to measure it after drawing it back. This expedient succeeded admirably. We found the breadth to be eighteen feet; but, as I proposed to give the bridge strength by having three feet, at least, resting on each shore, we chose some planks of twenty-four feet in length. How we were to get these across the river was [pg 058] another question, which we prepared to discuss during dinner, to which my wife now summoned us.

Our dinner consisted of a dish of crawfish, and some very good rice-milk. But, before we began, we admired her work. She had made a pair of bags for the ass, sewed with packthread; but having no large needles, she had been obliged to pierce holes with a nail, a tedious and painful process. Well satisfied with her success, we turned to our repast, talking of our bridge, which the boys, by anticipation, named the Nonpareil. We then went to work.

There happened to be an old trunk of a tree standing on the shore. To this I tied my main beam by a strong cord, loose enough to turn round the trunk. Another cord was attached to the opposite end of the beam, long enough to cross the river twice. I took the end of my rope over the stream, where we had previously fixed the block, used in our boat, to a tree, by the hook which usually suspended it. I passed my rope, and returned with the end to our own side. I then harnessed my cow and ass to the end of my rope, and drove them forcibly from the shore. The beam turned slowly round the trunk, then advanced, and was finally lodged over the river, amidst the shouts of the boys; its own weight keeping it firm. Fritz and Jack leaped on it immediately to run across, to my great fear.

We succeeded in placing four strong beams in the same way; and, by the aid of my sons, I arranged them at a convenient distance from each other, that we might have a broad and good bridge. We then laid down planks close together [pg 059] across the beams; but not fixed, as in time of danger it might be necessary rapidly to remove the bridge. My wife and I were as much excited as the children, and ran across with delight. Our bridge was at least ten feet broad.

Thoroughly fatigued with our day of labour, we returned home, supped, and offered thanks to God, and went to rest.

CHAPTER IX.

The next morning, after prayers, I assembled my family. We took a solemn leave of our first place of refuge. I cautioned my sons to be prudent, and on their guard;

and especially to remain together during our journey. We then prepared for departure. We assembled the cattle: the bags were fixed across the backs of the cow and the ass, and loaded with all our heavy baggage; our cooking utensils; and provisions, consisting of biscuits, butter, cheese, and portable soup; our hammocks and blankets; the captain's service of plate, were all carefully packed in the bags, equally poised on each side the animals.

All was ready, when my wife came in haste with her inexhaustible bag, requesting a place for it. Neither would she consent to leave the poultry, as food for the jackals; above all, Francis must have a place; he could not possibly walk all the way. I was amused with the exactions of the sex; but consented to all, and made a good place for Francis between the bags, on the back of the ass.

[pg 060]
The elder boys returned in despair,--they could not succeed in catching the fowls; but the experienced mother laughed at them, and said she would soon capture them.

"If you do," said my pert little Jack, "I will be contented to be roasted in the place of the first chicken taken."

"Then, my poor Jack," said his mother, "you will soon be on the spit. Remember, that intellect has always more power than mere bodily exertion. Look here!" She scattered a few handfuls of grain before the tent, calling the fowls; they soon all assembled, including the pigeons; then throwing more down inside the tent, they followed her. It was now only necessary to close the entrance; and they were all soon taken, tied by the wings and feet, and, being placed in baskets covered with nets, were added to the rest of our luggage on the backs of the animals.

Finally, we conveyed inside the tent all we could not carry away, closing the entrance, and barricading it with chests and casks, thus confiding all our possessions to the care of God. We set out on our pilgrimage, each carrying a game-bag and a gun. My wife and her eldest son led the way, followed by the heavily-laden cow and ass; the third division consisted of the goats, driven by Jack, the little monkey seated on the back of its nurse, and grimacing, to our great amusement; next came Ernest, with the sheep; and I followed, superintending the whole. Our gallant dogs acted as aides-de-camp, and were continually passing from the front to the rear rank.

[pg 061]
Our march was slow, but orderly, and quite patriarchal. "We are now travelling across the deserts, as our first fathers did," said I, "and as the Arabs, Tartars, and other nomade nations do to this day, followed by their flocks and herds. But these people generally have strong camels to bear their burdens, instead of a poor ass and cow. I hope this may be the last of our pilgrimages." My wife also hoped that,

48

once under the shade of her marvellous trees, we should have no temptation to travel further.

We now crossed our new bridge, and here the party was happily augmented by a new arrival. The sow had proved very mutinous at setting out, and we had been compelled to leave her; she now voluntarily joined us, seeing we were actually departing; but continued to grunt loudly her disapprobation of our proceedings. After we had crossed the river, we had another embarrassment. The rich grass tempted our animals to stray off to feed, and, but for our dogs, we should never have been able to muster them again. But, for fear of further accident, I commanded my advanced guard to take the road by the coast, which offered no temptation to our troops.

We had scarcely left the high grass when our dogs rushed back into it, barking furiously, and howling as if in combat; Fritz immediately prepared for action, Ernest drew near his mother, Jack rushed forward with his gun over his shoulder, and I cautiously advanced, commanding them to be discreet and cool. But Jack, with his usual impetuosity, leaped among the high grass to the dogs; and immediately returned, clapping his hands, and crying out, "Be quick, [pg 062] papa! a huge porcupine, with quills as long as my arm!"

When I got up, I really found a porcupine, whom the dogs were warmly attacking. It made a frightful noise, erecting its quills so boldly, that the wounded animals howled with pain after every attempt to seize it. As we were looking at them Jack drew a pistol from his belt, and discharged it directly into the head of the porcupine, which fell dead. Jack was very proud of his feat, and Fritz, not a little jealous, suggested that such a little boy should not be trusted with pistols, as he might have shot one of the dogs, or even one of us. I forbade any envy or jealousy among the brothers, and declared that all did well who acted for the public good. Mamma was now summoned to see the curious animal her son's valour had destroyed. Her first thought was to dress the wounds made by the quills which had stuck in the noses of the dogs during their attack. In the mean time, I corrected my son's notions on the power of this animal to lance its darts when in danger. This is a popular error; nature has given it a sufficient protection in its defensive and offensive armour.

As Jack earnestly desired to carry his booty with him, I carefully imbedded the body in soft grass, to preserve the quills; then packed it in strong cloth, and placed it on the ass behind Francis.

At last, we arrived at the end of our journey,--and, certainly, the size of the trees surpassed anything I could have imagined. Jack was certain they were gigantic walnut-trees; for my own part, I believed them to be a species of fig-tree-- probably [pg 063] the Antilles fig. But all thanks were given to the kind mother who had sought out such a pleasant home for us; at all events, we could find a

49

convenient shelter among the roots. And, if we should ever succeed in perching on the branches, I told her we should be safe from all wild beasts. I would defy even the bears of our native mountains to climb these immense trunks, totally destitute of branches.

We released our animals from their loads, tying their fore legs together, that they might not stray; except the sow, who, as usual, did her own way. The fowls and pigeons we released, and left to their own discretion. We then sat down on the grass, to consider where we should establish ourselves. I wished to mount the tree that very night. Suddenly we heard, to our no slight alarm, the report of a gun. But the next moment the voice of Fritz re-assured us. He had stolen out unnoticed, and shot a beautiful tiger-cat, which he displayed in great triumph.

"Well done, noble hunter!" said I; "you deserve the thanks of the fowls and pigeons; they would most probably have all fallen a sacrifice to-night, if you had not slain their deadly foe. Pray wage war with all his kind, or we shall not have a chicken left for the pot."

Ernest then examined the animal with his customary attention, and declared that the proper name was the margay, a fact Fritz did not dispute, only requesting that Jack might not meddle with the skin, as he wished to preserve it for a belt. I recommended them to skin it immediately, and give the flesh to the dogs. Jack, at the same time, determined to skin his porcupine, to make [pg 064] dog-collars. Part of its flesh went into the soup-kettle, and the rest was salted for the next day. We then sought for some flat stones in the bed of the charming little river that ran at a little distance from us, and set about constructing a cooking-place. Francis collected dry wood for the fire; and, while my wife was occupied in preparing our supper, I amused myself by making some packing-needles for her rude work from the quills of the porcupine. I held a large nail in the fire till it was red-hot, then, holding the head in wet linen, I pierced the quills, and made several needles, of various sizes, to the great contentment of our indefatigable workwoman.

Still occupied with the idea of our castle in the air, I thought of making a ladder of ropes; but this would be useless, if we did not succeed in getting a cord over the lower branches, to draw it up. Neither my sons nor myself could throw a stone, to which I had fastened a cord, over these branches, which were thirty feet above us. It was necessary to think of some other expedient. In the mean time, dinner was ready. The porcupine made excellent soup, and the flesh was well-tasted, though rather hard. My wife could not make up her mind to taste it, but contented herself with a slice of ham and some cheese.

CHAPTER X.

After dinner, as I found we could not ascend at present, I suspended our hammocks under the arched roots of our tree, and, covering the whole [pg 065] with sailcloth, we had a shelter from the dew and the insects.

While my wife was employed making harness for the cow and ass, I went with my sons to the shore, to look for wood fit for our use next day. We saw a great quantity of wreck, but none fit for our purpose, till Ernest met with a heap of bamboo canes, half buried in sand and mud. These were exactly what I wanted. I drew them out of the sand, stripped them of their leaves, cut them in pieces of about four or five feet long, and my sons each made up a bundle to carry home. I then set out to seek some slender stalks to make arrows, which I should need in my project.

We went towards a thick grove, which appeared likely to contain something for my purpose. We were very cautious, for fear of reptiles or other dangerous animals, allowing Flora to precede us. When we got near, she darted furiously among the bushes, and out flew a troop of beautiful flamingoes, and soared into the air. Fritz, always ready, fired at them. Two fell; one quite dead, the other, slightly wounded in the wing, made use of its long legs so well that it would have escaped, if Flora had not seized it and held it till I came up to take possession. The joy of Fritz was extreme, to have this beautiful creature alive. He thought at once of curing its wound, and domesticating it with our own poultry.

"What splendid plumage!" said Ernest; "and you see he is web-footed, like the goose, and has long legs like the stork; thus he can run as fast on land as he can swim in the water,"

"Yes," said I, "and fly as quickly in the air. These birds are remarkable for the power and [pg 066] strength of their wings. Few birds have so many advantages."

My boys occupied themselves in binding their captive and dressing his wound; while I sought some of the canes which had done flowering, to cut off the hard ends, to point my arrows. These are used by the savages of the Antilles. I then selected the highest canes I could meet with, to assist me in measuring, by a geometrical process, the height of the tree. Ernest took the canes, I had the wounded flamingo, and Fritz carried his own game. Very loud were the cries of joy and astonishment at our approach. The boys all hoped the flamingo might be tamed, of which I felt no doubt; but my wife was uneasy, lest it should require more food than she could spare. However, I assured her, our new guest would need no attention, as he would provide for himself at the river-side, feeding on small fishes, worms, and insects. His wounds I dressed, and found they would soon be healed; I then tied him to a stake, near the river, by a cord long enough to allow him to fish at his pleasure, and, in fact, in a few days, he learned to know us, and was quite domesticated. Meantime, my boys had been trying to measure the tree with the long canes I had brought, and came laughing to report to me, that I ought to have got them ten times as long to reach even the lowest branches. "There is a simpler mode than that," said I, "which geometry teaches us, and by which the highest mountains can be measured."

I then showed the method of measuring heights by triangles and imaginary lines, using canes of different lengths and cords instead of mathematical [pg 067] instruments. My result was thirty feet to the lowest branches. This experiment filled the boys with wonder and desire to become acquainted with this useful, exact science, which, happily, I was able to teach them fully.

I now ordered Fritz to measure our strong cord, and the little ones to collect all the small string, and wind it. I then took a strong bamboo and made a bow of it, and some arrows of the slender canes, filling them with wet sand to give them weight, and feathering them from the dead flamingo. As soon as my work was completed, the boys crowded round me, all begging to try the bow and arrows. I begged them to be patient, and asked my wife to supply me with a ball of thick strong thread. The enchanted bag did not fail us; the very ball I wanted appeared at her summons. This, my little ones declared, must be magic; but I explained to them, that prudence, foresight, and presence of mind in danger, such as their good mother had displayed, produced more miracles than magic.

I then tied the end of the ball of thread to one of my arrows, fixed it in my bow, and sent it directly over one of the thickest of the lower branches of the tree, and, falling to the ground, it drew the thread after it. Charmed with this result, I hastened to complete my ladder. Fritz had measured our ropes, and found two of forty feet each,--exactly what I wanted. These I stretched on the ground at about one foot distance from each other; Fritz cut pieces of cane two feet long, which Ernest passed to me. I placed these in knots which I had made in the cords, at about a foot distance from each other, [pg 068] and Jack fastened each end with a long nail, to prevent it slipping. In a very short time our ladder was completed; and, tying it to the end of the cord which went over the branch, we drew it up without difficulty. All the boys were anxious to ascend; but I chose Jack, as the lightest and most active. Accordingly, he ascended, while his brothers and myself held the ladder firm by the end of the cord. Fritz followed him, conveying a bag with nails and hammer. They were soon perched on the branches, huzzaing to us. Fritz secured the ladder so firmly to the branch, that I had no hesitation in ascending myself. I carried with me a large pulley fixed to the end of a rope, which I attached to a branch above us, to enable us to raise the planks necessary to form the groundwork of our habitation. I smoothed the branches a little by aid of my axe, sending the boys down to be out of my way. After completing my day's work, I descended by the light of the moon, and was alarmed to find that Fritz and Jack were not below; and still more so, when I heard their clear, sweet voices, at the summit of the tree, singing the evening hymn, as if to sanctify our future

52

abode. They had climbed the tree, instead of descending, and, filled with wonder and reverence at the sublime view below them, had burst out into the hymn of thanksgiving to God.

I could not scold my dear boys, when they descended, but directed them to assemble the animals, and to collect wood, to keep up fires during the night, in order to drive away any wild beasts that might be near.

My wife then displayed her work,--complete [pg 069] harness for our two beasts of burden, and, in return, I promised her we would establish ourselves next day in the tree. Supper was now ready, one piece of the porcupine was roasted by the fire, smelling deliciously; another piece formed a rich soup; a cloth was spread on the turf; the ham, cheese, butter, and biscuits, were placed upon it.

My wife first assembled the fowls, by throwing some grain to them, to accustom them to the place. We soon saw the pigeons fly to roost on the higher branches of the trees, while the fowls perched on the ladder; the beasts we tied to the roots, close to us. Now, that our cares were over, we sat down to a merry and excellent repast by moonlight. Then, after the prayers of the evening, I kindled our watch-fires, and we all lay down to rest in our hammocks. The boys were rather discontented, and complained of their cramped position, longing for the freedom of their beds of moss; but I instructed them to lie, as the sailors do, diagonally, and swinging the hammock, and told them that brave Swiss boys might sleep as the sailors of all nations were compelled to sleep. After some stifled sighs and groans, all sank to rest except myself, kept awake by anxiety for the safety of the rest.

CHAPTER XI.

My anxiety kept me awake till near morning, when, after a short sleep, I rose, and we were soon all at work. My wife, after milking the cow and goats, harnessed the cow and ass, and set out to [pg 070] search for drift-wood for our use. In the mean time, I mounted the ladder with Fritz, and we set to work stoutly, with axe and saw, to rid ourselves of all useless branches. Some, about six feet above our foundation, I left, to suspend our hammocks from, and others, a little higher, to support the roof, which, at present, was to be merely sailcloth. My wife succeeded in collecting us some boards and planks, which, with her assistance, and the aid of the pulley, we hoisted up. We then arranged them on the level branches close to each other, in such a manner as to form a smooth and solid floor. I made a sort of parapet round, to prevent accidents. By degrees, our dwelling began to assume a distinct form; the sailcloth was raised over the high branches, forming a roof; and, being brought down on each side, was nailed to the parapet. The immense trunk protected the back of our apartment, and the front was open to admit the breeze from the sea, which was visible from this elevation. We hoisted our hammocks and blankets by the pulley, and suspended them; my son and I then descended, and, as our day was not yet exhausted, we set about constructing a rude table and some benches, from the remainder of our wood, which we placed beneath the roots of the tree, henceforward to be our dining-room. The little boys collected the chips and pieces of wood for fire-wood; while their mamma prepared supper, which we needed much after the extraordinary fatigues of this day.

The next day, however, being Sunday, we looked forward to as a day of rest, of recreation, and thanksgiving to the great God who had preserved us.

[pg 071]
Supper was now ready, my wife took a large earthen pot from the fire, which contained a good stew, made of the flamingo, which Ernest had told her was an old bird, and would not be eatable, if dressed any other way. His brothers laughed heartily, and called him the cook. He was, however, quite right, the stew, well seasoned, was excellent, and we picked the very bones. Whilst we were thus occupied, the living flamingo, accompanying the rest of the fowls, and free from bonds, came in, quite tame, to claim his share of the repast, evidently quite unsuspicious that we were devouring his mate; he did not seem at all inclined to quit us. The little monkey, too, was quite at home with the boys, leaping from one to another for food, which he took in his forepaws, and ate with such absurd mimicry of their actions, that he kept us in continual convulsions of laughter. To augment our satisfaction, our great sow, who had deserted us for two days, returned of her own accord, grunting her joy at our re-union. My wife welcomed her with particular distinction, treating her with all the milk we had to spare; for, as she had no dairy utensils to make cheese and butter, it was best thus to dispose of our superfluity. I promised her, on our next voyage to the ship, to procure all these necessaries. This she could not, however, hear of, without shuddering.

The boys now lighted the fires for the night. The dogs were tied to the roots of the tree, as a protection against invaders, and we commenced our ascent. My three eldest sons soon ran up the ladder, my wife followed, with more deliberation, but arrived safely; my own journey was more difficult, [pg 072] as, besides having to carry Francis on my back, I had detached the lower part of the ladder from the roots, where it was nailed; in order to be able to draw it up during the night. We were thus as safe in our castle as the knights of old, when their drawbridge was raised. We retired to our hammocks free from care, and did not wake till the sun shone brightly in upon us.

CHAPTER XII.

Next morning, all awoke in good spirits; I told them that on this, the Lord's day, we would do no work. That it was appointed, not only for a day of rest, but a day when we must, as much as possible, turn our hearts from the vanities of the world, to God himself; thank him, worship him, and serve him. Jack thought we could not do this without a church and a priest; but Ernest believed that God would hear our prayers under his own sky, and papa could give them a sermon; Francis wished to know if God would like to hear them sing the beautiful hymns mamma had taught them, without an organ accompaniment.

"Yes, my dear children," said I, "God is everywhere; and to bless him, to praise him in all his works, to submit to his holy will, and to obey him,--is to serve him. But everything in its time. Let us first attend to the wants of our animals, and breakfast, and we will then begin the services of the day by a hymn."

We descended, and breakfasted on warm milk, [pg 073] fed our animals, and then, my children and their mother seated on the turf, I placed myself on a little eminence before them, and, after the service of the day, which I knew by heart, and singing some portions of the 119th Psalm, I told them a little allegory.

"There was once on a time a great king, whose kingdom was called the Land of Light and Reality, because there reigned there constant light and incessant activity. On the most remote frontier of this kingdom, towards the north, there was another large kingdom, equally subject to his rule, and of which none but himself knew the immense extent. From time immemorial, an exact plan of this kingdom had been preserved in the archives. It was called the Land of Obscurity, or Night, because everything in it was dark and inactive.

"In the most fertile and agreeable part of the empire of Reality, the king had a magnificent residence, called The Heavenly City, where he held his brilliant court. Millions of servants executed his wishes--still more were ready to receive his orders. The first were clothed in glittering robes, whiter than snow--for white was the colour of the Great King, as the emblem of purity. Others were clothed in armour, shining like the colours of the rainbow, and carried flaming swords in their hands. Each, at his master's nod, flew like lightning to accomplish his will. All his servants--faithful, vigilant, bold, and ardent--were united in friendship, and could imagine no happiness greater than the favour of their master. There were some, less elevated, who were still good, rich, and happy [pg 074] in the favours of their sovereign, to whom all his subjects were alike, and were treated by him as his children.

"Not far from the frontiers, the Great King possessed a desert island, which he desired to people and cultivate, in order to make it, for a time, the abode of those of his subjects whom he intended to admit, by degrees, into his Heavenly City--a favour he wished to bestow on the greatest number possible.

"This island was called Earthly Abode; and he who had passed some time there, worthily, was to be received into all the happiness of the heavenly city. To attain this, the Great King equipped a fleet to transport the colonists, whom he chose from the kingdom of Night, to this island, where he gave them light and activity-- advantages they had not known before. Think how joyful their arrival would be! The island was fertile when cultivated; and all was prepared to make the time pass agreeably, till they were admitted to their highest honours.

"At the moment of embarkation, the Great King sent his own son, who spoke thus to them in His name:--

"'My dear children, I have called you from inaction and insensibility to render you happy by feeling, by action, by life. Never forget I am your king, and obey my commands, by cultivating the country I confide to you. Every one will receive his portion of land, and wise and learned men are appointed to explain my will to you. I wish you all to acquire the knowledge of my laws, and that every father should keep a copy, to read daily to his children, that they may never be forgotten. [pg 075] And on the first day of the week you must all assemble, as brothers, in one place, to hear these laws read and explained. Thus it will be easy for every one to learn the best method of improving his land, what to plant, and how to cleanse it from the tares that might choke the good seed. All may ask what they desire, and every reasonable demand will be granted, if it be conformable to the great end.

"'If you feel grateful for these benefits, and testify it by increased activity, and by occupying yourself on this day in expressing your gratitude to me, I will take care this day of rest shall be a benefit, and not a loss. I wish that all your useful animals, and even the wild beasts of the plains, should on this day repose in peace.

"'He who obeys my commands in Earthly Abode, shall receive a rich reward in the Heavenly City; but the idle, the negligent, and the evil-disposed, shall be condemned to perpetual slavery, or to labour in mines, in the bowels of the earth.

"'From time to time, I shall send ships, to bring away individuals, to be rewarded or punished, as they have fulfilled my commands. None can deceive me; a magic mirror will show me the actions and thoughts of all,'

"The colonists were satisfied, and eager to begin their labour. The portions of land and instruments of labour were distributed to them, with seeds, and useful plants, and fruit-trees. They were then left to turn these good gifts to profit.

"But what followed? Every one did as he wished. Some planted their ground with groves and gardens, pretty and useless. Others planted wild fruit, instead of the good fruit the Great [pg 076] King had commanded. A third had sowed good seed; but, not knowing the tares from the wheat, he had torn up all before they reached maturity. But the most part left their land uncultivated; they had lost their seeds, or spoiled their implements. Many would not understand the orders of the great king; and others tried, by subtlety, to evade them.

"A few laboured with courage, as they had been taught, rejoicing in the hope of the promise given them. Their greatest danger was in the disbelief of their teachers. Though every one had a copy of the law, few read it; all were ready, by some excuse, to avoid this duty. Some asserted they knew it, yet never thought on it: some called these the laws of past times; not of the present. Other said the Great King did not regard the actions of his subjects, that he had neither mines nor dungeons, and that all would certainly be taken to the Heavenly City. They began to neglect the duties of the day dedicated to the Great King. Few assembled; and of these, the most part were inattentive, and did not profit by the instruction given them.

"But the Great King was faithful to his word. From time to time, frigates arrived, bearing the name of some disease. These were followed by a large vessel called The Grave, bearing the terrible flag of the Admiral Death; this flag was of two colours, green and black; and appeared to the colonists, according to their state, the smiling colour of Hope, or the gloomy hue of Despa'r.

"This fleet always arrived unexpectedly, and was usually unwelcome. The officers were sent out, [pg 077] by the admiral, to seize those he pointed out: many who were unwilling were compelled to go; and others whose land was prepared, and even the harvest ripening, were summoned; but these went joyfully, sure that they went to happiness. The fleet being ready, sailed for the Heavenly City. Then the Great King, in his justice, awarded the punishments and recompenses. Excuses were now too late; the negligent and disobedient were sent to labour in the dark mines; while the faithful and obedient, arrayed in bright robes, were received into their glorious abodes of happiness.

"I have finished my parable, my dear children; reflect on it, and profit by it. Fritz, what do you think of it?"

"I am considering the goodness of the Great King, and the ingratitude of his people," answered he.

"And how very foolish they were," said Ernest, "with a little prudence, they might have kept their land in good condition, and secured a pleasant life afterwards."

"Away with them to the mines!" cried Jack, "they richly deserved such a doom."

"How much I should like," said Francis, "to see those soldiers in their shining armour!"

"I hope you will see them some day, my dear boy, if you continue to be good and obedient." I then explained my parable fully, and applied the moral to each of my sons directly.

"You, Fritz, should take warning from the people who planted wild fruit, and wished to make them pass for good fruit. Such are those who are proud of natural virtues, easy to exercise,--such as bodily [pg 078] strength, or physical courage; and place these above the qualities which are only attained by labour and patience.

"You, Ernest, must remember the subjects who laid out their land in flowery gardens; like those who seek the pleasures of life, rather than the duties. And you, my thoughtless Jack, and little Francis, think of the fate of those who left their land untilled, or heedlessly sowed tares for wheat. These are God's people who neither study nor reflect; who cast to the winds all instruction, and leave room in their minds for evil. Then let us all be, like the good labourers of the parable, constantly cultivating our ground, that, when Death comes for us, we may willingly follow him to the feet of the Great King, to hear these blessed words: 'Good and faithful servants! enter into the joy of your Lord!'"

This made a great impression on my children. We concluded by singing a hymn. Then my good wife produced from her unfailing bag, a copy of the Holy Scripture, from which I selected such passages as applied to our situation; and explained them to my best ability. My boys remained for some time thoughtful and serious, and though they followed their innocent recreations during the day, they did not lose sight of the useful lesson of the morning, but, by a more gentle and amiable manner, showed that my words had taken effect.

The next morning, Ernest had used my bow, which I had given him, very skilfully; bringing down some dozens of small birds, a sort of ortolan, from the branches of our tree, where they assembled to feed on the figs. This induced them all [pg 079] to wish for such a weapon. I was glad to comply with their wishes, as I wished them to become skilful in the use of these arms of our forefathers, which might be of great value to us, when our ammunition failed. I made two bows; and two quivers, to contain their arrows, of a flexible piece of bark, and, attaching a strap to them, I soon armed my little archers.

Fritz was engaged in preparing the skin of the margay, with more care than Jack had shown with that of the jackal. I showed him how to clean it, by rubbing it with sand in the river, till no vestige of fat or flesh was left; and then applying butter, to render it flexible.

These employments filled up the morning till dinner-time came. We had Ernest's ortolans, and some fried ham and eggs, which made us a sumptuous repast. I gave my boys leave to kill as many ortolans as they chose, for I knew that, half-roasted, and put into casks, covered with butter, they would keep for a length of time, and prove an invaluable resource in time of need. As I continued my work, making arrows, and a bow for Francis, I intimated to my wife that the abundant supply of figs would save our grain, as the poultry and pigeons would feed on them, as well as the ortolans. This was a great satisfaction to her. And thus another day passed, and we mounted to our dormitory, to taste the sweet slumber that follows a day of toil.

[pg 080]

CHAPTER XIII.

The next morning, all were engaged in archery: I completed the bow for Francis, and at his particular request made him a quiver too. The delicate bark of a tree, united by glue, obtained from our portable soup, formed an admirable quiver; this I suspended by a string round the neck of my boy, furnished with arrows; then taking his bow in his hand, he was as proud as a knight armed at all points.

After dinner, I proposed that we should give names to all the parts of our island known to us, in order that, by a pleasing delusion, we might fancy ourselves in an inhabited country. My proposal was well received, and then began the discussion of names. Jack wished for something high-sounding and difficult, such as Monomotapa or Zanguebar; very difficult words, to puzzle any one that visited our island. But I objected to this, as we were the most likely to have to use the names ourselves, and we should suffer from it. I rather suggested that we should give, in our own language, such simple names as should point out some circumstance connected with the spot. I proposed we should begin with the bay where we landed, and called on Fritz for his name.

"The Bay of Oysters" said he,--"we found so many there."

"Oh, no!" said Jack, "let it be Lobster Bay; for there I was caught by the leg."

MAP OF THE HAPPY ISLAND.
"MAP OF THE HAPPY ISLAND."

"Then we ought to call it the Bay of Tears," [pg 081] said Ernest, "to commemorate those you shed on the occasion."

"My advice," said my wife, "is, that in gratitude to God we should name it Safety

Bay."

We were all pleased with this name, and proceeded to give the name of Tent House to our first abode; Shark Island, to the little island in the bay, where we had found that animal; and, at Jack's desire, the marshy spot where we had cut our arrows was named Flamingo Marsh. There the height from which we had vainly sought traces of our shipmates, received the name of Cape Disappointment. The river was to be Jackal River, and the bridge, Family Bridge. The most difficult point was, to name our present abode. At last we agreed on the name of Falcon's Nest (in German Falken-hoist). This was received with acclamations, and I poured out for my young nestlings each a glass of sweet wine, to drink Prosperity to Falcon's Nest. We thus laid the foundation of the geography of our new country, promising to forward it to Europe by the first post.

After dinner, my sons returned to their occupation as tanners, Fritz to complete his belt, and Jack to make a sort of cuirass, of the formidable skin of the porcupine, to protect the dogs. He finished by making a sort of helmet from the head of the animal, as strange as the cuirasses.

The heat of the day being over, we prepared to set out to walk to Tent House, to renew our stock of provisions, and endeavour to bring the geese and ducks to our new residence; but, instead of going by the coast, we proposed to go up the river till we reached the chain of rocks, and continue under [pg 082] their shade till we got to the cascade, where we could cross, and return by Family Bridge.

This was approved, and we set out. Fritz, decorated with his beautiful belt of skin, Jack in his porcupine helmet. Each had a gun and game-bag; except Francis, who, with his pretty fair face, his golden hair, and his bow and quiver, was a perfect Cupid. My wife was loaded with a large butter-pot for a fresh supply. Turk walked before us with his coat of mail, and Flora followed, peeping at a respectful distance from him, for fear of the darts. Knips, as my boys called the monkey, finding this new saddle very inconvenient, jumped off, with many contortions, but soon fixed on Flora, who, not being able to shake him off, was compelled to become his palfrey.

The road by the river was smooth and pleasant. When we reached the end of the wood, the country seemed more open; and now the boys, who had been rambling about, came running up, out of breath; Ernest was holding a plant with leaves and flowers, and green apples hanging on it.

"Potatoes!" said he; "I am certain they are potatoes!"

"God be praised," said I; "this precious plant will secure provision for our colony."

"Well," said Jack, "if his superior knowledge discovered them, I will be the first to

60

dig them up;" and he set to work so ardently, that we had soon a bag of fine ripe potatoes, which we carried on to Tent House.

[pg 083]

CHAPTER XIV.

We had been much delighted with the new and lovely scenery of our road: the prickly cactus, and aloe, with its white flowers; the Indian fig; the white and yellow jasmine; the fragrant vanilla, throwing round its graceful festoons. Above all, the regal pineapple grew in profusion, and we feasted on it, for the first time, with avidity.

Among the prickly stalks of the cactus and aloes, I perceived a plant with large pointed leaves, which I knew to be the karata. I pointed out to the boys its beautiful red flowers; the leaves are an excellent application to wounds, and thread is made from the filaments, and the pith of the stem is used by the savage tribes for tinder.

When I showed the boys, by experiment, the use of the pith, they thought the tinder-tree would be almost as useful as the potatoes.

"At all events," I said, "it will be more useful than the pine-apples; your mother will be thankful for thread, when her enchanted bag is exhausted."

"How happy it is for us," said she, "that you have devoted yourself to reading and study. In our ignorance we might have passed this treasure, without suspecting its value."

Fritz inquired of what use in the world all the rest of these prickly plants could be, which wounded every one that came near.

"All these have their use, Fritz," said I; "some contain juices and gums, which are daily made [pg 084] use of in medicine; others are useful in the arts, or in manufactures. The Indian fig, for instance, is a most interesting tree. It grows in the most arid soil. The fruit is said to be sweet and wholesome."

In a moment, my little active Jack was climbing the rocks to gather some of these figs; but he had not remarked that they were covered with thousands of slender thorns, finer than the finest needles, which terribly wounded his fingers. He returned, weeping bitterly and dancing with pain. Having rallied him a little for his greediness, I extracted the thorns, and then showed him how to open the fruit,

61

by first cutting off the pointed end, as it lay on the ground; into this I fixed a piece of stick, and then pared it with my knife. The novelty of the expedient recommended it, and they were soon all engaged eating the fruit, which they declared was very good.

In the mean time, I saw Ernest examining one of the figs very attentively. "Oh! papa!" said he, "what a singular sight; the fig is covered with a small red insect. I cannot shake them off. Can they be the Cochineal?" I recognized at once the precious insect, of which I explained to my sons the nature and use. "It is with this insect," said I, "that the beautiful and rich scarlet dye is made. It is found in America, and the Europeans give its weight in gold for it."

Thus discoursing on the wonders of nature, and the necessity of increasing our knowledge by observation and study, we arrived at Tent House, and found it in the same state as we left it.

We all began to collect necessaries. Fritz loaded himself with powder and shot, I opened the butter-cask, and my wife and little Francis [pg 085] filled the pot. Ernest and Jack went to try and secure the geese and ducks; but they had become so wild that it would have been impossible, if Ernest had not thought of an expedient. He tied pieces of cheese, for bait, to threads, which he floated on the water. The voracious creatures immediately swallowed the cheese and were drawn out by the thread. They were then securely tied, and fastened to the game-bags, to be carried home on our backs. As the bait could not be recovered, the boys contented themselves with cutting off the string close to the beak, leaving them to digest the rest.

Our bags were already loaded with potatoes, but we filled up the spaces between them with salt; and, having relieved Turk of his armour, we placed the heaviest on his back. I took the butter-pot; and, after replacing everything, and closing our tent, we resumed our march, with our ludicrous incumbrances. The geese and ducks were very noisy in their adieu to their old marsh; the dogs barked; and we all laughed so excessively, that we forgot our burdens till we sat down again under our tree. My wife soon had her pot of potatoes on the fire. She then milked the cow and goat, while I set the fowls at liberty on the banks of the river. We then sat down to a smoking dish of potatoes, a jug of milk, and butter and cheese. After supper we had prayers, thanking God especially for his new benefits; and we then sought our repose among the leaves.

[pg 086]

CHAPTER XV.

I had observed on the shore, the preceding day, a quantity of wood, which I thought would suit to make a sledge, to convey our casks and heavy stores from Tent House to Falcon's Nest. At dawn of day I woke Ernest, whose inclination to indolence I wished to overcome, and leaving the rest asleep, we descended, and harnessing the ass to a strong branch of a tree that was lying near, we proceeded to the shore. I had no difficulty in selecting proper pieces of wood; we sawed them the right length, tied them together, and laid them across the bough, which the patient animal drew very contentedly. We added to the load a small chest we discovered half buried in the sand, and we returned homewards, Ernest leading the ass, and I assisted by raising the load with a lever when we met with any obstruction. My wife had been rather alarmed; but seeing the result of our expedition, and hearing of the prospect of a sledge, she was satisfied. I opened the chest, which contained only some sailors' dresses and some linen, both wetted with sea-water; but likely to be very useful as our own clothes decayed. I found Fritz and Jack had been shooting ortolans; they had killed about fifty, but had consumed so much powder and shot, that I checked a prodigality so imprudent in our situation. I taught them to make snares for the birds of the threads we drew from the karata leaves we had brought home. My wife and her [pg 087] two younger sons busied themselves with these, while I, with my two elder boys, began to construct the sledge. As we were working, we heard a great noise among the fowls, and Ernest, looking about, discovered the monkey seizing and hiding the eggs from the nests; he had collected a good store in a hole among the roots, which Ernest carried to his mother; and Knips was punished by being tied up, every morning, till the eggs were collected.

Our work was interrupted by dinner, composed of ortolans, milk, and cheese. After dinner, Jack had climbed to the higher branches of the trees to place his snares, and found the pigeons were making nests. I then told him to look often to the snares, for fear our own poor birds should be taken; and, above all, never in future to fire into the tree.

"Papa," said little Francis, "can we not sow some gunpowder, and then we shall have plenty?" This proposal was received with shouts of laughter, which greatly discomposed the little innocent fellow. Professor Ernest immediately seized the opportunity to give a lecture on the composition of gunpowder.

At the end of the day my sledge was finished. Two long curved planks of wood, crossed by three pieces, at a distance from each other, formed the simple conveyance. The fore and hind parts were in the form of horns, to keep the load from falling off. Two ropes were fastened to the front, and my sledge was complete. My wife was delighted with it, and hoped I would now set out immediately to Tent House for the butter-cask. [pg 088] I made no objection to this; and Ernest and I prepared to go, and leave Fritz in charge of the family.

CHAPTER XVI.

When we were ready to set out, Fritz presented each of us with a little case he had made from the skin of the margay. They were ingeniously contrived to contain knife, fork, and spoon, and a small hatchet. We then harnessed the ass and the cow to the sledge, took a flexible bamboo cane for a whip, and, followed by Flora, we departed, leaving Turk to guard the tree.

We went by the shore, as the better road for the sledge, and crossing Family Bridge, were soon at Tent House. After unharnessing the animals, we began to load. We took the cask of butter, the cheese, and the biscuit; all the rest of our utensils, powder, shot, and Turk's armour, which we had left there. These labours had so occupied us, that we had not observed that our animals, attracted by the pasturage, had crossed the bridge, and wandered out of sight. I sent Ernest to seek them, and in the mean time went to the bay, where I discovered some convenient little hollows in the rock, that seemed cut out for baths. I called Ernest to come, and till he arrived, employed myself in cutting some rushes, which I thought might be useful. When my son came, I found he had ingeniously removed the first planks from the bridge, to prevent the animals straying over again. We then had a [pg 089] very pleasant bath, and Ernest being out first, I sent him to the rock, where the salt was accumulated, to fill a small bag, to be transferred to the large bags on the ass. He had not been absent long, when I heard him cry out, "Papa! papa! a huge fish! I cannot hold it; it will break my line." I ran to his assistance, and found him lying on the ground on his face, tugging at his line, to which an enormous salmon was attached, that had nearly pulled him into the water. I let it have a little more line, then drew it gently into a shallow, and secured it. It appeared about fifteen pounds weight; and we pleased ourselves with the idea of presenting this to our good cook. Ernest said, he remembered having remarked how this place swarmed with fish, and he took care to bring his rod with him; he had taken about a dozen small fishes, which he had in his handkerchief, before he was overpowered by the salmon. I cut the fishes open, and rubbed the inside with salt, to preserve them; then placing them in a small box on the sledge, and adding our bags of salt, we harnessed our animals, and set off homewards.

When we were about half-way, Flora left us, and, by her barking, raised a singular animal, which seemed to leap instead of ran. The irregular bounds of the animal disconcerted my aim, and, though very near, I missed it. Ernest was more fortunate; he fired at it, and killed it. It was an animal about the size of a sheep, with the tail of a tiger; its head and skin were like those of a mouse, ears longer than the hare; there was a curious pouch on the belly; the fore legs were short, as if imperfectly developed, and armed with [pg 090] strong claws, the hind legs long, like a pair of stilts. After Ernest's pride of victory was a little subdued, he fell back on his science, and began to examine his spoil.

"By its teeth," said he, "it should belong to the family of rodentes, or gnawers; by its legs, to the jumpers; and by its pouch, to the opossum tribe."

This gave me the right clue. "Then," said I, "this must be the animal Cook first discovered in New Holland, and it is called the kangaroo."

We now tied the legs of the animal together, and, putting a stick through, carried it to the sledge very carefully, for Ernest was anxious to preserve the beautiful skin. Our animals were heavily laden; but, giving them a little rest and some fresh grass, we once more started, and in a short time reached Falcon's Nest.

My wife had been employed during our absence in washing the clothes of the three boys, clothing them in the mean time from the sailor's chest we had found a few days before. Their appearance was excessively ridiculous, as the garments neither suited their age nor size, and caused great mirth to us all; but my wife had preferred this disguise to the alternative of their going naked.

We now began to display our riches, and relate our adventures. The butter and the rest of the provisions were very welcome, the salmon still more so, but the sight of the kangaroo produced screams of admiration. Fritz displayed a little jealousy, but soon surmounted it by an exertion of his nobler feelings; and only the keen eye of a father could have discovered it. He congratulated [pg 091] Ernest warmly, but could not help begging to accompany me next time.

"I promise you that," said I, "as a reward for the conquest you have achieved over your jealousy of your brother. But, remember, I could not have given you a greater proof of my confidence, than in leaving you to protect your mother and brothers. A noble mind finds its purest joy in the accomplishment of its duty, and to that willingly sacrifices its inclination. But," I added, in a low tone, lest I should distress my wife, "I propose another expedition to the vessel, and you must accompany me."

We then fed our tired animals, giving them some salt with their grass, a great treat to them. Some salmon was prepared for dinner, and the rest salted. After dinner, I hung up the kangaroo till next day, when we intended to salt and smoke the flesh. Evening arrived, and an excellent supper of fish, ortolans, and potatoes refreshed us; and, after thanks to God, we retired to rest.

CHAPTER XVII.

I rose early, and descended the ladder, a little uneasy about my kangaroo, and found I was but just in time to save it, for my dogs had so enjoyed their repast on the entrails, which I had given them the night before, that they wished to appropriate the rest. They had succeeded in tearing off the head, which was in their reach, and were devouring it in a sort of growling partnership. As we had no store-room [pg 092] for our provision, I decided to administer a little correction, as a warning to these gluttons. I gave them some smart strokes with a cane, and they fled howling to the stable under the roots. Their cries roused my wife, who came down; and, though she could not but allow the chastisement to be just and prudent, she was so moved by compassion, that she consoled the poor sufferers with some remains of last night's supper.

I now carefully stripped the kangaroo of his elegant skin, and washing myself, and changing my dress after this unpleasant operation, I joined my family at breakfast. I then announced my plan of visiting the vessel, and ordered Fritz to make preparations. My wife resigned herself mournfully to the necessity. When we were ready to depart, Ernest and Jack were not to be found; their mother suspected they had gone to get potatoes. This calmed my apprehension; but I charged her to reprimand them for going without leave. We set out towards Tent House, leaving Flora to protect the household, and taking our guns as usual.

We had scarcely left the wood, and were approaching Jackal River, when we heard piercing cries, and suddenly Ernest and Jack leaped from a thicket, delighted, as Jack said, in having succeeded in their plan of accompanying us, and, moreover, in making us believe we were beset with savages. They were, however, disappointed. I gave them a severe reproof for their disobedience, and sent them home with a message to their mother that I thought we might be detained all night, and begged she would not be uneasy.

They listened to me in great confusion, and [pg 093] were much mortified at their dismissal; but I begged Fritz to give Ernest his silver watch, that they might know how the time passed; and I knew that I could replace it, as there was a case of watches in the ship. This reconciled them a little to their lot, and they left us. We went forward to our boat, embarked, and, aided by the current, soon reached the vessel.

My first care was to construct some more convenient transport-vessel than our boat. Fritz proposed a raft, similar to those used by savage nations, supported on skins filled with air. These we had not; but we found a number of water-hogsheads, which we emptied, and closed again, and threw a dozen of them into the sea, between the ship and our boat. Some long planks were laid on these, and secured with ropes. We added a raised edge of planks to secure our cargo, and thus had a solid raft, capable of conveying any burden. This work occupied us the whole day, scarcely interrupted by eating a little cold meat from our game-bags. Exhausted by fatigue, we were glad to take a good night's rest in the captain's cabin on an elastic mattress, of which our hammocks had made us forget the comfort. Early next morning we began to load our raft.

We began by entirely stripping our own cabin and that of the captain. We carried away even the doors and windows. The chests of the carpenter and the gunner followed. There were cases of rich jewellery, and caskets of money, which at first tempted us, but were speedily relinquished for objects of real utility. I preferred a case of young plants of European fruits, carefully packed in moss for transportation. I saw, with delight, among [pg 094] these precious plants, apple, pear, plum, orange, apricot, peach, almond, and chesnut trees, and some young shoots of vines. How I longed to plant these familiar trees of home in a foreign soil. We secured some bars of iron and pigs of lead, grindstones, cart-wheels ready for mounting, tongs, shovels, plough-shares, packets of copper and iron wire, sacks of maize, peas, oats, and vetches; and even a small hand-mill. The vessel had been, in fact, laden with everything likely to be useful in a new colony. We found a saw-mill in pieces, but marked, so that it could be easily put together. It was difficult to select, but we took as much as was safe on the raft, adding a large fishing-net and the ship's compass. Fritz begged to take the harpoons, which he hung by the ropes over the bow of our boat; and I indulged his fancy. We were now loaded as far as prudence would allow us; so, attaching our raft firmly to the boat, we hoisted our sail, and made slowly to the shore.

CHAPTER XVIII.

The wind was favourable, but we advanced slowly, the floating mass that we had to tug retarding us. Fritz had been some time regarding a large object in the water; he called me to steer a little towards it, that he might see what it was. I went to the rudder, and made the movement; immediately I heard the whistling of the cord, and felt a shock; then a second, which was followed by a rapid motion of the boat.

[pg 095]
"We are going to founder!" cried I. "What is the matter?"

"I have caught it," shouted Fritz; "I have harpooned it in the neck. It is a turtle."

I saw the harpoon shining at a distance, and the turtle was rapidly drawing us along by the line. I lowered the sail, and rushed forward to cut the line; but Fritz besought me not to do it. He assured me there was no danger, and that he himself would release us if necessary. I reluctantly consented, and saw our whole convoy drawn by an animal whose agony increased its strength. As we drew near the shore, I endeavoured to steer so that we might not strike and be capsized. I saw after a few minutes that our conductor again wanted to make out to sea; I therefore hoisted the sail, and the wind being in our favour, he found resistance vain, and, tugging as before, followed up the current, only taking more to the left, towards Falcon's Nest, and landing us in a shallow, rested on the shore. I leaped out of the boat, and with a hatchet soon put our powerful conductor out of his misery.

Fritz uttered a shout of joy, and fired off his gun, as a signal of our arrival. All came running to greet us, and great was their surprise, not only at the value of our cargo, but at the strange mode by which it had been brought into harbour. My first care was to send them for the sledge, to remove some of our load without delay, and as the ebbing tide was leaving our vessels almost dry on the sand, I profited by the opportunity to secure them. By the aid of the jack-screw and levers, we raised and brought to the shore two large pieces of lead from the raft. These served for anchors, [pg 096] and, connected to the boat and raft by strong cables, fixed them safely.

As soon as the sledge arrived, we placed the turtle with some difficulty on it, as it weighed at least three hundredweight. We added some lighter articles, the mattresses, some small chests, &c., and proceeded with our first load to Falcon's Nest in great spirits. As we walked on, Fritz told them of the wondrous cases of jewellery we had abandoned for things of use; Jack wished Fritz had brought him a gold snuff-box, to hold curious seeds; and Francis wished for some of the money to buy gingerbread at the fair! Everybody laughed at the little simpleton, who could not help laughing himself, when he remembered his distance from fairs. Arrived at home, our first care was to turn the turtle on his back, to get the excellent meat out of the shell. With my hatchet I separated the cartilages that unite the shells: the upper shell is convex, the lower one nearly flat.

We had some of the turtle prepared for dinner, though my wife felt great repugnance in touching the green fat, notwithstanding my assurance of its being the chief delicacy to an epicure.

We salted the remainder of the flesh, and gave the offal to the dogs. The boys were all clamorous to possess the shell; but I said it belonged to Fritz, by right of conquest, and he must dispose of it as he thought best.

"Then," said he, "I will make a basin of it, and place it near the river, that my mother may always keep it full of fresh water."

"Very good," said I, "and we will fill our [pg 097] basin, as soon as we find some clay to make a solid foundation."

"I found some this morning," said Jack,--"a whole bed of clay, and I brought these balls home to show you."

"And I have made a discovery too," said Ernest. "Look at these roots, like radishes; I have not eaten any, but the sow enjoys them very much."

"A most valuable discovery, indeed," said I; "if I am not mistaken, this is the root of the manioc, which with the potatoes will insure us from famine. Of this root they make in the West Indies a sort of bread, called cassava bread. In its natural state it contains a violent poison, but by a process of heating it becomes wholesome. The nutritious tapioca is a preparation from this root."

By this time we had unloaded, and proceeded to the shore to bring a second load before night came on. We brought up two chests of our own clothes and property, some chests of tools, the cart-wheels, and the hand-mill, likely now to be of use for the cassava. After unloading, we sat down to an excellent supper of turtle, with potatoes, instead of bread. After supper, my wife said, smiling, "After such a hard day, I think I can give you something to restore you." She then brought a bottle and glasses, and filled us each a glass of clear, amber-coloured wine. I found it excellent Malaga. She had been down to the shore the previous day, and there found a small cask thrown up by the waves. This, with the assistance of her sons, she had rolled up to the [pg 098] foot of our tree, and there covered it with leaves to keep it cool till our arrival.

We were so invigorated by this cordial, that we set briskly to work to hoist up our mattresses to our dormitory, which we accomplished by the aid of ropes and pulleys. My wife received and arranged them, and after our usual evening devotions, we gladly lay down on them, to enjoy a night of sweet repose.

CHAPTER XIX.

I rose before daylight, and, leaving my family sleeping, descended, to go to the shore to look after my vessels. I found all the animals moving. The dogs leaped about me; the cocks were crowing; the goats browsing on the dewy grass. The ass alone was sleeping; and, as he was the assistant I wanted, I was compelled to rouse him, a preference which did not appear to flatter him. Nevertheless, I harnessed him to the sledge, and, followed by the dogs, went forward to the coast, where I found my boat and raft safe at anchor. I took up a moderate load and came home to breakfast; but found all still as I left them. I called my family, and they sprung up ashamed of their sloth; my wife declared it must have been the good mattress that had charmed her.

I gave my boys a short admonition for their sloth. We then came down to a hasty breakfast, and returned to the coast to finish the unloading the boats, that I might, at high water, take them round to moor at the usual place in the Bay of [pg 099] Safety. I sent my wife up with the last load, while Fritz and I embarked, and, seeing Jack watching us, I consented that he should form one of the crew, for I had determined to make another visit to the wreck before I moored my craft. When we reached the vessel, the day was so far advanced that we had only time to collect hastily anything easy to embark. My sons ran over the ship. Jack came trundling a wheelbarrow, which he said would be excellent for fetching the potatoes in.

But Fritz brought me good news: he had found, between decks, a beautiful pinnace (a small vessel, of which the prow is square), taken to pieces, with all its fittings, and even two small guns. I saw that all the pieces were numbered, and placed in order; nothing was wanting. I felt the importance of this acquisition; but it would take days of labour to put it together; and then how could we launch it? At present, I felt I must renounce the undertaking. I returned to my loading. It consisted of all sorts of utensils: a copper boiler, some plates of iron, tobacco-graters, two grindstones, a barrel of powder, and one of flints. Jack did not forget his wheelbarrow; and we found two more, which we added to our cargo, and then sailed off speedily, to avoid the land-wind, which rises in the evening.

As we drew near, we were astonished to see a row of little creatures standing on the shore, apparently regarding us with much curiosity. They were dressed in black, with white waistcoats, and thick cravats; their arms hung down carelessly; but from time to time they raised them as if they wished to bestow on us a fraternal embrace.

[pg 100]
"I believe," said I, laughing, "this must be the country of pigmies, and they are coming to welcome us."

"They are the Lilliputians, father," said Jack; "I have read of them; but I thought they had been less."

"As if Gulliver's Travels was true!" said Fritz, in a tone of derision.

"Then are there no pigmies?" asked he.

"No, my dear boy," said I; "all these stories are either the invention or the mistakes of ancient navigators, who have taken troops of monkeys for men, or who have wished to repeat something marvellous. But the romance of Gulliver is an allegory, intended to convey great truths."

"And now," said Fritz, "I begin to see our pigmies have beaks and wings."

"You are right," said I; "they are penguins, as Ernest explained to us some time since. They are good swimmers; but, unable to fly, are very helpless on land."

I steered gently to the shore, that I might not disturb them; but Jack leaped into the water up to his knees, and, dashing among the penguins, with a stick struck right and left, knocking down half a dozen of the poor stupid birds before they were aware. Some of these we brought away alive. The rest, not liking such a reception, took to the water, and were soon out of sight. I scolded Jack for his useless rashness, for the flesh of the penguin is by no means a delicacy.

We now filled our three wheelbarrows with such things as we could carry, not forgetting the sheets of iron and the graters, and trudged home. Our dogs announced our approach, and all rushed [pg 101] out to meet us. A curious and merry examination commenced. They laughed at my graters; but I let them laugh, for I had a project in my head. The penguins I intended for our poultry-yard; and, for the present, I ordered the boys to tie each of them by a leg to one of our geese or ducks, who opposed the bondage very clamorously; but necessity made them submissive.

My wife showed me a large store of potatoes and manioc roots, which she and her children had dug up the evening before. We then went to supper, and talked of all we had seen in the vessel, especially of the pinnace, which we had been obliged to leave. My wife did not feel much regret on this account, as she dreaded maritime expeditions, though she agreed she might have felt less uneasiness if we had had a vessel of this description. I gave my sons a charge to rise early next morning, as we had an important business on hand; and curiosity roused them all in very good time. After our usual preparations for the day, I addressed them thus: "Gentlemen, I am going to teach you all a new business,--that of a baker. Give me the plates of iron and the graters we brought yesterday." My wife was astonished; but I requested her to wait patiently and she should have bread, not perhaps light buns, but eatable flat cakes. But first she was to make me two small bags of sailcloth. She obeyed me; but, at the same time, I observed she put the potatoes on the fire, a proof she had not much faith in my bread-making. I then spread a cloth over the ground, and, giving each of the boys a grater, we began to grate the carefully-washed manioc roots, resting the end on the cloth. In a [pg 102] short time we had a heap of what appeared to be moist white sawdust; certainly not tempting to the appetite; but the little workmen were amused with their labour, and jested no little about the cakes made of scraped radishes.

"Laugh now, boys," said I; "we shall see, after a while. But you, Ernest, ought to know that the manioc is one of the most precious of alimentary roots, forming the

71

principal sustenance of many nations of America, and often preferred by Europeans, who inhabit those countries, to wheaten bread."

When all the roots were grated, I filled the two bags closely with the pollard, and my wife sewed the ends up firmly. It was now necessary to apply strong pressure to extract the juice from the root, as this juice is a deadly poison. I selected an oak beam, one end of which we fixed between the roots of our tree; beneath this I placed our bags on a row of little blocks of wood; I then took a large bough, which I had cut from a tree, and prepared for the purpose, and laid it across them. We all united then in drawing down the opposite end of the plank over the bough, till we got it to a certain point, when we suspended to it the heaviest substances we possessed; hammers, bars of iron, and masses of lead. This acting upon the manioc, the sap burst through the cloth, and flowed on the ground copiously. When I thought the pressure was complete, we relieved the bags from the lever, and opening one, drew out a handful of the pollard, still rather moist, resembling coarse maize-flour.

"It only wants a little heat to complete our [pg 103] success," said I, in great delight. I ordered a fire to be lighted, and fixing one of our iron plates, which was round in form, and rather concave, on two stones placed on each side of the fire, I covered it with the flour which we took from the bag with a small wooden shovel. It soon formed a solid cake, which we turned, that it might be equally baked.

It smelled so good, that they all wished to commence eating immediately; and I had some difficulty in convincing them that this was only a trial, and that our baking was still imperfect. Besides, as I told them there were three kinds of manioc, of which one contained more poison than the rest, I thought it prudent to try whether we had perfectly extracted it, by giving a small quantity to our fowls. As soon, therefore, as the cake was cold, I gave some to two chickens, which I kept apart; and also some to Master Knips, the monkey, that he might, for the first time, do us a little service. He ate it with so much relish, and such grimaces of enjoyment, that my young party were quite anxious to share his feast; but I ordered them to wait till we could judge of the effect, and, leaving our employment, we went to our dinner of potatoes, to which my wife had added one of the penguins, which was truly rather tough and fishy; but as Jack would not allow this, and declared it was a dish fit for a king, we allowed him to regale on it as much as he liked. During dinner, I talked to them of the various preparations made from the manioc; I told my wife we could obtain an excellent starch from the expressed juice; but this did not interest her much, as at present she usually wore the [pg 104] dress of a sailor, for convenience, and had neither caps nor collars to starch.

The cake made from the root is called by the natives of the Antilles cassava, and in no savage nation do we find any word signifying bread; an article of food unknown to them.

We spoke of poisons; and I explained to my sons the different nature and effects of them. Especially I warned them against the manchineel, which ought to grow in this part of the world. I described the fruit to them, as resembling a tempting yellow apple, with red spots, which is one of the most deadly poisons: it is said that even to sleep under the tree is dangerous. I forbade them to taste any unknown fruit, and they promised to obey me.

On leaving the table, we went to visit the victims of our experiment. Jack whistled for Knips, who came in three bounds from the summit of a high tree, where he had doubtless been plundering some nest; and his vivacity, and the peaceful cackling of the fowls, assured us our preparation was harmless.

"Now, gentlemen," said I, laughing, "to the bakehouse, and let us see what we can do." I wished them each to try to make the cakes. They immediately kindled the fire and heated the iron plate. In the mean time, I broke up the grated cassava, and mixed it with a little milk; and giving each of them a cocoa-nut basin filled with the paste, I showed them how to pour it with a spoon upon the plate, and spread it about; when the paste began to puff up, I judged it was baked on one side, and turned it, like a pancake, with a fork; and after a little time, we had a quantity of [pg 105] nice yellow biscuits, which, with a jug of milk, made us a delicious collation; and determined us, without delay, to set about cultivating the manioc.

The rest of the day was employed in bringing up the remainder of our cargo, by means of the sledge and the useful wheelbarrows.

CHAPTER XX.

The next morning I decided on returning to the wreck. The idea of the pinnace continually haunted my mind, and left me no repose. But it was necessary to take all the hands I could raise, and with difficulty I got my wife's consent to take my three elder sons, on promising her we would return in the evening. We set out, taking provision for the day, and soon arrived at the vessel, when my boys began to load the raft with all manner of portable things. But the great matter was the pinnace. It was contained in the after-hold of the vessel, immediately below the officers' berths. My sons, with all the ardour of their age, begged to begin by clearing a space in the vessel to put the pinnace together, and we might afterwards think how we should launch it. Under any other circumstances I should have shown them the folly of such an undertaking; but in truth, I had myself a vague hope of success, that encouraged me, and I cried out, "To work! to work!" The hold was lighted by some chinks in the ship's side. We set diligently to work, hacking, cutting, and sawing away all obstacles, and before evening we had a clear space round us. But now [pg 106] it was necessary to return, and we put to sea with our cargo, purposing to continue our work daily. On reaching the Bay of Safety, we had the pleasure of finding my wife and Francis, who had established themselves at Tent House, intending to continue there till our visits to the vessel were concluded; that they might always keep us in sight, and spare us the unnecessary labour of a walk after our day's work.

I thanked my wife tenderly for this kind sacrifice, for I knew how much she enjoyed the cool shade of Falcon's Nest; and in return I showed her the treasures we had brought her from the vessel, consisting of two barrels of salt butter, three hogsheads of flour, several bags of millet, rice, and other grains, and a variety of useful household articles, which she conveyed with great delight to our storehouse in the rocks.

For a week we spent every day in the vessel, returning in the evening to enjoy a good supper, and talk of our progress; and my wife, happily engrossed with her poultry and other household cares, got accustomed to our absence. With much hard labour, the pinnace was at last put together. Its construction was light and elegant, it looked as if it would sail well; at the head was a short half-deck; the masts and sails were like those of a brigantine. We carefully caulked all the seams with tow dipped in melted tar; and we even indulged ourselves by placing the two small guns in it, fastened by chains.

And there stood the beautiful little bark, immovable on the stocks. We admired it incessantly; but what could we do to get it afloat? The difficulty of forcing a way through the mighty [pg 107] timbers lined with copper, that formed the side of the ship, was insurmountable.

Suddenly, suggested by the excess of my despair, a bold but dangerous idea presented itself to me, in which all might be lost, as well as all gained. I said nothing about this to my children, to avoid the vexation of a possible disappointment, but began to execute my plan.

I found a cast-iron mortar, exactly fitted for my purpose, which I filled with gunpowder. I then took a strong oak plank to cover it, to which I fixed iron hooks, so that they could reach the handles of the mortar. I cut a groove in the side of the plank, that I might introduce a long match, which should burn at least two hours before it reached the powder. I placed the plank then over the mortar, fastened the hooks through the handles, surrounded it with pitch, and then bound some strong chains round the whole, to give it greater solidity. I proceeded to suspend this infernal machine against the side of the ship near our work, taking care to place it where the recoil from the explosion should not injure the pinnace. When all was ready, I gave the signal of departure, my sons having been employed in the boat, and not observing my preparations. I remained a moment to fire the match, and then hastily joined them with a beating heart, and proceeded to the shore.

As soon as we reached our harbour, I detached the raft, that I might return in the boat as soon as I heard the explosion. We began actively to unload the boat, and while thus employed, a report like thunder was heard. All trembled, and threw down their load in terror.

[pg 108]
"What can it be?" cried they. "Perhaps a signal from some vessel in distress. Let us go to their assistance."

"It came from the vessel," said my wife. "It must have blown up. You have not been careful of fire; and have left some near a barrel of gunpowder."

"At all events," said I, "we will go and ascertain the cause. Who'll go with me?"

By way of reply, my three sons leaped into the boat, and consoling the anxious mother by a promise to return immediately, away we rowed. We never made the voyage so quickly. Curiosity quickened the movements of my sons, and I was all impatience to see the result of my project. As we approached, I was glad to see no appearance of flames, or even smoke. The position of the vessel did not seem altered. Instead of entering the vessel as usual, we rounded the prow, and came opposite the other side. The greater part of the side of the ship was gone. The sea was covered with the remains of it. In its place stood our beautiful pinnace, quite uninjured, only leaning a little over the stocks. At the sight I cried out, in a transport that amazed my sons, "Victory! victory! the charming vessel is our own; it will be easy now to launch her."

"Ah! I comprehend now," said Fritz. "Papa has blown up the ship; but how could you manage to do it so exactly?"

I explained all to him, as we entered through the broken side of the devoted vessel. I soon ascertained that no fire remained; and that the pinnace had escaped any injury. We set to work to clear away all the broken timbers in our way, and, [pg 109] by the aid of the jack-screw and levers, we moved the pinnace, which we had taken care to build on rollers, to the opening; then attaching a strong cable to her head, and fixing the other end to the most solid part of the ship, we easily launched her. It was too late to do any more now, except carefully securing our prize. And we returned to the good mother, to whom, wishing to give her an agreeable surprise, we merely said, that the side of the vessel was blown out with powder; but we were still able to obtain more from it; at which she sighed, and, in her heart, I have no doubt, wished the vessel, and all it contained, at the bottom of the sea.

We had two days of incessant labour in fitting and loading the pinnace; finally, after putting up our masts, ropes, and sails, we selected a cargo of things our boats could not bring. When all was ready, my boys obtained permission, as a reward for their industry, to salute their mamma, as we entered the bay, by firing our two guns. Fritz was captain, and Ernest and Jack, at his command, put their matches to the guns, and fired. My wife and little boy rushed out in alarm; but our joyful shouts soon re-assured them; and they were ready to welcome us with astonishment and delight. Fritz placed a plank from the pinnace to the shore, and, assisting his mother, she came on board. They gave her a new salute, and christened the vessel The Elizabeth, after her.

My wife praised our skill and perseverance, but begged we would not suppose that Francis and she had been idle during our long absence. We moored the little fleet safely to the shore, and followed [pg 110] her up the river to the cascade, where we saw a neat garden laid out in beds and walks.

"This is our work," said she; "the soil here, being chiefly composed of decayed leaves, is light and easy to dig. There I have my potatoes; there manioc roots: these are sown with peas, beans and lentils; in this row of beds are sown lettuces, radishes, cabbages, and other European vegetables. I have reserved one part for sugar-canes; on the high ground I have transplanted pine-apples, and sown melons. Finally, round every bed, I have sown a border of maize, that the high, bushy stems may protect the young plants from the sun."

I was delighted with the result of the labour and industry of a delicate female and a child, and could scarcely believe it was accomplished in so short a time.

"I must confess I had no great hope of success at first," said my wife, "and this made me averse to speaking of it. Afterwards, when I suspected you had a secret, I determined to have one, too, and give you a surprise."

After again applauding these useful labours, we returned to discharge our cargo; and as we went, my good Elizabeth, still full of horticultural plans, reminded me of the young fruit-trees we had brought from the vessel. I promised to look after them next day, and to establish my orchard near her kitchen-garden.

We unloaded our vessels; placed on the sledge all that might be useful at Falcon's Nest; and, arranging the rest under the tent, fixed our pinnace to the shore, by means of the anchor and a cord fastened to a heavy stone; and at length set [pg 111] out to Falcon's Nest, where we arrived soon, to the great comfort of my wife, who dreaded the burning plain at Tent House.

CHAPTER XXI.

After our return to Falcon's Nest, I requested my sons to continue their exercises in gymnastics. I wished to develope all the vigour and energy that nature had given them; and which, in our situation, were especially necessary. I added to archery, racing, leaping, wrestling, and climbing trees, either by the trunks, or by a rope suspended from the branches, as sailors climb. I next taught them to use the lasso, a powerful weapon, by aid of which the people of South America capture savage animals. I fixed two balls of lead to the ends of a cord about a fathom in length. The Patagonians, I told them, used this weapon with wonderful dexterity. Having no leaden balls, they attach a heavy stone to each end of a cord about thirty yards long. If they wish to capture an animal, they hurl one of the stones at it with singular address. By the peculiar art with which the ball is thrown, the rope makes a turn or two round the neck of the animal, which remains entangled, without the power of escaping. In order to show the power of this weapon, I took aim at the trunk of a tree which they pointed out. My throw was quite successful. The end of the rope passed two or three times round the trunk of the tree, and remained firmly fixed to it. If the tree had been the neck of a tiger, I should have [pg 112] been absolute master of it. This experiment decided them all to learn the use of the lasso. Fritz was soon skilful in throwing it, and I encouraged the rest to persevere in acquiring the same facility, as the weapon might be invaluable to us when our ammunition failed.

The next morning I saw, on looking out, that the sea was too much agitated for any expedition in the boats; I therefore turned to some home employments. We looked over our stores for winter provision. My wife showed me a cask of ortolans she had preserved in butter, and a quantity of loaves of cassava bread, carefully prepared. She pointed out, that the pigeons had built in the tree, and were sitting on their eggs. We then looked over the young fruit-trees brought from Europe, and my sons and I immediately laid out a piece of ground, and planted them.

The day passed in these employments; and as we had lived only on potatoes, cassava bread, and milk for this day, we determined to go off next morning in pursuit of game to recruit our larder. At dawn of day we all started, including little Francis and his mother, who wished to take this opportunity of seeing a little more of the country. My sons and I took our arms, I harnessed the ass to the sledge which contained our provision for the day, and was destined to bring back the products of the chase. Turk, accoutred in his coat of mail, formed the advanced guard; my sons followed with their guns; then came my wife with Francis leading the ass; and at a little distance I closed the procession, with Master Knips mounted on the patient Flora.

We crossed Flamingo Marsh, and there my [pg 113] wife was charmed with the richness of the vegetation and the lofty trees. Fritz left us, thinking this a favourable spot for game. We soon heard the report of his gun, and an enormous bird fell a few paces from us. I ran to assist him, as he had much difficulty in securing his prize, which was only wounded in the wing, and was defending itself vigorously with its beak and claws. I threw a handkerchief over its head, and, confused by the darkness, I had no difficulty in binding it, and conveying it in triumph to the sledge. We were all in raptures at the sight of this beautiful creature, which Ernest pronounced to be a female of the bustard tribe. My wife hoped that the bird might be domesticated among her poultry, and, attracting some more of its species, might enlarge our stock of useful fowls. We soon arrived at the Wood of Monkeys, as we called it, where we had obtained our cocoa-nuts; and Fritz related the laughable scene of the stratagem to his mother and brothers. Ernest looked up wistfully at the nuts, but there were no monkeys to throw them down.

"Do they never fall from the trees?" and hardly had he spoken, when a large cocoa-nut fell at his feet, succeeded by a second, to my great astonishment, for I saw no animal in the tree, and I was convinced the nuts in the half-ripe state, as these were, could not fall of themselves.

"It is exactly like a fairy tale," said Ernest; "I had only to speak, and my wish was accomplished."

"And here comes the magician," said I, as, after a shower of nuts, I saw a huge land-crab descending the tree quietly, and quite regardless [pg 114] of our presence. Jack boldly struck a blow at him, but missed, and the animal, opening its enormous claws, made up to its opponent, who fled in terror. But the laughter of his brothers made him ashamed, and recalling his courage, he pulled off his coat, and threw it over the back of the crab; this checked its movements, and going to his assistance, I killed it with a blow of my hatchet.

They all crowded round the frightful animal, anxious to know what it was. I told them it was a land-crab--which we might call the cocoa-nut crab, as we owed such a store to it. Being unable to break the shell of the nut, of which they are very fond, they climb the tree, and break them off, in the unripe state. They then descend to enjoy their feast, which they obtain by inserting their claw through the small holes in the end, and abstracting the contents. They sometimes find them broken by the fall, when they can eat them at pleasure.

The hideousness of the animal, and the mingled terror and bravery of Jack, gave us subject of conversation for some time. We placed our booty on the sledge, and continued to go on through the wood. Our path became every instant more intricate, from the amazing quantity of creeping plants which choked the way, and obliged us to use the axe continually. The heat was excessive, and we got on slowly, when Ernest, always observing, and who was a little behind us, cried out, "Halt! a new and important discovery!" We returned, and he showed us, that from the stalk of one of the creepers we had cut with our axe, there was issuing clear, pure water. It was the [pg 115] liane rouge, which, in America, furnishes the hunter such a precious resource against thirst. Ernest was much pleased; he filled a cocoa-nut cup with the water, which flowed from the cut stalks like a fountain, and carried it to his mother, assuring her she might drink fearlessly; and we all had the comfort of allaying our thirst, and blessing the Gracious Hand who has placed this refreshing plant in the midst of the dry wilderness for the benefit of man.

 Suddenly we saw Ernest running to us, in great terror,
crying, 'A wild boar, papa! a great wild boar!.
"Suddenly we saw Ernest running to us, in great terror, crying, 'A wild boar, papa! a great wild boar!.'"

We now marched on with more vigour, and soon arrived at the Gourd Wood, where my wife and younger sons beheld with wonder the growth of this remarkable fruit. Fritz repeated all the history of our former attempts, and cut some gourds to make his mother some egg-baskets, and a large spoon to cream the milk. But we first sat down under the shade, and took some refreshment; and afterwards, while we all worked at making baskets, bowls, and flasks, Ernest, who had no taste for such labour, explored the wood. Suddenly we saw him running to us, in great terror, crying, "A wild boar! Papa; a great wild boar!" Fritz and I seized our guns, and ran to the spot he pointed out, the dogs preceding us. We soon heard barking and loud grunting, which proved the combat had begun, and, hoping for a good prize, we hastened forward; when, what was our vexation, when we found the dogs holding by the ears, not a wild boar, but our own great sow, whose wild and intractable disposition had induced her to leave us, and live in the woods! We could not but laugh at our disappointment, after a while, and I made the dogs release the poor sow, who immediately resumed her feast on [pg 116] a small fruit, which had fallen from the trees, and, scattered on the ground, had evidently tempted the voracious beast to this part. I took up one of these apples, which somewhat resembled a medlar, and opening it, found the contents of a rich and juicy nature, but did not venture to taste it till we had put it to the usual test. We collected a quantity--I even broke a loaded branch from the tree, and we returned to our party. Master Knips no sooner saw them than he seized on some, and crunched them up with great enjoyment. This satisfied me that the fruit was wholesome, and we regaled ourselves with some. My wife was especially delighted when I told her this must be the guava, from which the delicious jelly is obtained, so much prized in America.

"But, with all this," said Fritz, "we have a poor show of game. Do let us leave mamma with the young ones, and set off, to see what we can meet with."

I consented, and we left Ernest with his mother and Francis, Jack wishing to accompany us. We made towards the rocks at the right hand, and Jack preceded us a little, when he startled us by crying out, "A crocodile, papa!--a crocodile!"

"You simpleton!" said I, "a crocodile in a place where there is not a drop of water!"

"Papa!--I see it!" said the poor child, his eyes fixed on one spot; "it is there, on this rock, sleeping. I am sure it is a crocodile!"

As soon as I was near enough to distinguish it, I assured him his crocodile was a very harmless lizard, called the iguana, whose eggs and flesh were excellent food. Fritz would immediately have shot at this frightful creature, which was [pg 117] about five feet in length. I showed him that his scaly coat rendered such an attempt useless. I then cut a strong stick and a light wand. To the end of the former I attached a cord with a noose; this I held in my right hand, keeping the wand in my left. I approached softly, whistling. The animal awoke, apparently listening with pleasure. I drew nearer, tickling him gently with the wand. He lifted up his head, and opened his formidable jaws. I then dexterously threw the noose round his neck, drew it, and, jumping on his back, by the aid of my sons, held him down, though he succeeded in giving Jack a desperate blow with his tail. Then, plunging my wand up his nostrils, a few drops of blood came, and he died apparently without pain.

We now carried off our game. I took him on my back, holding him by the fore-claws, while my boys carried the tail behind me; and, with shouts of laughter, the procession returned to the sledge.

Poor little Francis was in great dismay when he saw the terrible monster we brought, and began to cry; but we rallied him out of his cowardice, and his mother, satisfied with our exploits, begged to return home. As the sledge was heavily laden, we decided to leave it till the next day, placing on the ass, the iguana, the crab, our gourd vessels, and a bag of the guavas, little Francis being also mounted. The bustard we loosed, and, securing it by a string tied to one of its legs, led it with us.

We arrived at home in good time. My wife prepared part of the iguana for supper, which was pronounced excellent. The crab was rejected as tough and tasteless. Our new utensils were then tried, the egg-baskets and the milk-bowls, and [pg 118] Fritz was charged to dig a hole in the earth, to be covered with boards, and serve as a dairy, till something better was thought of. Finally, we ascended our leafy abode, and slept in peace.

CHAPTER XXII.

I projected an excursion with my eldest son, to explore the limits of our country, and satisfy ourselves that it was an island, and not a part of the continent. We set out, ostensibly, to bring the sledge we had left the previous evening. I took Turk and the ass with us, and left Flora with my wife and children, and, with a bag of provisions, we left Falcon's Nest as soon as breakfast was over.

In crossing a wood of oaks, covered with the sweet, eatable acorn, we again met with the sow; our service to her in the evening did not seem to be forgotten, for she appeared tamer, and did not run from us. A little farther on, we saw some beautiful birds. Fritz shot some, among which I recognized the large blue Virginian jay, and some different kinds of parrots. As he was reloading his gun, we heard at a distance a singular noise, like a muffled drum, mingled with the sound made in sharpening a saw. It might be savages; and we plunged into a thicket, and there discovered the cause of the noise in a brilliant green bird, seated on the withered trunk of a tree. It spread its wings and tail, and strutted about with strange contortions, to the great delight of its mates, who seemed lost in admiration of him. At the same [pg 119] time, he made the sharp cry we heard, and, striking his wing against the tree, produced the drum-like sound. I knew this to be the ruffed grouse, one of the greatest ornaments of the forests of America. My insatiable hunter soon put an end to the scene; he fired at the bird, who fell dead, and his crowd of admirers, with piercing cries, took to flight.

I reprimanded my son for so rashly killing everything we met with without consideration, and for the mere love of destruction. He seemed sensible of his error, and, as the thing was done, I thought it as well to make the best of it, and sent him to pick up his game.

"What a creature!" said he, as he brought it; "how it would have figured in our poultry-yard, if I had not been in such a hurry."

We went on to our sledge in the Gourd Wood, and, as the morning was not far advanced, we determined to leave all here, and proceed in our projected excursion beyond the chain of rocks. But we took the ass with us to carry our provisions, and any game or other object we should meet with in the new country we hoped to penetrate. Amongst gigantic trees, and through grass of a prodigious height, we travelled with some labour, looking right and left to avoid danger, or to make discoveries. Turk walked the first, smelling the air; then came the donkey, with his grave and careless step; and we followed, with our guns in readiness. We met with plains of potatoes and of manioc, amongst the stalks of which were sporting tribes of agoutis; but we were not tempted by such game.

We now met with a new kind of bush covered [pg 120] with small white berries about the size of a pea. On pressing these berries, which adhered to my fingers, I discovered that this plant was the Myrica cerifera, or candle-berry myrtle, from which a wax is obtained that may be made into candles. With great pleasure I gathered a bag of these berries, knowing how my wife would appreciate this acquisition; for she often lamented that we were compelled to go to bed with the birds, as soon as the sun set.

We forgot our fatigue, as we proceeded, in contemplation of the wonders of nature, flowers of marvellous beauty, butterflies of more dazzling colours than the flowers, and birds graceful in form, and brilliant in plumage. Fritz climbed a tree, and succeeded in securing a young green parrot, which he enveloped in his handkerchief, with the intention of bringing it up, and teaching it to speak. And now we met with another wonder: a number of birds who lived in a community, in nests, sheltered by a common roof, in the formation of which they had probably laboured jointly. This roof was composed of straw and dry sticks, plastered with clay, which rendered it equally impenetrable to sun or rain. Pressed as we were for time, I could not help stopping to admire this feathered colony. This leading us to speak of natural history, as it relates to animals who live in societies, we recalled in succession the ingenious labours of the beavers and the marmots; the not less marvellous constructions of the bees, the wasps, and the ants; and I mentioned particularly those immense ant-hills of America, of which the masonry is finished with such skill and [pg 121] solidity that they are sometimes used for ovens, to which they bear a resemblance.

We had now reached some trees quite unknown to us. They were from forty to sixty feet in height, and from the bark, which was cracked in many places, issued small balls of a thick gum. Fritz got one off with difficulty, it was so hardened by the sun. He wished to soften it with his hands, but found that heat only gave it the power of extension, and that by pulling the two extremities, and then releasing them, it immediately resumed its first form.

Fritz ran to me, crying out, "I have found some India-rubber!"

"If that be true," said I, "you have made a most valuable discovery."

He thought I was laughing at him, for we had no drawing to rub out here.

I told him this gum might be turned to many useful purposes; among the rest we might make excellent shoes of it. This interested him. How could we accomplish this?

"The caoutchouc," said I, "is the milky sap which is obtained from certain trees of the Euphorbium kind, by incisions made in the bark. It is collected in vessels, care being taken to agitate them, that the liquid may not coagulate. In this state they cover little clay bottles with successive layers of it, till it attains the required thickness. It is then dried in smoke, which gives it the dark brown colour. Before it is quite dry, it is ornamented by lines and flowers drawn with the knife. Finally, they break the clay form, and extract it from the mouth; and there remains the [pg 122] India-rubber bottle of commerce, soft and flexible. Now, this is my plan for shoemaking; we will fill a stocking with sand, cover it with repeated layers of the gum till it is of the proper thickness; then empty out the sand, and, if I do not deceive myself, we shall have perfect boots or shoes."

Comfortable in the hope of new boots, we advanced through an interminable forest of various trees. The monkeys on the cocoa-nut trees furnished us with pleasant refreshment, and a small store of nuts besides. Among these trees I saw some lower bushes, whose leaves were covered with a white dust. I opened the trunk of one of these, which had been torn up by the wind, and found in the interior a white farinaceous substance, which, on tasting, I knew to be the sago imported into Europe. This, as connected with our subsistence, was a most important affair, and my son and I, with our hatchets, laid open the tree, and obtained from it twenty-five pounds of the valuable sago.

This occupied us an hour; and, weary and hungry, I thought it prudent not to push our discoveries farther this day. We therefore returned to the Gourd Wood, placed all our treasures on the sledge, and took our way home. We arrived without more adventures, and were warmly greeted, and our various offerings gratefully welcomed, especially the green parrot. We talked of the caoutchouc, and new boots, with great delight during supper; and, afterwards, my wife looked with exceeding content at her bag of candle-berries, anticipating the time when we should not have to go to bed, as we did now, as soon as the sun set.

[pg 123]

CHAPTER XXIII.

The next morning my wife and children besought me to begin my manufacture of candles. I remembered having seen the chandler at work, and I tried to recall all my remembrances of the process. I put into a boiler as many berries as it would hold, and placed it over a moderate fire: the wax melted from the berries, and rose to the surface, and this I carefully skimmed with a large flat spoon and put in a separate vessel placed near the fire; when this was done, my wife supplied me with some wicks she had made from the threads of sailcloth; these wicks were attached, four at a time, to a small stick; I dipped them into the wax, and placed them on two branches of a tree to dry; I repeated this operation as often as necessary to make them the proper thickness, and then placed them in a cool spot to harden. But we could not forbear trying them that very night; and, thought somewhat rude in form, it was sufficient that they reminded us of our European home, and prolonged our days by many useful hours we had lost before.

This encouraged me to attempt another enterprise. My wife had long regretted that she had not been able to make butter. She had attempted to beat her cream in a vessel, but either the heat of the climate, or her want of patience, rendered her trials unsuccessful. I felt that I had not skill enough to make a churn; but I fancied that by some simple method, like that used by the Hottentots, who put their cream in a skin and shake [pg 124] it till they produce butter, we might obtain the same result. I cut a large gourd in two, filled it with three quarts of cream, then united the parts, and secured them closely. I fastened a stick to each corner of a square piece of sailcloth, placed the gourd in the middle, and, giving a corner to each of my sons, directed them to rock the cloth with a slow, regular motion, as you would a child's cradle. This was quite an amusement for them; and at the end of an hour, my wife had the pleasure of placing before us some excellent butter. I then tried to make a cart, our sledge being unfitted for some roads; the wheels I had brought from the wreck rendered this less difficult; and I completed a very rude vehicle, which was, nevertheless, very useful to us.

While I was thus usefully employed, my wife and children were not idle. They had transplanted the European trees, and thoughtfully placed each in the situation best suited to it. I assisted with my hands and counsels. The vines we planted round the roots of our trees, and hoped in time to form a trellis-work. Of the chesnut, walnut, and cherry-trees, we formed an avenue from Falcon's Nest to Family Bridge, which, we hoped, would ultimately be a shady road between our two mansions. We made a solid road between the two rows of trees, raised in the middle and covered with sand, which we brought from the shore in our wheelbarrows. I also made a sort of tumbril, to which we harnessed the ass, to lighten this difficult labour.

We then turned our thoughts to Tent House, our first abode, and which still might form our [pg 125] refuge in case of danger. Nature had not favoured it; but our labour soon supplied all deficiencies. We planted round it every tree that requires ardent heat; the citron, pistachio, the almond, the mulberry, the Siamese orange, of which the fruit is as large as the head of a child, and the Indian fig, with its long prickly leaves, all had a place here. These plantations succeeding admirably, we had, after some time, the pleasure of seeing the dry and sandy desert converted into a shady grove, rich in flowers and fruit. As this place was the magazine for our arms, ammunition, and provisions of all sorts; we made a sort of fortress of it, surrounding it with a high hedge of strong, thorny trees; so that not only to wild beasts, but even to human enemies, it was inaccessible. Our bridge was the only point of approach, and we always carefully removed the first planks after crossing it. We also placed our two cannon on a little elevation within the enclosure; and, finally, we planted some cedars, near our usual landing-place, to which we might, at a future time, fasten our vessels. These labours occupied us three months, only interrupted by a strict attention to the devotions and duties of the Sunday. I was most especially grateful to God for the robust health we all enjoyed, in the midst of our employments. All went on well in our little colony. We had an abundant and certain supply of provisions; but our wardrobe, notwithstanding the continual repairing my wife bestowed on it, was in a most wretched state, and we had no means of renewing it, except by again visiting the wreck, which I knew still contained some chests of clothes, and [pg 126] bales of cloth. This decided me to make another voyage; besides I was rather anxious to see the state of the vessel.

We found it much in the same condition we had left it, except being much more shattered by the winds and waves.

We selected many useful things for our cargo; the bales of linen and woollen cloth were not forgotten; some barrels of tar; and everything portable that we could remove; doors, windows, tables, benches, locks and bolts, all the ammunition, and even such of the guns as we could move. In fact we completely sacked the vessel; carrying off, after several days' labour, all our booty, with the exception of some weighty articles, amongst which were three or four immense boilers, intended for a sugar-manufactory. These we tied to some large empty casks, which we pitched completely over, and hoped they would be able to float in the water.

When we had completed our arrangements, I resolved to blow up the ship. We placed a large barrel of gunpowder in the hold, and arranging a long match from it, which would burn some hours, we lighted it, and proceeded without delay to Safety Bay to watch the event. I proposed to my wife to sup on a point of land where we could distinctly see the vessel. Just as the sun was going down, a majestic rolling, like thunder, succeeded by a column of fire, announced the destruction of the vessel, which had brought us from Europe, and bestowed its great riches on us. We could not help shedding tears, as we heard the last mournful cry of this sole remaining bond that connected [pg 127] us with home. We returned sorrowfully to Tent House, and felt as if we had lost an old friend.

We rose early next morning, and hastened to the shore, which we found covered with the wreck, which, with a little exertion, we found it easy to collect. Amongst the rest, were the large boilers. We afterwards used these to cover our barrels of gunpowder, which we placed in a part of the rock, where, even if an explosion took place, no damage could ensue.

My wife, in assisting us with the wreck, made the agreeable discovery, that two of our ducks, and one goose, had hatched each a brood, and were leading their noisy young families to the water. This reminded us of all our poultry and domestic comfort, at Falcon's Nest, and we determined to defer, for some time, the rest of our work at Tent House, and to return the next day to our shady summer home.

CHAPTER XXIV.

As we went along the avenue of fruit-trees, I was concerned to see my young plants beginning to droop, and I immediately resolved to proceed to Cape Disappointment the next morning, to cut bamboos to make props for them. It was determined we should all go, as, on our arrival at Falcon's Nest, we discovered many other supplies wanting. The candles were failing: we must have more berries, for now my wife sewed by candlelight, while I wrote my journal. She wanted, [pg 128] also, some wild-fowls' eggs to set under her hens. Jack wanted some guavas, and Francis wished for some sugar-canes. So we made a family tour of it, taking the cart, with the cow and ass, to contain our provision, and a large sailcloth, to make a tent. The weather was delightful, and we set out singing, in great spirits.

We crossed the potato and manioc plantations, and the wood of guavas, on which my boys feasted to their great satisfaction. The road was rugged, but we assisted to move the cart, and rested frequently. We stopped to see bird colony, which greatly delighted them all, and Ernest declared they belonged to the species of Loxia gregaria, the sociable grosbeak. He pointed out to us their wonderful instinct in forming their colony in the midst of the candle-berry bushes, on which they feed. We filled two bags with these berries, and another with guavas, my wife proposing to make jelly from them.

We then proceeded to the caoutchouc-tree, and here I determined to rest awhile, to collect some of the valuable gum. I had brought some large gourd-shells with me for the purpose. I made incisions in the trees, and placed these bowls to receive the gum, which soon began to run out in a milky stream, and we hoped to find them filled on our return. We turned a little to the left, and entered a beautiful and fertile plain, bounded on one side by the sugar-canes, behind which rose a wood of palms, on the other by the bamboos; and before us was Cape Disappointment, backed by the ocean--a magnificent picture.

We at once decided to make this our resting-place; [pg 129] we even thought of transferring our residence from Falcon's Nest to this spot; but we dismissed the thought, when we reflected on the perfect security of our dear castle in the air. We contented ourselves with arranging to make this always our station for refreshment in our excursions. We loosed our animals, and allowed them to graze on the rich grass around us. We arranged to spend the night here, and, taking a light repast, we separated on our several employments--some to cut sugar-canes, others bamboos, and, after stripping them, to make them into bundles, and place them in the cart. This hard work made the boys hungry; they refreshed themselves with sugar-canes, but had a great desire to have some cocoa-nuts. Unfortunately, there were neither monkeys nor crabs to bestow them, and the many attempts they made to climb the lofty, bare trunk of the palm ended only in disappointment and confusion. I went to their assistance. I gave them pieces of the rough skin of the shark, which I had brought for the purpose, to brace on their legs, and showing them how to climb, by the aid of a cord fastened round the tree with a running noose, a method practised with success by the savages, my little climbers soon reached the summit of the trees; they then used their hatchets, which they had carried up in their girdles, and a shower of cocoa-nuts fell down. These furnished a pleasant dessert, enlivened by the jests of Fritz and Jack, who, being the climbers, did not spare Doctor Ernest, who had contented himself with looking up at them; and even now, regardless of their banter, he was lost in some new idea. [pg 130] Rising suddenly, and looking at the palms, he took a cocoa-nut cup, and a tin flask with a handle, and gravely addressed us thus:--

"Gentlemen and lady! this exercise of climbing is really very disagreeable and difficult; but since it confers so much honour on the undertakers, I should like also to attempt an adventure, hoping to do something at once glorious and agreeable to the company."

He then bound his legs with the pieces of shark's skin, and with singular vigour and agility sprung up a palm which he had long been attentively examining. His brothers laughed loudly at his taking the trouble to ascend a tree that had not a single nut on it. Ernest took no notice of their ridicule, but, as soon as he reached the top, struck with his hatchet, and a tuft of tender yellow leaves fell at our feet, which I recognized as the product of the cabbage-palm, a delicate food, highly valued in America. His mother thought it a mischievous act, to destroy the tree thus; but he assured her his prize was worth many cocoa-nuts. But our hero did not descend; and I asked him if he wanted to replace the cabbage he had cut off?

"Wait a little," said he; "I am bringing you some wine to drink my health; but it comes slower than I could wish."

He now descended, holding his cocoa-cup, into which he poured from the flask a clear rose-coloured liquor, and, presenting it to me, begged me to drink. It was, indeed, the true palm-wine, which is as pleasant as champaign, and, taken moderately, a great restorative.

We all drank; and Ernest was praised and [pg 131] thanked by all, till he forgot all the scoffs he had received.

As it was getting late, we set about putting up our tent for the night, when suddenly our ass, who had been quietly grazing near us, began to bray furiously, erected his ears, kicking right and left, and, plunging into the bamboos, disappeared. This made us very uneasy. I could not submit to lose the useful animal; and, moreover, I was afraid his agitation announced the approach of some wild beast. The dogs and I sought for any trace of it in vain; I therefore, to guard against any danger, made a large fire before our tent, which I continued to watch till midnight, when, all being still, I crept into the tent, to my bed of moss, and slept undisturbed till morning.

In the morning we thanked God for our health and safety, and then began to lament our poor donkey, which, I hoped, might have been attracted by the light of our fire, and have returned; but we saw nothing of him, and we decided that his services were so indispensable, that I should go, with one of my sons, and the two dogs, in search of him, and cross the thickets of bamboo. I chose to take Jack with me, to his great satisfaction, for Fritz and Ernest formed a better guard for their mother in a strange place. We set out, well armed, with bags of provisions on our back, and after an hour's fruitless search among the canes, We emerged beyond them, in an extensive plain on the borders of the great bay. We saw that the ridge of rocks still extended on the right till it nearly reached the shore, when it abruptly terminated in a perpendicular precipice. A considerable [pg 132] river flowed into the bay here, and between the river and the rock was a narrow passage, which at high water would be overflowed. We thought it most likely that our ass had passed by this defile; and I wished to see whether these rocks merely bordered or divided the island; we therefore went forward till we met with a stream, which fell in a cascade from a mass of rocks into the river. We ascended the stream till we found a place shallow enough to cross. Here we saw the shoemarks of our ass, mingled with the footsteps of other animals, and at a distance we saw a herd of animals, but could not distinguish what they were. We ascended a little hill, and, through our telescope, saw a most beautiful and fertile country, breathing peace and repose. To our right rose the majestic chain of rocks that divided the island. On our left a succession of beautiful green hills spread to the horizon. Woods of palms and various unknown trees were scattered over the scene. The beautiful stream meandered across the valley like a silver ribbon, bordered by rushes and other aquatic plants. There was no trace of the footstep of man. The country had all the purity of its first creation; no living creatures but some beautiful birds and brilliant butterflies appeared.

But, at a distance, we saw some specks, which I concluded were the animals we had first seen, and I resolved to go nearer, in hopes our ass might have joined them. We made towards the spot, and, to shorten the road, crossed a little wood of bamboos, the stalks of which, as thick as a man's thigh, rose to the height of thirty feet. I suspected this to be the giant reed of America, so useful for [pg 133] the masts of boats and canoes. I promised Jack to allow him to cut some on our return; but at present the ass was my sole care. When we had crossed the wood, we suddenly came face to face on a herd of buffaloes, not numerous certainly, but formidable in appearance. At the sight, I was absolutely petrified, and my gun useless. Fortunately the dogs were in the rear, and the animals, lifting their heads, and fixing their large eyes on us, seemed more astonished than angry--we were the first men probably they had ever seen.

We drew back a little, prepared our arms, and endeavoured to retreat, when the dogs arrived, and, notwithstanding our efforts to restrain them, flew at the buffaloes. It was no time now to retreat; the combat was begun. The whole troop uttered the most frightful roars, beat the ground with their feet, and butted with their horns. Our brave dogs were not intimidated, but marched straight upon the enemy, and, falling on a young buffalo that had strayed before the rest, seized it by the ears. The creature began to bellow, and struggle to escape; its mother ran to its assistance, and, with her, the whole herd. At that moment,--I tremble as I write it, I gave the signal to my brave Jack, who behaved with admirable coolness, and at the same moment we fired on the herd. The effect was wonderful: they paused a moment, and then, even before the smoke was dissipated, took to flight with incredible rapidity, forded the river, and were soon out of sight. My dogs still held their prize, and the mother, though wounded by our shot, tore up the ground in her fury, and was advancing on the dogs to destroy them; but I stepped forward, and discharging [pg 134] a pistol between the horns, put an end to her life.

We began to breathe. We had looked death in the face,--a most horrible death; and thanked God for our preservation. I praised Jack for his courage and presence of mind; any fear or agitation on his part would have unnerved me, and rendered our fate certain. The dogs still held the young calf by the ears, it bellowed incessantly, and I feared they would either be injured or lose their prize. I went up to their assistance. I hardly knew how to act. I could easily have killed it; but I had a great desire to carry it off alive, and try to tame it, to replace our ass, whom I did not intend to follow farther. A happy idea struck Jack: he always carried his lasso in his pocket; he drew it out, retired a little, and flung it so dexterously that he completely wound it round the hind legs of the calf, and threw it down. I now approached; I replaced the lasso by a stronger cord, and used another to bind his fore legs loosely. Jack cried victory, and already thought how his mother and brothers would be delighted, when we presented it; but that was no easy matter. At last I thought of the method used in Italy to tame the wild bulls, and I resolved to try it, though it was a little cruel.

I began by tying to the foot of a tree the cords that held the legs; then making the dogs seize him again by the ears, I caught hold of his mouth, and with a sharp knife perforated the nostril, and quickly passed a cord through the opening. This cord was to serve as my rein, to guide the animal. The operation was successful; and, as soon as the blood ceased to flow, I took [pg 135] the cord, uniting the two ends, and the poor suffering creature, completely subdued, followed me without resistance.

I was unwilling to abandon the whole of the buffalo I had killed, as it is excellent meat; I therefore cut out the tongue, and some of the best parts from the loin, and covered them well with salt, of which we had taken a provision with us. I then carefully skinned the four legs, remembering that the American hunters use these skins for boots, being remarkably soft and flexible. We permitted the dogs to feast on the remainder; and while they were enjoying themselves, we washed ourselves, and sat down under a tree to rest and refresh ourselves. But the poor beasts had soon many guests at their banquet. Clouds of birds of prey came from every part; an incessant combat was kept up; no sooner was one troop of brigands satisfied, than another succeeded; and soon all that remained of the poor buffalo was the bones. I noticed amongst these ravenous birds the royal vulture, an elegant bird, remarkable for a brilliant collar of down. We could easily have killed some of these robbers, but I thought it useless to destroy for mere curiosity, and I preferred employing our time in cutting, with a small saw we had brought, some of the gigantic reeds that grew round us. We cut several of the very thick ones, which make excellent vessels when separated at the joints; but I perceived that Jack was cutting some of small dimensions, and I inquired if he was going to make a Pandean pipe, to celebrate his triumphal return with the buffalo.

"No," said he; "I don't recollect that Robinson [pg 136] Crusoe amused himself with music in his island; but I have thought of something that will be useful to mamma. I am cutting these reeds to make moulds for our candles."

"An excellent thought, my dear boy!" said I; "and if even we break our moulds in getting out the candles, which I suspect we may, we know where they grow, and can come for more."

We collected all our reeds in bundles, and then set out. The calf, intimidated by the dogs, and galled by the rein, went on tolerably well. We crossed the narrow pass in the rocks, and here our dogs killed a large jackal which was coming from her den in the rock. The furious animals then entered the den, followed by Jack, who saved, with difficulty, one of the young cubs, the others being immediately worried. It was a pretty little gold-coloured creature, about the size of a cat. Jack petitioned earnestly to have it to bring up; and I made him happy by granting his request.

In the mean time I had tied the calf to a low tree, which I discovered was the thorny dwarf palm, which grows quickly, and is extremely useful for fences. It bears an oblong fruit, about the size of a pigeon's egg, from which is extracted an oil which is an excellent substitute for butter. I determined to return for some young plants of this palm to plant at Tent House.

It was almost night when we joined our family; and endless were the questions the sight of the buffalo produced, and great was the boasting of Jack the dauntless. I was compelled to lower his pride a little by an unvarnished statement, though I gave him much credit for his coolness and resolution; and, supper-time arriving, my wife had [pg 137] time to tell me what had passed while we had been on our expedition.

CHAPTER XXV.

My wife began by saying they had not been idle in my absence. They had collected wood, and made torches for the night. Fritz and Ernest had even cut down an immense sago-palm, seventy feet high, intending to extract its precious pith; but this they had been unable to accomplish alone, and waited for my assistance. But while they were engaged in this employment, a troop of monkeys had broken into the tent and pillaged and destroyed everything; they had drunk or overturned the milk, and carried off or spoiled all our provisions; and even so much injured the palisade I had erected round the tent, that it took them an hour, after they returned, to repair the damage. Fritz had made also a beautiful capture, in a nest he had discovered in the rocks at Cape Disappointment. It was a superb bird, and, though very young, quite feathered. Ernest had pronounced it to be the eagle of Malabar, and I confirmed his assertion; and as this species of eagle is not large, and does not require much food, I advised him to train it as a falcon, to chase other birds. I took this opportunity to announce that henceforward every one must attend to his own live stock, or they should be set at liberty, mamma having sufficient to manage in her own charge.

We then made a fire of green wood, in the [pg 138] smoke of which we placed the buffalo-meat we had brought home, leaving it during the night, that it might be perfectly cured. We had had some for supper, and thought it excellent. The young buffalo was beginning to graze, and we gave him a little milk to-night, as well as to the jackal. Fritz had taken the precaution to cover the eyes of his eagle, and tying it fast by the leg to a branch, it rested very tranquilly. We then retired to our mossy beds, to recruit our strength for the labours of another day.

At break of day we rose, made a light breakfast, and I was about to give the signal of departure, when my wife communicated to me the difficulty they had had in cutting down the palm-tree, and the valuable provision that might be obtained from it with a little trouble. I thought she was right, and decided to remain here another day; for it was no trifling undertaking to split up a tree seventy feet long. I consented the more readily, as I thought I might, after removing the useful pith from the trunk, obtain two large spouts or channels to conduct the water from Jackal River to the kitchen garden.

Such tools as we had we carried to the place where the tree lay. We first sawed off the head; then, with the hatchet making an opening at each end, we took wedges and mallets, and the wood being tolerably soft, after four hours' labour, we succeeded in splitting it completely. When parted, we pressed the pith with our hands, to get the whole into one division of the trunk, and began to make our paste. At one end of the spout we nailed one of the graters, through which we intended to force the paste, to form the round seeds. My little bakers [pg 139] set vigorously to work, some pouring water on the pith, while the rest mixed it into paste. When sufficiently worked, I pressed it strongly with my hand against the grater; the farinaceous parts passed easily through the holes, while the ligneous part, consisting of splinters of wood, &c, was left behind. This we threw into a heap, hoping mushrooms might spring from it. My wife now carefully spread the grains on sailcloth, in the sun, to dry them. I also formed some vermicelli, by giving more consistence to the paste, and forcing it through the holes in little pipes. My wife promised with this, and the Dutch cheese, to make us a dish equal to Naples maccaroni. We were now contented; we could at any time obtain more sago by cutting down a tree, and we were anxious to get home to try our water-pipes. We spent the rest of the day in loading the cart with our utensils and the halves of the tree. We retired to our hut at sunset, and slept in peace.

The next morning the whole caravan began to move at an early hour. The buffalo, harnessed to the cart, by the side of his nurse, the cow, took the place of our lost ass, and began his apprenticeship as a beast of draught. We took the same road on our return, that we might carry away the candle-berries and the vessels of India-rubber. The vanguard was composed of Fritz and Jack, who pioneered our way, by cutting down the underwood to make a road for the cart. Our water-pipes, being very long, somewhat impeded our progress; but we happily reached the candle-berry trees without accident, and placed our sacks on the cart. We did not find more than a quart [pg 140] of the caoutchouc gum; but it would be sufficient for our first experiment, and I carried it off.

In crossing the little wood of guavas, we suddenly heard our dogs, who were before us with Fritz and Jack, uttering the most frightful howlings. I was struck with terror lest they should have encountered a tiger, and rushed forward ready to fire. The dogs were endeavouring to enter a thicket, in the midst of which Fritz declared he had caught a glimpse of an animal larger than the buffalo, with a black, bristly skin. I was just about to discharge my gun into the thicket, when Jack, who had lain down on the ground, to look under the bushes, burst into a loud laugh. "It is another trick of that vexatious animal, our old sow! she is always making fools of us," cried he. Half merry and half angry, we made an opening into the thicket, and there discovered the lady lying, surrounded by seven little pigs, only a few days old. We were very glad to see our old friend so attended, and stroked her. She seemed to recognize us, and grunted amicably. We supplied her with some potatoes, sweet acorns, and cassava bread; intending, in return, to eat her young ones, when they were ready for the spit, though my dear wife cried out against the cruelty of the idea. At present we left them with her, but proposed afterwards to take away two, to be brought up at home, and leave the rest to support themselves on acorns in the woods, where they would become game for us. At length we arrived at Falcon's Nest, which we regarded with all the attachment of home. Our domestic animals crowded round us, and noisily welcomed us. We tied up the buffalo and jackal, [pg 141] as they were not yet domesticated. Fritz fastened his eagle to a branch by a chain long enough to allow it to move freely, and then imprudently uncovered its eyes; it immediately raised its head, erected its feathers, and struck on all sides with its beak and claws; our fowls took to flight, but the poor parrot fell in his way, and was torn to pieces before we could assist it. Fritz was very angry, and would have executed the murderer; but Ernest begged he would not be so rash, as parrots were more plentiful than eagles, and it was his own fault for uncovering his eyes; the falconers always keeping their young birds hooded six weeks, till they are quite tamed. He offered to train it, if Fritz would part with it; but this Fritz indignantly refused. I told them the fable of the dog in the manger, which abashed Fritz; and he then besought his brother to teach him the means of training this noble bird, and promised to present him with his monkey.

Ernest then told him that the Caribs subdue the largest birds by making them inhale tobacco smoke. Fritz laughed at this; but Ernest brought a pipe and some tobacco he had found in the ship, and began to smoke gravely under the branch where the bird was perched. It was soon calm, and on his continuing to smoke it became quite motionless. Fritz then easily replaced the bandage, and thanked his brother for his good service.

The next morning we set out early to our young plantation of fruit-trees, to fix props to support the weaker plants. We loaded the cart with the thick bamboo canes and our tools, and harnessed the cow to it, leaving the buffalo in the stable, as I wished the wound in his nostrils to be perfectly [pg 142] healed before I put him to any hard work. I left Francis with his mother, to prepare our dinner, begging them not to forget the maccaroni.

We began at the entrance of the avenue to Falcon's Nest, where all the trees were much bent by the wind. We raised them gently by a crowbar; I made a hole in the earth, in which one of my sons placed the bamboo props, driving them firmly down with a mallet, and we proceeded to another, while Ernest and Jack tied the trees to them with a long, tough, pliant plant, which I suspected was a species of llana. As we were working, Fritz inquired if these fruit-trees were wild.

"A pretty question!" cried Jack. "Do you think that trees are tamed like eagles or buffaloes? You perhaps could teach them to bow politely, so that we might gather the fruit!"

"You fancy you are a wit," said I, "but you speak like a dunce. We cannot make trees bow at our pleasure; but we can make a tree, which by nature bears sour and uneatable fruit, produce what is sweet and wholesome. This is effected by grafting into a wild tree a small branch, or even a bud, of the sort you wish. I will show you this method practically at some future time, for by these means we can procure all sorts of fruit; only we must remember, that we can only graft a tree with one of the same natural family; thus, we could not graft an apple on a cherry-tree, for one belongs to the apple tribe, and the other to the plum tribe."

"Do we know the origin of all these European fruits?" asked the inquiring Ernest.

"All our shell fruits," answered I, "such as the [pg 143] nut, the almond, and the chesnut, are natives of the East; the peach, of Persia; the orange and apricot, of Armenia; the cherry, which was unknown in Europe sixty years before Christ, was brought by the proconsul Lucullus from the southern shores of the Euxine; the olives come from Palestine. The first olive-trees were planted on Mount Olympus, and from thence were spread through the rest of Europe; the fig is from Lydia; the plums, your favourite fruit, with the exception of some natural sorts that are natives of our forests, are from Syria, and the town of Damascus has given its name to one sort, the Damascene, or Damson. The pear is a fruit of Greece; the ancients called it the fruit of Peloponnesus; the mulberry is from Asia; and the quince from the island of Crete."

Our work progressed as we talked thus, and we had soon propped all our valuable plants. It was now noon, and we returned to Falcon's Nest very hungry, and found an excellent dinner prepared, of smoked beef, and the tender bud of the cabbage-palm, the most delicious of vegetables.

After dinner, we began to discuss a plan I had long had in my head; but the execution of it presented many difficulties. It was, to substitute a firm and solid staircase for the ladder of ropes, which was a source of continual fear to my wife. It is true, that we only had to ascend it to go to bed; but bad weather might compel us to remain in our apartment; we should then have frequently to ascend and descend, and the ladder was very unsafe. But the immense height of the tree, and the impossibility of procuring beams to sustain a staircase round it, threw me into despair. However, [pg 144] looking at the monstrous trunk of the tree, I thought, if we cannot succeed outside, could we not contrive to mount within?

"Have you not said there was a swarm of bees in the trunk of the tree?" I inquired of my wife. "Yes," said little Francis, "they stung my face dreadfully the other day, when I was on the ladder. I was pushing a stick into the hole they came out of, to try how deep it was."

"Now, then," cried I, "I see through my difficulties. Let us find out how far the tree is hollow; we can increase the size of the tunnel, and I have already planned the sort of staircase I can construct." I had hardly spoken, when the boys leaped like squirrels, some upon the arched roots, some on the steps of the ladder, and began to strike with sticks and mallets to sound the tree. This rash proceeding had nearly been fatal to Jack, who, having placed himself just before the opening, and striking violently, the whole swarm, alarmed at an attack, which probably shook their palace of wax, issued forth, and revenged themselves amply on all the assailants. Nothing was heard but cries and stamping of feet. My wife hastened to cover the stings with moist earth, which rather relieved them; but it was some hours before they could open their eyes. They begged me to get them the honey from their foes, and I prepared a hive, which I had long thought of--a large gourd, which I placed on a board nailed upon a branch of our tree, and covered with straw to shelter it from the sun and wind. But it was now bedtime, and we deferred our attack on the fortress till next day.

[pg 145]

CHAPTER XXVI.

An hour before day, I waked my sons to assist me in removing the bees to the new abode I had prepared for them. I commenced by plastering up the entrance to their present dwelling with clay, leaving only room to admit the bowl of my pipe. This was necessary, because I had neither masks nor gloves, as the regular bee-takers have. I then began to smoke briskly, to stupify the bees. At first we heard a great buzzing in the hollow, like the sound of a distant storm: the murmur ceased by degrees, and a profound stillness succeeded, and I withdrew my pipe without a single bee appearing. Fritz and I then, with a chisel and small axe, made an opening about three feet square, below the bees' entrance. Before we detached this, I repeated the fumigation, lest the noise and the fresh air should awake the bees; but there was no fear of such a thing,--they were quite stupified. We removed the wood, and through this opening beheld, with wonder and admiration, the work of this insect nation. There was such a store of wax and honey, that we feared we should not have vessels to contain it. The interior of the tree was filled with the honeycombs; I cut them carefully, and placed them in the gourds the boys brought me. As soon as I had made a little space, I placed the upper comb, on which the bees were hanging in clusters, in the new hive, and put it on the plank prepared for it; I then descended with the rest of the honeycomb, and filled a cask with it, which I had previously washed [pg 146] in the stream; this we covered with sailcloth and planks, lest the bees, attracted by the smell, should come to claim their own. We left out some comb for a treat at dinner, and my wife carefully put by the rest.

To prevent the bees returning to their old abode, we placed some burning tobacco in the hollow, the smell and fumes of which drove them from the tree, when they wished to enter; and, finally, they settled in the new hive, where the queen bee, doubtless, had fixed herself.

We now began our work; we emptied the cask of honey into a large boiler, except a little reserved for daily use; we added a little water, placed the boiler on a slow fire, and reduced it to a liquid mass; this was strained through a bag into the cask, and left standing all night to cool. The next morning the wax had risen to the top, and formed a hard and solid cake, which we easily removed; and beneath was the most pure and delicious honey. The barrel was then carefully closed, and placed in a cool place. We now proceeded to examine the interior of the tree. I took a long pole, and tried the height from the window I had made; and tied a stone to a string to sound the depth. To my surprise, the pole penetrated without resistance to the very branches where our dwelling was, and the stone went to the roots. It was entirely hollow, and I thought I could easily fix a winding staircase in this wide tunnel. It would seem, that this huge tree, like the willow of our country, is nourished through the bark, for it was flourishing in luxuriant beauty.

We began by cutting a doorway, on the side facing the sea, of the size of the door we had [pg 147] brought from the captain's cabin, with its framework, thus securing ourselves from invasion on that side. We then cleansed, and perfectly smoothed the cavity, fixing in the middle the trunk of a tree about ten feet high, to serve for the axis of the staircase. We had prepared, the evening before, a number of boards from the staves of a large barrel, to form our steps. By the aid of the chisel and mallet, we made deep notches in the inner part of our tree, and corresponding notches in the central pillar; I placed my steps in these notches, riveting them with large nails; I raised myself in this manner step after step, but always turning round the pillar, till we got to the top. We then fixed on the central pillar another trunk of the same height, prepared beforehand, and continued our winding steps. Four times we had to repeat this operation, and, finally, we reached our branches, and terminated the staircase on the level of the floor of our apartment. I cleared the entrance by some strokes of my axe. To render it more solid, I filled up the spaces between the steps with planks, and fastened two strong cords from above, to each side of the staircase, to hold by. Towards different points, I made openings; in which were placed the windows taken from the cabin, which gave light to the interior, and favoured our observations outside.

The construction of this solid and convenient staircase occupied us during a month of patient industry; not that we laboured like slaves, for we had no one to constrain us; we had in this time completed several works of less importance; and many events had amused us amidst our toil.

A few days after we commenced, Flora produced [pg 148] six puppies; but the number being too large for our means of support, I commanded that only a male and female should be preserved, that the breed might be perpetuated; this was done, and the little jackal being placed with the remainder, Flora gave it the same privileges as her own offspring. Our goats also, about this time, gave us two kids; and our sheep some lambs. We saw this increase of our flock with great satisfaction; and for fear these useful animals should take it into their heads to stray from us, as our ass had done, we tied round their necks some small bells we had found on the wreck, intended to propitiate the savages, and which would always put us on the track of the fugitives.

The education of the young buffalo was one of the employments that varied our labour as carpenters. Through the incision in his nostrils, I had passed a small stick, to the ends of which I attached a strap. This formed a kind of bit, after the fashion of those of the Hottentots; and by this I guided him as I chose; though not without much rebellion on his part. It was only after Fritz had broken it in for mounting, that we began to make it carry. It was certainly a remarkable instance of patience and perseverance surmounting difficulties, that we not only made it bear the wallets we usually placed on the ass, but Ernest, Jack, and even little Francis, took lessons in horsemanship, by riding him, and, henceforward, would have been able to ride the most spirited horse without fear; for it could not be worse than the buffalo they had assisted to subdue.

In the midst of this, Fritz did not neglect the training of his young eagle. The royal bird began [pg 149] already to pounce very cleverly on the dead game his master brought, and placed before him; sometimes between the horns of the buffalo, sometimes on the back of the great bustard, or the flamingo; sometimes he put it on a board, or on the end of a pole, to accustom it to pounce, like the falcon, on other birds. He taught it to settle on his wrist at a call, or a whistle; but it was some time before he could trust it to fly, without a long string attached to its leg, for fear its wild nature should carry it from us for ever. Even the indolent Ernest was seized with the mania of instructing animals. He undertook the education of his little monkey, who gave him sufficient employment. It was amusing to see the quiet, slow, studious Ernest obliged to make leaps and gambols with his pupil to accomplish his instruction. He wished to accustom Master Knips to carry a pannier, and to climb the cocoa-nut trees with it on his back; Jack and he wove a small light pannier of rushes, and fixed it firmly on his back with three straps. This was intolerable to him at first; he ground his teeth, rolled on the ground, and leaped about in a frantic manner, trying in vain to release himself. They left the pannier on his back night and day, and only allowed him to eat what he had previously put into it. After a little time, he became so accustomed to it, that he rebelled if they wished to remove it, and threw into it everything they gave him to hold. He was very useful to us, but he obeyed only Ernest, who had very properly taught him equally to love and fear him.

Jack was not so successful with his jackal; for, though he gave him the name of "The Hunter," [pg 150] yet, for the first six months, the carnivorous animal chased only for himself, and, if he brought anything to his master, it was only the skin of the animal he had just devoured; but I charged him not to despair, and he continued zealously his instructions.

During this time I had perfected my candle manufacture; by means of mixing the bees' wax with that obtained from the candle-berry, and by using cane moulds, which Jack first suggested to me, I succeeded in giving my candles the roundness and polish of those of Europe. The wicks were for some time an obstacle. I did not wish to use the small quantity of calico we had left, but my wife happily proposed to me to substitute the pith of a species of elder, which answered my purpose completely.

I now turned myself to the preparation of the caoutchouc, of which we had found several trees. I encouraged the boys to try their ingenuity in making flasks and cups, by covering moulds of clay with the gum, as I had explained to them. For my part, I took a pair of old stockings, and filled them with sand for my mould, which I covered with a coating of mud, and left to dry in the sun. I cut out a pair of soles of buffalo leather, which I first hammered well, and then fastened with small tacks to the sole of the stocking, filling up the spaces left with the gum, so as to fix it completely. Then, with a brush of goats hair, I covered it with layer upon layer of the elastic gum, till I thought it sufficiently thick. It was easy after this to remove the sand, the stocking, and the hardened mud, to shake out the dust, [pg 151] and I had a pair of water-proof boots, without seam, and fitting as well as if I had employed an English shoemaker. My boys were wild with joy, and all begged for a pair; but I wished first to try their durability, compared with those of buffalo leather. I began to make a pair of boots for Fritz, using the skin drawn from the legs of the buffalo we had killed; but I had much more difficulty than with the caoutchouc. I used the gum to cover the seams, so that the water might not penetrate. They were certainly not elegant as a work of art, and the boys laughed at their brother's awkward movements in them; but their own productions, though useful vessels, were not models of perfection.

We then worked at our fountain, a great source of pleasure to my wife and to all of us. We raised, in the upper part of the river, a sort of dam, made with stakes and stones, from whence the water flowed into our channels of the sago-palm, laid down a gentle declivity nearly to our tent, and there it was received into the shell of the turtle, which we had raised on some stones of a convenient height, the hole which the harpoon had made serving to carry off the waste water through a cane that was fitted to it. On two crossed sticks were placed the gourds that served us for pails, and thus we had always the murmuring of the water near us, and a plentiful supply of it, always pure and clean, which the river, troubled by our water-fowl and the refuse of decayed leaves, could not always give us. The only inconvenience of these open channels was, that the water reached us warm and unrefreshing; but this I hoped to remedy in time, by using bamboo pipes buried in [pg 152] the earth. In the mean time, we were grateful for this new acquisition, and gave credit to Fritz, who had suggested the idea.

CHAPTER XXVII.

One morning, as we were engaged in giving the last finish to our staircase, we were alarmed at hearing at a distance strange, sharp, prolonged sounds, like the roars of a wild beast, but mingled with an unaccountable hissing. Our dogs erected their ears, and prepared for deadly combat. I assembled my family; we then ascended our tree, closing the lower door, loaded our guns, and looked anxiously round, but nothing appeared. I armed my dogs with their porcupine coats of mail and collars, and left them below to take care of our animals.

The horrible howlings seemed to approach nearer to us; at length, Fritz, who was leaning forward to listen as attentively as he could, threw down his gun, and bursting into a loud laugh, cried out, "It is our fugitive, the ass, come back to us, and singing his song of joy on his return!" We listened, and were sure he was right, and could not but feel a little vexation at being put into such a fright by a donkey. Soon after, we had the pleasure of seeing him appear among the trees; and, what was still better, he was accompanied by another animal of his own species, but infinitely more beautiful. I knew it at once to be the onagra, or wild ass, a most important capture, if we could make it; though all naturalists have [pg 153] declared it impossible to tame this elegant creature, yet I determined to make the attempt.

I went down with Fritz, exhorting his brothers to remain quiet, and I consulted with my privy counsellor on the means of taking our prize. I also prepared, as quickly as possible, a long cord with a noose, kept open by a slight stick, which would fall out as soon as the animal's head entered, while any attempt to escape would only draw the noose closer; the end of this cord was tied to the root of a tree. I took then a piece of bamboo, about two feet long, and splitting it up, tied it firmly at one end, to form a pair of pincers for the nose of the animal. In the mean time, the two animals had approached nearer, our old Grizzle apparently doing the honours to his visitor, and both grazing very comfortably.

By degrees we advanced softly to them, concealed by the trees; Fritz carrying the lasso, and I the pincers. The onagra, as soon as he got sight of Fritz, who was before me, raised his head, and started back, evidently only in surprise, as it was probably the first man the creature had seen. Fritz remained still, and the animal resumed his browsing. Fritz went up to our old servant, and offered him a handful of oats mixed with salt; the ass came directly to eat its favourite treat; its companion followed, raised its head, snuffed the air, and came so near, that Fritz adroitly threw the noose over its head. The terrified animal attempted to fly, but that drew the cord so tight as almost to stop his respiration, and he lay down, his tongue hanging out. I hastened up and relaxed the cord, lest he should be strangled. I threw the halter of the ass round his neck, and [pg 154] placed the split cane over his nose, tying it firmly below with a string. I subdued this wild animal by the means that blacksmiths use the first time they shoe a horse. I then took off the noose, and tied the halter by two long cords to the roots of two separate trees, and left him to recover himself.

In the mean time, the rest of the family had collected to admire this noble animal, whose graceful and elegant form, so superior to that of the ass, raises it almost to the dignity of a horse. After a while it rose, and stamped furiously with its feet, trying to release itself; but the pain in its nose obliged it to lie down again. Then my eldest son and I, approaching gently, took the two cords, and led or dragged it between two roots very near to each other, to which we tied the cords so short, that it had little power to move, and could not escape. We took care our own donkey should not stray again, by tying his fore-feet loosely, and putting on him a new halter, and left him near the onagra.

I continued, with a patience I had never had in Europe, to use every means I could think of with our new guest, and at the end of a month he was so far subdued, that I ventured to begin his education. This was a long and difficult task. We placed some burdens on his back; but the obedience necessary before we could mount him, it seemed impossible to instil into him. At last, I recollected the method they use in America to tame the wild horses, and I resolved to try it. In spite of the bounds and kicks of the furious animal, I leaped on his back, and seizing one of his long ears between my teeth, I bit it till the [pg 155] blood came. In a moment he reared himself almost erect on his hind-feet, remained for a while stiff and motionless, then came down on his fore-feet slowly, I still holding on his ear. At last I ventured to release him; he made some leaps, but soon subsided into a sort of trot, I having previously placed loose cords on his fore-legs. From that time we were his masters; my sons mounted him one after another; they gave him the name of Lightfoot, and never animal deserved his name better. As a precaution, we kept the cords on his legs for some time; and as he never would submit to the bit, we used a snaffle, by which we obtained power over his head, guiding him by a stick, with which we struck the right or left ear, as we wished him to go.

During this time, our poultry-yard was increased by three broods of chickens. We had at least forty of these little creatures chirping and pecking about, the pride of their good mistress's heart. Part of these were kept at home, to supply the table, and part she allowed to colonize in the woods, where we could find them when we wanted them. "These," she said, "are of more use than your monkeys, jackals, and eagles, who do nothing but eat, and would not be worth eating themselves, if we were in need." However, she allowed there was some use in the buffalo, who carried burdens, and Lightfoot, who carried her sons so well. The fowls, which cost us little for food, would be always ready, she said, either to supply us with eggs or chickens, when the rainy season came on--the winter of this climate.

This reminded me that the approach of that dreary season permitted me no longer to defer a very [pg 156] necessary work for the protection of our animals. This was to construct, under the roots of the trees, covered houses for them. We began by making a kind of roof above the vaulted roots of our tree. We used bamboo canes for this purpose; the longer and stouter were used for the supports, like columns, the slighter ones bound together closely formed the roof. The intervals we filled up with moss and clay, and spread over the whole a coating of tar. The roof was so firm, that it formed a platform, which we surrounded with a railing; and thus we had a balcony, and a pleasant promenade. By the aid of some boards nailed to the roots, we made several divisions in the interior, each little enclosure being appropriated to some useful purpose; and thus, stables, poultry-houses, dairy, larder, hay-house, store-room, &c., besides our dining-room, were all united under one roof. This occupied us some time, as it was necessary to fill our store-room before the bad weather came; and our cart was constantly employed in bringing useful stores.

One evening, as we were bringing home a load of potatoes on our cart, drawn by the ass, the cow, and the buffalo, I saw the cart was not yet full; I therefore sent home the two younger boys with their mother, and went on with Fritz and Ernest to the oak wood, to collect a sack of sweet acorns--Fritz mounted on his onagra, Ernest followed by his monkey, and I carrying the bag. On arriving at the wood, we tied Lightfoot to a tree, and all three began to gather the dropped acorns, when we were startled by the cries of birds, and a loud flapping of wings, and we concluded that a brisk combat was going on between Master Knips [pg 157] and the tenants of the thickets, from whence the noise came. Ernest went softly to see what was the matter, and we soon heard him calling out, "Be quick! a fine heath-fowl's nest, full of eggs! Knips wants to suck them, and the mother is beating him."

Fritz ran up, and secured the two beautiful birds, who fluttered, and cried out furiously, and returned, followed by Ernest, carrying a large nest filled with eggs. The monkey had served us well on this occasion; for the nest was so hidden by a bush with long leaves, of which Ernest held his hand full, that, but for the instinct of the animal, we could never have discovered it. Ernest was overjoyed to carry the nest and eggs for his dear mamma, and the long, pointed leaves he intended for Francis, to serve as little toy-swords.

We set out on our return, placing the sack of acorns behind Fritz on Lightfoot; Ernest carried the two fowls, and I charged myself with the care of the eggs, which I covered up, as I found they were warm, and I hoped to get the mother to resume her brooding when we got to Falcon's Nest. We were all delighted with the good news we should have to carry home, and Fritz, anxious to be first, struck his charger with a bunch of the pointed leaves he had taken from Ernest: this terrified the animal so much, that he took the bit in his teeth, and flew out of sight like an arrow. We followed, in some uneasiness, but found him safe. Master Lightfoot had stopped of himself when he reached his stable. My wife placed the valuable eggs under a sitting hen, the true mother refusing to fulfil her office. She was then put [pg 158] into the cage of the poor parrot, and hung in our dining-room, to accustom her to society. In a few days the eggs were hatched, and the poultry-yard had an increase of fifteen little strangers, who fed greedily on bruised acorns, and soon became as tame as any of our fowls, though I plucked the large feathers out of their wings when they were full-grown, lest their wild nature should tempt them to quit us.

CHAPTER XXVIII.

Francis had soon become tired of playing with the long leaves his brother had brought him, and they were thrown aside. Fritz happened to take some of the withered leaves up, which were soft and flexible as a ribbon, and he advised Francis to make whiplashes of them, to drive the goats and sheep with, for the little fellow was the shepherd. He was pleased with the idea, and began to split the leaves into strips, which Fritz platted together into very good whiplashes. I remarked, as they were working, how strong and pliant these strips seemed, and, examining them closely, I found they were composed of long fibres, or filaments, which made me suspect it to be Phormium tenax, or New Zealand flax, a most important discovery to us, and which, when I communicated it to my wife, almost overwhelmed her with joy. "Bring me all the leaves you can without delay," cried she, "and I will make you stockings, shirts, coats, sewing-thread, cords--in fact, give me but flax and work-tools, and I can manage all." I could [pg 159] not help smiling at the vivacity of her imagination, roused at the very name of flax; but there was still great space between the leaves lying before us and the linen she was already sewing in idea. But my boys, always ready to second the wishes of their beloved mother, soon mounted their coursers, Fritz on Lightfoot, and Jack on the great buffalo, to procure supplies.

Whilst we waited for these, my wife, all life and animation, explained to me all the machines I must make, to enable her to spin and weave, and make linen to clothe us from head to foot; her eyes sparkled with delight as she spoke, and I promised her all she asked.

In a short time, our young cavaliers returned from their foraging expedition, conveying on their steeds huge bundles of the precious plant, which they laid at the feet of their mother. She gave up everything to begin her preparation. The first operation necessary was to steep the flax, which is usually done by exposing it in the open air in the rain, the wind, and the dew, so as, in a certain degree, to dissolve the plant, rendering the separation of the fibrous and ligneous parts more easy. It can then be cleaned and picked for spinning. But, as the vegetable glue that connects the two parts is very tenacious, and resists for a long time the action of moisture, it is often advisable to steep it in water, and this, in our dry climate, I considered most expedient.

My wife agreed to this, and proposed that we should convey it to Flamingo Marsh; and we spent the rest of the day in tying up the leaves in bundles. Next morning, we loaded our cart, and proceeded to the marsh: we there untied our bundles, [pg 160] and spread them in the water, pressing them down with stones, and leaving them till it was time to take them out to dry. We could not but admire here the ingenious nests of the flamingo; they are of a conical form, raised above the level of the marsh, having a recess above, in which the eggs are deposited, out of the reach of danger, and the female can sit on them with her legs in the water. These nests are of clay, and so solid, that they resist the water till the young are able to swim.

In a fortnight the flax was ready to be taken out of the water; we spread it in the sun, which dried it so effectually, that we brought it to Falcon's Nest the same evening, where it was stored till we were ready for further operations. At present we laboured to lay up provision for the rainy season, leaving all sedentary occupations to amuse us in our confinement. We brought in continually loads of sweet acorns, manioc, potatoes, wood, fodder for the cattle, sugar-canes, fruit, indeed everything that might be useful during the uncertain period of the rainy season. We profited by the last few days to sow the wheat and other remaining European grains, that the rain might germinate them. We had already had some showers; the temperature was variable, the sky became cloudy, and the wind rose. The season changed sooner than we expected; the winds raged through the woods, the sea roared, mountains of clouds were piled in the heavens. They soon burst over our heads, and torrents of rain fell night and day, without intermission; the rivers swelled till their waters met, and turned the whole country around us into an immense [pg 161] lake. Happily we had formed our little establishment on a spot rather elevated above the rest of the valley; the waters did not quite reach our tree, but surrounded us about two hundred yards off, leaving us on a sort of island in the midst of the general inundation. We were reluctantly obliged to descend from our aërial abode; the rain entered it on all sides, and the hurricane threatened every moment to carry away the apartment, and all that were in it. We set about our removal, bringing down our hammocks and bedding to the sheltered space under the roots of the trees that we had roofed for the animals. We were painfully crowded in the small space; the stores of provisions, the cooking-utensils, and especially the neighbourhood of the animals, and the various offensive smells, made our retreat almost insupportable. We were choked with smoke if we lighted a fire, and inundated with rain if we opened a door. For the first time since our misfortune, we sighed for the comforts of our native home; but action was necessary, and we set about endeavouring to amend our condition.

The winding staircase was very useful to us; the upper part was crowded with things we did not want, and my wife frequently worked in the lower part, at one of the windows. We crowded our beasts a little more, and gave a current of air to the places they had left. I placed outside the enclosure the animals of the country, which could bear the inclemency of the season; thus I gave a half-liberty to the buffalo and the onagra, tying their legs loosely, to prevent them straying, the boughs of the tree affording them a shelter. We made as few fires as possible, as, fortunately it [pg 162] was never cold, and we had no provisions that required a long process of cookery. We had milk in abundance, smoked meat, and fish, the preserved ortolans, and cassava cakes. As we sent out some of our animals in the morning, with bells round their necks, Fritz and I had to seek them and bring them in every evening, when we were invariably wet through. This induced my ingenious Elizabeth to make us a sort of blouse and hood out of old garments of the sailors, which we covered with coatings of the caoutchouc, and thus obtained two capital water-proof dresses; all that the exhausted state of our gum permitted us to make.

The care of our animals occupied us a great part of the morning, then we prepared our cassava, and baked our cakes on iron plates. Though we had a glazed door to our hut, the gloominess of the weather, and the obscurity caused by the vast boughs of the tree, made night come on early. We then lighted a candle, fixed in a gourd on the table, round which we were all assembled. The good mother laboured with her needle, mending the clothes; I wrote my journal, which Ernest copied, as he wrote a beautiful hand; while Fritz and Jack taught their young brother to read and write, or amused themselves with drawing the animals or plants they had been struck with. We read the lessons from the Bible in turns, and concluded the evening with devotion. We then retired to rest, content with ourselves and with our innocent and peaceful life. Our kind housekeeper often made us a little feast of a roast chicken, a pigeon, or a duck, and once in four or five days we had fresh butter made in the gourd [pg 163] churn; and the delicious honey which we ate to our cassava bread might have been a treat to European epicures.

The remains of our repast was always divided among our domestic animals. We had four dogs, the jackal, the eagle, and the monkey, who relied on their masters, and were never neglected. But if the buffalo, the onagra, and the sow had not been able to provide for themselves, we must have killed them, for we had no food for them.

We now decided that we would not expose ourselves to another rainy season in such an unsuitable habitation; even my gentle Elizabeth got out of temper with the inconveniences, and begged we would build a better winter house; stipulating, however, that we should return to our tree in summer. We consulted a great deal on this matter; Fritz quoted Robinson Crusoe, who had cut a dwelling out of the rock, which sheltered him in the inclement season; and the idea of making our home at Tent House naturally came into my mind. It would probably be a long and difficult undertaking, but with time, patience, and perseverance, we might work wonders. We resolved, as soon as the weather would allow us, to go and examine

104

the rocks at Tent House.

The last work of the winter was, at my wife's incessant request, a beetle for her flax, and some carding-combs. The beetle was easily made, but the combs cost much trouble. I filed large nails till they were round and pointed, I fixed them, slightly inclined, at equal distances, in a sheet of tin, and raised the edge like a box; I then poured melted lead between the nails and the edge, to fix them more firmly. I nailed this on a [pg 164] board, and the machine was fit for use, and my wife was all anxiety to begin her manufacture.

CHAPTER XXIX.

I cannot describe our delight when, after long and gloomy weeks, we saw at length the sky clear, and the sun, dispersing the dark clouds of winter, spread its vivifying rays over all nature; the winds were lulled, the waters subsided, and the air became mild and serene. We went out, with shouts of joy, to breathe the balmy air, and gratified our eyes with the sight of the fresh verdure already springing up around us. Nature seemed in her youth again, and amidst the charms that breathed on every side, we forgot our sufferings, and, like the children of Noah coming forth from the ark, we raised a hymn of thanksgiving to the Giver of all good.

All our plantations and seeds had prospered. The corn was springing, and the trees were covered with leaves and blossoms. The air was perfumed with the odour of countless beautiful flowers; and lively with the songs and cries of hundreds of brilliant birds, all busy building their nests. This was really spring in all its glory.

We began our summer occupation by cleaning and putting in order our dormitory in the tree, which the rain and the scattered leaves had greatly deranged; and in a few days we were able to inhabit it again. My wife immediately began with her flax; while my sons were leading the cattle to the pasture, I took the bundles of flax into the [pg 165] open air, where I constructed a sort of oven of stone, which dried it completely. We began that very evening to strip, beat, and comb it; and I drew out such handfuls of soft, fine flax, ready for spinning, that my wife was overjoyed, and begged me to make her a wheel, that she might commence.

I had formerly had a little taste for turning, and though I had now neither lathe nor any other of the tools, yet I knew how a spinning-wheel and reel should be made, and, by dint of application, I succeeded in completing these two machines to her satisfaction. She began to spin with so much earnestness, that she would hardly take a walk, and reluctantly left her wheel to make dinner ready. She employed

Francis to reel off the thread as she spun it, and would willingly have had the elder boys to take her place when she was called off; but they rebelled at the effeminate work, except Ernest, whose indolent habits made him prefer it to more laborious occupation.

In the mean time we walked over to Tent House to see the state of things, and found that winter had done more damage there than at Falcon's Nest. The storm had overthrown the tent, carried away some of the sailcloth, and injured our provisions so much, that great part was good for nothing, and the rest required to be immediately dried. Fortunately our beautiful pinnace had not suffered much,--it was still safe at anchor, and fit for use; but our tub boat was entirely destroyed.

Our most important loss was two barrels of gunpowder, which had been left in the tent, instead of under the shelter of the rock, and which the [pg 166] rain had rendered wholly useless. This made us feel still more strongly the necessity of securing for the future a more suitable shelter than a canvas tent, or a roof of foliage. Still I had small hope from the gigantic plan of Fritz or the boldness of Jack. I could not be blind to the difficulties of the undertaking. The rocks which surrounded Tent House presented an unbroken surface, like a wall without any crevice, and, to all appearance, of so hard a nature as to leave little hopes of success. However, it was necessary to try to contrive some sort of cave, if only for our gunpowder. I made up my mind, and selected the most perpendicular face of the rock as the place to begin our work. It was a much pleasanter situation than our tent, commanding a view of the whole bay, and the two banks of Jackal River, with its picturesque bridge. I marked out with chalk the dimension of the entrance I wished to give to the cave; then my sons and I took our chisels, pickaxes, and heavy miner's hammers, and began boldly to hew the stone.

Our first blows produced very little effect; the rock seemed impenetrable, the sun had so hardened the surface; and the sweat poured off our brows with the hard labour. Nevertheless, the efforts of my young workmen did not relax. Every evening we left our work advanced, perhaps, a few inches; and every morning returned to the task with renewed ardour. At the end of five or six days, when the surface of the rock was removed, we found the stone become easier to work; it then seemed calcarious, and, finally, only a sort of hardened clay, which we could remove [pg 167] with spades; and we began to hope. After a few days' more labour, we found we had advanced about seven feet. Fritz wheeled out the rubbish, and formed a sort of terrace with it before the opening; while I was working at the higher part, Jack, as the least, worked below. One morning he was hammering an iron bar, which he had pointed at the end, into the rock, to loosen the earth, when he suddenly cried out--

"Papa! papa! I have pierced through!"

"Not through your hand, child?" asked I.

"No, papa!" cried he; "I have pierced through the mountain! Huzza!"

Fritz ran in at the shout, and told him he had better have said at once that he had pierced through the earth! But Jack persisted that, however his brother might laugh, he was quite sure he had felt his iron bar enter an empty space behind. I now came down from my ladder, and, moving the bar, I felt there was really a hollow into which the rubbish fell, but apparently very little below the level we were working on. I took a long pole and probed the cavity, and found that it must be of considerable size. My boys wished to have the opening enlarged and to enter immediately, but this I strictly forbade; for, as I leaned forward to examine it through the opening, a rush of mephitic air gave me a sort of vertigo. "Come away, children," cried I, in terror; "the air you would breathe there is certain death." I explained to them that, under certain circumstances, carbonic acid gas was frequently accumulated in caves or grottoes, rendering the air unfit for respiration; producing giddiness of the head, fainting, and eventually death. I sent them to collect [pg 168] some hay, which I lighted and threw into the cave; this was immediately extinguished; we repeated the experiment several times with the same result. I now saw that more active means must be resorted to.

We had brought from the vessel a box of fireworks, intended for signals; I threw into the cave, by a cord, a quantity of rockets, grenades, &c., and scattered a train of gunpowder from them; to this I applied a long match, and we retired to a little distance. This succeeded well; a great explosion agitated the air, a torrent of the carbonic acid gas rushed through the opening, and was replaced by the pure air; we sent in a few more rockets, which flew round like fiery dragons, disclosing to us the vast extent of the cave. A shower of stars, which concluded our experiment, made us wish the duration had been longer. It seemed as if a crowd of winged genii, carrying each a lamp, were floating about in that enchanted cavern. When they vanished, I threw in some more lighted hay, which blazed in such a lively manner, that I knew all danger was over from the gas; but, for fear of deep pits, or pools of water, I would not venture in without lights. I therefore despatched Jack, on his buffalo, to report this discovery to his mother, and bring all the candles she had made. I purposely sent Jack on the errand, for his lively and poetic turn of mind would, I hoped, invest the grotto with such charms, that his mother would even abandon her wheel to come and see it.

This succeeded well; a great explosion agitated the
air--a torrent of the carbonic acid gas rushed through the opening.
"This succeeded well; a great explosion agitated the air--a torrent of the carbonic acid gas rushed through the opening."

Delighted with his commission, Jack leaped upon his buffalo, and, waving his whip, galloped off with an intrepidity that made my hair stand on [pg 169] end.

During his absence, Fritz and I enlarged the opening, to make it easy of access, removed all the rubbish, and swept a road for mamma. We had just finished, when we heard the sound of wheels crossing the bridge, and the cart appeared, drawn by the cow and ass, led by Ernest. Jack rode before on his buffalo, blowing through his hand to imitate a horn, and whipping the lazy cow and ass. He rode up first, and alighted from his huge courser, to help his mother out.

I then lighted our candles, giving one to each, with a spare candle and flint and steel in our pockets. We took our arms, and proceeded in a solemn manner into the rock. I walked first, my sons followed, and their mother came last, with Francis. We had not gone on above a few steps, when we stopped, struck with wonder and admiration; all was glittering around us; we were in a grotto of diamonds! From the height of the lofty vaulted roof hung innumerable crystals, which, uniting with those on the walls, formed colonnades, altars, and every sort of gothic ornament of dazzling lustre, creating a fairy palace, or an illuminated temple.

When we were a little recovered from our first astonishment, we advanced with more confidence. The grotto was spacious, the floor smooth, and covered with a fine dry sand. From the appearance of these crystals, I suspected their nature, and, on breaking off a piece and tasting it, I found, to my great joy, that we were in a grotto of rock salt, which is found in large masses in the earth, usually above a bed of gypsum, and surrounded by fossils. We were charmed with this discovery, of which we could no longer have a doubt. What [pg 170] an advantage this was to our cattle, and to ourselves! We could now procure this precious commodity without care or labour. The acquisition was almost as valuable as this brilliant retreat was in itself, of which we were never tired of admiring the beauty. My wife was struck with our good fortune in opening the rock precisely at the right spot; but I was of opinion, that this mine was of great extent, and that we could not well have missed it. Some blocks of salt were scattered on the ground, which had apparently fallen from the vaulted roof. I was alarmed; for such an accident might destroy one of my children; but, on examination, I found the mass above too solid to be detached spontaneously, and I concluded that the explosion of the fireworks had given this shock to the subterranean palace, which had not been entered since the creation of the world. I feared there might yet be some pieces loosened; I therefore sent out my wife and younger sons. Fritz and I remained, and, after carefully examining the suspected parts, we fired our guns, and watched the effect; one or two pieces fell, but the rest remained firm, though we struck with long poles as high as we could reach. We were now satisfied of the security of our magnificent abode, and began to plan our arrangements for converting it into a convenient and pleasant habitation. The majority were for coming here immediately, but the wiser heads determined that, for this year, Falcon's Nest was to continue our home. There we went every night, and spent the day at Tent House, contriving and arranging our future winter dwelling.

[pg 171]

CHAPTER XXX.

The last bed of rock, before we reached the cave which Jack had pierced, was so soft, and easy to work, that we had little difficulty in proportioning and opening the place for our door; I hoped that, being now exposed to the heat of the sun, it would soon become as hard as the original surface. The door was that we had used for the staircase at Falcon's Nest; for as we only intended to make a temporary residence of our old tree, there was no necessity for solid fittings; and, besides, I intended to close the entrance of the tree by a door of bark, more effectually to conceal it, in case savages should visit us. I then laid out the extent of the grotto at pleasure, for we had ample space. We began by dividing it into two parts; that on the right of the entrance was to be our dwelling; on the left were, first, our kitchen, then the workshop and the stables; behind these were the store-rooms and the cellar. In order to give light and air to our apartments, it was necessary to insert in the rock the windows we had brought from the ship; and this cost us many days of labour. The right-hand portion was subdivided into three rooms: the first our own bedroom; the middle, the common sitting-room, and beyond the boys' room. As we had only three windows, we appropriated one to each bedroom, and the third to the kitchen, contenting ourselves, at present, with a grating in the dining-room. I constructed a sort of chimney in the kitchen, formed of four boards, and conducted the smoke thus, through a [pg 172] hole made in the face of the rock. We made bur work-room spacious enough for us to carry on all our manufactures, and it served also for our cart-house. Finally, all the partition-walls were put up, communicating by doors, and completing our commodious habitation. These various labours, the removal of our effects, and arranging them again, all the confusion of a change when it was necessary to be at once workmen and directors, took us a great part of summer; but the recollection of the vexations we should escape in the rainy season gave us energy.

We passed nearly all our time at Tent House, the centre of our operations; and, besides the gardens and plantations which surrounded it, we found many advantages which we profited by. Large turtles often came to deposit their eggs in the sand, a pleasant treat for us; but we raised our desires to the possession of the turtles themselves, living, to eat when we chose. As soon as we saw one on the shore, one of my sons ran to cut off its retreat. We then hastened to assist, turned the creature on its back, passed a long cord through its shell, and tied it firmly to a post close to the water. We then placed it on its legs, when of course it made for the water, but could only ramble the length of its cord; it seemed, however, very content, and we had it in readiness when we wanted it. The lobsters, crabs, muscles, and every sort of fish which abounded on the coast, plentifully supplied our table. One morning, we were struck with an extraordinary spectacle: a large portion of the sea appeared in a state of ebullition, and immense flocks of marine birds were hovering [pg 173] over it, uttering piercing cries, and plunging into the waves. From time to time the surface, on which the rising sun now shone, seemed covered with little flames, which rapidly appeared and vanished. Suddenly, this extraordinary mass advanced to the bay; and we ran down, fall of curiosity. We found, on our arrival, that this strange phenomenon was caused by a shoal of herrings. These shoals are so dense, that they are often taken for sand-banks, are many leagues in extent, and several feet in depth: they spread themselves over the seas, carrying to barren shores the resources that nature has denied them.

These brilliant, scaly creatures had now entered the bay, and my wife and children were lost in admiration of the wonderful sight; but I reminded them, that when Providence sends plenty, we ought to put forth our hands to take it. I sent immediately for the necessary utensils, and organized my fishery. Fritz and Jack stood in the water, and such was the thickness of the shoal, that they filled baskets, taking them up as you would water in a pail; they threw them on the sand; my wife and Ernest cut them open, cleaned them, and rubbed them with salt; I arranged them in small barrels, a layer of herrings and a layer of salt; and when the barrel was full, the ass, led by Francis, took them up to the storehouse. This labour occupied us several days, and at the end of that time we had a dozen barrels of excellent salt provision against the winter season.

The refuse of this fishery, which we threw into the sea, attracted a number of sea-dogs; we killed several for the sake of the skin and the oil, which [pg 174] would be useful to burn in lamps, or even as an ingredient in soap, which I hoped to make at some future time.

At this time I greatly improved my sledge, by placing it on two small wheels belonging to the guns of the ship, making it a light and commodious carriage, and so low, that we could easily place heavy weights on it. Satisfied with our labours, we returned very happy to Falcon's Nest, to spend our Sunday, and to thank God heartily for all the blessings he had given us.

CHAPTER XXXI.

We went on with our labours but slowly, as many employments diverted us from the great work. I had discovered that the crystals of salt in our grotto had a bed of gypsum for their base, from which I hoped to obtain a great advantage. I was fortunate enough to discover, behind a projecting rock, a natural passage leading to our store-room, strewed with fragments of gypsum. I took some of it to the kitchen, and by repeated burnings calcined it, and reduced it to a fine white powder, which I put into casks, and carefully preserved for use. My intention was, to form our partition-walls of square stones, cemented with the gypsum. I employed my sons daily to collect this, till we had amassed a large quantity; using some, in the first place, effectually to cover our herring-barrels. Four barrels were salted and covered in this way; the rest my wife smoked in a little hut of reeds and branches, in the midst of which the [pg 175] herrings were laid on sticks, and exposed to the smoke of a fire of green moss kindled below. This dried them, and gave them the peculiar flavour so agreeable to many.

We were visited by another shoal of fish a month after that of the herrings. Jack first discovered them at the mouth of Jackal River, where they had apparently come to deposit their eggs among the scattered stones. They were so large, that he was sure they must be whales. I found them to be pretty large sturgeons, besides salmon, large trout, and many other fishes. Jack immediately ran for his bow and arrows, and told me he would kill them all. He fastened the end of a ball of string to an arrow, with a hook at the end of it; he tied the bladders of the dog-fish at certain distances to the string; he then placed the ball safe on the shore, took his bow, fixed the arrow in it, and aiming at the largest salmon, shot it in the side; the fish tried to escape; I assisted him to draw the cord; it was no easy task, for he struggled tremendously; but at length, weakened by loss of blood, we drew him to land, and despatched him.

The other boys came running up to congratulate the young fisherman on his invention, and as it was to be feared that the rest, alarmed by this attack, might take their departure, we determined to abandon everything for the fishery. Fritz threw his harpoon, and landed, by means of the reel, some large salmon; Ernest took his rod, and caught trout; and I, armed like Neptune with an iron trident, succeeded in striking, amongst the stones, some enormous fish. The greatest difficulty was to land our booty; Fritz had struck a sturgeon at least eight feet long, which resisted [pg 176] our united efforts, till my wife brought the buffalo, which we harnessed to the line, and made ourselves masters of this immense prize.

We had a great deal of labour in opening and cleaning all our fish: some we dried and salted; some my wife boiled in oil, as they preserve the tunny. The spawn of the sturgeon, a huge mass, weighing not less than thirty pounds, I laid aside to prepare as caviare, a favourite dish in Holland and Russia. I carefully cleansed the eggs from the skin and fibres that were mixed with them, washed them thoroughly in sea-water, slightly sprinkled them with salt, then put them in a gourd pierced with small holes to let the water escape, and placed weights on them to press them completely for twenty-four hours. We then removed the caviare in solid masses, like cheeses, took it to the smoking-hut to dry, and in a few days had this large addition to our winter provision.

My next employment was the preparation of the valuable isinglass. I took the air-bladder and sounds of the fish, cut them in strips, twisted them in rolls, and dried them in the sun. This is all that is necessary to prepare this excellent glue. It becomes very hard, and, when wanted for use, is cut up in small pieces, and dissolved over a slow fire. The glue was so white and transparent, that I hoped to make window-panes from it instead of glass.

After this work was finished, we began to plan a boat to replace our tub raft. I wished to try to make one of bark, as the savage nations do, and I proposed to make an expedition in search of a tree for our purpose. All those in our own neighbourhood [pg 177] were too precious to destroy; some for their fruits, others for their shade. We resolved to search at a distance for trees fit for our purpose, taking in our road a survey of our plantations and fields. Our garden at Tent House produced abundantly continual successions of vegetables in that virgin soil, and in a climate which recognized no change of season. The peas, beans, lentils, and lettuces were flourishing, and only required water, and our channels from the river brought this plentifully to us. We had delicious cucumbers and melons; the maize was already a foot high, the sugar-canes were prospering, and the pine-apples on the high ground promised us a rich treat.

We hoped our distant plantations were going on as well, and all set out one fine morning to Falcon's Nest, to examine the state of things there. We found my wife's corn-fields were luxuriant in appearance, and for the most part ready for cutting. There were barley, wheat, oats, beans, millet, and lentils. We cut such of these as were ready, sufficient to give us seeds for another year. The richest crop was the maize, which suited the soil. But there were a quantity of gatherers more eager to taste these new productions than we were; these were birds of every kind, from the bustard to the quail, and from the various establishments they had formed round, it might be presumed they would not leave much for us.

After our first shock at the sight of these robbers, we used some measures to lessen the number of them. Fritz unhooded his eagle, and pointed out the dispersing bustards. The well-trained bird immediately soared, and pounced on a superb bustard, and laid it at the feet of its master. The [pg 178] jackal, too, who was a capital pointer, brought to his master about a dozen little fat quails, which furnished us with an excellent repast; to which my wife added a liquor of her own invention, made of the green maize crushed in water, and mingled with the juice of the sugar-cane; a most agreeable beverage, white as milk, sweet and refreshing.

We found the bustard, which the eagle had struck down, but slightly wounded; we washed his hurts with a balsam made of wine, butter, and water, and tied him by the leg in the poultry-yard, as a companion to our tame bustard.

We passed the remainder of the day at Falcon's Nest, putting our summer abode into order, and thrashing out our grain, to save the precious seed for another year.

The Turkey wheat was laid by in sheaves, till we should have time to thrash and winnow it; and then I told Fritz that it would be necessary to put the hand-mill in order, that we had brought from the wreck. Fritz thought we could build a mill ourselves on the river; but this bold scheme was, at present, impracticable.

The next day we set out on an excursion in the neighbourhood. My wife wished to establish colonies of our animals at some distance from Falcon's Nest, at a convenient spot, where they would be secure, and might find subsistence. She selected from her poultry-yard twelve young fowls; I took four young pigs, two couple of sheep, and two goats. These animals were placed in the cart, in which we had previously placed our provisions of every kind, and the tools and utensils we might need, not forgetting the rope ladder and the portable tent; we then harnessed the buffalo, the cow, and the ass, and departed on our tour.

[pg 179]
Fritz rode before on Lightfoot, to reconnoitre the ground, that we might not plunge into any difficulties; as, this time, we went in a new direction, exactly in the midst between the rocks and the shore, that we might get acquainted with the whole of the country that stretched to Cape Disappointment. We had the usual difficulty, at first, in getting through the high grass, and the underwood embarrassed our road, till we were compelled to use the axe frequently. I made some trifling discoveries that were useful, while engaged in this labour; amongst others, some roots of trees curved like saddles, and yokes for beasts of draught. I cut away several of these, and placed them on the cart. When we had nearly passed the wood, we were struck with the singular appearance of a little thicket of low bushes, apparently covered with snow. Francis clapped his hands with joy, and begged to get out of the cart that he might make some snowballs. Fritz galloped forward, and returned, bringing me a branch loaded with this beautiful white down, which, to my great joy, I recognized to be cotton. It was a discovery of inestimable value to us, and my wife began immediately to enumerate all the advantages we should derive from it, when I should have constructed for her the machines for spinning and weaving the cotton. We soon gathered as much as filled three bags, intending afterwards to collect the seeds of this marvellous plant, to sow in the neighbourhood of Tent House.

After crossing the plain of the cotton-trees, we reached the summit of a hill, from which the eye rested on a terrestrial paradise. Trees of every sort covered the sides of the hill, and a murmuring [pg 180] stream crossed the plain, adding to its beauty and fertility. The wood we had just crossed formed a shelter against the north winds, and the rich pasture offered food for our cattle. We decided at once that this should be the site of our farm.

We erected our tent, made a fireplace, and set about cooking our dinner. While this was going on, Fritz and I sought a convenient spot for our structure; and we met with a group of beautiful trees, at such a distance one from another, as to form natural pillars for our dwelling; we carried all our tools here; but as the day was far advanced, we delayed commencing our work till next day. We returned to the tent, and found my wife and her boys picking cotton, with which they made some very comfortable beds, and we slept peacefully under our canvass roof.

CHAPTER XXXII.

The trees which I had chosen for my farmhouse were about a foot in diameter in the trunk. They formed a long square; the long side facing the sea. The dimensions of the whole were about twenty-four feet by sixteen. I cut deep mortices in the trees, about ten feet distant from the ground, and again ten feet higher, to form a second story; I then placed in them strong poles: this was the skeleton of my house--solid, if not elegant; I placed over this a rude roof of bark, cut in squares, and placed sloping, that the rain might run off. We fastened these with the thorn of the acacia, as our nails were too precious to be lavished. While [pg 181] procuring the bark, we made many discoveries. The first was that of two remarkable trees,-- the Pistacia terebinthus and the Pistacia atlantica; the next, the thorny acacia, from which we got the substitute for nails.

The instinct of my goats led us also to find out, among the pieces of bark, that of the cinnamon, not perhaps equal to that of Ceylon, but very fragrant and agreeable. But this was of little value, compared to the turpentine and mastic I hoped to procure from the pistachios, to compose a sort of pitch to complete our intended boat.

We continued our work at the house, which occupied us several days. We formed the walls of thin laths interwoven with long pliant reeds for about six feet from the ground; the rest was merely a sort of light trellis-work, to admit light and air. The door opened on the front to the sea. The interior consisted simply of a series of compartments, proportioned to the guests they were to contain. One small apartment was for ourselves, when we chose to visit our colony. On the upper story was a sort of hayloft for the fodder. We projected plastering the walls with clay; but these finishing touches we deferred to a future time, contented that we had provided a shelter for our cattle and fowls. To accustom them to come to this shelter of themselves, we took care to fill their racks with the food they liked best, mingled with salt; and this we proposed to renew at intervals, till the habit of coming to their houses was fixed. We all laboured ardently, but the work proceeded slowly, from our inexperience; and the provisions we had brought were nearly exhausted. I did not wish to return to Falcon's Nest till I had [pg 182] completed my new establishment, and therefore determined to send Fritz and Jack to look after the animals at home, and bring back a fresh stock of provisions. Our two young couriers set out, each on his favourite steed, Fritz leading the ass to bring back the load, and Jack urging the indolent animal forward with his whip.

During their absence, Ernest and I made a little excursion, to add to our provision--if we could meet with them, some potatoes and cocoa-nuts. We ascended the stream for some time, which led us to a large marsh, beyond which we discovered a lake abounding with water-fowl. This lake was surrounded by tall, thick grass, with ears of a grain, which I found to be a very good, though small, sort of rice. As to the lake itself, it is only a Swiss, accustomed from his infancy to look on such smooth, tranquil waters, that can comprehend the happiness we felt on looking upon this. We fancied we were once more in Switzerland, our own dear land; but the majestic trees and luxuriant vegetation soon reminded us we were no longer in Europe, and that the ocean separated us from our native home.

In the mean time, Ernest had brought down several birds, with a skill and success that surprised me. A little after, we saw Knips leap off the back of his usual palfrey, Flora, and, making his way through the rich grass, collect and carry rapidly to his mouth something that seemed particularly to please his palate. We followed him, and, to our great comfort, were able to refresh ourselves with that delicious strawberry called in Europe the Chili or pineapple strawberry. We ate plentifully of this fruit, which was of enormous [pg 183] size; Ernest especially enjoyed them, but did not forget the absent; he filled Knips's little pannier with them, and I covered them with large leaves, which I fastened down with reeds, lest he should take a fancy to help himself as we went home. I took, also, a specimen of rice, for the inspection of our good housekeeper, who would, I knew, rejoice in such an acquisition.

We proceeded round the lake, which presented a different scene on every side. This was one of the most lovely and fertile parts we had yet seen of this country. Birds of all kinds abounded; but we were particularly struck with a pair of black swans, sailing majestically on the water. Their plumage was perfectly black and glossy, except the extremity of the wings, which was white. Ernest would have tried his skill again, but I forbade him to disturb the profound tranquillity of this charming region.

But Flora, who probably had not the same taste for the beauties of nature that I had, suddenly darted forward like an arrow, pounced upon a creature that was swimming quietly at the edge of the water, and brought it to us. It was a most curious animal. It resembled an otter in form, but was web-footed, had an erect bushy tail like the squirrel, small head, eyes and ears almost invisible. A long, flat bill, like that of a duck, completed its strange appearance. We were completely puzzled--even Ernest, the naturalist, could not give its name. I boldly gave it the name of the beast with a bill. I told Ernest to take it, as I wished to stuff and preserve it.

"It will be," said the little philosopher, "the first natural object for our museum."

[pg 184]
"Exactly," replied I; "and, when the establishment is fully arranged, we will appoint you curator."

But, thinking my wife would grow uneasy at our protracted absence, we returned by a direct road to the tent. Our two messengers arrived about the same time, and we all sat down together to a cheerful repast. Every one related his feats. Ernest dwelt on his discoveries, and was very pompous in his descriptions, and I was obliged to promise to take Fritz another time. I learnt, with pleasure, that all was going on well at Falcon's Nest, and that the boys had had the forethought to leave the animals with provisions for ten days. This enabled me to complete my farmhouse. We remained four days longer, in which time I finished the interior, and my wife arranged in our own apartment the cotton mattresses, to be ready for our visits, and put into the houses the fodder and grain for their respective tenants. We then loaded our cart, and began our march. The animals wished to follow us, but Fritz, on Lightfoot, covered our retreat, and kept them at the farm till we were out of sight.

We did not proceed directly, but went towards the wood of monkeys. These mischievous creatures assaulted us with showers of the fir-apples; but a few shots dispersed our assailants.

Fritz collected some of these new fruits they had flung at us, and I recognized them as those of the stone Pine, the kernel of which is good to eat, and produces an excellent oil. We gathered a bag of these, and continued our journey till we reached the neighbourhood of Cape Disappointment. There we ascended a little hill, from the summit [pg 185] of which we looked upon rich plains, rivers, and woods clothed with verdure and brilliant flowers, and gay birds that fluttered among the bushes. "Here, my children," cried I, "here we will build our summer house. This is truly Arcadia." Here we placed our tent, and immediately began to erect a new building, formed in the same manner as the Farm House, but now executed more quickly. We raised the roof in the middle, and made four sloped sides. The interior was divided into eating and sleeping apartments, stables, and a store-room for provisions; the whole was completed and provisioned in ten days; and we had now another mansion for ourselves, and a shelter for new colonies of animals. This new erection received the name of Prospect Hill, to gratify Ernest, who thought it had an English appearance.

However, the end for which our expedition was planned was not yet fulfilled. I had not yet met with a tree likely to suit me for a boat. We returned then to inspect the trees, and I fixed on a sort of oak, the bark of which was closer than that of the

European oak, resembling more that of the cork-tree. The trunk was at least five feet in diameter, and I fancied its coating, if I could obtain it whole, would perfectly answer my purpose. I traced a circle at the foot, and with a small saw cut the bark entirely through; Fritz, by means of the rope ladder we had brought with us, and attached to the lower branches of the tree, ascended, and cut a similar circle eighteen feet above mine. We then cut out, perpendicularly, a slip the whole length, and, removing it, we had room to insert the necessary tools, and, with [pg 186] wedges, we finally succeeded in loosening the whole. The first part was easy enough, but there was greater difficulty as we advanced. We sustained it as we proceeded with ropes, and then gently let it down on the grass. I immediately began to form my boat while the bark was fresh and flexible. My sons, in their impatience, thought it would do very well if we nailed a board at each end of the roll; but this would have been merely a heavy trough, inelegant and unserviceable; I wished to have one that would look well by the side of the pinnace; and this idea at once rendered my boys patient and obedient. We began by cutting out at each end of the roll of bark a triangular piece of about five feet long; then, placing the sloping parts one over the other, I united them with pegs and strong glue, and thus finished the ends of my boat in a pointed form. This operation having widened it too much in the middle, we passed strong ropes round it, and drew it into the form we required. We then exposed it to the sun, which dried and fixed it in the proper shape.

As many things were necessary to complete my work, I sent Fritz and Jack to Tent House for the sledge, to convey it there, that we might finish it more conveniently. I had the good fortune to meet with some very hard, crooked wood, the natural curve of which would be admirably suitable for supporting the sides of the boat. We found also a resinous tree, which distilled a sort of pitch, easy to manage, and which soon hardened in the sun. My wife and Francis collected sufficient of it for my work. It was almost night when [pg 187] our two messengers returned. We had only time to sup and retire to our rest.

We were all early at work next morning. We loaded the sledge, placing on it the canoe, the wood for the sides, the pitch, and some young trees, which I had transplanted for our plantation at Tent House, and which we put into the boat. But, before we set out, I wished to erect a sort of fortification at the pass of the rock, for the double purpose of securing us against the attacks of wild beasts or of savages, and for keeping enclosed, in the savannah beyond the rocks, some young pigs, that we wished to multiply there, out of the way of our fields and plantations.

As we crossed the sugar-cane plantation, I saw some bamboos larger than any I had ever met with, and we cut down one for a mast to our canoe. We now had the river to our left, and the chain of rocks to our right, which here approached the river, leaving only a narrow pass. At the narrowest part of this we raised a rampart before a deep ditch, which could only be crossed by a drawbridge we placed there. Beyond the bridge, we put a narrow gate of woven bamboos, to enable us to enter

117

the country beyond, when we wished. We planted the side of the rampart with dwarf palms, India fig, and other thorny shrubs, making a winding path through the plantation, and digging in the midst a hidden pitfall, known to ourselves by four low posts, intended to support a plank bridge when we wished to cross it. After this was completed, we built a little chalet of bark in that part of the plantation that faced the stream, and gave it the name of the Hermitage, [pg 188] intending it for a resting-place. After several days of hard labour, we returned to Prospect Hill, and took a little relaxation. The only work we did was to prepare the mast, and lay it on the sledge with the rest.

The next morning we returned to Tent House, where we immediately set to work on our canoe with such diligence that it was soon completed. It was solid and elegant, lined through with wood, and furnished with a keel. We provided it with brass rings for the oars, and stays for the mast. Instead of ballast, I laid at the bottom a layer of stones covered with clay, and over this a flooring of boards. The benches for the rowers were laid across, and in the midst the bamboo mast rose majestically, with a triangular sail. Behind I fixed the rudder, worked by a tiller; and I could boast now of having built a capital canoe.

Our fleet was now in good condition. For distant excursions we could take the pinnace, but the canoe would be invaluable for the coasting service.

Our cow had, in the mean time, given us a young male calf, which I undertook to train for service, as I had done the buffalo, beginning by piercing its nostrils; and the calf promised to be docile and useful; and, as each of the other boys had his favourite animal to ride, I bestowed the bull on Francis, and intrusted him with its education, to encourage him to habits of boldness and activity. He was delighted with his new charger, and chose to give him the name of Valiant.

We had still two months before the rainy season, and this time we devoted to completing the [pg 189] comforts of our grotto. We made all the partitions of wood, except those which divided us from the stables, which we built of stone, to exclude any smell from the animals. We soon acquired skill in our works; we had a plentiful supply of beams and planks from the ship; and by practice we became very good plasterers. We covered the floors with a sort of well-beaten mud, smoothed it, and it dried perfectly hard. We then contrived a sort of felt carpet. We first covered the floor with sailcloth; we spread over this wool and goats' hair mixed, and poured over it isinglass dissolved, rolling up the carpet, and beating it well. When this was dry, we repeated the process, and in the end had a felt carpet. We made one of these for each room, to guard against any damp that we might be subject to in the rainy season.

The privations we had suffered the preceding winter increased the enjoyment of our present comforts. The rainy season came on; we had now a warm, well-lighted, convenient habitation, and abundance of excellent provision for ourselves and our cattle. In the morning, we could attend to their wants without trouble, for the rain-water, carefully collected in clean vessels, prevented the necessity of going to the river. We then assembled in the dining-room to prayers. After that we went to our work-room. My wife took her wheel, or her loom, which was a rude construction of mine, but in which she had contrived to weave some useful cloth of wool and cotton, and also some linen, which she had made up for us. Everybody worked; the workshop was never empty. I contrived, with the wheel of a gun, to arrange a sort [pg 190] of lathe, by means of which I and my sons produced some neat furniture and utensils. Ernest surpassed us all in this art, and made some elegant little things for his mother.

After dinner, our evening occupations commenced; our room was lighted up brilliantly; we did not spare our candles, which were so easily procured, and we enjoyed the reflection in the elegant crystals above us. We had partitioned off a little chapel in one corner of the grotto, which we had left untouched, and nothing could be more magnificent than this chapel lighted up, with its colonnades, portico, and altars. We had divine service here every Sunday. I had erected a sort of pulpit, from which I delivered a short sermon to my congregation, which I endeavoured to render as simple and as instructive as possible.

Jack and Francis had a natural taste for music. I made them flageolets of reeds, on which they acquired considerable skill. They accompanied their mother, who had a very good voice; and this music in our lofty grotto had a charming effect.

We had thus made great steps towards civilization; and, though condemned, perhaps, to pass our lives alone on this unknown shore, we might yet be happy. We were placed in the midst of abundance. We were active, industrious, and content; blessed with health, and united by affection, our minds seemed to enlarge and improve every day. We saw around us on every side traces of the Divine wisdom and beneficence; and our hearts overflowed with love and veneration for that Almighty hand which had so miraculously saved, and [pg 191] continued to protect us. I humbly trusted in Him, either to restore us to the world, or send some beings to join us in this beloved island, where for two years we had seen no trace of man. To Him we committed our fate. We were happy and tranquil, looking with resignation to the future.

END OF THE FIRST PART OF THE JOURNAL.

POSTSCRIPT BY THE EDITOR.

It is necessary to explain how this first part of the journal of the Swiss pastor came into my hands.

Three or four years after the family had been cast on this desert coast, where, as we see, they lived a happy and contented life, an English transport was driven by a storm upon the same shore. This vessel was the Adventurer, Captain Johnson, and was returning from New Zealand to the eastern coast of North America, by Otaheite, to fetch a cargo of furs for China, and then to proceed from Canton to England. A violent storm, which lasted several days, drove them out of their course. For many days they wandered in unknown seas, and the ship was so injured by the storm, that the captain looked out for some port to repair it. They discovered a rocky coast, and, as the violence of the wind was lulled, ventured to approach the shore. At a short distance they anchored, and sent a boat to examine the coast. Lieutenant Bell, who went with the boat, knew a little German. They were some time before they [pg 192] could venture to land among the rocks which guarded the island, but, turning the promontory, they saw Safety Bay, and entering it, were astonished to see a handsome pinnace and boat at anchor, near the strand a tent, and in the rock doors and windows, like those of a European house.

They landed, and saw a middle-aged man coming to meet them, clothed in European fashion, and well armed. After a friendly salutation, they first spoke in German and then in English. This was the good father; the family were at Falcon's Nest, where they were spending the summer. He had seen the vessel in the morning through his telescope, but, unwilling to alarm, or to encourage hopes that might be vain, he had not spoken of it, but come alone towards the coast.

After much friendly conference, the party were regaled with all hospitality at Tent House, the good Swiss gave the Lieutenant this first part of his journal for the perusal of Captain Johnson, and, after an hour's conversation, they separated, hoping to have a pleasant meeting next day.

But Heaven decreed it otherwise. During the night, another fearful storm arose; the Adventurer lost its anchor, and was driven out to sea; and, after several days of anxiety and danger, found itself so far from the island, and so much shattered, that all thoughts of returning were given up for that time, and Captain Johnson reluctantly relinquished the hope of rescuing the interesting family.

Thus it happened that the first part of this journal was brought to England, and from thence sent to me, a friend of the family, in Switzerland, accompanied by a letter from the Captain, declaring, [pg 193] that he could have no rest till he found, and became acquainted with, this happy family; that he would search for the island in his future voyages, and either bring away the family, or, if they preferred to remain, he would send out from England some colonists, and everything that might be necessary to promote their comfort. A rough map of the island is added to the journal, executed by Fritz, the eldest son.

[pg 194]

CONTINUATION OF THE JOURNAL.

CHAPTER XXXIII.

I left the reader at the moment in which I had placed the first part of my journal in the hands of Lieutenant Bell, to deliver to Captain Johnson, of the English vessel the Adventurer, expecting him to return the next day with Lieutenant Bell. We separated in this hope, and I thought it necessary to inform my family of this expected visit, which might decide their future lot. My wife and elder sons might wish to seize this only occasion that might occur to revisit their native country--to quit their beloved island, which would doubtless cost them much sorrow at the last moment, but was necessary to their future comfort. I could not help feeling distressed at the prospect of my dear children's solitary old age, and I determined, if they did not wish to return with Captain Johnson, to request him to send some colonists out to people our island.

It will be remembered that I had left home alone, and at an early hour, having perceived a vessel from the top of our tree with my telescope. I had set out without breakfast, without giving my sons their tasks, or making any arrangements for the labours of the day. My conference with Lieutenant Bell had been long; it was now past noon, and knowing how prompt my wife was to [pg 195] alarm herself, I was surprised that I did not meet her, nor any of my sons. I began to be uneasy, and on my arrival I hastily mounted the tree, and found my faithful partner extended on her bed, surrounded by her four sons, and apparently in great pain. I demanded, with a cry of grief, what had happened; all wished to speak at once, and it was with some difficulty I learned, that my dear wife, in descending the staircase, had been seized with a giddiness in her head, and had fallen down and injured herself so much, that she was unable to rise without assistance; she was now enduring great pain in her right leg and in her left foot. "Ernest and I," added Fritz, "carried her without delay to her bed, though not without difficulty, for the staircase is so narrow; but she continued to get worse, and we did not know what to do."

Jack. I have rubbed her foot continually, but it swells more and more, as well as her leg, which I dare not touch, it hurts her so much.

Ernest. I remember, father, that of the chests that we brought from the ship there is one unopened, which is marked "medicines,"--may it not contain something that

121

will relieve mamma?

Father. Perhaps it may, my son. You did well to remember it; we will go to Tent House for it. Fritz, you shall accompany me to assist in bringing it.

I wished to be alone with Fritz, to consult him about the English vessel, and was glad of this opportunity. Before I left my wife, I intended to examine her leg and foot, which were exceedingly painful. When I was preparing to enter the Church, I had studied medicine and practical surgery, [pg 196] in order to be able to administer to the bodily afflictions of my poor parishioners, as well as to their spiritual sorrows. I knew how to bleed, and could replace a dislocated limb. I had often made cures; but since my arrival at the island I had neglected my medical studies, which happily had not been needed. I hoped now, however, to recall as much of my knowledge as would be sufficient to cure my poor wife. I examined her foot first, which I found to be violently sprained. She begged me then to look at her leg, and what was my distress when I saw it was fractured above the ancle; however, the fracture appeared simple, without splinters, and easy to cure. I sent Fritz without delay to procure me two pieces of the bark of a tree, between which I placed the leg, after having, with the assistance of my son, stretched it till the two pieces of broken bone united; I then bound it with bandages of linen, and tied the pieces of bark round the leg, so that it might not be moved. I bound the sprained foot very tightly, till I could procure the balsam which I expected to find in the chest. I felt assured, that the giddiness of the head, which had caused her fall, proceeded from some existing cause, which I suspected, from the pulse and the complexion, must be a fulness of blood; and it appeared to be necessary to take away some ounces, which I persuaded her to allow me to do, when I should have brought my medicine-chest and instruments from Tent House. I left her, with many charges, to the care of my three younger sons, and proceeded to Tent House with Fritz, to whom I now related my morning adventure, and consulted him how we should mention it to his mother. Fritz was astonished. [pg 197] I saw how his mind was employed; he looked round on our fields and plantations, increasing and prospering.

"We must not tell her, father," said he. "I will be at Tent House early in the morning; you must give me some commission to execute; I will await the arrival of the Captain, and tell him that my dear mother is ill,--and that he may return as he came."

"You speak rashly, Fritz," answered I. "I have told you that this ship has suffered much from the storm, and needs repairs. Have you not often read the golden rule of our divine Master, Do unto others as you would have others do unto you? Our duty is to receive the Captain into our island, and to assist him in repairing and refitting his vessel."

"And he will find," said he, "we know something of that kind of work. Did you show him our beautiful pinnace and canoe? But can such a large vessel enter our Bay of Safety?"

"No," replied I; "I fear there will not be sufficient water; but we will show the captain the large bay at the other end of the island, formed by Cape Disappointment; he will find there a beautiful harbour."

"And he and his officers may live at the farm, and we can go over every day to assist in repairing their vessel," continued Fritz.

"Very well," said I; "and when it is finished, he will, in return, give us a place in it to return to Europe."

"To return to Europe, father!" cried he; "to leave our beautiful winter dwelling, Tent House, and our charming summer residence, [pg 198] Falcon's Nest; our dear, good animals; our crystals of salt; our farms; so much that is our own, and which nobody covets, to return into Europe to poverty, to war, to those wicked soldiers who have banished us! We want nothing. Dear father, can you consent to leave our beloved island?"

"You are right, my dear son," said I. "Would to God we might always remain here happily together; but we are of different ages, and by the law of nature we must one day be separated. Consider, my dear son, if you should survive your brothers, how cheerless it would be to live quite alone on this desert island, without any one to close your eyes. But let us look at these trees; I see they are tamarind-trees; their fruit contains a pulp which is very useful in medicine, and which will suit your mother, I think, as well as the juice of the orange or lemon. We shall find some of the latter at our plantation near Tent House; but, in the mean time, do you climb the tamarind-tree, and gather some of those pods which resemble those of beans, fill one side of the bag with them, the other we will reserve for the oranges and lemons. Not to lose any time, I will go on to Tent House to seek for the two chests, and you can follow me."

Fritz was up the tamarind-tree in a moment. I crossed Family Bridge, and soon reached the grotto. I lighted a candle, which I always kept ready, entered the magazine, and found the two chests, labelled.

They were neither large nor heavy, and, having tied cords round them for the convenience of carrying them, I proceeded to visit the orange [pg 199] and lemon trees, where I found the fruit sufficiently ripe for lemonade. Fritz came to meet me, with a good supply of tamarinds. We filled the other end of his sack with oranges and lemons. He threw it over his shoulder, and, neither of us being overloaded, we pursued our way homewards very quickly, notwithstanding the heat, which was excessively oppressive, though the sun was hidden under the thick clouds, which entirely concealed the sea from us. Nothing was to be seen but the waves breaking against the rocks. Fritz expressed his fears that a storm was coming on, which might prove fatal to the vessel, and wished to take out the pinnace and endeavour to assist Captain Johnson. Delighted as I felt with his fearless humanity, I could not consent; I reminded him of the situation of his mother. "Forgive me, dear father," said he; "I had forgotten everything but the poor vessel. But the captain may do as we did, leave his ship between the rocks, and come, with all in the vessel, to establish themselves here. We will give them up a corner of our islands; and if there should be any ladies amongst them, how pleasant it would be for mamma to have a friend!"

The rain now fell in torrents, and we proceeded with great difficulty. After crossing the bridge, we saw at a distance a very extraordinary figure approaching us; we could not ascertain what species of animal it was. It appeared taller than any of the monkeys we had seen, and much larger, of a black or brown colour. We could not distinguish the head, but it seemed to have two thick and moveable horns before it. We had fortunately taken no gun with us, or Fritz would [pg 200] certainly have fired at this singular animal. But as it rapidly approached us, we soon recognized the step, and the cry of pleasure which hailed us. "It is Jack," we exclaimed; and in fact it was he, who was hurrying to meet us with my large cloak and water-proof caoutchouc boots. I had neglected to take them, and my dear little fellow had volunteered to bring them to Tent House. To protect himself on the way, he had put the cloak on, covering his head with the hood, and my boots being too large for him, he had put one on each arm, which he held up to secure the hood. Conceive what a singular figure he made. Notwithstanding our uneasiness, and our wretched condition, for we were wet to the skin, we could not but laugh heartily at him. I would not consent to use the coverings he had brought; neither Fritz nor I could be worse for the distance we had to go, and Jack was younger and more delicate; I obliged him therefore to retain his curious protection; and asked how he had left his mother. "Very uneasy," said he, "about you; else I think she must be much better, for her cheeks are very red, and her eyes very bright, and she talks incessantly. She would have come herself to seek you, but could not rise; and when I told her I would come, she bid me be very quick; but when I was coming down stairs, I heard her call me back for fear of the rain and the thunder; I would not hear her, but ran as fast as I could, hoping to reach Tent House. Why did you come back so soon?"

"To spare you half your journey, my brave little man," said I, hastening on; for Jack's account of his mother made me uneasy. I perceived [pg 201] she must be labouring under fever, and the blood ascending to her head. My children followed me, and we soon reached the foot of our castle in the air.

CHAPTER XXXIV.

We entered our apartment literally as if we had come out of the sea, and I found my poor Elizabeth much agitated. "Heaven be praised!" said she; "but where is Jack, that rash little fellow?"

"Here I am, mamma," said he, "as dry as when I left you. I have left my dress below, that I might not terrify you; for if Mr. Fritz had had his gun, I might have been shot as a rhinoceros, and not been here to tell you my story."

The good mother then turned her thoughts on Fritz and me, and would not suffer us to come near her till we had changed our drenched garments. To oblige her, we retired to a little closet I had contrived between two thick branches at the top of the staircase, which was used to contain our chests of linen, our dresses, and our provisions. Our dress was soon changed; we hung up the wet garments, and I returned to my companion, who was suffering from her foot, but still more from a frightful headache. She had a burning fever. I concluded that bleeding was urgently needed, but commenced by assuaging her thirst with some lemonade. I then opened my box of surgical instruments, and approached the opening to the east which served us for a window, [pg 202] and which we could close by means of a curtain, that was now entirely raised to give air to our dear invalid, and to amuse my children, who were watching the storm. The mighty waves that broke against the rocks, the vivid lightning bursting through the castles of murky clouds, the majestic and incessant rolling of the thunder, formed one of those enchanting spectacles to which they had been from infancy accustomed. As in the Swiss mountains we are liable to frightful storms, to which it is necessary to familiarize oneself, as one cannot avoid them, I had accustomed my wife and children, by my own example, to behold, not only without fear, but even with admiration, these great shocks of the elements,--these convulsions of nature.

I had opened the chest, and my children had directed their attention to the instruments it contained; the first were a little rusty, and I handed them to Ernest, who, after examining them, placed them on a table inside the window. I was searching for a lancet in good condition, when a clap of thunder, such as I had never heard in my life, terrified us all so much, that we nearly fell down. This burst of thunder had not been preceded by any lightning, but was accompanied by two immense forked columns of fire, which seemed to stretch from the sky to our very feet. We all cried out, even my poor wife; but the silence of terror succeeded, and seemed to be the silence of death. I flew to the bedside, and found my dear patient in a state of total insensibility. I was convinced that she was dead, and I was dumb with despair. I was roused from my stupor by the voice of my children. I then remembered [pg 203] that I had not lost all: there still remained duties to fulfil, and affection to console me. "My children," cried I, extending my arms to them, "come and comfort your unfortunate father: come and lament with him the best of wives and mothers." Terrified at the appearance of their mother, they surrounded her bed, calling on her in piercing accents. At that moment I saw my little Francis was missing, and my grief was augmented by the fear that he had been killed by the lightning. I hastily turned to the window, expecting to find my child dead, and our dwelling in flames. Fortunately, all was safe; but, in my distraction, I scarcely thanked God for His mercy, at the very moment even when he graciously restored to me my lost treasures. Francis, frightened by the storm, had hidden himself in his mother's bed, and fallen asleep; awaked by the thunder, he had not dared to move, fearing it announced the arrival of the savages; but at last, the cries of his brothers roused him, and raising his pretty fair head, supposing his mother sleeping, he flung his arms round her neck, saying, "Wake, mamma, we are all here,--papa, my brothers, and the storm, too, which is very beautiful, but frightens me. Open your eyes, mamma; look at the bright lightning, and kiss your little Francis." Either his sweet voice, or the cries of her elder children, restored her faculties: she gradually recovered, and called me to her. The excess of my joy threatened to be almost as fatal as my grief. With difficulty I controlled my own feelings and those of my boys; and, after I had sent them from the bed, I ascertained that she was not only really living, but much better. The pulse was calm, [pg 204] and the fever had subsided, leaving only a weakness that was by no means alarming. I relinquished, joyfully, the intention of bleeding her, the necessity of which I had trembled to contemplate, and contented myself with employing the boys to prepare a cooling mixture, composed of the juice of the lemon, of barley, and tamarinds, which they completed to the great satisfaction of their mother. I then ordered Fritz to descend to the yard, to kill a fowl, pluck and boil it, to make broth,--a wholesome and light nourishment for our dear invalid. I told one of his brothers to assist him, and Jack and Francis, frequently employed under their mother, were ready in a moment. Ernest alone remained quietly on his seat, which I attributed to his usual indolence, and tried to make him ashamed of it. "Ernest," said I, "you are not very anxious to oblige your mother; you sit as if the thunderbolt had struck you."

"It has, indeed, rendered me unfit to be of any service to my good mother," said he, quietly; and, drawing his right hand from under his waistcoat, he showed it to me, most frightfully black and burnt.

This dear child, who must have suffered very much, had never uttered a complaint, for fear of alarming his mother; and even now he made a sign to me to be silent, lest she should hear, and discover the truth. She soon, however, fell into a sleep, which enabled me to attend to poor Ernest, and to question him about the accident. I learned that a long and pointed steel instrument, which he was examining near the large window, stooping over it to see it better, had [pg 205] attracted the lightning, which, falling partly on the hand in which he held it, had caused the misfortune. There were traces on his arm of the electric fire, and his hair was burnt on one side. By what miracle the electric fluid had been diverted, and how we, dwelling in a tree, had been preserved from a sudden and general

126

conflagration, I knew not. My son assured me he had seen the fire run along the instrument he held, and from thence fall perpendicularly to the earth, where it seemed to burst with a second explosion. I was impatient to examine this phenomenon, and to see if any other traces were left, except those on the hand of my son, which it was necessary, in the first place, to attend to. I remembered frequently to have applied with success in burns the most simple and easy of remedies, which everybody can command: this is, to bathe the hand affected in cold water, taking care to renew it every eight or ten minutes. I placed Ernest between two tubs of cold water, and, exhorting him to patience and perseverance, I left him to bathe his hand, and approached the opening, to try and discover what had preserved us, by averting the direction of the lightning, which one might have expected would have killed my son, and destroyed our dwelling. I saw only some light traces on the table; but, on looking more attentively, I found that the greater part of the surgical instruments which Ernest had placed upon it were either melted or much damaged. In examining them separately, I remarked one much longer than the rest, which projected beyond the edge of the table, and was much marked by the fire. I could not easily take it up; it had adhered somewhat in [pg 206] melting, and, in endeavouring to disengage it, I saw that the point, which was beyond the opening, touched a thick wire, which seemed to be suspended from the roof of our tent. All was now explained to me; except that I could in no way account for this wire, placed expressly to serve as a conductor for the lightning. It seemed to be the work of magic. The evening was too far advanced for me to distinguish how it was fastened, and what fixed it below; therefore, enjoining Ernest to call loudly if he needed me, I hastened down. I saw my three cooks very busy, as I passed through, preparing the broth for their mother--they assured me it would be excellent. Fritz boasted that he had killed the fowl with all speed, Jack that he had plucked it without tearing it much, and Francis that he had lighted and kept up the fire. They had nothing to employ them just then, and I took them with me to have some one to talk to on the phenomenon of the lightning. Below the window I found a large packet of iron wire, which I had brought from Tent House some days before, intending on some leisure day to make a sort of grating before our poultry-yard. By what chance was it here, and hooked by one end to the roof of our house? Some time before I had replaced our cloth canopy by a sort of roof covered with bark nailed upon laths; the cloth still enclosed the sides and front; all was so inflammable, that, but for the providential conductor, we must have been in flames in an instant. I thanked God for our preservation; and little Francis, seeing me so happy, said--

"Is it quite true, papa, that this wire has preserved us?"

[pg 207]
"Yes, it is true, my darling; and I wish to know what good genius has placed it there, that I may be thankful," said I.

"Ah! father," said my little fellow, "embrace me, but do not thank me; for I did not

127

know that I was doing good."

Astonished at this information, I requested my boy to tell me why and how he had fixed the wire?

"I wanted to reach some figs," said he, "when you and Fritz were at Tent House, and Jack and Ernest were nursing mamma; I wished to do some good for her. I thought she would like some of our sweet figs; but there were none in my reach, and I had no stick long enough to beat them down. I went below, and found that great roll of wire. I tried to break a piece off, but could not; and I then determined to carry the whole up to our dwelling, and to bend one end into a hook, by which I might catch some of the branches, and bring them near me to gather the figs. I was very successful at first, and secured one or two figs. I had my packet of wire on the table by the window, and stood near it myself. I thought I could reach a branch that hung over our roof, loaded with fruit. I leaned forward, and extended my hook to the branch; I felt I had secured it, and joyfully began to pull. You know, papa, they bend, and don't break; but it remained immovable, as well as my hook, which was held by one of the laths of the roof. I pulled with all my strength, and, in my efforts, I struck my foot against the roll of wire, which fell down to the ground without detaching the hook. You may judge how firm it is, for it is no trifling leap from our house to the ground."

[pg 208]
"A good work, indeed, my boy," said I, "is yours, for it has saved us. God has inspired you, and has made use of the hand of a child for our preservation. Your conductor shall remain where you have so happily placed it; we may still have need of it. The sky still looks very threatening; let us return to your mother, and take a light with us."

I had contrived a sort of portable lantern, made of isinglass, which lighted us in our offices. Moreover, a calibash pierced with small holes, with a candle inside, was placed at the top of the winding staircase, and lighted it entirely, so that we were able to descend without danger by night as w ell as by day. I was, however, uneasy about the way we should bring my wife down, if we found it necessary to remove her during her sickness; I named it to Fritz.

"Have no uneasiness, father," said he, "Ernest and I are very strong now, and we can carry mamma like a feather."

"You and I might, my dear boy," said I; "but Ernest cannot be of much assistance to us at present."

I then related his misfortune to them. They were distressed and astonished, not comprehending the cause, which I promised to explain. They wished now, however, to see their brother. Fritz then requested, in a low tone of voice, that he

128

might go to Tent House, to see if the vessel and the captain had arrived. Seeing his brothers listening with curiosity, I thought it best to tell them the affair, requesting them, however, not to name it to their mother at present. Jack, who was now about fourteen years of age, listened with the [pg 209] most intense interest, his eyes sparkling with joy and surprise.

"A vessel!--people from Europe! Do you think they have come to seek us? Perhaps they are our relations and friends."

"How glad should I be," said Francis, "if my good grandmamma were there; she loved me so much, and was always giving me sweetmeats." This was the mother of my dear wife, from whom she had parted with extreme regret; I knew that a single word from the child would have revived all her sorrows, and would in her present state be dangerous. I therefore forbade him naming such a thing to his mother, even if we mentioned the vessel.

We ascended, and found our dear patient awake, with Ernest at her side, his hand tied up, and somewhat relieved; though, from not having applied the water immediately, there were several blisters, which he requested me to open. It was necessary to tell his mother he had had a burn; she named several remedies, and I was hesitating which to use, when Fritz, giving me a significant glance, said, "Don't you think, father, that the leaves of the karata, which cured Jack's leg so well, would be is serviceable to Ernest's hand?"

"I have no doubt of it," said I; "but we have none here."

"I know very well where they grow," said he. "Come, Jack, we shall soon be there; we shall have a little rain, but what of that? we shall not be melted, and we can have a bath."

My wife was divided between her desire to relieve Ernest, and her fear of the boys venturing out in such a stormy night. She agreed at last, [pg 210] provided Jack had my cloak, and Fritz the boots, and that they should take the lantern. Thus equipped, they set out; I accompanied them outside the tree; Fritz assuring me they would be back in three hours, at most. He intended to proceed along the rocks towards Tent House, to make what observations he could; for, as he told me, he could not get the poor captain and his vessel out of his head. It was now seven o'clock; I gave them my blessing, and left them with injunctions to be prudent, and returned with an anxious heart to my invalids.

CHAPTER XXXV.

On entering, I found Francis sitting on his mother's bed, telling her the story of the lightning, of the wire which was called a conductor, of the figs that he was going to gather for her, and that papa had called him--little Francis--the preserver of the whole family. Having briefly explained to them the results of Francis's fortunate device, I procured some raw potato to apply to Ernest's hand, which still gave him great pain, and bathed my wife's foot with some eau d'arquebusade, which I procured from my medicine-chest; here I also met with some laudanum, a few drops of which I infused into the lemonade, wishing her to sleep till her sons returned. She soon was in a sweet slumber; the boys followed her example, and I was left alone with my anxieties; happy, however, to see them at rest after such an evening of agitation. The hours passed, still my children returned [pg 211] not. I was continually at the window, listening for their steps or the sound of their voices; I heard only the rain falling in torrents, the waves breaking against the rocks, and the wind howling frightfully. I could not help thinking of the danger they ran, having twice to cross the river, which was doubtless swoln by the rain. I was not so much alarmed for Fritz, a strong, bold youth of nineteen years of age, and a determined hunter: as for poor Jack, bold even to rashness, and having neither strength nor experience to secure him, I could not help fancying him carried away by the stream, and his brother not daring to return without him. My wife occasionally awoke, but the narcotic stupified her; she did not perceive the absence of her sons. Francis slept tranquilly; but when Ernest awoke, and heard the tempest so terribly augmented, he was almost distracted; all his selfishness, all his indolence disappeared. He entreated me to allow him to go in search of his brothers, and with difficulty I detained him. To convince him that he was not the sole cause of the danger of Fritz and Jack, I related to him, for the first time, the history of the boat and the vessel, and assured him that the great cause of their anxiety to go over to Tent House, was to search for some traces of the unfortunate seamen and their vessel, exposed to that furious sea.

"And Fritz, also, is exposed to that sea," cried Ernest. "I know it; I am sure that he is at this moment in his canoe, struggling against the waves!"

"And Jack, my poor Jack!" sighed I, infected with his fears.

"No, father," added Ernest; "be composed; [pg 212] Fritz will not be so imprudent; he will have left Jack in our house at the rock; and, probably, seeing the hopelessness of his undertaking, he is returned himself now, and is waiting there till the stream subsides a little; do allow me to go, dear father; you have ordered me cold water for my burnt hand, and it will certainly cure it to get well wet."

I could not consent to expose my third son to the tempest, which was now become frightful; the sailcloth which covered our window was torn into a thousand pieces, and carried away; the rain, like a deluge, forced itself into our dwelling, even to the bed where my wife and child were lying. I could neither make up my mind to leave them myself in this perilous situation, nor to spare my boy, who could not even be of any use to his brothers. I commanded him to remain, succeeded in persuading him of their probable safety, and induced him to lie down to rest. Now, in my terrible solitude, I turned to Him, "who tempers the wind to the shorn lamb;" who forbids us not to address Him in the trials he sends us, to beseech Him to soften them, or to give us strength to bear them. Kneeling down, I dared to supplicate Him to restore me my children, submissively adding, after the example of our blessed Saviour, "Yet, not my will, but thine be done, O Lord."

My prayers appeared to be heard; the storm gradually abated, and the day began to break. I awoke Ernest, and having dressed his wounded hand, he set out for Tent House, in search of his brothers. I followed him with my eyes as far as I could see; the whole country appeared one vast lake, and the road to Tent House was like the bed [pg 213] of a river; but, protected by his good gaiters of buffalo-skin, he proceeded fearlessly, and was soon out of my sight.

I was recalled from the window by the voice of my wife, who was awake, and anxiously inquiring for her sons.

"They are gone," said I, "to gather the leaves of the karata for Ernest's burnt hand, and he wished to go too."

Her deep sleep had entirely chased from her memory all the events of the previous evening, and I was glad to allow Francis to repeat his little tale of the burn and his conductor in order to gain time. She was astonished and uneasy to hear of Ernest's accident, and was afraid they would get wet in searching for the karata, little aware of the hours of anguish I had endured waiting and watching for those she believed had only just left home. At that moment, the dear and well-known voices were heard under the great window.

"Father, I am bringing back my brothers," cried Ernest.

"Yes, papa, we are all alive, and as wet as fishes," added the sweet voice of Jack.

"But not without having had our troubles," said the manly voice of Fritz.

I rushed down the staircase to meet them, and, embracing them, I led them, trembling with emotion, to the bed of their mother, who could not comprehend the transport of joy I expressed.

"Dear Elizabeth," said I, "here are our sons; God has given them to us a second time."

"Have we then been in any danger of losing them?" said she. "What is the meaning of this?"

They saw their mother was unconscious of their [pg 214] long absence, and assured her it was only the storm which had so completely wetted them, that had alarmed me. I hastened to get them to change their clothes, and go to bed a little while to rest themselves; as, however anxious I was myself, I wished to prepare my wife for their recital, and also to tell her of the vessel. Jack would not go till he had produced his bundle of the karata leaves.

"There is enough for six-and-thirty thunderstorms," said he; "and I will prepare them. I have had some experience with my own, and I know the best method."

He soon divided one of the leaves with his knife, after cutting away the triangular thorn from the end, and applied it to his brother's hand, binding it with his handkerchief. Having completed this dressing, he threw off his clothes, and, jumping into his bed, he and his brothers were sound asleep in ten minutes.

I then sat down by my wife, and began my tale; from my first view of the vessel, and my anxious watching for intercourse with it, in order that we might take the opportunity to return to Europe.

"But why should we return to Europe?" said she; "we want nothing here now, since I have got flax, cotton, and a wheel. Our children lead an active, healthy, and innocent life, and live with us, which they might not do in the world. For four years we have been happy here, and what shall we find in Europe to compensate us for what we leave here?--poverty, war, and none of those things which we have here abundantly."

"But we should find grandmamma," said little Francis; and stopped, recollecting my prohibition.

[pg 215]
He had, however, said sufficient to bring tears to his mother's eyes.

"You are right, my darling," said she, "that is my sole regret; but my dear parent was aged and infirm, in all probability I should no longer find her in this world; and if removed to Heaven, she watches over us in this island, as well as if we were in Europe."

After my dear wife had subdued the agitation this remembrance caused her, I pursued the conversation as follows:--

132

CHAPTER XXXVI.

"I see, my dear wife," said I, "that you, as well as the rest of my family, are contented to remain on this island, where it seems it is the will of God for us to dwell, as it is improbable that in such a tempest Captain Johnson would risk approaching the island, if indeed it has not been already fatal to him. I am impatient to learn if Fritz has any tidings of him; for it was on the shore near Tent House that he and Jack passed the night."

"Well done, my good and courageous boys!" said their mother; "they might at any rate have given assistance to them if wrecked."

"You are more courageous than I am, my dear Elizabeth," answered I; "I have passed the whole night mourning for my children, and you think only of the good they might have done to their fellow-creatures."

My sons were awake by this time, and I eagerly [pg 216] inquired if they had discovered any traces of the vessel. Fritz said they had not; but he feared it would never be able to resist the fury of the tempest.

"No, indeed," said Jack; "those mountains of waves, which were not fixtures like other mountains, came full gallop to swallow up Fritz the great, Jack the little, and their fine canoe."

My wife nearly fainted when she heard they had ventured on that terrible sea; and I reminded Fritz that I had forbidden him to do this.

"But you have often said to me, papa," said he, "do unto others as you would they should do unto you; and what a happiness it would have been to us, when our vessel was wrecked, if we had seen a canoe!"

"With two bold men coming to our assistance," said Jack;--"but go on with your story, Fritz."

Fritz continued: "We proceeded first to the rocks, and, with some difficulty, and not until Jack had shed some blood in the cause, we secured the karata-leaves, with their ugly thorns at the end. When our sack was full, we proceeded along the rocks towards Tent House. From this height I tried to discover the ship, but the darkness obscured everything. Once I thought I perceived at a great distance a fixed light, which was neither a star nor the lightning, and which I lost sight of occasionally. We had now arrived at the cascade, which, from the noise, seemed much swollen by the rain--our great stones were quite hidden by a boiling foam. I would have attempted to cross, if I had been alone; but, with Jack on my

133

shoulders, I was afraid of the risk. I [pg 217] therefore prepared to follow the course of the river to Family Bridge. The wet ground continually brought us on our knees, and with great difficulty we reached the bridge. But judge of our consternation! the river had risen so much that the planks were covered, and, as we conceived, the whole was destroyed. I then told Jack to return to Falcon's Nest with the karata-leaves, and I would swim across the river. I returned about a hundred yards up the stream to find a wider and less rapid part, and easily crossed. Judge of my surprise when I saw a human figure approaching to meet me; I had no doubt it was the captain of the vessel, and--"

"And it was Captain Jack, sans peur et sans reproche," said the bold little fellow. "I was determined not to return home a poltroon who was afraid of the water." When Fritz was gone, I tried the bridge, and soon found there was not sufficient water over it to risk my being drowned. I took off my boots, which might have made me slip, and my cloak, which was too heavy, and, making a dart, I ran with all my strength across, and reached the other side. I put on my boots, which I had in my hands, and advanced to meet Fritz, who called out, as soon as he saw me, "Is it you, captain?" I tried to say, "Yes, certainly," in a deep tone, but my laughter betrayed me.

"To my great regret;" said Fritz, "I should truly have preferred meeting Captain Johnson; but I fear he and his people are at the bottom of the sea. After meeting with Jack, we proceeded to Tent House, where we kindled a good fire, and dried ourselves a little. We then refreshed ourselves [pg 218] with some wine which remained on the table where you had entertained the captain, and proceeded to prepare a signal to inform the vessel we were ready to receive them. We procured a thick bamboo cane from the magazine; I fixed firmly to one end of it the large lantern of the fish's bladder you gave us to take; I filled the lamp with oil, and placed in it a thick cotton-wick, which, when lighted, was very brilliant. Jack and I then placed it on the shore, at the entrance of the bay. We fixed it before the rock, where the land-wind would not reach it, sunk it three or four feet into the ground, steadied it with stones, and then went to rest over our fire, after this long and difficult labour. After drying ourselves a little, we set out on our return, when, looking towards the sea, we were startled by the appearance of the same light we had noticed before; we heard, at the same time, the distant report of a gun, which was repeated three or four times at irregular intervals. We were persuaded that it was the vessel calling to us for aid, and, remembering the command of our Saviour, we thought you would forgive our disobedience if we presented to you in the morning the captain, the lieutenant, and as many as our canoe would contain. We entered it then without any fear, for you know how light and well-balanced it is; and, rowing into the bay, the sail was spread to the wind, and we had no more trouble. I then took the helm; my own signal-light shone clearly on the shore; and, except for the rain which fell in torrents, the waves which washed over our canoe, and uneasiness about the ship and about you, and our fear that the wind might carry us into the [pg 219] open sea, we should have had a delightful little maritime excursion. When we got out of the bay, I perceived the wind was driving us towards Shark's Island, which, being directly before the bay, forms two entrances to it. I intended to go round it, and disembark there, if possible, that I might look out for some trace of the ship, but we found this impossible; the sea ran too high; besides, we should have been unable to moor our canoe, the island not affording a single tree or anything we could lash it to, and the waves would soon have carried it away. We had now lost sight of the light, and hearing no more signals, I began to think on your distress when we did not arrive at the hour we promised. I therefore resolved to return by the other side of the bay, carefully avoiding the current, which would have carried us into the open sea. I lowered the sail by means of the ropes you had fixed to it, and we rowed into port. We carefully moored the canoe, and, without returning to Tent House, took the road home. We crossed the bridge as Jack had done, found the water-proof cloak and bag of karata-leaves where he had left them, and soon after met Ernest. As it was daylight, I did not take him for the captain, but knew him immediately, and felt the deepest remorse when I heard from him in what anxiety and anguish you had passed the night. Our enterprise was imprudent, and altogether useless; but we might have saved life, which would have been an ample remuneration. I fear all is hopeless. What do you think, father, of their fate?"

"I hope they are far from this dangerous coast," said I; "but if still in our neighbourhood, [pg 220] we will do all we can to assist them. As soon as the tempest is subsided, we will take the pinnace and sail round the island. You have long urged me to this, Fritz; and who knows but on the opposite side we may find some traces of our own poor sailors,--perhaps even meet with them?"

The weather gradually clearing, I called my sons to go out with me. My wife earnestly besought me not to venture on the sea; I assured her it was not sufficiently calm, but we must examine our plantations, to ascertain what damage was done, and at the same time we might look out for some traces of the wreck; besides, our animals were becoming clamorous for food; therefore, leaving Ernest with her, we descended to administer in the first place to their wants.

CHAPTER XXXVII.

Our animals were impatiently expecting us; they had been neglected during the storm, and were ill-supplied with food, besides being half-sunk in water. The ducks and the flamingo liked it well enough, and were swimming comfortably in the muddy water; but the quadrupeds were complaining aloud, each in his own proper language, and making a frightful confusion of sounds. Valiant, especially,--

the name Francis had bestowed on the calf I had given him to bring up,--bleated incessantly for his young master, and could not be quieted till he came. It is wonderful how this child, only twelve years old, had tamed and attached this animal; though sometimes so [pg 221] fierce, with him he was mild as a lamb. The boy rode on his back, guiding him with a little stick, with which he just touched the side of his neck as he wished him to move; but if his brothers had ventured to mount, they would have been certainly thrown off. A pretty sight was our cavalry: Fritz on his handsome onagra, Jack on his huge buffalo, and Francis on his young bull. There was nothing left for Ernest but the donkey, and its slow and peaceful habits suited him very well.

Francis ran up to his favourite, who showed his delight at seeing him as well as he was able, and at the first summons followed his master from the stable. Fritz brought out Lightfoot Jack his buffalo, and I followed with the cow and the ass. We left them to sport about at liberty on the humid earth, till we removed the water from their stable, and supplied them with fresh food. We then drove them in, considering it advisable to pursue our expedition on foot, lest the bridge should still be overflowed. Francis was the superintendent of the fowls, and knew every little chicken by name; he called them out and scattered their food for them, and soon had his beautiful and noisy family fluttering round him.

After having made all our animals comfortable, and given them their breakfast, we began to think of our own. Francis made a fire and warmed some chicken broth for his mother; for ourselves, we were contented with some new milk, some salt herrings, and cold potatoes. I had often searched in my excursions for the precious bread-fruit tree, so highly spoken of by modern travellers, which I had hoped might be found in our island, from its favourable situation; but I had hitherto been [pg 222] unsuccessful. We were unable to procure the blessing of bread, our ship biscuit had long been exhausted, and though we had sown our European corn, we had not yet reaped any.

After we had together knelt down to thank God for his merciful protection through the terrors of the past night, and besought him to continue it, we prepared to set out. The waves still ran high, though the wind had subsided, and we determined merely to go along the shore, as the roads still continued impassable from the rain, and the sand was easier to walk on than the wet grass; besides, our principal motive for the excursion was to search for any traces of a recent shipwreck. At first we could discover nothing, even with the telescope; but Fritz, mounting a high rock, fancied he discovered something floating towards the island. He besought me to allow him to take the canoe, which was still where he left it the preceding night. As the bridge was now easy to cross, I consented, only insisting on accompanying him to assist in managing it. Jack, who was much afraid of being left behind, was the first to leap in and seize an oar. There was, however, no need of it; I steered my little boat into the current, and we were carried away with such velocity as almost to take our breath. Fritz was at the helm, and appeared to have no fear; I will not say that his father was so tranquil. I held Jack, for fear of accidents, but he only laughed, and observed to his brother that the canoe galloped better than Lightfoot. We were soon in the open sea, and directed our canoe towards the object we had remarked, and which we still had in sight. We were afraid it was the boat upset, [pg 223] but it proved to be a tolerably large cask, which had probably been thrown overboard to lighten the distressed vessel; we saw several others, but neither mast nor plank to give us any idea that the vessel and boat had perished. Fritz wished much to have made the circuit of the island, to assure ourselves of this, but I would not hear of it; I thought of my wife's terror; besides, the sea was still too rough for our frail bark, and we had, moreover, no provisions. If my canoe had not been well built, it would have run great risk of being overset by the waves, which broke over it. Jack, when he saw one coming, lay down on his face, saying he preferred having them on his back rather than in his mouth; he jumped up as soon as it passed, to help to empty the canoe, till another wave came to fill it again; but, thanks to my out-riggers, we preserved our balance very well, and I consented to go as far as Cape Disappointment, which merited the name a second time, for we found no trace here of the vessel, though we mounted the hill, and thus commanded a wide extent of view. As we looked round the country, it appeared completely devastated: trees torn up by the roots, plantations levelled with the ground, water collected into absolute lakes,--all announced desolation; and the tempest seemed to be renewing. The sky was darkened, the wind arose, and was unfavourable for our return; nor could I venture the canoe on the waves, every instant becoming more formidable. We moored our bark to a large palm-tree we found at the foot of the hill, near the shore, and set out by land to our home. We crossed the Gourd Wood and the Wood of Monkeys, and arrived at our farm, which [pg 224] we found, to our great satisfaction, had not suffered much from the storm. The food we had left in the stables was nearly consumed; from which we concluded that the animals we had left here had sheltered themselves during the storm. We refilled the mangers with the hay we had preserved in the loft, and observing the sky getting more and more threatening, we set out without delay for our house, from which we were yet a considerable distance. To avoid Flamingo Marsh, which was towards the sea, and Rice Marsh, towards the rock, we determined to go through Cotton Wood, which would save us from the wind, which was ready to blow us off our feet. I was still uneasy about the ship, which the lieutenant had told me was out of repair; but I indulged a hope that they might have taken refuge in some bay, or found anchorage on some hospitable shore, where they might get their vessel into order.

Jack was alarmed lest they should fall into the hands of the anthropophagi, who eat men like hares or sheep, of whom he had read in some book of travels, and excited the ridicule of his brother, who was astonished at his ready belief of travellers' tales, which he asserted were usually false.

"But Robinson Crusoe would not tell a falsehood," said Jack, indignantly; "and there were cannibals came to his island, and were going to eat Friday, if he had not saved him."

"Oh! Robinson could not tell a falsehood," said Fritz, "because he never existed. The whole history is a romance--is not that the name, father, that is given to works of the imagination?"

"It is," said I; "but we must not call Robinson Crusoe a romance; though Robinson himself, [pg 225] and all the circumstances of his history are probably fictitious, the details are all founded on truth--on the adventures and descriptions of voyagers who may be depended on, and unfortunate individuals who have actually been wrecked on unknown shores. If ever our journal should be printed, many may believe that it is only a romance--a mere work of the imagination."

My boys hoped we should not have to introduce any savages into our romance, and were astonished that an island so beautiful had not tempted any to inhabit it; in fact, I had often been myself surprised at this circumstance; but I told them many voyagers had noticed islands apparently fertile, and yet uninhabited; besides, the chain of rocks which surrounded this might prevent the approach of savages, unless they had discovered the little Bay of Safety where we had landed. Fritz said he anxiously desired to circumnavigate the island, in order to ascertain the size of it, and if there were similar chains of rocks on the opposite side. I promised him, as soon as the stormy weather was past, and his mother well enough to remove to Tent House, we would take our pinnace, and set out on our little voyage.

We now approached the marsh, and he begged me to let him go and cut some canes, as he projected making a sort of carriage for his mother. As we were collecting them, he explained his scheme to me. He wished to weave of these reeds, which were very strong, a large and long sort of pannier, in which his mother might sit or recline, and which might be suspended between two strong bamboo-canes by handles of rope. He then purposed to yoke two of our most gentle [pg 226] animals, the cow and the ass, the one before and the other behind, between these shafts, the leader to be mounted by one of the children as director; the other would follow naturally, and the good mother would thus be carried, as if in a litter, without any danger of jolting. I was pleased with this idea, and we all set to work to load ourselves each with a huge burden of reeds. They requested me not to tell my wife, that they might give her an agreeable surprise. It needed such affection as ours to induce us to the undertaking in such unpropitious weather. It rained in torrents, and the marsh was so soft and wet, that we were in danger of sinking at every step. However, I could not be less courageous than my sons, whom nothing daunted, and we soon made up our bundles, and, placing them on our heads, they formed a sort of umbrella, which was not without its benefits. We soon arrived at Falcon's Nest. Before we reached the tree, I saw a fire shine to such a distance, that I was alarmed; but soon found it was only meant for our benefit by our kind friends at home. When my wife saw the rain falling, she had instructed her little assistant to make a fire in our usual cooking-place, at a little distance from the tree, and protected by a canopy of water-proof cloth from the rain. The young cook had not only kept up a good fire to dry us on our return, but had taken the opportunity of roasting two dozen of those excellent little birds which his mother had preserved in butter, and which, all ranged on the old sword which served us for a spit, were just ready on our arrival, and the fire and feast were equally grateful to the [pg 227] hungry, exhausted, and wet travellers, who sat down to enjoy them.

However, before we sat down to our repast, we went up to see our invalids, whom we found tolerably well, though anxious for our return. Ernest, with his sound hand, and the assistance of Francis, had succeeded in forming a sort of rampart before the opening into the room, composed of the four hammocks in which he and his brothers slept, placed side by side, on end. This sufficiently protected them from the rain, but excluded the light, so that they had been obliged to light a candle, and Ernest had been reading to his mother in a book of voyages that had formed part of the captain's small library. It was a singular coincidence, that while we were talking of the savages on the way home, they were also reading of them; and I found my dear wife much agitated by the fears these accounts had awakened in her mind. After soothing her terrors, I returned to the fire to dry myself, and to enjoy my repast. Besides the birds, Francis had prepared fresh eggs and potatoes for us. He told me that his mamma had given up her office of cook to him, and assured me that he would perform the duties to our satisfaction, provided he was furnished with materials. Fritz was to hunt, Jack to fish, I was to order dinner, and he would make it ready. "And when we have neither game nor fish," said Jack, "we will attack your poultry-yard." This was not at all to the taste of poor little Francis, who could not bear his favourites to be killed, and who had actually wept over the chicken that was slaughtered to make broth for [pg 228] his mother. We were obliged to promise him that, when other resources failed, we would apply to our barrels of salt-fish. He, however, gave us leave to dispose as we liked of the ducks and geese, which were too noisy for him.

After we had concluded our repast, we carried a part of it to our friends above, and proceeded to give them an account of our expedition. I then secured the hammocks somewhat more firmly, to save us from the storm that was still raging, and the hour of rest being at hand, my sons established themselves on mattresses of cotton, made by their kind mother, and in spite of the roaring of the winds, we were soon in profound repose.

CHAPTER XXXVIII.

The storm continued to rage the whole of the following day, and even the day after, with the same violence. Happily our tree stood firm, though several branches were broken; amongst others, that to which Francis's wire was suspended. I replaced it with more care, carried it beyond our roof, and fixed at the extremity the pointed instrument which had attracted the lightning. I then substituted for the hammocks before the window, strong planks, which remained from my building, and which my sons assisted me to raise with pulleys, after having sawed them to the proper length. Through these I made loop-holes, to admit the light and air. In order to carry off the rain, I fixed a sort of spout, made of the wood of a tree I had met with, which was unknown to me, though apparently [pg 229] somewhat like the elder. The whole of the tree, almost to the bark, was filled up with a sort of pith, easily removed. From this tree I made the pipes for our fountain, and the remainder was now useful for these rain-spouts. I employed those days in which I could not go out, in separating the seeds and grain, of which I saw we should have need, and in mending our work-tools; my sons, in the mean time, nestled under the tree among the roots, were incessantly employed in the construction of the carriage for their mother. The karatas had nearly completed the cure of Ernest's hand, and he was able to assist his brothers preparing the canes, which Fritz and Jack wove between the flat wooden wands, with which they had made the frame of their pannier; they succeeded in making it so strong and close, that they might have carried liquids in it. My dear wife's foot and leg were gradually improving; and I took the opportunity of her confinement, to reason with her on her false notion of the dangers of the sea, and to represent to her the gloomy prospect of our sons, if they were left alone in the island. She agreed with me, but could not resolve to leave it; she hoped God would send some vessel to us, which might leave us some society; and after all, if our sons were left, she pointed out to me, that they had our beautiful pinnace, and might at any time, of their own accord, leave the island.

"And why should we anticipate the evils of futurity, my dear friend?" said she. "Let us think only of the present. I am anxious now to know if the storm has spared my fine kitchen-garden."

[pg 230]
"You must wait a little," said I. "I am as uneasy as you, for my maize-plantations, my sugar-canes, and my corn-fields."

At last, one night, the storm ceased, the clouds passed away, and the moon showed herself in all her glory. How delighted we were! My wife got me to remove the large planks I had placed before the opening, and the bright moonbeams streamed through the branches of the tree into our room; a gentle breeze refreshed us, and so delighted were we in gazing on that sky of promise, that we could scarcely bear to go to bed, but spent half the night in projects for the morrow; the good mother alone said, that she could not join in our excursions. Jack and Francis smiled at

140

each other, as they thought of their litter, which was now nearly finished.

A bright sun awoke us early next morning. Fritz and Jack had requested me to allow them to finish their carriage; so, leaving Ernest with his mother, I took Francis with me to ascertain the damage done to the garden at Tent House, about which his mother was so anxious. We easily crossed the bridge, but the water had carried away some of the planks; however, my little boy leaped from one plank to another with great agility, though the distance was sometimes considerable. He was so proud of being my sole companion, that he scarcely touched the ground as he ran on before me; but he had a sad shock when he got to the garden; of which we could not find the slightest trace. All was destroyed; the walks, the fine vegetable-beds, the plantations of pines and melons--all had vanished. Francis [pg 231] stood like a marble statue, as pale and still; till, bursting into tears, he recovered himself.

"Oh! my good mamma," said he; "what will she say when she hears of this misfortune? But she need not know it, papa," added he, after a pause; "it would distress her too much; and if you and my brothers will help me, we will repair the damage before she can walk. The plants may not be so large; but the earth is moist, and they will grow quickly, and I will work hard to get it into order."

I embraced my dear boy, and promised him this should be our first work. I feared we should have many other disasters to repair; but a child of twelve years old gave me an example of resignation and courage. We agreed to come next day to begin our labour, for the garden was too well situated for me to abandon it. It was on a gentle declivity, at the foot of the rocks, which sheltered it from the north wind, and was conveniently watered from the cascade. I resolved to add a sort of bank, or terrace, to protect it from the violent rains; and Francis was so pleased with the idea, that he began to gather the large stones which were scattered over the garden, and to carry them to the place where I wished to build my terrace. He would have worked all day, if I would have allowed him; but I wanted to look after my young plantations, my sugar-canes, and my fields, and, after the destruction I had just witnessed, I had everything to fear. I proceeded to the avenue of fruit-trees that led to Tent House, and was agreeably surprised. All were half-bowed to the ground, as well as the bamboos that supported [pg 232] them, but few were torn up; and I saw that my sons and I, with the labour of two or three days, could restore them. Some of them had already begun to bear fruit, but all was destroyed for this year. This was, however, a trifling loss, compared with what I had anticipated; for, having no more plants of European fruits, I could not have replaced them. Besides, having resolved to inhabit Tent House at present, entirely,--being there defended from storms,--it was absolutely necessary to contrive some protection from the heat. My new plantations afforded little shade yet, and I trembled to propose to my wife to come and inhabit these burning rocks. Francis was gathering some of the beautiful unknown flowers of the island for his mother, and when he had formed his nosegay, bringing it to me,--

"See, papa," said he, "how the rain has refreshed these flowers. I wish it would rain still, it is so dreadfully hot here. Oh! if we had but a little shade."

"That is just what I was thinking of, my dear," said I; "we shall have shade enough when my trees are grown; but, in the mean time--"

"In the mean time, papa," said Francis, "I will tell you what you must do. You must make a very long, broad colonnade before our house, covered with cloth, and open before, so that mamma may have air and shade at once."

I was pleased with my son's idea, and promised him to construct a gallery soon, and call it the Franciade in honour of him. My little boy was delighted that his suggestion should be thus approved, and begged me not to tell his mamma, as [pg 233] he wished to surprise her, as much as his brothers did with their carriage; and he hoped the Franciade might be finished before she visited Tent House. I assured him I would be silent; and we took the road hence, talking about our new colonnade. I projected making it in the most simple and easy way. A row of strong bamboo-canes planted at equal distances along the front of our house, and united by a plank of wood at the top cut into arches between the canes; others I would place sloping from the rock, to which I would fasten them by iron cramps; these were to be covered with sailcloth, prepared with the elastic gum, and well secured to the plank. This building would not take much time, and I anticipated the pleasure of my wife when she found out that it was an invention of her little favourite, who, of a mild and reflecting disposition, was beloved by us all. As we walked along, we saw something approaching, that Francis soon discovered to be his brothers, with their new carriage; and, concluding that his mamma occupied it, he hastened to meet them, lest they should proceed to the garden. But on our approach, we discovered that Ernest was in the litter, which was borne by the cow before, on which Fritz was mounted, and by the ass behind, with Jack on it. Ernest declared the conveyance was so easy and delightful that he should often take his mother's place.

"I like that very much," said Jack; "then I will take care that we will harness the onagra and the buffalo for you, and they will give you a pretty jolting, I promise you. The cow and ass are only for mamma. Look, papa, is it not complete? [pg 234] We wished to try it as soon as we finished it, so we got Ernest to occupy it, while mother was asleep."

Ernest declared it only wanted two cushions, one to sit upon, the other to recline against, to make it perfect; and though I could not help smiling at his love of ease, I encouraged the notion, in order to delay my wife's excursion till our plans were completed. I then put Francis into the carriage beside his brother; and ordering Fritz and Jack to proceed with their equipage to inspect our corn-fields, I returned to my wife, who was still sleeping. On her awaking, I told her the garden and plantations would require a few days' labour to set them in order, and I should leave Ernest, who was not yet in condition to be a labourer, to nurse her and read to her. My sons returned in the evening, and gave me a melancholy account of our corn-fields; the corn was completely destroyed, and we regretted this the more, as we had very little left for seed. We had anticipated a feast of real bread, but we were obliged to give up all hope for this year, and to content ourselves with our cakes of cassava, and with potatoes. The maize had suffered less, and might have been a resource for us, but the large, hard grain was so very difficult to reduce to flour fine enough for dough. Fritz often recurred to the necessity of building a mill near the cascade at Tent House; but this was not the work of a moment, and we had time to consider of it; for at present we had no corn to grind. As I found Francis had let his brothers into all our secrets, it was agreed that I, with Fritz, Jack, and Francis, should proceed to Tent House next morning. [pg 235] Francis desired to be of the party, that he might direct the laying out of the garden, he said, with an important air, as he had been his mother's assistant on its formation. We arranged our bag of vegetable-seeds, and having bathed my wife's foot with a simple embrocation, we offered our united prayers, and retired to our beds to prepare ourselves for the toils of the next day.

CHAPTER XXXIX.

We rose early; and, after our usual morning duties, we left our invalids for the whole day, taking with us, for our dinner, a goose and some potatoes, made ready the evening before. We harnessed the bull and the buffalo to the cart, and I sent Fritz and Jack to the wood of bamboos, with orders to load the cart with as many as it would contain; and, especially, to select some very thick ones for my colonnade; the rest I intended for props for my young trees; and this I proposed to be my first undertaking. Francis would have preferred beginning with the Franciade, or the garden, but he was finally won over by the thoughts of the delicious fruits, which we might lose by our neglect; the peaches, plums, pears, and, above all, the cherries, of which he was very fond. He then consented to assist me in holding the trees whilst I replaced the roots; after which he went to cut the reeds to tie them. Suddenly I heard him cry, "Papa, papa, here is a large chest come for us; come and take it." I ran to him, and saw it was the very chest we had seen [pg 236] floating, and which we had taken for the boat at a distance; the waves had left it in our bay, entangled in the reeds, which grew abundantly here. It was almost buried in the sand. We could not remove it alone, and, notwithstanding our curiosity, we were compelled to wait for the arrival of my sons. We returned to our work, and it was pretty well advanced when the tired and hungry party returned with their cart-load of bamboos. We rested, and sat down to eat our goose. Guavas and sweet acorns, which had escaped the storm, and which my sons brought, completed our repast. Fritz had killed a large bird in the marsh, which I took at first for a young flamingo; but it was a young cassowary, the first I had seen in the island. This bird is remarkable for its extraordinary size, and for its plumage, so short and fine that it seems rather to be hair than feathers. I should have liked to have had it alive to ornament our poultry-yard, and it was so young we might have tamed it; but Fritz's unerring aim had killed it at once. I wished to let my wife see this rare bird, which, if standing on its webbed feet, would have been four feet high; I therefore forbade them to meddle with it.

Fritz, with a strong hatchet forced the chest open,
and we all eagerly crowded to see the contents.
"Fritz, with a strong hatchet forced the chest open, and we all eagerly crowded to see the contents."

As we ate, we talked of the chest, and our curiosity being stronger than our hunger, we swallowed our repast hastily, and then ran down to the shore. We were obliged to plunge into the water up to the waist, and then had some difficulty to extricate it from the weed and slime, and to push it on shore. No sooner had we placed it in safety than Fritz, with a strong hatchet, forced it open, and we all eagerly crowded to see the contents. Fritz hoped it would be powder and fire-arms; [pg 237] Jack, who was somewhat fond of dress, and had notions of elegance, declared in favour of clothes, and particularly of linen, finer and whiter than that which his mother wove; if Ernest had been there, books would have been his desire; for my own part, there was nothing I was more anxious for than European seeds, particularly corn; Francis had a lingering wish that the chest might contain some of those gingerbread cakes which his grandmamma used to treat him with in Europe, and which he had often regretted; but he kept this wish to himself, for fear his brothers should call him "little glutton," and assured us that he should like a little pocket-knife, with a small saw, better than anything in the world; and he was the only one who had his wish. The chest was opened, and we saw that it was filled with a number of trifling things likely to tempt savage nations, and to become the means of exchange,--principally glass and iron ware, coloured beads, pins, needles, looking-glasses, children's toys, constructed as models, such as carts, and tools of every sort; amongst which we found some likely to be useful, such as hatchets, saws, planes, gimlets, &c.; besides a collection of knives, of which Francis had the choice; and scissors, which were reserved for mamma, her own being nearly worn out. I had, moreover, the pleasure of finding a quantity of nails of every size and kind, besides iron hooks, staples, &c, which I needed greatly. After we had examined the contents, and selected what we wanted immediately, we closed up the chest, and conveyed it to our magazine at Tent House. We had spent so much time in our examination, that we had some difficulty to finish [pg 238] propping our trees, and to arrive at home before it was dark. We found my wife somewhat uneasy at our lengthened absence, but our appearance soon calmed her. "Mother," said I, "I have brought back all your chickens to crowd under your wing."

"And we have not come back empty-handed," said Jack. "Look, mamma; here are a beautiful pair of scissors, a large paper of needles, another of pins, and a thimble! How rich you are now! And when you get well, you can make me a pretty waistcoat and a pair of trousers, for I am in great want of them."

"And I, mamma," said Francis, "have brought you a mirror, that you may arrange your cap; you have often been sorry papa did not remember to bring one from the ship. This was intended for the savages, and I will begin with you."

"I believe I rather resemble one now," said my good Elizabeth, arranging the red and yellow silk handkerchief which she usually wore on her head.

"Only, mamma," said Jack, "when you wear the comical pointed bonnet which Ernest made you."

"What matters it," said she, "whether it be pointed or round? It will protect me from the sun, and it is the work of my Ernest, to whom I am much obliged."

Ernest, with great ingenuity and patience, had endeavoured to plait his mother a bonnet of the rice-straw; he had succeeded; but not knowing how to form the round crown, he was obliged to finish it in a point, to the great and incessant diversion of his brothers.

[pg 239]
"Mother," said Ernest, in his usual grave and thoughtful tone, "I should not like you to look like a savage; therefore, as soon as I regain the use of my hand, my first work shall be to make you a bonnet, which I will take care shall be formed with a round crown, as you will lend me one of your large needles, and I will take, to sew the crown on, the head of either Jack or Francis."

"What do you mean? My head!" said they both together.

"Oh, I don't mean to take it off your shoulders," said he; "it will only be necessary that one of you should kneel down before me, for a day perhaps, while I use your head as a model; and you need not cry out much if I should chance to push my needle in."

This time the philosopher had the laugh on his side, and his tormentors were silenced.

We now explained to my wife where we had found the presents we had brought her. My offerings to her were a light axe, which she could use to cut her fire-wood

145

with, and an iron kettle, smaller and more convenient than the one she had. Fritz had retired, and now came in dragging with difficulty his huge cassowary. "Here, mamma," said he, "I have brought you a little chicken for your dinner;" and the astonishment and laughter again commenced. The rest of the evening was spent in plucking the bird, to prepare part of it for next day. We then retired to rest, that we might begin our labour early next morning. Ernest chose to remain with his books and his mother, for whom he formed with the mattresses a sort of reclining chair, in which she was able to sit up in bed and sew. Thus she endured [pg 240] a confinement of six weeks, without complaint, and in that time got all our clothes put into good order. Francis had nearly betrayed our secret once, by asking his mamma to make him a mason's apron. "A mason's apron!" said she; "are you going to build a house, child?"

"I meant to say a gardener's apron," said he.

His mamma was satisfied, and promised to comply with his request.

In the mean time, my three sons and I laboured assiduously to get the garden into order again, and to raise the terraces, which we hoped might be a defence against future storms. Fritz had also proposed to me to construct a stone conduit, to bring the water to our kitchen-garden from the river, to which we might carry it back, after it had passed round our vegetable-beds. This was a formidable task, but too useful an affair to be neglected; and, aided by the geometrical skill of Fritz, and the ready hands of my two younger boys, the conduit was completed. I took an opportunity, at the same time, to dig a pond above the garden, into which the conduit poured the water; this was always warm with the sun, and, by means of a sluice, we were able to disperse it in little channels to water the garden. The pond would also be useful to preserve small fish and crabs for use. We next proceeded to our embankment. This was intended to protect the garden from any extraordinary overflow of the river, and from the water running from the rocks after heavy rains. We then laid out our garden on the same plan as before, except that I made the walks wider, and not so flat; I carried one directly to our house, which, in the autumn, I intended to [pg 241] plant with shrubs, that my wife might have a shady avenue to approach her garden; where I also planned an arbour, furnished with seats, as a resting-place for her. The rocks were covered with numerous climbing plants, bearing every variety of elegant flower, and I had only to make my selection.

All this work, with the enclosing the garden with palisades of bamboo, occupied us about a fortnight, in which time our invalids made great progress towards their recovery. After the whole was finished, Francis entreated me to begin his gallery. My boys approved of my plan, and Fritz declared that the house was certainly comfortable and commodious, but that it would be wonderfully improved by a colonnade, with a little pavilion at each end, and a fountain in each pavilion.

"I never heard a word of these pavilions," said I.

"No," said Jack, "they are our own invention. The colonnade will be called the Franciade; and we wish our little pavilions to be named, the one Fritzia, the other Jackia, if you please."

I agreed to this reasonable request, and only begged to know how they would procure water for their fountains. Fritz undertook to bring the water, if I would only assist them in completing this little scheme, to give pleasure to their beloved mother. I was charmed to see the zeal and anxiety of my children to oblige their tender mother. Her illness seemed to have strengthened their attachment; they thought only how to console and amuse her. She sometimes told me she really blessed the accident, which had taught her how much she was valued by all around her.

[pg 242]

CHAPTER XL.

The next day was Sunday,--our happy Sabbath for repose and quiet conversation at home. After passing the day in our usual devotions and sober reading, my three elder boys requested my permission to walk towards our farm in the evening. On their return, they informed me it would be necessary to give a few days' labour to our plantations of maize and potatoes. I therefore determined to look to them.

Though I was out early next morning, I found Fritz and Jack had been gone some time, leaving only the ass in the stables, which I secured for my little Francis. I perceived, also, that they had dismounted my cart, and carried away the wheels, from which I concluded that they had met with some tree in their walk the preceding evening, suitable for the pipes for their fountains, and that they had now returned to cut it down, and convey it to Tent House. As I did not know where to meet with them, I proceeded with Francis on the ass to commence his favourite work. I drew my plan on the ground first. At the distance of twelve feet from the rock which formed the front of our house, I marked a straight line of fifty feet, which I divided into ten spaces of five feet each for my colonnade; the two ends were to be reserved for the two pavilions my sons wished to build. I was busy in my calculations, and Francis placing stakes in the places where I wished to dig, when the cart drove up with our two good labourers. They had, as I expected, found the [pg 243] evening before a species of pine, well adapted for their pipes. They had cut down four, of fifteen or twenty feet in length, which they had brought on the wheels of the cart, drawn by the four animals. They had had some difficulty in transporting them to the place; and the greatest still remained--the

147

boring the trunks, and then uniting them firmly. I had neither augers nor any tools fit for the purpose. I had, certainly, constructed a little fountain at Falcon's Nest; but the stream was near at hand, and was easily conveyed by cane pipes to our tortoise-shell basin. Here the distance was considerable, the ground unequal, and, to have the water pure and cool, underground pipes were necessary. I thought of large bamboos, but Fritz pointed out the knots, and the difficulty of joining the pieces, and begged me to leave it to him, as he had seen fountains made in Switzerland, and had no fears of success. In the mean time, all hands set to work at the arcade. We selected twelve bamboos of equal height and thickness, and fixed them securely in the earth, at five feet from each other. These formed a pretty colonnade, and were work enough for one day.

We took care to divert all inquiries at night, by discussing the subjects which our invalids had been reading during the day. The little library of our captain was very choice; besides the voyages and travels, which interested them greatly, there was a good collection of historians, and some of the best poets, for which Ernest had no little taste. However, he requested earnestly that he might be of our party next day, and Francis, good-naturedly, offered to stay with mamma, expecting, no doubt, Ernest's congratulations on the forward state of [pg 244] the Franciade. The next morning Ernest and I set out, his brothers having preceded us. Poor Ernest regretted, as we went, that he had no share in these happy schemes for his mother. I reminded him, however, of his dutiful care of her during her sickness, and all his endeavours to amuse her. "And, besides," added I, "did you not make her a straw bonnet?"

"Yes," said he, "and I now remember what a frightful shape it was. I will try to make a better, and will go to-morrow morning to choose my straw."

As we approached Tent House, we heard a most singular noise, echoing at intervals amongst the rocks. We soon discovered the cause; in a hollow of the rocks I saw a very hot fire, which Jack was blowing through a cane, whilst Fritz was turning amidst the embers a bar of iron. When it was red hot, they laid it on an anvil I had brought from the ship, and struck it alternately with hammers to bring it to a point.

"Well done, my young smiths," said I; "we ought to try all things, and keep what is good. Do you expect to succeed in making your auger? I suppose that is what you want."

"Yes, father," said Fritz; "we should succeed well enough if we only had a good pair of bellows; you see we have already got a tolerable point."

Now Fritz could not believe anything was impossible. He had killed a kangaroo the evening before, and skinned it. The flesh made us a dinner; of the skin he determined to make a pair of bellows. He nailed it, with the hair out, not having time to tan it, to two flat pieces of wood, [pg 245] with holes in them; to this he added a reed for the pipe; he then fixed it by means of a long cord and a post, to the side of his fire, and Jack, with his hand or his foot, blew the fire, so that the iron was speedily red hot, and quite malleable. I then showed them how to twist the iron into a screw,--rather clumsy, but which would answer the purpose tolerably well. At one end they formed a ring, in which we placed a piece of wood transversely, to enable them to turn the screw. We then made a trial of it. We placed a tree on two props, and Fritz and I managed the auger so well, that we had our tree pierced through in a very little time, working first at one end and then at the other. Jack, in the mean time, collected the shavings we made, which he deposited in the kitchen for his mother's use, to kindle the fire. Ernest, meanwhile, was walking about, making observations, and giving his advice to his brothers on the architecture of their pavilions, till, seeing they were going to bore another tree, he retired into the garden to see the embankment. He returned delighted with the improvements, and much disposed to take some employment. He wanted to assist in boring the tree, but we could not all work at it. I undertook this labour myself, and sent him to blow the bellows, while his brothers laboured at the forge, the work not being too hard for his lame hand. My young smiths were engaged in flattening the iron to make joints to unite their pipes; they succeeded very well, and then began to dig the ground to lay them. Ernest, knowing something of geometry and land-surveying, was able to give them some useful hints, which enabled them to [pg 246] complete their work successfully. Leaving them to do this, I employed myself in covering in my long colonnade. After I had placed on my columns a plank cut in arches, which united them, and was firmly nailed to them, I extended from it bamboos, placed sloping against the rock, and secured to it by cramps of iron, the work of my young smiths. When my bamboo roof was solidly fixed, the canes as close as possible, I filled the interstices with a clay I found near the river, and poured gum over it; I had thus an impervious and brilliant roof, which appeared to be varnished, and striped green and brown. I then raised the floor a foot, in order that there might be no damp, and paved it with the square stones I had preserved when we cut the rock. It must be understood that all this was the work of many days. I was assisted by Jack and Fritz, and by Ernest and Francis alternately, one always remaining with his mother, who was still unable to walk. Ernest employed his time, when at home, in making the straw bonnet, without either borrowing his brother's head for a model, or letting any of them know what he was doing. Nevertheless, he assisted his brothers with their pavilions by his really valuable knowledge. They formed them very elegantly,-- something like a Chinese pagoda. They were exactly square, supported on four columns, and rather higher than the gallery. The roofs terminated in a point, and resembled a large parasol. The fountains were in the middle; the basins, breast-high, were formed of the shells of two turtles from our reservoir, which were mercilessly sacrificed for the purpose, and furnished our table abundantly for some days. [pg 247] They succeeded the cassowary, which had supplied us very seasonably: its flesh tasted like beef, and made excellent soup.

But to return to the fountains. Ernest suggested the idea of ornamenting the end of the perpendicular pipe, which brought the water to the basin, with shells; every sort might be collected on the shore, of the most brilliant colours, and curious and varied shapes. He was passionately devoted to natural history, and had made a collection of these, endeavouring to classify them from the descriptions he met with in the books of voyages and travels. Some of these, of the most dazzling beauty, were placed round the pipe, which had been plastered with clay; from thence the water was received into a volute, shaped like an antique urn, and again was poured gracefully into the large turtle-shell; a small channel conveyed it then out of the pavilions. The whole was completed in less time than I could have imagined, and greatly surpassed my expectations; conferring an inestimable advantage on our dwelling, by securing us from the heat. All honour was rendered to Master Francis, the inventor, and The Franciade was written in large letters on the middle arch; Fritzia and Jackia were written in the same way over the pavilions. Ernest alone was not named; and he seemed somewhat affected by it. He had acquired a great taste for rambling and botanizing, and had communicated it also to Fritz, and now that our labours were ended at Tent House, they left us to nurse our invalid, and made long excursions together, which lasted sometimes whole days. As they generally returned with some game, or some new fruit, we pardoned [pg 248] their absence, and they were always welcome. Sometimes they brought a kangaroo, sometimes an agouti, the flesh of which resembles that of a rabbit, but is richer; sometimes they brought wild ducks, pigeons, and even partridges. These were contributed by Fritz, who never went out without his gun and his dogs. Ernest brought us natural curiosities, which amused us much,-- stones, crystals, petrifactions, insects, butterflies of rare beauty, and flowers, whose colours and fragrance no one in Europe can form an idea of. Sometimes he brought fruit, which we always administered first to our monkey, as taster: some of them proved very delicious. Two of his discoveries, especially, were most valuable acquisitions,--the guajaraba, on the large leaf of which one may write with a pointed instrument, and the fruit of which, a sort of grape, is very good to eat; also the date-palm, every part of which is so useful, that we were truly thankful to Heaven, and our dear boys, for the discovery. Whilst young, the trunk contains a sort of marrow, very delicious. The date-palm is crowned by a head, formed of from forty to eighty leafy branches, which spread round the top. The dates are particularly good about half-dried; and my wife immediately began to preserve them. My sons could only bring the fruit now, but we purposed to transplant some of the trees themselves near our abode. We did not discourage our sons in these profitable expeditions; but they had another aim, which I was yet ignorant of. In the mean time, I usually walked with one of my younger sons towards Tent House, to attend to our garden, and to see if our works continued in good condition to receive mamma, who daily improved; but [pg 249] I insisted on her being completely restored, before she was introduced to them. Our dwelling looked beautiful amongst the picturesque rocks, surrounded by trees of every sort, and facing the smooth and lovely Bay of Safety. The garden was not so forward as I could have wished; but we were obliged to be patient, and hope for the best.

CHAPTER XLI.

One day, having gone over with my younger sons to weed the garden, and survey our possessions, I perceived that the roof of the gallery wanted a little repair, and called Jack to raise for me the rope ladder which I had brought from Falcon's Nest, and which had been very useful while we were constructing the roof; but we sought for it everywhere; it could not be found; and as we were quite free from robbers in our island, I could only accuse my elder sons, who had doubtless carried it off to ascend some tall cocoa-nut tree. Obliged to be content, we walked into the garden by the foot of the rocks. Since our arrival, I had been somewhat uneasy at hearing a dull, continued noise, which appeared to proceed from this side. The forge we had passed, now extinguished, and our workmen were absent. Passing along, close to the rocks, the noise became more distinct, and I was truly alarmed. Could it be an earthquake? Or perhaps it announced some volcanic explosion. I stopped before that part of the rock where the noise was loudest; the surface was firm and level; [pg 250] but from time to time, blows and falling stones seemed to strike our ears. I was uncertain what to do; curiosity prompted me to stay, but a sort of terror urged me to remove my child and myself. However, Jack, always daring, was unwilling to go till he had discovered the cause of the phenomenon. "If Francis were here," said he, "he would fancy it was the wicked gnomes, working underground, and he would be in a fine fright. For my part, I believe it is only people come to collect the salt in the rock."

"People!" said I; "you don't know what you are saying, Jack; I could excuse Francis and his gnomes,--it would be at least a poetic fancy, but yours is quite absurd. Where are the people to come from?"

"But what else can it be?" said he. "Hark! you may hear them strike the rock."

"Be certain, however," said I, "there are no people." At that moment, I distinctly heard human voices, speaking, laughing, and apparently clapping their hands. I could not distinguish any words; I was struck with a mortal terror; but Jack, whom nothing could alarm, clapped his hands also, with joy, that he had guessed right. "What did I say, papa? Was I not right? Are there not people within the rock?-- friends, I hope." He was approaching the rock, when it appeared to me to be shaking; a stone soon fell down, then another. I seized hold of Jack, to drag him away, lest he should be crushed by the fragments of rock. At that moment another stone fell, and we saw two heads appear through the opening,--the heads of Fritz and Ernest. Judge of our surprise and joy! Jack was soon [pg 251] through the opening, and assisting his brothers to enlarge it. As soon as I could enter, I stepped in, and found myself in a real grotto, of a round form, with a vaulted roof, divided by a narrow crevice, which admitted the light and air. It was, however, better lighted by two large gourd lamps. I saw my long ladder of ropes suspended from the opening at the top, and thus comprehended how my sons had penetrated into this recess, which it was impossible to suspect the existence of from the outside. But how had they discovered it? and what were they making of it? These were my two questions. Ernest replied at once to the last. "I wished," said he, "to make a resting-place for my mother, when she came to her garden. My brothers have each built some place for her, and called it by their name. I had a desire that some place in our island might be dedicated to Ernest, and I now present you the Grotto Ernestine."

"And after all," said Jack, "it will make a pretty dwelling for the first of us that marries."

"Silence, little giddy-pate," said I; "where do you expect to find a wife in this island? Do you think you shall discover one among the rocks, as your brothers have discovered the grotto? But tell me, Fritz, what directed you here."

"Our good star, father," said he. "Ernest and I were walking round these rocks, and talking of his wish for a resting-place for my mother on her way to the garden. He projected a tent; but the path was too narrow to admit it; and the rock, heated by the sun, was like a stove. We were considering what we should do, when I saw on the summit of the rock a very beautiful little unknown [pg 252] quadruped. From its form I should have taken it for a young chamois, if I had been in Switzerland; but Ernest reminded me that the chamois was peculiar to cold countries, and he thought it was a gazelle or antelope; probably the gazelle of Guinea or Java, called by naturalists the chevrotain. You may suppose I tried to climb the rock on which this little animal remained standing, with one foot raised, and its pretty head turning first to one side and then to the other; but it was useless to attempt it here, where the rock was smooth and perpendicular; besides, I should have put the gazelle to flight, as it is a timid and wild animal. I then remembered there was a place near Tent House where a considerable break occurred in the chain of rocks, and we found that, with a little difficulty, the rock might be scaled by ascending this ravine. Ernest laughed at me, and asked me if I expected the antelope would wait patiently till I got to it? No matter, I determined to try, and I told him to remain; but he soon determined to accompany me, for he fancied that in the fissure of a rock he saw a flower of a beautiful rose-colour, which was unknown to him. My learned botanist thought it must be an erica, or heath, and wished to ascertain the fact. One helping the other, we soon got through all difficulties, and arrived at the summit; and here we were amply repaid by the beautiful prospect on every side. We will talk of that afterwards, father; I have formed some idea of the country which these rocks separate us from. But to return to our grotto. I went along, first looking for my pretty gazelle, which I saw licking a piece of rock, where doubtless she [pg 253] found some salt. I was hardly a hundred yards from her, my gun ready, when I was suddenly stopped by a crevice, which I could not cross, though the opening was not very wide. The pretty quadruped was on the rock opposite to me; but of what use would it have been to shoot it, when I could not secure it. I was obliged to defer it till a better opportunity offered, and turned to examine the opening, which appeared deep; still I could see that the bottom of the cavity was white, like that of our former grotto. I called Ernest, who was behind me, with his plants and stones, to impart to him an idea that suddenly struck me. It was, to make this the retreat for my mother. I told him that I believed the floor of the cave was nearly on a level with the path that led to the garden, and we had only to make an opening in the form of a natural grotto, and it would be exactly what he wished. Ernest was much pleased with the idea, and said he could easily ascertain the level by means of a weight attached to a string; but though he was startled at the difficulty of descending to our labour every day, and returning in the evening, he would not agree to my wish of beginning at the outside of the rock, as we had done in our former grotto, He had several reasons for wishing to work from within. 'In the first place,' said he, 'it will be so much cooler this summer weather; we should be soon unable to go on labouring before the burning rock; then our path is so narrow, that we should not know how to dispose of the rubbish; in the interior, it will serve us to make a bench round the grotto; besides, I should have such pleasure in completing it secretly, and [pg 254] unsuspected, without any assistance or advice except yours, my dear Fritz, which I accept with all my heart; so pray find out some means of descending and ascending readily.'

"I immediately recollected your rope ladder, father; it was forty feet long, and we could easily fasten it to the point of the rock. Ernest was delighted and sanguine. We returned with all speed. We took first a roll of cord and some candles; then the rope ladder, which we rolled up as well as we could, but had great difficulty in conveying it up the rock; once or twice, when the ascent was very difficult, we were obliged to fasten a cord to it, and draw it up after us; but determination, courage, and perseverance overcame all obstacles. We arrived at the opening, and, on sounding it, we were glad to find our ladder would be long enough to reach the bottom. We then measured the outside of the rock, and ascertained that the floor of the grotto was near the same level as the ground outside. We remembered your lessons, father, and made some experiments to discover if it contained mephitic air. We first lighted some candles, which were not extinguished; we then kindled a large heap of sticks and dried grass, which burned well, the smoke passing through the opening like a chimney. Having no uneasiness about this, we deferred our commencement till the next day. Then we lighted the forge, and pointed some iron bars we found in the magazine; these were to be our tools to break open the rock. We secured, also, your chisel, as well as some hammers, and all our tools were thrown down below; we then arranged two gourds to serve us for lamps; and when all was [pg 255] ready, and our ladder firmly fixed, we descended ourselves; and we have nothing more to tell you, except that we were very glad when we heard your voices outside, at the very time when our work was drawing to an end.

We were sure, when we distinguished your voices so clearly, that we must be near the external air; we redoubled our efforts, and here we are. Now tell us, father, are you pleased with our idea? and will you forgive us for making a mystery of it?"

I assured them of my forgiveness, and my cordial approbation of their manly and useful enterprise; and made Ernest happy by declaring that it should always be called the Grotto Ernestine.

"Thanks to you all, my dear children," said I; "your dear mamma will now prefer Tent House to Falcon's Nest, and will have no occasion to risk breaking a limb in descending the winding staircase. I will assist you to enlarge the opening, and as we will leave it all the simplicity of a natural grotto, it will soon be ready."

We all set to work; Jack carried away the loosened stones and rubbish, and formed benches on each side the grotto. With what had fallen outside, he also made two seats in the front of the rock, and before evening all was complete. Fritz ascended to unfasten the ladder, and to convey it by an easier road to Tent House; he then rejoined us, and we returned to our castle in the air, which was henceforward only to be looked on as a pleasure-house. We resolved, however, to establish here, as we had done at our farm, a colony of our cattle, which increased daily: we had now a number of young cows, which were most useful for our support. We wished, however, for [pg 256] a female buffalo, as the milk of that animal makes excellent cheese. Conversing on our future plans, we soon reached home, and found all well.

CHAPTER XLII.

In a few days we completed the Grotto Ernestine. It contained some stalactites; but not so many as our former grotto. We found, however, a beautiful block of salt, which resembled white marble, of which Ernest formed a sort of altar, supported by four pillars, on which he placed a pretty vase of citron-wood, which he had turned himself, and in which he arranged some of the beautiful erica which had been the cause of his discovering the grotto. It was one of those occasions when his feelings overcame his natural indolence, when he became for a time the most active of the four, and brought forward all his resources, which were many. This indolence was merely physical; when not excited by any sudden circumstance, or by some fancy which soon assumed the character of a passion, he loved ease, and to enjoy life tranquilly in study. He improved his mind continually, as well by his excellent memory, as by natural talent and application. He reflected, made experiments, and was always successful. He had at last succeeded in making his mother a very pretty bonnet. He had also composed some verses, which were intended to celebrate her visit to Tent House; and this joyful day being at last fixed, the boys all went over, the evening before, to make their preparations. [pg 257] The flowers that the storm had spared were gathered to ornament the fountains, the altar, and the table, on which was placed an excellent cold dinner, entirely prepared by themselves. Fritz supplied and roasted the game,--a fine bustard, the flesh of which resembles a turkey, and a brace of partridges. Ernest brought pines, melons, and figs; Jack should have supplied the fish, but was able only to procure oysters, crabs, and turtles' eggs. Francis had the charge of the dessert, which consisted of a dish of strawberries, honeycomb, and the cream of the cocoa-nut. I had contributed a bottle of Canary wine, that we might drink mamma's health. All was arranged on a table in the middle of the Franciade, and my sons returned to accompany the expedition next day.

The morning was beautiful, and the sun shone brightly on our emigration. My wife was anxious to set out, expecting she should have to return to her aërial dwelling. Though her leg and foot were better, she still walked feebly, and she begged us to harness the cow and ass to the cart, and to lead them as gently as possible.

"I will only go a little way the first day," said she, "for I am not strong enough to visit Tent House yet."

We felt quite convinced she would change her opinion when once in her litter. I wished to carry her down the staircase; but she declined, and descended very well with the help of my arm. When the door was opened, and she found herself once more in the open air, surrounded by her children, she thanked God, with tears of gratitude, for her recovery, and all his mercies to us. Then [pg 258] the pretty osier carriage arrived. They had harnessed the cow and young bull to it; Francis answering for the docility of Valiant, provided he guided him himself. Accordingly, he was mounted before, his cane in his hand, and his bow and quiver on his back, very proud to be mamma's charioteer. My other three boys mounted on their animals, were ready before, to form the advanced guard, while I proposed to follow, and watch over the whole. My wife was moved even to tears, and could not cease admiring her new carriage, which Fritz and Jack presented to her as their own work. Francis, however, boasted that he had carded the cotton for the soft cushion on which she was to sit, and I, that I had made it. I then lifted her in, and as soon as she was seated Ernest came to put her new bonnet on her head, which greatly delighted her; it was of fine straw, and so thick and firm that it might even defend her from the rain. But what pleased her most was, that it was the shape worn by the Swiss peasants in the Canton of Vaud, where my dear wife had resided some time in her youth. She thanked all her dear children, and felt so easy and comfortable in her new conveyance, that we arrived at Family Bridge without her feeling the least fatigue. Here we stopped.

"Would you like to cross here, my dear?" said I; "and as we are very near, look in at your convenient Tent House, where you will have no staircase to ascend. And we should like to know, too, if you approve of our management of your garden,"

"As you please," said she; "in fact, I am so comfortable in my carriage, that if it were necessary, [pg 259] I could make the tour of the island. I should like to see my house again; but it will be so very hot at this season, that we must not stay long."

"But you must dine there, my dear mother," said Fritz; "it is too late to return to dinner at Falcon's Nest; consider, too, the fatigue it would occasion you."

"I would be very glad, indeed, my dear," said she; "but what are we to dine on? We have prepared no provision, and I fear we shall all be hungry."

"What matter," said Jack, "provided you dine with us? You must take your chance. I will go and get some oysters, that we may not die with hunger;" and off he galloped on his buffalo. Fritz followed him, on some pretence, on Lightfoot. Mamma wished she had brought a vessel to carry some water from the river, for she knew we could get none at Tent House. Francis reminded her we could milk the cow, and she was satisfied, and enjoyed her journey much. At last we arrived before the colonnade. My wife was dumb with wonder for some moments.

"Where am I, and what do I see?" said she, when she could speak.

"You see the Franciade, mamma," said her little boy; "this beautiful colonnade was my invention, to protect you from the heat; stay, read what is written above: Francis to his dear mother. May this colonnade, which is called the Franciade, be to her a temple of happiness. Now mamma, lean on me, and come and see my brothers' gifts--much better than mine;" and he led her to Jack's pavilion, who was standing by the [pg 260] fountain. He held a shell in his hand, which he filled with water, and drank, saying, "To the health of the Queen of the Island; may she have no more accidents, and live as long as her children! Long live Queen Elizabeth, and may she come every day to Jackia, to drink her son Jack's health."

I supported my wife, and was almost as much affected as herself. She wept and trembled with joy and surprise. Jack and Ernest then joined their hands, and carried her to the other pavilion, where Fritz was waiting to receive her, and the same scene of tenderness ensued. "Accept this pavilion, dear mother," said he; "and may Fritzia ever make you think on Fritz."

The delighted mother embraced them all, and observing Ernest's name was not commemorated by any trophy, thanked him again for her beautiful bonnet. She then drank some of the delicious water of the fountain, and returned to seat herself at the repast, which was another surprise for her. We all made an excellent dinner; and at the dessert, I handed my Canary wine round in shells; and then Ernest rose and sung us very prettily, to a familiar air, some little verses he had composed:--

On this festive happy day,
Let us pour our grateful lay;
Since Heaven has hush'd our mother's pain,
And given her to her sons again.
Then from this quiet, lovely home
Never, never, may we roam.
All we love around us smile:
Joyful is our desert isle.

When o'er our mother's couch we bent,
Fervent prayers to Heaven we sent,
[pg 261] And God has spared that mother dear,
To bless her happy children here.
Then from this quiet, lovely home,
Never, never, may we roam;
All we love around us smile,
Joyful is our desert isle.

We all joined in the chorus, and none of us thought of the ship, of Europe, or of anything that was passing in the world. The island was our universe, and Tent House was a palace we would not have exchanged for any the world contained. This was one of those happy days that God grants us sometimes on earth, to give us an idea of the bliss of Heaven; and most fervently did we thank Him, at the end of our repast, for all his mercies and blessings to us.

After dinner, I told my wife she must not think of returning to Falcon's Nest, with all its risks of storms and the winding staircase, and she could not better recompense her sons for their labours than by living among them. She was of the same opinion, and was very glad to be so near her kitchen and her stores, and to be able to walk alone with the assistance of a stick in the colonnade, which she could do already; but she made me promise to leave Falcon's Nest as it was. It would be a pretty place to walk to, and besides, this castle in the air was her own invention. We agreed that this very evening she should take possession of her own pretty room, with the good felt carpet, on which she could walk without fear; and that the next day, I should go with my elder sons and the animals to bring the cart, such utensils as we needed, and above all, the poultry. Our dogs always followed their masters, as well as [pg 262] the monkey and jackal, and they were so domesticated, we had no trouble with them.

I then prevailed on my wife to go into her room and rest for an hour, after which we were to visit the garden. She complied, and after her repose found her four sons ready to carry her in her litter as in a sedan-chair. They took care to bring her straight to the grotto, where I was waiting for her. This was a new surprise for the good mother. She could not sufficiently express her astonishment and delight, when Jack and Francis, taking their flageolets, accompanied their brothers, who sung the following verse, which Ernest had added to his former attempt.

Dear mother, let this gift be mine,
Accept the Grotto Ernestine.
May all your hours be doubly blest
Within this tranquil place of rest.
Then from this quiet, lovely home
Never, never may we roam;
All we love around us smile.
Joyful is our desert isle!
What cause had we to rejoice in our children! we could not but shed tears to witness their affection and perfect happiness.

Below the vase of flowers, on the block of salt, Ernest had written:--

Ernest, assisted by his brother Fritz,
  Has prepared this grotto,
As a retreat for his beloved mother,
  When she visits her garden.
Ernest then conducted his mother to one of the benches, which he had covered with soft moss, as a seat for her, and there she rested at her ease to hear the history of the discovery of the grotto. It was now my turn to offer my present; the garden, [pg 263] the embankment, the pond, and the arbour. She walked, supported by my arm, to view her little empire, and her delight was extreme; the pond, which enabled her to water her vegetables, particularly pleased her, as well as her shady arbour, under which she found all her gardening tools, ornamented with flowers, and augmented by two light watering-pans, constructed by Jack and Francis, from two gourds. They had canes for spouts, with the gourd bottles at the end, pierced with holes, through which the water came in the manner of a watering-pan. The embankment was also a great surprise; she proposed to place plants of pines and melon on it, and I agreed to it. Truly did she rejoice at the appearance of the vegetables, which promised us some excellent European provision, a great comfort to her. After expressing her grateful feelings, she returned to the grotto, and seating herself in her sedan-chair, returned to Tent House, to enjoy the repose she needed, after such a day of excitement. We did not, however, lie down before we had together thanked God for the manifold blessings he had given us, and for the pleasure of that day.

"If I had been in Europe," said my dear wife, "on the festival of my recovery, I should have received a nosegay, a ribbon, or some trinket; here I have had presented a carriage, a colonnade, pavilions, ornamental fountains, a large grotto, a garden, a pond, an arbour, and a straw bonnet!"

[pg 264]

CHAPTER XLIII.

THE next and following days were spent in removing our furniture and property, particularly our poultry, which had multiplied greatly. We also constructed a poultry-yard, at a sufficient distance from our house to save our sleep from disturbance, and still so near that we could easily tend them. We made it as a continuation of the colonnade, and on the same plan, but enclosed in the front by a sort of wire trellis-work, which Fritz and Jack made wonderfully well. Fritz, who had a turn for architecture and mechanics, gave me some good hints, especially one, which we put into execution. This was to carry the water from the basin of the fountain through the poultry-yard, which enabled us also to have a little pond for our ducks. The pigeons had their abode above the hen-roosts, in some pretty baskets, which Ernest and Francis made, similar to those made by the savages of the Friendly Isles, of which they had seen engravings in Cook's Voyages. When all was finished, my wife was delighted to think that even in the rainy season she could attend to her feathered family and collect their eggs.

"What a difference," said she, admiring the elegance of our buildings,--"what a difference between this Tent House and the original dwelling that suggested the name to us, and which was our only shelter four years ago. What a surprising progress luxury has made with us in that time! Do you remember, my dear, the barrel [pg 265] which served us for a table, and the oyster-shells for spoons, the tent where we slept, crowded together on dried leaves, and without undressing, and the river half a mile off, where we were obliged to go to drink if we were thirsty? Compared to what we were then, we are now great lords"

"Kings, you mean, mamma," said Jack, "for all this island is ours, and it is quite like a kingdom."

"And how many millions of subjects does Prince Jack reckon in the kingdom of his august father?" said I.

Prince Jack declared he had not yet counted the parrots, kangaroos, agoutis, and monkeys. The laughter of his brothers stopped him. I then agreed with my wife that our luxuries had increased; but I explained to her that this was the result of our industry. All civilized nations have commenced as we did; necessity has developed the intellect which God has given to man alone, and by degrees the arts have progressed, and knowledge has extended more perhaps than is conducive to happiness. What appeared luxury to us now was still simplicity compared with the luxury of towns, or even villages, among civilized nations. My wife declared she had everything she wished for, and should not know what more to ask for, as we now had only to rest and enjoy our happiness.

I declared against spending our time in rest and indolence, as the sure means of ending our pleasure; and I well knew my dear wife was, like myself, an enemy to idleness; but she dreaded any more laborious undertakings.

"But, mamma," said Fritz, "you must let me make a mill under the cascade; it will be so useful when our corn grows, and even now for the maize. [pg 266] I also think of making an oven in the kitchen, which will be very useful for you to bake your bread in."

"These would indeed be useful labours," said the good mother, smiling; "but can you accomplish them?"

"I hope so," said Fritz, "with the help of God and that of my dear brothers."

Ernest promised his best aid, in return for his brother's kind services in forming his grotto, only requesting occasional leisure for his natural history collections. His mother did not see the utility of these collections, but, willing to indulge her kind and attentive Ernest, she offered, till she could walk well, to assist him in arranging and labelling his plants, which were yet in disorder, and he gratefully consented. In procuring her some paper for the purpose, of which I had brought a large quantity from the vessel, I brought out an unopened packet, amongst which was a piece of some fabric, neither paper nor stuff apparently. We examined it together, and at length remembered it was a piece of stuff made at Otaheite, which our captain had bought of a native at an island where we had touched on our voyage. Fritz appearing much interested in examining this cloth, Ernest said gravely, "I can teach you how to make it;" and immediately bringing Cook's Voyages, where a detailed description is given, he proceeded to read it. Fritz was disappointed to find it could only be made of the bark of three trees--of these our island produced only one. These trees were the mulberry-tree, the bread fruit, and the wild fig. We had the last in abundance, but of the two former we had not yet discovered a single [pg 267] plant. Fritz was not, however, discouraged. "They ought to be here," said he, "since they are found in all the South-Sea Islands. Perhaps we may find them on the other side of the rocks, where I saw some superb unknown trees from the height where we discovered the grotto; and who knows but I may find my pretty gazelle there again. The rogue can leap better than I can over those rocks. I had a great wish to descend them, but found it impossible; some are very high and perpendicular; others have overhanging summits; I might, however, get round as you did by the pass, between the torrent and the rocks at the Great Bay."

Jack offered to be his guide, even with his eyes shut, into that rich country where he conquered and captured his buffalo; and Ernest begged to be of the party. As this was an expedition I had long projected, I agreed to accompany them next day, their mother being content to have Francis left with her as a protector. I cautioned

Fritz not to fire off his gun when we approached the buffaloes, as any show of hostility might render them furious; otherwise the animals, unaccustomed to man, have no fear of him, and will not harm him. "In general," added I, "I cannot sufficiently recommend to you to be careful of your powder; we have not more than will last us a year, and there may be a necessity to have recourse to it for our defence."

"I have a plan for making it," said Fritz, who never saw a difficulty in anything. "I know it is composed of charcoal, saltpetre, and sulphur--and we ought to find all these materials in the island. It is only necessary to combine them, and [pg 268] to form it into little round grains. This is my only difficulty; but I will consider it over; and I have my mill to think on first. I have a confused recollection of a powder manufactory at Berne: there was some machinery which went by water; this machinery moved some hammers, which pounded and mixed the ingredients-- was not this the case, father?"

"Something like it," said I; "but we have many things to do before making powder. First, we must go to sleep; we must set out before daybreak, if we intend to return to-morrow evening." We did indeed rise before the sun, which would not rise for us. The sky was very cloudy, and shortly we had an abundant and incessant rain, which obliged us to defer our journey, and put us all in bad humour, but my wife, who was not sorry to keep us with her, and who declared this gracious rain would water her garden, and bring it forward. Fritz was the first who consoled himself; he thought on nothing but building mills, and manufacturing gunpowder. He begged me to draw him a mill; this was very easy, so far as regards the exterior,-- that is, the wheel, and the waterfall that sets it in motion; but the interior,--the disposition of the wheels, the stones to bruise the grain, the sieve, or bolter, to separate the flour from the bran; all this complicated machinery was difficult to explain; but he comprehended all, adding his usual expression,--"I will try, and I shall succeed." Not to lose any time, and to profit by this rainy day, he began by making sieves of different materials, which he fastened to a circle of pliant wood, and tried by passing through them the flour of the cassava; he made some with [pg 269] sailcloth, others with the hair of the onagra, which is very long and strong, and some of the fibres of bark. His mother admired his work, which he continued to improve more and more; she assured him the sieve would be sufficient for her; it was useless to have the trouble of building a mill.

"But how shall we bruise the grain, mamma?" said he; "it would be tedious and hard work."

"And you think there will be no hard work in building your mill?" said Jack. "I am curious to see how you will contrive to form that huge stone, which is called the millstone."

"You shall see," said Fritz; "only find me the stone, and it shall soon be done. Do

161

you think, father, that of our rock would be suitable?"

I told him I thought it would be hard enough, but it would be difficult to cut from the rock a piece large enough for the purpose. He made his usual reply,-- "I will try. Ernest and Jack will assist me; and perhaps you, papa."

I declared my willingness, but named him the master-mason; we must only be his workmen. Francis was impatient to see the mill in operation. "Oh!" said Jack, "you shall soon have that pleasure. It is a mere trifle; we only want stone, wood, tools, and science."

At the word "science," Ernest, who was reading in a corner, without listening to us, raised his head suddenly, saying,-- "What science are you in need of?"

"Of one you know nothing of, Mr. Philosopher," said Jack. "Come, tell us, do you know how to build a mill?"

"A mill?" answered Ernest; "of what description? [pg 270] There are many sorts. I was just looking in my dictionary for it. There are corn-mills, and powder-mills, oil-mills, wind-mills, water-mills, hand-mills, and saw-mills; which do you want?"

Fritz would have liked them all.

"You remind me," said I, "that we brought from the vessel a hand-mill and a saw-mill, taken to pieces, to be sure, but numbered and labelled, so that they could be easily united: they should be in the magazine, where you found the anvil and iron bars; I had forgotten them."

"Let us go and examine them," said Fritz, lighting his lantern; "I shall get some ideas from them."

"Rather," said his mother, "they will spare you the trouble of thinking and labouring."

I sent them all four to seek these treasures, which, heaped in an obscure corner of the store-room, had escaped my recollection. When we were alone, I seriously besought my wife not to oppose any occupations our children might plan, however they might seem beyond their power; the great point being, to keep them continually occupied, so that no evil or dangerous fancies might fill their minds. "Let them," I said, "cut stone, fell trees, or dig fountains, and bless God that their thoughts are so innocently directed." She understood me, and promised not to discourage them, only fearing the excessive fatigue of these undertakings.

Our boys returned from the magazine, delighted with what they had found, and loaded with work-tools. Those of the masons,--the chisel, the short hammer, and the trowel, were not to be found, and rarely are taken out to sea; but they [pg 271] had collected a great number of carpenters' tools,--saws, planes, rules, &c. And now that Fritz was a smith, he had no difficulty in making any tool he wanted. He was loaded on each shoulder, and in each hand he brought a specimen of gunpowder; one sort was in good condition, and they had found a barrel of it; the other was much damaged by the water. Jack and Francis were also bending under the weight of various articles; among which I saw some pieces of the hand-mill Fritz wished to examine. Ernest, always rather idle, came proudly on, with a leather belt across his shoulders, to which was suspended a large tin box for plants, and a leather portmanteau for stones, minerals, and shells. His brothers, even Francis, rallied him unmercifully on his immense burden; one offered to help him, another to go and bring the ass; he preserved his grave and thoughtful air, and extended himself on a seat near his mother, who was occupied with his specimens of natural history. Jack deposited his load in a corner, and ran out; we soon saw him return with a huge screw-machine on his head, which he placed before Ernest, saying, with an air of respect,--

"I have the honour to bring for his Highness the Prince of the Idle Penguins, the press for his august plants, which his Highness doubtless found too heavy; and, truly, it is no little weight."

Ernest did not know whether to thank him or to be angry, but he decided to join in the jest, and, therefore, answered gravely that he was distressed that his Highness the Prince of the Monkeys should have taken so much trouble to oblige him, that he ought to have employed some of his docile [pg 272] subjects to do it; after all, he confessed that the press, which he had not noticed, gave him great pleasure, and he placed some plants in it immediately, which he had collected the evening before.

The rain ceasing for a short time, I went with Fritz and Jack to examine our embankment, and to open the sluices of the pond. We found all right, and our garden looking beautiful after the rain. On our return, we looked in at the Grotto Ernestine, which we found inundated from the opening above. We proposed to make a trench, or little channel, to carry off the rain-water from it. We returned home, and retired to bed, in hopes of being able to set out next morning. We were, however, again disappointed, and for a longer period than we expected. The rain continued some days, and the country was again a complete lake; we had, however, no storm or wind, and our possessions did not suffer; so we resolved to wait patiently till the weather would permit us to go. My wife was delighted to be in her comfortable abode, and to have us round her; neither did we waste the time. Ernest finished the arrangement of his collection with his mother and Francis. Fritz and Jack prepared the tools that would be wanted in their great undertaking-- the first attempt was to be a saw-mill. In order to prepare the planks they wished, a very large saw, which they had found amongst the tools, would serve their

163

purpose; but it was necessary to set it in motion by water, and here was the difficulty. Fritz made several models from the thin wood of our chests, and the wheels of our guns, but they were too small. In the mean [pg 273] time, the mind of my young mechanic was exercised, his ideas were enlarged and improved; and, as this science was so necessary in our situation, I allowed him to go on with his experiments. Notwithstanding the rain, protected by my cloak, he went several times to the cascade to look out for a place where he should place his mills to the best advantage, and have a constant supply of water. Ernest assisted him by his advice, and promised his labour when it should be needed. Jack and Francis were helping their mother to card cotton, of which she had made a large collection, intending to spin it for our clothing; and I exercised my mechanical talents in turning a large wheel for her, which it was necessary should revolve very easily, her leg being still stiff; and a reel, by which four bobbins were filled at once by turning a handle.

These different occupations aided us to pass the rainy season, which visited us earlier this year, and did not remain so long. My wife knew something of dyeing cloth; and, some of the plants she had helped Ernest to dry having left their colour on the papers, she made some experiments, and succeeded in obtaining a very pretty blue to dye our clothes with; and, with the cochineal from our fig-tree, a beautiful red brown, with which she had dyed for herself a complete dress.

Thus passed several weeks. Ernest read to us from some amusing or instructive work every evening; and, when his collections were all put in order, he worked at his lathe, or at the business of weaving. At last the sun appeared; we spent some days enjoying it in our delightful colonnade. [pg 274] We went to visit the grotto and the garden, where all was going on well--the embankment had prevented the inundation. Satisfied with our work, we now fixed our departure for the next day, once more hoping the rain would not come again to disappoint us.

CHAPTER XLIV.

The next day the weather was delightful. We rose before daybreak. My eldest sons took their work-tools, which we might want, and their guns also, but under the condition that they should not use them till I gave the word, "Fire!" I carried the bag of provisions. Our flock of sheep had increased so much at the farm, that we allowed ourselves to kill one, and my wife had roasted a piece for us the preceding evening; to this we added a cake of cassava, and for our dessert we depended on the fruits of the trees we might discover. But, previous to our departure, while I was taking leave of my wife and Francis, I heard a dispute in the colonnade, which I hastened to learn the cause of. I found it was a question between Fritz and Jack, whether we should make the tour of the island by sea or land; and each was anxious for my support. Fritz complained that, since their two expeditions in the canoe, Jack believed himself the first sailor in the world, and that they had given him the name of Lord of the Waves, because he was constantly saying--"When I was under the waves--when the waves were washing over me, do you think that they left me dry?"

[pg 275]
"No, Mr. Sportsman," said Jack, "you got enough of them, and that's the reason you don't wish to try them again. For my part, I love the waves, and I sing, 'The sea! the sea! it was the sea that brought us here!'"

"What a boaster you are," said Fritz: "it was only yesterday you said to me, 'I will guide you; I know the way by the rocks; I got my buffalo there, and I intend to have another.' Was it in the pinnace you intended to pass the defile, and pursue buffaloes?"

"No, no! I meant on foot," said Jack; "but I thought we should be only two then. But, as we are four--papa at the helm, and three bold rowers, why should we fatigue ourselves in making the tour of the island on our legs, when we have a good vessel to carry us? What says Mr. Philosopher, the prince of idlers, to it?"

"For my part," said Ernest, quietly, "I am quite indifferent whether I use my legs in walking, or my arms in rowing, it is equally fatiguing; but walking gives me more chance of filling my plant-box and my game-bag."

"And does he think," added Fritz, "that the mulberry and bread-fruit trees, which we shall certainly find on the other side, grow on the sea? without naming my gazelle, which does not run over the waves."

"No, it is waiting, without moving, for you to shoot it," said Jack; "and Ernest, perhaps you may find on the sea some of those curious things half plants, half animals, which you were showing me in a book."

"The zoophytes, or polypi; for they are the same family, though there are more than a thousand [pg 276] species," said Ernest, charmed to display his knowledge; but I stopped him by saying: "We will dispense with the thousand names at present. After hearing all your arguments, attend to mine; even Jack must yield to them. Our principal aim now being to search for the trees we are in need of, and to examine the productions of the island, our most sensible plan will be to walk."

Jack still contended that we might land occasionally; but I showed him the danger of this, the island being, in all probability, surrounded by reefs, which might extend so far into the sea as to take us out of the sight of the island; this I intended to ascertain some day; and in the mean time I proposed to them that we should endeavour to find a pass round the rocks on our side, from whence we could walk to the defile at the other end, take our canoe, which we had left at anchor near the Great Bay, and return to Tent House.

Jack was in ecstasies; he declared the pass must be very well concealed that escaped his search, and, seizing his lasso and his bow, rushed out the first, singing "The sea! the sea!"

"There goes a sailor formed by nature," thought I, as we followed the course of the chain of rocks to the left of our dwelling. It conducted us first to the place of our landing, that little uncultivated plain of triangular form, of which the base was washed by the sea, and the point was lost among the rocks. I found here some traces of our first establishment; but how wretched all appeared, compared with our present comforts! We tried here in vain to find a passage to cross the rocks-- the chain was everywhere like an impenetrable wall. We arrived at the ravine Fritz [pg 277] and Ernest had scaled when they discovered their grotto; and, truly, nothing but the courage and rashness of youth could have undertaken this enterprise, and continued it daily for three weeks. It appeared to me almost impossible; Fritz offered to ascend, to show me how they accomplished it; but I would not consent, as it could serve no useful purpose. I thought it better for us to proceed to the border of the island, where it was not impossible there might be a small space on the strand between the rocks and the sea, round which we could pass; from my sons being able to distinguish from the summit the country on the other side, it was evident the chain of rocks could not be very broad. Suddenly Fritz struck his forehead, and, seizing Ernest by the arm--"Brother," said he, "what fools we have been!"

Ernest inquired what folly they had been guilty of.

"Why did we not," said Fritz, "when we were working within our grotto, attempt to make the opening on the other side? We should not have had much difficulty, I am persuaded, and if our tools had not been sufficient, a little powder would have opened us a door on the other side. Only consider, father, the convenience of bringing the cart loaded with the trees we wanted through our grotto, and to be able to go a-hunting without having I don't know how many miles to go."

"Well, we can still do that," said Ernest, in his usual calm, grave manner; "if we do not find another passage, we will make one through the Grotto Ernestine, with mamma's permission, as it is her property."

This idea of my son appeared good. It was [pg 278] quite certain, from our experience at Tent House and in the grotto, that the cavity in the rocks was of very great extent, and it did not appear difficult to pierce through to the other side; but some other chain of rocks, some gigantic tree, some hill, at the end of our tunnel,

166

might render all our labour useless. I proposed that we should defer our work till we had examined the nature of the ground on the other side; my sons agreed, and we proceeded with renewed courage, when we were suddenly checked by the sight of the sea beating against a perpendicular rock of terrific height, which terminated our island on this side, and did not give us a chance of going on. I saw the rock did not extend far; but how to get round it, I could not devise. I did not conceive we could get the pinnace round, as the coast seemed surrounded by reefs; masses of rock stood up in the sea, and the breakers showed that more were hidden. After much consideration and many plans, Ernest proposed that we should swim out to the uncovered rocks, and endeavour to pass round. Fritz objected, on account of his arms and ammunition; but Ernest suggested that the powder should be secured in the pockets of his clothes, which he might carry on his head, holding his gun above the water.

With some difficulty we arranged our incumbrances, and succeeded in reaching the range of outer rocks, without swimming, as the water was not above our shoulders. We rested here awhile, and, putting on some of our clothes, we commenced our walk over sharp stones, which wounded our feet. In many places, where the rocks lay low, we were up to the waist in the [pg 279] water. Ernest, the proposer of the plan, encouraged us, and led the way for some time; but at last he fell behind, and remained so long, that I became alarmed, and calling aloud, for I had lost sight of him, he answered me, and at last I discovered him stretched on the rock, endeavouring to separate a piece from it with his knife.

"Father," said he, "I am now certain that this bed of rocks, over which we are walking, and which we fancied was formed of stone or flints, is nothing but the work of those remarkable zoophytes, called coral insects, which form coral and many other extraordinary things; they can even make whole islands. Look at these little points and hollows, and these stars of every colour and every form; I would give all the world to have a specimen of each kind."

He succeeded in breaking off a piece, which was of a deep orange-colour inside; he collected also, and deposited in his bag, some other pieces, of various forms and colours. These greatly enriched his collection; and, idle as he was, he did not complain of any difficulty in obtaining them. He had given his gun to Jack, who complained much of the ruggedness of our road. Our march was truly painful, and I repented more than once of having yielded to the idea; besides the misery of walking along these shelly rocks, which presented points like the sharp teeth of a saw, tearing our shoes and even our skin, the sea, in some of the lower places, was so high as to bar our passage, and we were obliged, in the interval between two waves, to rush across, with the water to our chins. We had some difficulty to avoid being carried away. I trembled especially for Jack; though small and [pg 280] light, he preferred facing the wave to avoiding it. I was several times obliged to catch hold of him, and narrowly escaped destruction along with him. Happily, our march was not above half a mile, and we gained the shore at last without any serious accident, but much fatigued and foot-sore; and we made a resolution never more to cross the coral reefs.

After dressing ourselves, resting, and taking a slight refreshment on the beach, we resumed our march more at our ease into the interior of the island; but though the long grass was not so sharp as the coral, it was almost as troublesome, twisting round our legs, and threatening to throw us down every step we took. Ernest, loaded with his bag of fragments of rock, coral, and zoophytes, had given his gun to Jack; and, fearing an accident among the long grass, I thought it prudent to discharge it. In order to profit by it, I fired at a little quadruped, about the size of a squirrel, and killed it. It appeared to me to be the animal called by naturalists the palm-squirrel, because it climbs the cocoa and date-palms, hooks itself by its tail, which is very long and flexible, to the upper branches, and feeds at pleasure on the fruit, of which it is very fond. We amused ourselves by details of the habits of this animal, occasionally separating to make more discoveries, but agreeing on a particular call, which was to assemble us when necessary,--a precaution by no means useless, as it turned out.

Fritz, with his head raised, went on examining all the trees, and occasionally giving a keen look after his gazelle. Ernest, stooping down, examined plants, insects, and, occasionally pursuing [pg 281] rare and beautiful butterflies, was filling his bag and plant-box with various curiosities. Jack, with his lasso in his hand, prepared himself to fling it round the legs of the first buffalo he met with, and was vexed that he did not see any. For my own part, I was engaged in surveying the chain of rocks, in order to discover that which contained the Grotto Ernestine. It was easy to recognize it, from its summit cleft in two; and I wished to ascertain, as nearly as possible, if the cleft extended to the base of the rock, as this would render our work much easier. This side of the island did not resemble that near the Great Bay, with which Jack and I had been so much charmed. The island was much narrower here, and instead of the wide plain, crossed by a river, divided by delightful woods, giving an idea of paradise on earth; we were journeying through a contracted valley, lying between the rocky wall which divided the island, and a chain of sandy hills, which hid the sea and sheltered the valley from the wind. Fritz and I ascended one of these hills, on which a few pines and broom were growing, and perceived beyond them a barren tract, stretching to the sea, where the coral reefs rose to the level of the water, and appeared to extend far into the sea. Any navigators, sailing along these shores, would pronounce the island inaccessible and entirely barren. This is not the fact; the grass is very thick, and the trees of noble growth; we found many unknown to us, some loaded with fruit; also, several beautiful shrubs covered with flowers; the dwarf orange-tree, the elegant melaleuca, the nutmeg-tree, and the Bengal rose blending its flowers with the fragrant jasmine. I should never finish, if I were to [pg 282] try and name all the plants found in this shady valley, which might be called the botanic garden of Nature. Ernest was in ecstasies; he wished to carry away everything, but he did not know how to dispose of them.

"Ah!" said he, "if only our grotto were open to this side!"

At this moment Fritz came running out of breath, crying out, "The bread-fruit tree! I have found the bread-fruit tree! Here is the fruit,--excellent, delicious bread. Taste it, father; here, Ernest; here, Jack;" and he gave us each a part of an oval fruit, about the size of an ordinary melon, which really seemed very good and nourishing.

"There are many of these trees," continued he, "loaded with fruit. Would that we had our grotto opened, that we might collect a store of them, now that they are ripe."

My boys pointed out to me exactly the situation of the grotto, judging from the rock above, and longed for their tools, that they might commence the opening directly. We proceeded to make our way through a border of trees and bushes, that separated us from the rock, that we might examine it, and judge of the difficulties of our undertaking. Jack preceded us, as usual, after giving Ernest his gun; Fritz followed him, and suddenly turning to me, said,--

"I believe kind Nature has saved us much trouble; the rock appears to be divided from top to bottom; at the foot I see a sort of cave, or grotto, already made."

We saw at the entrance of the cave two large brown bears.
"We saw at the entrance of the cave two large brown bears."

At this moment Jack uttered a piercing cry, and came running to us, his lasso in his hand: [pg 283] "Two monstrous beasts!" cried he. "Help! help!" We rushed forward, our guns ready, and saw at the entrance of the cave two large brown bears. The black bear, whose fur is most valued, is only found in cold and mountainous countries; but the brown prefers the south. It is a carnivorous animal, considered very ferocious. The black bear lives only on vegetables and honey. Of these, the one I judged to be the female seemed much irritated, uttering deep growls, and furiously gnashing her teeth. As I knew something of these animals, having met with them on the Alps, I remembered having heard that a sharp whistling terrifies and checks them. I therefore whistled as long and loudly as I could, and immediately saw the female retire backwards into the cave, while the male, raising himself on his hind legs, stood quite still, with his paws closed. My two elder sons fired into his breast: he fell down, but being only wounded, turned furiously on us. I fired a third shot at him, and finished him. We then hastened to load our guns again, to be ready to receive his companion. Jack wished to use his lasso; but I explained to him that the legs of the bear were too short and thick for such a measure to be successful. He related to us, that having entered the cave, he saw something moving at the bottom; he took up a stone, and threw it with all his strength at the object; immediately he heard a frightful growling, and saw two large beasts coming towards him; he had barely time to escape and call for help, and then to hide himself behind a tree. To save ourselves from the other bear, it was necessary that we should take some prompt measures; we therefore advanced, and formed a line [pg 284] of battle before the entrance of the cave, I then gave the word—Fire! and we all three fired off our pieces at the same moment. A ferocious roar made us hope the bullets had taken effect but to make sure, and to prevent the escape of the animal if it was still living, we gathered a large heap of dried branches and leaves before the opening, to which I set fire. As soon as it blazed, we saw by the light the bear laid motionless on its side, but it is well known that this animal is crafty enough sometimes to feign itself dead till its enemy approaches near enough to be in its power, when it seizes him in its enormous paws and strangles him. We took a lighted branch, and approached with great precaution. The cave did not extend far; the animal was lying on a heap of dried leaves prepared for its young ones. I ascertained that it was really dead. I then, with the assistance of my sons, drew it out of the cave which was too dark for work, and I wished to secure the rich and beautiful skins which might be useful to us in winter. We set to work, and, as the animals were still warm, we succeeded more easily than I could have expected, but the skins were so heavy it was almost impossible to remove them. We therefore left them in the cave, the bottom of which was sandy, closing the entrance with boughs that no animal might enter to devour them, and abandoned the two bodies, only regretting the abundance of fat which would have been useful for many domestic purposes. [pg 285]

CHAPTER XLV.

We resumed our search, thanking God for our preservation from this danger, in which my dear Jack at any rate, might have perished. As a proof and trophy of our adventure, we cut off the fore paws of the animal, to carry to my wife. It is said that these form a very delicious dish, fit for the table of a king. The valley now began to expand, and presented a more varied appearance. It was intersected with beautiful plains or savannas, of which the grass had evidently been eaten, and with more extensive woods, through which we had great difficulty in forcing a passage; so thick and entangled were the lianas and underwood. We succeeded in passing them by keeping at the borders, where we also felt in greater safety from the wild beasts and reptiles, of which we saw many species that had their abode at the foot of the rocks. Besides the fatigue of our journey, we were tormented with thirst, never having seen any water since we left the sea. The soil was so moist, that I was of opinion we might have found water by digging; but having been compelled to leave our spades when we came along the reef, we had no tools suitable for the purpose. We were also impatient to wash ourselves after the butchery of the bears, when, to our great satisfaction, we heard the murmur of waters, which I concluded was the river Jack and I had seen in our former expedition. He had frequently inquired about it, and we had foolishly thought it had extended along the whole

170

valley, which could not be. It was a gentle stream, gushing from a perpendicular rock, which reminded me of the source of the river Orbe, in the Canton of Vaud; it issued forth in its full width, rolling at first over a rocky bed; then forming a graceful bend, it took its course towards the great bay, and fell in a cascade into the sea. We remained some time here to fill our gourds, drinking moderately, and taking a bath, which refreshed us all greatly.

[pg 286]
The evening was approaching, and we began to fear we should not reach home before night. I had warned my wife that there was a possibility that we might be delayed, though I could not then anticipate the cause of our delay. We endeavoured, however, by walking as quickly as we could, and resting no more, to reach our farm at any rate. We followed the course of the river, on the opposite shore of which rose a wide plain, where we saw the herd of buffaloes quietly grazing, ruminating, and drinking, without paying the slightest attention to us. We thought we distinguished some other quadrupeds amongst them, which Fritz was certain were zebras or onagras; but certainly not his dear gazelle, for which he had incessantly looked round. Jack was in despair that the river separated us from the buffaloes, so that he could not cast his lasso round the legs of one of them, as he had promised Ernest. He even wished to swim across the stream, to have a hunt; but I forbade him, encouraging him to hope that perhaps a single buffalo might cross to our side, and throw itself in the way of his lasso. I was far from wishing such a thing myself, for we had no time to lose, nor [pg 287] any means to secure and lead it home, should we succeed in capturing one, not having any cords with us; and moreover, intending to return from the bay in the canoe. When we arrived at the bay, the night, which comes on rapidly in equinoctial countries, had almost closed. We were scarcely able to see, without terror, the changes that the late storm had occasioned; the narrow pass which led from the other side of the island, between the river and a deep stream that flowed from the rocks, was entirely obstructed with rocks and earth fallen upon it; and to render our passage practicable, it was necessary to undertake a labour that the darkness now prevented, and which would at any time be attended by danger. We were obliged then to spend the night in the open air, and separated from our dear and anxious friends at Tent House. Fortunately, Fritz had collected a store of bread-fruit for his mother, with which he had filled his own pockets and those of his brothers. These, with water from the river, formed our supper; for we had nothing but the bone of our leg of mutton left. We turned back a little way, to establish ourselves under a clump of trees, where we were in greater safety; we loaded our muskets, we kindled a large fire of dry branches, and recommending ourselves to the protection of God, we lay ourselves down on the soft moss to wait for the first rays of light. With the exception of Jack, who from the first slept as if he had been in his bed, we none of us could rest. The night was beautiful; a multitude of stars shone over our heads in the ethereal vault. Ernest was never tired of gazing on them. After some questions and suppositions [pg 288] on the plurality of worlds, their courses and their distances, he quitted us to wander on the borders of the river, which

171

reflected them in all their brilliancy. From this night his passion for astronomy commenced, a passion which he carried beyond all others. This became his favourite and continual study, nor did he fall far short of Duval, whose history he had read. Whilst he was engaged in contemplation, Fritz and I conversed on our projects for tunnelling to the grotto, and on the utility of such a passage, as this side of the island was quite lost to us, from the difficulty in reaching it. "And yet," said I, "it is to this difficulty we owe the safety we have enjoyed. Who can say that the bears and the buffaloes may not find the way through the grotto? I confess I am not desirous of their visits, nor even of those of the onagras. Who knows but they might persuade your favourite Lightfoot to return and live amongst them? Liberty has many charms. Till now, we have been very happy on our side of the island, without the productions of this. My dear boy, there is a proverb, 'Let well alone,' Let us not have too much ambition,--it has ruined greater states than ours."

Fritz seemed grieved to give up his plan, and suggested that he could forge some strong bars of iron to place before the opening, which could be removed at will.

"But," said I, "they will not prevent the snakes from passing underneath. I have noticed some with terror, as they are animals I have a great antipathy to; and if your mother saw one crawl into her grotto, she would never enter it again; even if she did not die of fright."

[pg 289]
"Well, we must give it up," said Fritz; "but it is a pity. Do you think, father, there are more bears in the island than those we killed?"

"In all probability," said I; "it is scarcely to be supposed that there should only be two. I cannot well account for their being here. They can swim very well, and perhaps the abundance of fruit in this part of the island may have attracted them." I then gave my son a short account of their manners and habits, from the best works on the history of these animals.

CHAPTER XLVI.

Whilst we continued to talk and to admire the beauty of the stars, they at length began to fade away before the first light of morning. Ernest returned to us, and we awoke Jack, who had slept uninterruptedly, and was quite unconscious where he was. We returned to the pass, which now, by the light of day, seemed to us in a more hopeless state than in the dusk of evening. I was struck with consternation: it appeared to me that we were entirely enclosed at this side; and I shuddered to think of crossing the island again, to pass round at the other end, of the risk we should run of meeting wild beasts, and of the painful and perilous passage along the coral reefs. At that moment I would gladly have consented to open a passage through the grotto, at the hazard of any visitors, in order to get through myself, that I might relieve the anxious feelings of my dear wife [pg 290] and boy. The thoughts of their agony unnerved me, and took away all courage for the commencement of a labour which seemed impossible, our only utensils being a small saw, and a little dibble for taking up plants, which Ernest had been unwilling to leave behind us. The path by which Jack and I had passed was covered with rocks and masses of soil, which obstructed even the course of the stream; we could not discover the place we had forded, the river had opened itself a wider course, far beyond its former one.

"It is impossible," said Fritz, gazing on the ruins, "that we can remove all these immense stones without proper tools; but, perhaps, with a little courage, we may cross over them, the rivulet being widened cannot be very deep. At all events, it cannot be worse than the coral reefs."

"Let us try; but I fear it will be impossible, at least for him," said I, pointing to Jack.

"Him, indeed, papa, and why not?" said the bold fellow; "he is perhaps as strong, and more active, than some of them; ask Fritz what he thinks of his workman. Shall I go the first to show you the way?"

And he was advancing boldly, but I checked him, and said, that before we undertook to scale these masses of rock, absolutely bare, where we had nothing to support us, or to hold by, it would be as well to examine if, by descending lower, we could not find a less dangerous road. We descended to the narrow pass, and found our drawbridge, plantation, all our fortification that my boys were so proud of, and where, at Fritz's request, I had even planted a small cannon, all, all destroyed; the cannon swallowed up with the [pg 291] rest. My boys deplored their disappointment; but I showed them how useless such a defence must ever be. Nature had provided us with a better fortification than we could construct, as we just now bitterly experienced.

We had descended several yards lower with incredible difficulty, plunged in a wet, heavy soil, and obliged to step across immense stones, when Fritz, who went first, cried out, joyfully--

"The roof, papa! the roof of our chalet! it is quite whole; it will be a bridge for us if we can only get to it."

"What roof? What chalet?" said I, in astonishment.

173

"The roof of our little hermitage," said he, "which we had covered so well with stones, like the Swiss chalets."

I then recollected that I had made this little hut, after the fashion of the Swiss chalet, of bark, with a roof nearly flat and covered with stones, to secure it against the winds. It was this circumstance, and its situation, that had saved it in the storm. I had placed it opposite the cascade, that we might see the fall in all its beauty, and, consequently, a little on one side of the passage filled up by the fall of the rocks. Some fragments reached the roof of the hut, and we certainly could not have entered it; but the chalet was supported by this means, and the roof was still standing and perfectly secure. We contrived to slide along the rock which sustained it; Jack was the first to stand on the roof and sing victory. It was very easy to descend on the other side, holding by the poles and pieces of bark, and we soon found ourselves safe in our own island. Ernest had lost [pg 292] his gun in the passage: not being willing to resign his bag of curiosities, he had dropped the gun into the abyss.

"You may take the gun I left in the canoe," said Fritz; "but, another time, throw away your stones, and keep your gun--you will find it a good friend in need."

"Let us embark in our canoe," cried Jack. "The sea! the sea! Long live the waves! they are not so hard as the stones."

I was very glad to have the opportunity of conveying my canoe back to the port of Tent House; our important occupations had prevented me till now, and everything favoured the plan: the sea was calm, the wind favourable, and we should arrive at home sooner, and with less fatigue, than by land. We skirted the great Bay to the Cabbage-palm Wood. I had moored the canoe so firmly to one of the palms, that I felt secure of it being there. We arrived at the place, and no canoe was there! The mark of the cord which fastened it was still to be seen round the tree, but the canoe had entirely disappeared. Struck with astonishment, we looked at each other with terror, and without being able to articulate a word. What was become of it?

"Some animal,--the jackals; a monkey, perhaps,--might have detached it," said Jack; "but they could not have eaten the canoe." And we could not find a trace of it, any more than of the gun Fritz had left in it.

This extraordinary circumstance gave me a great deal of thought. Savages, surely, had landed on our island, and carried off our canoe. We could no longer doubt it when we discovered on the [pg 293] sands the print of naked feet! It is easy to believe how uneasy and agitated I was. I hastened to take the road to Tent House, from which we were now more than three leagues distant. I forbade my sons to mention this event, or our suspicions, to their mother, as I knew it would rob her of all peace of mind. I tried to console myself. It was possible that chance had conducted them to the Bay, that they had seen our pretty canoe, and that, satisfied

174

with their prize, and seeing no inhabitants, they might not return. Perhaps, on the contrary, these islanders might prove kind and humane, and become our friends. There was no trace of their proceedings further than the shore. We called at The Farm, on purpose to examine. All appeared in order; and certainly, if they had reached here, there was much to tempt them: our cotton mattresses, our osier seats, and some household utensils that my wife had left here. Our geese and fowls did not appear to have been alarmed, but were pecking about as usual for worms and insects. I began to hope that we might get off with the loss of our canoe,--a loss which might be repaired. We were a sufficient number, being well armed, not to be afraid of a few savages, even if they penetrated further into the island, and showed hostile intentions. I exhorted my sons to do nothing to irritate them; on the contrary, to meet them with kindness and attention, and to commit no violence against them unless called on to defend their lives. I also recommended them to select from the wrecked chest, some articles likely to please the savages, and to carry them always about with them. "And I beseech you, once more," added I, "not to [pg 294] alarm your mother." They promised me; and we continued our road unmolested to Falcon's Nest. Jack preceded us, delighted, he said, to see our castle again, which he hoped the savages had not carried away. Suddenly, we saw him return, running, with terror painted on his countenance.

"They are there!" said he; "they have taken possession of it; our dwelling is full of them. Oh! how frightful they are! What a blessing mamma is not there; she would have died of fright to see them enter."

I confess I was much agitated; but, not wishing to expose my children to danger before I had done all in my power to prevent it, I ordered them to remain behind till I called them. I broke a branch from a tree hastily, which I held in one hand, and in the other some long nails, which I found by chance in the bottom of my pocket; and I advanced thus to my Tree-Castle. I expected to have found the door of my staircase torn open and broken, and our new guests ascending and descending; but I saw at once it was closed as I had left it; being of bark, it was not easily distinguished. How had these savages reached the dwelling, forty feet from the ground? I had placed planks before the great opening; they were no longer there; the greater part of them had been hurled down to the ground, and I heard such a noise in our house, that I could not doubt Jack's report. I advanced timidly, holding up in the air the branch and my offerings, when I discovered, all at once, that I was offering them to a troop of monkeys, lodged in the fortress, which they were amusing themselves by destroying. We had numbers of them in the island; some large [pg 295] and mischievous, against whom we had some difficulty in defending ourselves when crossing the woods, where they principally dwelt. The frequent report of fire-arms round our dwelling had kept them aloof till now, when, emboldened by our absence, and enticed by the figs on our tree, they had come in crowds. These vexatious animals had got through the roof, and, once in, had thrown down the planks that covered the opening; they made the most frightful grimaces, throwing down everything they could seize.

175

Although this devastation caused me much vexation, I could not help laughing at their antics, and at the humble and submissive manner in which I had advanced to pay homage to them. I called my sons, who laughed heartily, and rallied "the prince of the monkeys" without mercy, for not knowing his own subjects. Fritz wished much to discharge his gun amongst them, but I forbade him. I was too anxious to reach Tent House, to be able to turn my thoughts on these depredators just now.

We continued our journey--but I pause here; my heart is oppressed. My feelings when I reached home require another chapter to describe them, and I must summon courage for the task.

CHAPTER XLVII.

We soon arrived at Family Bridge, where I had some hopes of meeting Francis, and perhaps his mother, who was beginning to walk very well; but I was disappointed--they were not there. Yet [pg 296] I was not uneasy, for they were neither certain of the hour of our return, nor of the way we might take. I expected, however, to find them in the colonnade--they were not there. I hastily entered the house; I called aloud, "Elizabeth! Francis! where are you?" No one answered. A mortal terror seized me--and for a moment I could not move.

"They will be in the grotto," said Ernest.

"Or in the garden," said Fritz.

"Perhaps on the shore," cried Jack; "my mother likes to watch the waves, and Francis may be gathering shells."

These were possibilities. My sons flew in all directions in search of their mother and brother. I found it impossible to move, and was obliged to sit down. I trembled, and my heart beat till I could scarcely breathe. I did not venture to dwell on the extent of my fears, or, rather, I had no distinct notion of them. I tried to recover myself. I murmured, "Yes--at the grotto, or the garden--they will return directly." Still, I could not compose myself. I was overwhelmed with a sad presentiment of the misfortune which impended over me. It was but too soon realized. My sons returned in fear and consternation. They had no occasion to tell me the result of their search; I saw it at once, and, sinking down motionless, I cried, "Alas! they are not there!"

Jack returned the last, and in the most frightful state; he had been at the sea-shore, and, throwing himself into my arms, he sobbed out--

"The savages have been here, and carried away my mother and Francis; perhaps they have devoured [pg 297] them; I have seen the marks of their horrible feet on the sands, and the print of dear Francis's boots."

This account at once recalled me to strength and action.

"Come, my children, let us fly to save them. God will pity our sorrow, and assist us. He will restore them. Come, come!"

They were ready in a moment. But a distracting thought seized me. Had they carried off the pinnace? if so, every hope was gone. Jack, in his distress, had never thought of remarking this; but, the instant I named it, Fritz and he ran to ascertain the important circumstance, Ernest, in the mean time, supporting me, and endeavouring to calm me.

"Perhaps," said he, "they are still in the island. Perhaps they may have fled to hide themselves in some wood, or amongst the reeds. Even if the pinnace be left, it would be prudent to search the island from end to end before we leave it. Trust Fritz and me, we will do this; and, even if we find them in the hands of the enemy, we will recover them. Whilst we are off on this expedition, you can be preparing for our voyage, and we will search the world from one end to the other, every country and every sea, but we will find them. And we shall succeed. Let us put our whole trust in God. He is our Father, he will not try us beyond our strength."

I embraced my child, and a flood of tears relieved my overcharged heart. My eyes and hands were raised to Heaven; my silent prayers winged their flight to the Almighty, to him who tries us [pg 298] and consoles us. A ray of hope seemed to visit my mind, when I heard my boys cry out, as they approached--

"The pinnace is here! they have not carried that away!"

I fervently thanked God--it was a kind of miracle; for this pretty vessel was more tempting than the canoe. Perhaps, as it was hidden in a little creek between the rocks, it had escaped their observation; perhaps they might not know how to manage it; or they might not be numerous enough. No matter, it was there, and might be the means of our recovering the beloved objects those barbarians had torn from us. How gracious is God, to give us hope to sustain us in our afflictions! Without hope, we could not live; it restores and revives us, and, even if never realized below, accompanies us to the end of our life, and beyond the grave!

I imparted to my eldest son the idea of his brother, that they might be concealed in some part of the island; but I dared not rely on this sweet hope. Finally, as we

177

ought not to run the risk of abandoning them, if they were still here, and perhaps in the power of the savages, I consented that my two eldest sons should go to ascertain the fact. Besides, however impatient I was, I felt that a voyage such as we were undertaking into unknown seas might be of long duration, and it was necessary to make some preparations--I must think on food, water, arms, and many other things. There are situations in life which seize the heart and soul, rendering us insensible to the wants of the body--this we now experienced. We had just come from a painful journey, on foot, of twenty-four hours, [pg 299] during which we had had little rest, and no sleep. Since morning we had eaten nothing but some morsels of the bread-fruit; it was natural that we should be overcome with fatigue and hunger. But we none of us had even thought of our own state--we were supported, if I may use the expression, by our despair. At the moment that my sons were going to set out, the remembrance of their need of refreshment suddenly occurred to me, and I besought them to rest a little, and take something; but they were too much agitated to consent. I gave Fritz a bottle of Canary, and some slices of roast mutton I met with, which he put in his pocket. They had each a loaded musket, and they set out, taking the road along the rocks, where the most hidden retreats and most impenetrable woods lay; they promised me to fire off their pieces frequently to let their mother know they were there, if she was hidden among the rocks--they took also one of the dogs. Flora we could not find, which made us conclude she had followed her mistress, to whom she was much attached.

As soon as my eldest sons had left us, I made Jack conduct me to the shore where he had seen the footmarks, that I might examine them, to judge of their number and direction. I found many very distinct, but so mingled, I could come to no positive conclusion. Some were near the sea, with the foot pointing to the shore; and amongst these Jack thought he could distinguish the boot-mark of Francis. My wife wore very light boots also, which I had made for her; they rendered stockings unnecessary, and strengthened her ankles. I could not find the trace of these; but [pg 300] I soon discovered that my poor Elizabeth had been here, from a piece torn from an apron she wore, made of her own cotton, and dyed red. I had now not the least doubt that she was in the canoe with her son. It was a sort of consolation to think they were together; but how many mortal fears accompanied this consolation! Oh! was I ever to see again these objects of my tenderest affection!

Certain now that they were not in the island, I was impatient for the return of my sons, and I made every preparation for our departure. The first thing I thought of was the wrecked chest, which would furnish me with means to conciliate the savages, and to ransom my loved ones. I added to it everything likely to tempt them; utensils, stuffs, trinkets; I even took with me gold and silver coin, which was thrown on one side as useless, but might be of service to us on this occasion. I wished my riches were three times as much as they were, that I might give all in exchange for the life and liberty of my wife and son. I then turned my thoughts on those remaining to me: I took, in bags and gourds, all that we had left of cassava-bread, manioc-roots, and potatoes; a barrel of salt-fish, two bottles of rum, and several jars of fresh water. Jack wept as he filled them at his fountain, which he perhaps might never see again, any more than his dear Valiant, whom I set at liberty, as well as the cow, ass, buffalo, and the beautiful onagra. These docile animals were accustomed to us and our attentions, and they remained in their places, surprised that they were neither harnessed nor mounted. We opened the poultry-yard and pigeon-cote. The flamingo would not leave us, it went and came [pg 301] with us from the house to the pinnace. We took also oil, candles, fuel, and a large iron pot to cook our provisions in. For our defence, I took two more guns, and a small barrel of powder, all we had left. I added besides some changes of linen, not forgetting some for my dear wife, which I hoped might be needed. The time fled rapidly while we were thus employed; night came on, and my sons returned not. My grief was inconceivable; the island was so large and woody, that they might have lost themselves, or the savages might have returned and encountered them. After twenty hours of frightful terror, I heard the report of a gun--alas! only one report! it was the signal agreed on if they returned alone; two if they brought their mother; three if Francis also accompanied them; but I expected they would return alone, and I was still grateful. I ran to meet them; they were overcome with fatigue and vexation.

They begged to set out immediately, not to lose one precious moment; they were now sure the island did not contain those they lamented, and they hoped I would not return without discovering them, for what would the island be to us without our loved ones? Fritz, at that moment, saw his dear Lightfoot capering round him, and could not help sighing as he caressed him, and took leave of him.

"May I find thee here," said he, "where I leave thee in such sorrow; and I will bring back thy young master," added he, turning to the bull, who was also approaching him.

He then begged me again to set out, as the moon was just rising in all her majesty.

[pg 302]
"The queen of night," said Ernest; "will guide us to the queen of our island, who is perhaps now looking up to her, and calling on us to help her."

"Most assuredly," said I, "she is thinking on us; but it is on God she is calling for help. Let us join her in prayer, my dear children, for herself and our dear Francis."

They fell on their knees with me, and I uttered the most fervent and earnest prayer that ever human heart poured forth; and I rose with confidence that our prayers were heard. I proceeded with new courage to the creek that contained our pinnace, where Jack arranged all we had brought; we rowed out of the creek, and when we were in the bay, we held a council to consider on which side we were to commence our search. I thought of returning to the great bay, from whence our

179

canoe had been taken; my sons, on the contrary, thought that these islanders, content with their acquisition, had been returning homewards, coasting along the island, when an unhappy chance had led their mother and brother to the shore, where the savages had seen them, and carried them off. At the most, they could but be a day before us; but that was long enough to fill us with dreadful anticipations. I yielded to the opinion of my sons, which had a great deal of reason on its side, besides the wind was favourable in that direction; and, abandoning ourselves in full confidence to Almighty God, we spread our sails, and were soon in the open sea.

[pg 303]

CHAPTER XLVIII.

A gentle wind swelled our sails, and the current carried us rapidly into the open sea. I then seated myself at the helm, and employed the little knowledge I had gained during our voyage from Europe in directing our bark, so that we might avoid the rocks and coral banks that surrounded our island. My two oldest sons, overcome with fatigue, had no sooner seated themselves on a bench, than they fell into a profound sleep, notwithstanding their sorrows. Jack held out the best; his love of the sea kept him awake, and I surrendered the helm to him till I took a momentary slumber, my head resting against the stern. A happy dream placed me in the midst of my family in our dear island; but a shout from Ernest awoke me, he was calling on Jack to leave the helm, as he was contriving to run the vessel among the breakers on the coast. I seized the helm, and soon set all right, determined not to trust my giddy son again.

Jack, of all my sons, was the one who evinced most taste for the sea; but being so young when we made our voyage, his knowledge of nautical affairs was very scanty. My elder sons had learnt more. Ernest, who had a great thirst for knowledge of every kind, had questioned the pilot on all he had seen him do. He had learned a great deal in theory, but of practical knowledge he had none. The mechanical genius of Fritz had drawn conclusions from what he saw; this would have induced me to place much trust in him in case of [pg 304] that danger which I prayed Heaven might be averted. What a situation was mine for a father! Wandering through unknown and dangerous seas with my three sons, my only hope, in search of a fourth, and of my beloved helpmate; utterly ignorant which way we should direct our course, or where to find a trace of those we sought. How often do we allay the happiness granted us below by vain wishes! I had at one time regretted that we had no means of leaving our island; now we had left it, and our sole wish was to recover those we had lost, to bring them back to it, and never to leave it more. I sometimes regretted that I had led my sons into this danger. I might have ventured alone; but I reflected that I could not have left them, for Fritz had said, "If the savages had carried off the pinnace, I would have swum from isle to isle till I had found them." My boys all endeavoured to encourage and console me. Fritz placed himself at the rudder, observing that the pinnace was new and well built, and likely to resist a tempest. Ernest stood on the deck silently watching the stars, only breaking his silence by telling me he should be able by them to supply the want of the compass, and point out how we should direct our course. Jack climbed dexterously up the mast to let me see his skill; we called him the cabin-boy, Fritz was the pilot, Ernest the astronomer, and I was the captain and commander of the expedition. Daybreak showed us we had passed far from our island, which now only appeared a dark speck. I, as well as Fritz and Jack, was of opinion that it would be advisable to go round it, and try our fortune on the opposite coast; but [pg 305] Ernest, who had not forgotten his telescope, was certain he saw land in a direction he pointed out to us. We took the glass, and were soon convinced he was right. As day advanced, we saw the land plainly, and did not hesitate to sail towards it.

As this appeared the land nearest to our island, we supposed the savages might have conveyed their captives there. But more trials awaited us before we arrived there. It being necessary to shift the sail, in order to reach the coast in view, my poor cabin-boy, Jack, ran up the mast, holding by the ropes; but before he reached the sail, the rope which he held broke suddenly; he was precipitated into the sea, and disappeared in a moment; but he soon rose to the surface, trying to swim, and mingling his cries with ours. Fritz, who was the first to see the accident, was in the water almost as soon as Jack, and seizing him by the hair, swam with the other hand, calling on him to try and keep afloat, and hold by him. When I saw my two sons thus struggling with the waves, that were very strong from a land wind, I should, in my despair, have leaped in after them; but Ernest held me, and implored me to remain to assist in getting them into the pinnace. He had thrown ropes to them, and a bench which he had torn up with the strength of despair. Fritz had contrived to catch one of the ropes and fasten it round Jack, who still swam, but feebly, as if nearly exhausted. Fritz had been considered an excellent swimmer in Switzerland; he preserved all his presence of mind, calling to us to draw the rope gently, while he supported the poor boy, and pushed him towards the pinnace. At last I was [pg 306] able to reach and draw him up; and when I saw him extended, nearly lifeless, at the bottom of the pinnace, I fell down senseless beside him. How precious to us now was the composed mind of Ernest! In the midst of such a scene, he was calm and collected; promptly disengaging the rope from the body of Jack, he flung it back to Fritz, to help him in reaching the pinnace, attaching the other end firmly to the mast. This done, quicker than I can write it, he approached us, raised his brother so that he might relieve himself from the quantity of water he had swallowed; then turning to me, restored me to my senses by administering to me some drops of rum, and by saying, "Courage, father! you have saved Jack, and I will save Fritz. He has hold of the rope; he is swimming strongly; he is coming; he is here!"

He left me to assist his brother, who was soon in the vessel, and in my arms. Jack, perfectly recovered, joined him; and fervently did I thank God for granting me, in the midst of my trials, such a moment of happiness. We could not help fancying this happy preservation was an augury of our success in our anxious search, and that we should bring back the lost ones to our island.

"Oh, how terrified mamma would have been," said Jack, "to see me sink! I thought I was going, like a stone, to the bottom of the sea; but I pushed out my arms and legs with all my strength, and up I rose."

He as well as Fritz was quite wet. I had by chance brought some changes of clothes, which I made them put on, after giving each a little rum. They were so much fatigued, and I was so overcome [pg 307] by my agitation, that we were obliged to relinquish rowing, most unwillingly, as the skies threatened a storm. We gradually began to distinguish clearly the island we wished to approach; and the land-birds, which came to rest on our sails, gave us hopes that we should reach it before night; but, suddenly, such a thick fog arose, that it hid every object from us, even the sea itself, and we seemed to be sailing among the clouds. I thought it prudent to drop our anchor, as, fortunately, we had a tolerably strong one; but there appeared so little water, that I feared we were near the breakers, and I watched anxiously for the fog to dissipate, and permit us to see the coast. It finally changed into a heavy rain, which we could with difficulty protect ourselves from; there was, however, a half-deck to the pinnace, under which we crept, and sheltered ourselves. Here, crowded close together, we talked over the late accident. Fritz assured me he was never in any danger, and that he would plunge again into the sea that moment, if he had the least hope that it would lead him to find his mother and Francis. We all said the same; though Jack confessed that his friends, the waves, had not received his visit very politely, but had even beat him very rudely.

"But I would bear twice as much," said he, "to see mamma and dear Francis again. Do you think, papa, that the savages could ever hurt them? Mamma is so good, and Francis is so pretty! and then, poor mamma is so lame yet; I hope they would pity her, and carry her."

Alas! I could not hope as my boy did; I feared that they would force her to walk. I tried to conceal other horrible fears, that almost threw me [pg 308] into despair. I recalled all the cruelties of the cannibal nations, and shuddered to think that my Elizabeth and my darling child were perhaps in their ferocious hands. Prayer and confidence in God were the only means, not to console, but to support me, and teach me to endure my heavy affliction with resignation. I looked on my three sons, and endeavoured, for their sakes, to hope and submit. The darkness rapidly increased, till it became total; we concluded it was night. The rain having ceased, I went out to strike a light, as I wished to hang the lighted lantern to the mast, when

Ernest, who was on deck, called out loudly, "Father! brothers! come! the sea is on fire!" And, indeed, as far as the eye could reach, the surface of the water appeared in flames; this light, of the most brilliant, fiery red, reached even to the vessel, and we were surrounded by it. It was a sight at once beautiful, and almost terrific. Jack seriously inquired, if there was not a volcano at the bottom of the sea; and I astonished him much by telling him, that this light was caused by a kind of marine animals, which in form resembled plants so much, that they were formerly considered such; but naturalists and modern voyagers have entirely destroyed this error, and furnished proofs that they are organized beings, having all the spontaneous movements peculiar to animals. They feel when they are touched, seek for food, seize and devour it; they are of various kinds and colours, and are known under the general name of zoophytes.

"And this which glitters in such beautiful colours on the sea, is called pyrosoma," said Ernest. "See, here are some I have caught in my hat; [pg 309] you may see them move. How they change colour--orange, green, blue, like the rainbow; and when you touch them, the flame appears still more brilliant; now they are pale yellow."

They amused themselves some time with these bright and beautiful creatures, which appear to have but a half-life. They occupied a large space on the water, and their astonishing radiance, in the midst of the darkness of the atmosphere, had such a striking and magnificent effect, that for a few moments we were diverted from our own sad thoughts; but an observation from Jack soon recalled them.

"If Francis passed this way," said he, "how he would be amused with these funny creatures, which look like fire, but do not burn; but I know he would be afraid to touch them; and how much afraid mamma would be, as she likes no animals she does not know. Ah! how glad I shall be to tell her all about our voyage, and my excursion into the sea, and how Fritz dragged me by the hair, and what they call these fiery fishes; tell me again, Ernest; py--py--"

"Pyrosoma, Mr. Peron calls them," said Ernest. "The description of them is very interesting in his voyage, which I have read to mamma; and as she would recollect it, she would not be afraid."

"I pray to God," replied I, "that she may have nothing more to fear than the pyrosoma, and that we may soon see them again, with her and Francis."

We all said Amen; and, the day breaking, we decided to weigh the anchor, and endeavour to find a passage through the reefs to reach the island, which we now distinctly saw, and which seemed an uncultivated and rocky coast. I resumed [pg 310] my place at the helm, my sons took the oars, and we advanced cautiously, sounding every minute. What would have become of us if our pinnace had been injured! The sea was perfectly calm, and, after prayer to God, and a slight

183

refreshment, we proceeded forward, looking carefully round for any canoe of the savages--it might be, even our own; but, no! we were not fortunate enough to discover any trace of our beloved friends, nor any symptom of the isle being inhabited; however, as it was our only point of hope, we did not wish to abandon it. By dint of searching, we found a small bay, which reminded us of our own. It was formed by a river, broad and deep enough for our pinnace to enter. We rowed in; and having placed our vessel in a creek, where it appeared to be secure, we began to consider the means of exploring the whole island.

CHAPTER XLIX.

I did not disembark on this unknown shore without great emotion: it might be inhabited by a barbarous and cruel race, and I almost doubted the prudence of thus risking my three remaining children in the hazardous and uncertain search after our dear lost ones. I think I could have borne my bereavement with Christian resignation, if I had seen my wife and child die in my arms; I should then have been certain they were happy in the bosom of their God; but to think of them in the power of ferocious and idolatrous savages, [pg 311] who might subject them to cruel tortures and death, chilled my very blood. I demanded of my sons, if they felt courage to pursue the difficult and perilous enterprise we had commenced. They all declared they would rather die than not find their mother and brother. Fritz even besought me, with Ernest and Jack, to return to the island, in case the wanderers should come back, and be terrified to find it deserted; and to leave him the arms, and the means of trafficking with the savages, without any uneasiness about his prudence and discretion.

I assured him I did not distrust his courage and prudence, but I showed him the futility of hoping that the savages would voluntarily carry back their victims, or that they could escape alone. And should he meet with them here, and succeed, how could he carry his recovered treasures to the island?

"No, my children," said I, "we will all search, in the confidence that God will bless our efforts."

"And perhaps sooner than we think," said Ernest. "Perhaps they are in this island."

Jack was running off immediately to search, but I called my little madcap back, till we arranged our plans. I advised that two of us should remain to watch the coast, while the other two penetrated into the interior. The first thing necessary to ascertain was if the island was inhabited, which might easily be done, by climbing some tree that overlooked the country, and remarking if there were any traces of the natives, any huts, or fires lighted, &c. Those who made any discovery were immediately to inform the rest, that we might go in a body to recover our own. If nothing announced [pg 312] that the island was inhabited, we were to leave it immediately, to search elsewhere. All wished to be of the party of discovery. At length, Ernest agreed to remain with me, and watch for any arrivals by sea. Before we parted, we all knelt to invoke the blessing of God on our endeavours. Fritz and Jack, as the most active, were to visit the interior of the island, and to return with information as soon as possible. To be prepared for any chance, I gave them a game-bag filled with toys, trinkets, and pieces of money, to please the savages; I also made them take some food. Fritz took his gun, after promising me he would not fire it, except to defend his life, lest he should alarm the savages, and induce them to remove their captives. Jack took his lasso, and they set out with our benedictions, accompanied by the brave Turk, on whom I depended much to discover his mistress and his companion Flora, if she was still with her friends.

As soon as they were out of sight, Ernest and I set to work to conceal as much as possible our pinnace from discovery. We lowered the masts, and hid with great care under the deck the precious chest with our treasure, provisions, and powder. We got our pinnace with great difficulty, the water being low, behind a rock, which completely concealed it on the land-side, but it was still visible from the sea. Ernest suggested that we should entirely cover it with branches of trees, so that it might appear like a heap of bushes; and we began to cut them immediately with two hatchets we found in the chest, and which we speedily fitted with handles. We found also a large iron staple, which Ernest succeeded, with a hammer [pg 313] and pieces of wood, in fixing in the rock to moor the pinnace to. We had some difficulty in finding branches within our reach; there were many trees on the shore, but their trunks were bare. We found, at last, at some distance, an extensive thicket, composed of a beautiful shrub, which Ernest recognized to be a species of mimosa. The trunk of this plant is knotty and stunted, about three or four feet high, and spreads its branches horizontally, clothed with beautiful foliage, and so thickly interwoven, that the little quadrupeds who make their dwellings in these thickets are obliged to open covered roads out of the entangled mass of vegetation.

At the first blow of the hatchet, a number of beautiful little creatures poured forth on all sides. They resembled the kangaroos of our island, but were smaller, more elegant, and remarkable for the beauty of their skin, which was striped like that of the zebra.

"It is the striped kangaroo," cried Ernest, "described in the voyages of Peron. How I long to have one. The female should have a pouch to contain her young ones."

He lay down very still at the entrance of the thicket, and soon had the satisfaction of seizing two, which leaped out almost into his arms. This animal is timid as the hare of our country. They endeavoured to escape, but Ernest held them fast. One was a female, which had her young one in her pouch, which my son took out very cautiously. It was an elegant little creature, with a skin like its mother, only more brilliant--it was full of graceful antics. The poor mother no longer wished to escape; all her desire seemed to be to [pg 314] recover her offspring, and to replace it in its nest. At last, she succeeded in seizing and placing it carefully in security. Then her desire to escape was so strong, that Ernest could scarcely hold her. He wished much to keep and tame her, and asked my permission to empty one of the chests for a dwelling for her, and to carry her off in the pinnace; but I refused him decidedly. I explained to him the uncertainty of our return to the island, and the imprudence of adding to our cares, and, "certainly," added I, "you would not wish this poor mother to perish from famine and confinement, when your own mother is herself a prisoner?"

His eyes filled with tears, and he declared he would not be such a savage as to keep a poor mother in captivity. "Go, pretty creature," said he, releasing her, "and may my mother be as fortunate as you." She soon profited by his permission, and skipped off with her treasure.

We continued to cut down the branches of the mimosa; but they were so entangled, and the foliage so light, that we agreed to extend our search for some thicker branches.

As we left the shore, the country appeared more fertile: we found many unknown trees, which bore no fruit; but some covered with delicious flowers. Ernest was in his element, he wanted to collect and examine all, to endeavour to discover their names, either from analogy to other plants, or from descriptions he had read. He thought he recognized the melaleuca, several kinds of mimosa, and the Virginian pine, which has the largest and thickest branches. We loaded ourselves with as much as we could carry, and, in two or three [pg 315] journeys, we had collected sufficient to cover the vessel, and to make a shelter for ourselves, if we were obliged to pass the night on shore. I had given orders to my sons that both were to return before night, at all events; and if the least hope appeared, one was to run with all speed to tell us. All my fear was that they might lose their way in this unknown country: they might meet with lakes, marshes, or perplexing forests; every moment I was alarmed with the idea of some new danger, and never did any day seem so long. Ernest endeavoured, by every means in his power, to comfort and encourage me; but the buoyancy of spirit, peculiar to youth, prevented him dwelling long on one painful thought. He amused his mind by turning to search for the marine productions with which the rocks were covered: sea-weed, mosses of the most brilliant colours, zoophytes of various kinds, occupied his attention. He brought them to me, regretting that he could not preserve them.

"Oh! if my dear mother could see them," said he, "or if Fritz could paint them, how they would amuse Francis!"

186

This recalled our sorrows, and my uneasiness increased.

CHAPTER L.

All was so still around us, and our pinnace was so completely hidden with its canopy of verdure, that I could not help regretting that I had not accompanied my sons. It was now too late, but my [pg 316] steps involuntarily turned to the road I had seen them take, Ernest remaining on the rocks in search of natural curiosities; but I was suddenly recalled by a cry from Ernest--

"Father, a canoe! a canoe!"

"Alas! is it not ours?" I said, rushing to the shore, where, indeed, I saw beyond the reefs a canoe, floating lightly, apparently filled with the islanders, easy to distinguish from their dark complexion. This canoe did not resemble ours; it was longer, narrower, and seemed to be composed of long strips of bark, quite rough, tied together at each end, which gave somewhat of a graceful form to it, though it evidently belonged to the infancy of the art of navigation. It is almost inconceivable how these frail barks resist the slightest storm; but these islanders swim so well, that even if the canoe fills, they jump out, empty it, and take their places again. When landed, one or two men take up the canoe and carry it to their habitation. This, however, appeared to be provided with out-riggers, to preserve the equilibrium, and six savages, with a sort of oars, made it fly like the wind. When it passed the part of the island where we were, we hailed it as loudly as we could; the savages answered by frightful cries, but showed no intention of approaching us or entering the bay; on the contrary, they went on with great rapidity, continuing their cries. I followed them with my eyes as far as I could in speechless emotion; for either my fancy deceived me, or I faintly distinguished a form of fairer complexion than the dark-hued beings who surrounded him-- features or dress I could not see; on the whole, it was a vague impression, that I [pg 317] trembled alike to believe or to doubt. Ernest, more active than I, had climbed a sand-bank, and, with his telescope, had commanded a better view of the canoe. He watched it round a point of land, and then came down almost as much agitated as myself. I ran to him and said--

"Ernest, was it your mother?"

"No, papa; I am certain it was not my mother," said he. "Neither was it Francis."

Here he was silent: a cold shuddering came over me.

187

"Why are you silent?" said I; "what do you think?"

"Indeed, papa, I could distinguish nothing," said he, "even with the telescope, they passed so quickly. Would that it were my mother and brother, we should then be sure they were living, and might follow them. But a thought strikes me: let us free the pinnace, and sail after the canoe. We can go quicker than they with the sail; we shall overtake them behind the cape, and then we shall at least be satisfied."

I hesitated, lest my sons should come back; but Ernest represented to me that we were only fulfilling the wishes of Fritz; besides, we should return in a short time; he added, that he would soon disencumber the pinnace.

"Soon," cried I, "when we have been at least two hours in covering it."

"Yes," said he; "but we had a dozen journeys to make to the trees then; I will have it ready in less than half an hour."

I assisted him as actively as I could, though not with good heart, for I was uneasy about abandoning my sons. I would have given worlds [pg 318] to see them arrive before our departure; to have their assistance, which was of much consequence in the pinnace, and to know they were safe. I often left off my work to take a glance into the interior of the island, hoping to see them. Frequently I mistook the trees in the twilight, which was now coming on, for moving objects. At last, I was not deceived, I saw distinctly a figure walking rapidly.

"They are here!" I cried, running forward, followed by Ernest; and we soon saw a dark-coloured figure approaching. I concluded it was a savage, and, though disappointed, was not alarmed, as he was alone. I stopped, and begged Ernest to recollect all the words he had met with in his books, of the language of the savages. The black man approached; and conceive my surprise when I heard him cry, in my own language--

"Don't be alarmed, father, it is I, your son Fritz."

"Is it possible," said I; "can I believe it? and Jack? What have you done with my Jack? Where is he? Speak...."

Ernest did not ask. Alas! he knew too well; he had seen with his telescope that it was his dear brother Jack that was in the canoe with the savages; but he had not dared to tell me. I was in agony. Fritz, harassed with fatigue, and overwhelmed with grief, sunk down on the ground.

"Oh father!" said he, sobbing, "I dread to appear before you without my brother! I have lost him. Can you ever forgive your unfortunate Fritz?"

"Oh yes, yes; we are all equally unfortunate," cried I, sinking down beside my son, while Ernest [pg 319] seated himself on the other side to support me. I then besought Fritz to tell me if the savages had murdered my dear boy. He assured me that he was not killed, but carried off by the savages; still he hoped he was safe. Ernest then told me he had seen him seated in the canoe, apparently without clothes, but not stained black as Fritz was.

"I earnestly wish he had been," said Fritz; to that I attribute my escape. But I am truly thankful to God that you have seen him, Ernest. "Which way have the monsters gone?"

Ernest pointed out the cape, and Fritz was anxious that we should embark without delay, and endeavour to snatch him from them.

"And have you learned nothing of your mother and Francis?" said I.

"Alas! nothing," said he; "though I think I recognized a handkerchief, belonging to dear mamma, on the head of a savage. I will tell you all my adventure as we go. You forgive me, dear father?"

"Yes, my dear son," said I; "I forgive and pity you; but are you sure my wife and Francis are not on the island?"

"Quite sure," said he. "In fact the island is entirely uninhabited; there is no fresh water, nor game, and no quadrupeds whatever, but rats and kangaroos; but plenty of fruit. I have filled my bag with bread-fuit, which is all we shall need: let us go."

We worked so hard, that in a quarter of an hour the branches were removed, and the pinnace ready to receive us. The wind was favourable for carrying us towards the cape the savages had [pg 320] turned; we hoisted our sail, I took my place at the helm; the sea was calm, and the moon lighted our way. After recommending ourselves to the protection of God, I desired Fritz to commence his melancholy recital.

"It will be melancholy, indeed," said the poor boy, weeping; "if we do not find my dear Jack, I shall never forgive myself for not having stained his skin before my own; then he should have been with you now--"

"But I have you, my dear son, to console your father," said I. "I can do nothing myself, in my sorrow. I depend on you, my two eldest, to restore to me what I have lost. Go on, Fritz."

"We went on," continued he, "with courage and hope; and as we proceeded, we felt that you were right in saying we ought not to judge of the island by the

189

borders. You can form no idea of the fertility of the island, or of the beauty of the trees and shrubs we met with at every step, quite unknown to me; some were covered with fragrant flowers, others with tempting fruits; which, however, we did not venture to taste, as we had not Knips to try them."

"Did you see any monkeys?" asked Ernest.

"Not one," replied his brother, "to the great vexation of Jack; but we saw parrots, and all sorts of birds of the most splendid plumage. Whilst we were remarking these creatures, I did not neglect to look carefully about for any trace that might aid our search. I saw no hut, no sort of dwelling, nor anything that could indicate that the island was inhabited, and not the slightest appearance of fresh water; and we should have been tormented with thirst if we had not found [pg 321] some cocoa-nuts containing milk, and an acid fruit, full of juice, which we have in our own island--Ernest calls it the carambolier; we quenched our thirst with this, as well as with the plant, which we also have, and which contains water in the stem. The country is flat and open, and its beautiful trees stand at such a distance from each other, that no one could hide amongst them. But if we found no dwellings, we often discovered traces of the savages,--extinguished fires, remains of kangaroos and of fish, cocoa-nut shells, and even entire nuts, which we secured for ourselves; we remarked, also, footmarks on the sand. We both wished anxiously to meet with a savage, that we might endeavour to make him comprehend, by signs, whom we were in search of, hoping that natural affection might have some influence even with these untaught creatures. I was only fearful that my dress and the colour of my skin might terrify them. In the mean time, Jack, with his usual rashness, had climbed to the summit of one of the tallest trees, and suddenly cried out, 'Fritz, prepare your signs, the savages are landing. Oh! what black ugly creatures they are, and nearly naked! you ought to dress yourself like them, to make friends with them. You can stain your skin with these,' throwing me down branches of a sort of fruit of a dark purple colour, large as a plum, with a skin like the mulberry. 'I have been tasting them, they are very nauseous, and they have stained my fingers black; rub yourself well with the juice of this fruit, and you will be a perfect savage,'

"I agreed immediately. He descended from the tree while I undressed, and with his assistance I [pg 322] stained myself from head to foot, as you see me; but don't be alarmed, a single dip in the sea will make me a European again. The good-natured Jack then helped to dress me in a sort of tunic made of large leaves, and laughed heartily when he looked at me, calling me Omnibou, of whom he had seen a picture, which he declared I exactly resembled. I then wished to disguise him in the same way, but he would not consent; he declared that, when he met with mamma and Francis, he should fly to embrace them, and that he should alarm and disgust them in such a costume. He said I could protect him if the savages wished to devour him: they were now at hand, and we went forward, Jack following me with my bundle of clothes under his arm. I had slung my kangaroo-skin bag of powder and provision on my shoulders, and I was glad to see that most of the savages wore the skin of that animal, for the most part spread out like a mantle over their shoulders; few of them had other clothes, excepting one, who appeared to be the chief, and had a tunic of green rushes, neatly woven. I tried to recollect all the words of savage language I could, but very few occurred to me. I said at first 'tayo, tayo'. I don't know whether they comprehended me, but they paid me great attention, evidently taking me for a savage; only one of them wished to seize my gun; but I held it firmly, and on the chief speaking a word to him, he drew back. They spoke very rapidly, and I saw by their looks they spoke about us; they looked incessantly at Jack, repeating, 'To maiti tata.' Jack imitated all their motions, and made some grimaces which [pg 323] seemed to amuse them. I tried in vain to attract their attention. I had observed a handkerchief twisted round the head of him who seemed the chief, that reminded me much of the one my mother usually wore. I approached him, touched the handkerchief, saying expressively, 'Metoua aîné mère, et tata frère;' I added, pointing to the sea, 'pay canot.' But, alas! they did not appear to understand my words. The chief thought I wished to rob him of his handkerchief, and repelled me roughly. I then wished to retire, and I told Jack to follow me; but four islanders seized him, opened his waistcoat and shirt, and cried out together, 'Alea téa tata.' In an instant he was stripped, and his clothes and mine were put on in a strange fashion by the savages. Jack, mimicking all their contortions, recovered his shirt from one of them, put it on, and began to dance, calling on me to do the same, and, in a tone as if singing, repeated, 'Make your escape, Fritz, while I am amusing them; I will then run off and join you very soon,' As if I could for a moment think of leaving him in the hands of these barbarians! However, I recollected at that moment the bag you had given me of toys and trinkets; we had thoughtlessly left it under the great tree where I had undressed. I told Jack, in the same tone, I would fetch it, if he could amuse the savages till I returned, which he might be certain would be very soon. I ran off with all speed, and without opposition arrived at the tree, found my bag well guarded, indeed, father; for what was my surprise to find our two faithful dogs, Turk and Flora, sitting over it."

[pg 324]
"Flora!" cried I, "she accompanied my dear wife and child into their captivity; they must be in this island--why have we left it!"

"My dear father," continued Fritz, "depend on it, they are not there; but I feel convinced that the wretches who have carried off Jack, hold dear mamma and Francis in captivity; therefore we must, at all events, pursue them. The meeting between Flora and me was truly joyful, for I was now convinced that my mother and Francis were not far off, though certainly not on the same island, or their attached friend would not have quitted them. I concluded that the chief who had taken my mamma's handkerchief had also taken her dog, and brought her on this excursion, and that she had here met with her friend Turk, who had rambled from us.

191

"After caressing Flora, and taking up my bag, I ran off full speed to the spot where my dear Jack was trying to divert the barbarians. As I approached, I heard cries,-- not the noisy laughter of the savages, but cries of distress from my beloved brother,--cries for help, addressed to me. I did not walk--I flew till I reached the spot, and I then saw him bound with a sort of strong cord, made of gut; his hands were fastened behind his back, his legs tied together, and these cruel men were carrying him towards their canoe, while he was crying out, 'Fritz, Fritz, where are you?' I threw myself desperately on the six men who were bearing him off. In the struggle, my gun, which I held in my hand, caught something, and accidentally went off, and--O, father, it was my own dear Jack that I wounded! I cannot tell how I survived his cry of 'You have killed me!' [pg 325] And when I saw his blood flow, my senses forsook me, and I fainted. When I recovered, I was alone; they had carried him off. I rose, and following the traces of his blood, arrived fortunately at the shore just as they were embarking. God permitted me to see him again, supported by one of the savages, and even to hear his feeble voice cry, 'Console yourself, Fritz, I am not dead; I am only wounded in the shoulder; it is not your fault; go, my kind brother, as quick as possible to papa, and you will both'--the canoe sailed away so swiftly, that I heard no more; but I understood the rest--'you will both come and rescue me.' But will there be time? Will they dress his wound? Oh! father, what have I done! Can you forgive me?"

Overwhelmed with grief, I could only hold out my hand to my poor boy, and assure him I could not possibly blame him for this distressing accident.

Ernest, though greatly afflicted, endeavoured to console his brother; he told him a wound in the shoulder was not dangerous, and the savages certainly intended to dress his wound, or they would have left him to die. Fritz, somewhat comforted, begged me to allow him to bathe, to divest himself of the colouring, which was now become odious to him, as being that of these ruthless barbarians. I was reluctant to consent; I thought it might still be useful, in gaining access to the savages; but he was certain they would recognize him in that disguise as the bearer of the thunder, and would distrust him. I now recollected to ask what had become of his gun, and was sorry to learn that they had carried it off [pg 326] whilst he lay insensible; he himself considered that it would be useless to them, as they had fortunately left him the bag of ammunition. Ernest, however, regretted the loss to ourselves, this being the third we had lost--the one we had left in the canoe being also in the possession of the savages. The dogs we missed, too, and Fritz could give no account of them; we concluded they had either followed the savages, or were still in the island. This was another severe sorrow; it seemed as if every sort of misfortune was poured out upon us. I rested on the shoulder of Ernest in my anguish. Fritz took advantage of my silence, and leaped out of the pinnace to have a bath. I was alarmed at first; but he was such an excellent swimmer, and the sea was so calm, that I soon abandoned my fears for him.

CHAPTER LI.

Fritz was now swimming far before us, and appeared to have no idea of turning, so that I was at once certain he projected swimming on to the point where we had lost sight of the savages, to be the first to discover and aid his brother. Although he was an excellent swimmer, yet the distance was so great, that I was much alarmed; and especially for his arrival by night in the midst of the savages. This fear was much increased by a very extraordinary sound, which we now heard gradually approaching us; it was a sort of submarine tempest. The weather was beautiful; there was no wind, the moon shone in a cloudless sky, yet the waves [pg 327] were swoln as if by a storm, and threatened to swallow us; we heard at the same time a noise like violent rain. Terrified at these phenomena, I cried out aloud for Fritz to return; and though it was almost impossible my voice could reach him, we saw him swimming towards us with all his strength. Ernest and I used all our power in rowing to meet him, so that we soon got to him. The moment he leaped in, he uttered in a stifled voice, pointing to the mountains of waves, "They are enormous marine monsters! whales, I believe! such an immense shoal! They will swallow us up!"

"No," said Ernest, quietly; "don't be alarmed; the whale is a gentle and harmless animal, when not attacked. I am very glad to see them so near. We shall pass as quietly through the midst of these colossal creatures, as we did through the shining zoophytes: doubtless the whales are searching for them, for they constitute a principal article of their food."

They were now very near us, sporting on the surface of the water, or plunging into its abysses, and forcing out columns of water through their nostrils to a great height, which occasionally fell on us, and wetted us. Sometimes they raised themselves on their huge tail, and looked like giants ready to fall on us and crush us; then they went down again into the water, which foamed under their immense weight. Then they seemed to be going through some military evolutions, advancing in a single line, like a body of regular troops, one after another swimming with grave dignity; still more frequently they were in lines of two and two. This wonderful sight partly [pg 328] diverted us from our own melancholy thoughts. Fritz had, however, seized his oar, without giving himself time to dress, whilst I, at the rudder, steered as well as I could through these monsters, who are, notwithstanding their appearance, the mildest animals that exist. They allowed us to pass so closely, that we were wetted with the water they spouted up, and might have touched them; and with the power to overturn us with a stroke of their tail, they never noticed us; they seemed to be satisfied with each other's society. We were truly sorry to see their mortal enemy appear amongst them, the sword-fish of the south, armed with its long saw, remarkable for a sort of fringe of nine or ten inches long, which distinguishes it from the sword-fish of the north. They are both terrible enemies to the whale, and next to man, who wages an eternal war with them, its most formidable foes. The whales in our South Seas had only the sword-fish to dread; as soon as they saw him approach, they dispersed, or dived into the depths of the ocean. One only, very near us, did not succeed in escaping, and we witnessed a combat, of which, however, we could not see the event. These two monsters attacked each other with equal ferocity; but as they took an opposite direction to that we were going, we soon lost sight of them, but we shall never forget our meeting with these wonderful giants of the deep.

We happily doubled the promontory behind which the canoe had passed, and found ourselves in an extensive gulf, which narrowed as it entered the land, and resembled the mouth of a river. We did not hesitate to follow its course. We went round the bay, but found no traces of man, [pg 329] but numerous herds of the amphibious animal, called sometimes the sea-lion, the sea-dog, or the sea-elephant, or trunked phoca: modern voyagers give it the last name. These animals, though of enormous size, are gentle and peaceful, unless roused by the cruelty of man. They were in such numbers on this desert coast, that they would have prevented our approach if we had intended it. They actually covered the beach and the rocks, opening their huge mouths, armed with very sharp teeth, more frightful than dangerous. As it was night when we entered the bay, they were all sleeping, but they produced a most deafening noise with their breathing. We left them to their noisy slumber; for us, alas! no such comfort remained. The continual anxiety attending an affliction like ours destroys all repose, and for three days we had not slept an hour. Since the new misfortune of Jack's captivity, we were all kept up by a kind of fever. Fritz was in a most incredible state of excitement, and declared he would never sleep till he had rescued his beloved brother. His bath had partially removed the colouring from his skin, but he was still dark enough to pass for a savage, when arrayed like them. The shores of the strait we were navigating were very steep, and we had yet not met with any place where we could land; however, my sons persisted in thinking the savages could have taken no other route, as they had lost sight of their canoe round the promontory. As the strait was narrow and shallow, I consented that Fritz should throw off the clothes he had on, and swim to reconnoitre a place which seemed to be an opening in the rocks or hills that obstructed our passage, and we soon had [pg 330] the pleasure of seeing him standing on the shore, motioning for us to approach. The strait was now so confined, that we could not have proceeded any further with the pinnace; we could not even bring it to the shore. Ernest and I were obliged to step into the water up to the waist; but we took the precaution to tie a long and strong rope to the prow, and when we were aided by the vigorous arm of Fritz, we soon drew the pinnace near enough to fix it by means of the anchor.

There were neither trees nor rocks on that desert shore to which we could fasten the pinnace; but, to our great delight and encouragement, we found, at a short distance from our landing-place, a bark canoe, which my sons were certain was that in which Jack had been carried off. We entered it, but at first saw only the oars; at last, however, Ernest discovered, in the water which half filled the canoe, part of a handkerchief, stained with blood, which they recognized as belonging to Jack. This discovery, which relieved our doubts, caused Fritz to shed tears of joy. We were certainly on the track of the robbers, and might trust that they had not proceeded farther with their barbarity. We found on the sand, and in the boat, some cocoa-nut shells and fish-bones, which satisfied us of the nature of their repasts. We resolved to continue our search into the interior of the country, following the traces of the steps of the savages. We could not find any traces of Jack's foot, which would have alarmed us, if Fritz had not suggested that they had carried him, on account of his wound. We were about to set out, when the thoughts of the pinnace came over us; it was more than ever necessary for us to [pg 331] preserve this, our only means of return, and which moreover contained our goods for ransom, our ammunition, and our provisions, still untouched, for some bread-fruit Fritz had gathered, some muscles, and small, but excellent, oysters, had been sufficient for us. It was fortunate that we had brought some gourds of water with us, for we had not met with any. We decided that it would be necessary to leave one of our party to guard the precious pinnace, though this would be but an insufficient and dangerous defence, in case of the approach of the natives. My recent bereavements made me tremble at the idea of leaving either of my sons. I cannot yet reflect on the agony of that moment without horror--yet it was the sole means to secure our vessel; there was not a creek or a tree to hide it, and the situation of the canoe made it certain the savages must return there to embark. My children knew my thoughts, by the distracted glances with which I alternately regarded them and the pinnace, and, after consulting each other's looks, Ernest said--

"The pinnace must not remain here unguarded, father, to be taken, or, at any rate, pillaged by the natives, who will return for their canoe. Either we must all wait till they come, or you must leave me to defend it. I see, Fritz, that you could not endure to remain here."

In fact, Fritz impatiently stamped with his foot, saying--

"I confess, I cannot remain here; Jack may be dying of his wound, and every moment is precious. I will seek him--find him--and save him! I have a presentiment I shall; and if I discover him, as I expect, in the hands of the [pg 332] savages, I know the way to release him, and to prevent them carrying off our pinnace."

I saw that the daring youth, in the heat of his exasperation, exposed alone to the horde of barbarians, might also become their victim. I saw that my presence was necessary to restrain and aid him; and I decided, with a heavy heart, to leave

Ernest alone to protect the vessel. His calm and cool manner made it less dangerous for him to meet the natives. He knew several words of their language, and had read of the mode of addressing and conciliating them. He promised me to be prudent, which his elder brother could not be. We took the bag of toys which Fritz had brought, and left those in the chest, to use if necessary; and, praying for the blessing of Heaven on my son, we left him. My sorrow was great; but he was no longer a child, and his character encouraged me. Fritz embraced his brother, and promised him to bring Jack back in safety.

CHAPTER LII.

After having traversed for some time a desert, sandy plain without meeting a living creature, we arrived at a thick wood, where we lost the traces we had carefully followed. We were obliged to direct our course by chance, keeping no fixed road, but advancing as the interwoven branches permitted us. The wood was alive with the most beautiful birds of brilliant and varied plumage; but, in our anxious and distressed state, we should have been more interested in seeing a savage than [pg 333] a bird. We passed at last through these verdant groves, and reached an arid plain extending to the shore. We again discovered numerous footsteps; and, whilst we were observing them, we saw a large canoe pass rapidly, filled with islanders: and this time I thought that, in spite of the distance, I could recognize the canoe we had built, and which they had robbed us of. Fritz wished to swim after them, and was beginning to undress himself, and I only stopped him by declaring that if he did, I must follow him, as I had decided not to be separated from him. I even proposed that we should return to Ernest, as I was of opinion that the savages would stop at the place where we had disembarked, to take away the boat they had left, and we might then, by means of the words Ernest had acquired, learn from them what had become of my wife and children. Fritz agreed to this, though he still persisted that the easiest and quickest mode of return would have been by swimming. We were endeavouring to retrace our road, when, to our great astonishment, we saw, at a few yards' distance, a man clothed in a long black robe advancing towards us, whom we immediately recognized as a European.

"Either I am greatly deceived," said I, "or this is a missionary, a worthy servant of God, come into these remote regions to make Him known to the wretched idolators."

We hastened to him. I was not wrong. He was one of those zealous and courageous Christians who devote their energies and their lives to the instruction and eternal salvation of men born in another hemisphere, of another colour, uncivilized, but not less our brothers. I had quitted Europe [pg 334] with the same intention, but Providence had ordered it otherwise; yet I met with joy one of my Christian brethren, and, unable to speak from emotion, I silently embraced him. He spoke to me in English--a language I had fortunately learned myself, and taught to my children--and his words fell on my soul like the message of the angel to Abraham, commanding him to spare his son.

"You are the person I am seeking," said he, in a mild and tender tone, "and I thank Heaven that I have met with you. This youth is Fritz, your eldest son, I conclude; but where have you left your second son, Ernest?"

"Reverend man," cried Fritz, seizing his hands, "you have seen my brother Jack. Perhaps my mother? You know where they are. Oh! are they living?"

"Yes, they are living, and well taken care of," said the missionary; "come, and I will lead you to them."

It was, indeed, necessary to lead me; I was so overcome with joy, that I should have fainted, but the good missionary made me inhale some volatile salts which he had about him; and supported by him and my son, I managed to walk. My first words were a thanksgiving to God for his mercy; then I implored my good friend to tell me if I should indeed see my wife and children again. He assured me that an hour's walk would bring me to them; but I suddenly recollected Ernest, and refused to present myself before the beloved ones while he was still in danger. The missionary smiled, as he told me he expected this delay, and wished to know where we had left Ernest. I recounted [pg 335] to him our arrival in the island, and the purpose for which we had left Ernest; with our intention of returning to him as soon as we saw the canoe pass, hoping to obtain some intelligence from the savages.

"But how could you have made yourselves understood?" said he; "are you acquainted with their language?"

I told him Ernest had studied the vocabulary of the South Sea islanders.

"Doubtless that of Tahiti, or the Friendly Islands," said he; "but the dialect of these islanders differs much from theirs. I have resided here more than a year, and have studied it, so may be of use to you; let us go. Which way did you come?"

"Through that thick wood," replied I; "where we wandered a long time; and I fear we shall have some difficulty in finding our way back."

"You should have taken the precaution to notch the trees as you came," said our worthy friend; "without that precaution, you were in danger of being lost; but we will find my marks, which will lead us to the brook, and following its course we shall be safe."

"We saw no brook," remarked Fritz.

"There is a brook of excellent water, which you have missed in crossing the forest; if you had ascended the course of the stream, you would have reached the hut which contains your dear friends; the brook runs before it."

Fritz struck his forehead with vexation.

"God orders all for the best," said I to the good priest; "we might not have met with you; we should have been without Ernest; you might [pg 336] have sought us all day in vain. Ah! good man, it is under your holy auspices that our family ought to meet, in order to increase our happiness. Now please to tell me"--

"But first," interrupted Fritz, "pray tell me how Jack is? He was wounded, and"--

"Be composed, young man," said the calm man of God; "the wound, which he confesses he owes to his own imprudence, will have no evil consequences; the savages had applied some healing herbs to it, but it was necessary to extract a small ball, an operation which I performed yesterday evening. Since then he suffers less; and will be soon well, when his anxiety about you is relieved."

Fritz embraced the kind missionary, entreating his pardon for his rashness, and adding, "Did my brother talk to you of us, sir?"

"He did," answered his friend; "but I was acquainted with you before; your mother talked continually of her husband and children. What mingled pain and delight she felt yesterday evening when the savages brought to her dear Jack, wounded! I was fortunately in the hut to comfort her, and assist her beloved boy."

"And dear Francis," said I, "how rejoiced he would be to see his brother again!"

"Francis," said the missionary, smiling, "will be the protector of you all. He is the idol of the savages now; an idolatry permitted by Christianity."

We proceeded through the wood as we conversed, and at last reached the brook. I had a thousand questions to ask, and was very anxious to know how my wife and Francis had been brought to this island, and how they met with the [pg 337] missionary. The five or six days we had been separated seemed to me five or six months. We walked too quickly for me to get much information. The English minister said little, and referred me to my wife and son for all details. On the subject of his own noble mission he was less reserved.

"Thank God," said he, "I have already succeeded in giving this people some notions of humanity. They love their black friend, as they call me, and willingly listen to my preaching, and the singing of some hymns. When your little Francis was taken, he had his reed flageolet in his pocket, and his playing and graceful manners have so captivated them that I fear they will with reluctance resign him. The king is anxious to adopt him. But do not alarm yourself, brother; I hope to arrange all happily, with the divine assistance. I have gained some power over them, and I will avail myself of it. A year ago, I could not have answered for the life of the prisoners; now I believe them to be in safety. But how much is there yet to teach these simple children of nature, who listen only to her voice, and yield to every impression! Their first impulse is good, but they are so unsteady that affection may suddenly change to hatred; they are inclined to theft, violent in their anger, yet generous and affectionate. You will see an instance of this in the abode where a woman, more unfortunate than your wife, since she has lost her husband, has found an asylum."

He was silent, and I did not question him farther on this subject. We were approaching the arm of the sea where we had left our pinnace, and my heart, at ease about the rest, became now [pg 338] anxious solely for Ernest. Sometimes the hills concealed the water from us; Fritz climbed them, anxious to discover his brother, at last I heard him suddenly cry out "Ernest, Ernest...."

He was answered by shouts, or rather howls, amongst which I could not distinguish the voice of my son. Terror seized me.

"These are the islanders," said I to the missionary; "and these frightful cries...."

"Are cries of joy," said he, "which will be increased when they see you. This path will conduct us to the shore. Call Fritz; but I do not see him; he will, doubtless, have descended the hill, and joined them. Have no fears; recommend your sons to be prudent. The black friend will speak to his black friends, and they will hear him."

We proceeded towards the shore, when, at some distance, I perceived my two sons on the deck of the pinnace, which was covered with the islanders, to whom they were distributing the treasures of the chest, at least those we had put apart in the bag; they had not been so imprudent as to open the chest itself, which would soon have been emptied; it remained snugly below the deck, with the powder-barrel. At every new acquisition, the savages uttered cries of joy, repeating mona, mona signifying beautiful. The mirrors were at first received with the most delight, but this soon changed into terror; they evidently conceived there was something magical about them, and flung them all into the sea. The coloured glass beads had then the preference, but the distribution caused many disputes. Those who had not obtained any, wished to deprive the rest of them [pg 339] by force. The clamour and quarrelling were increasing, when the voice of the missionary was heard, and calmed them as if by enchantment. All left the pinnace, and crowded round him; he harangued them in their own language, and pointed me out to them, naming

199

me, me touatane, that is, father, which they repeated in their turn. Some approached me, and rubbed their noses against mine, which, the pastor had informed me, was a mark of respect. In the mean time, Fritz had informed Ernest that his mother and brothers were found, and that the man who accompanied us was a European. Ernest received the intelligence with a calm joy; it was only by the tears in his eyes you could discover how much his heart was affected; he leaped from the pinnace and came to thank the missionary. I had my share of his gratitude too, for coming to seek him, before I had seen the dear lost ones.

We had now to think of joining them. We unanimously decided to proceed by water; in the first place, that we might bring our pinnace as near as possible to my dear Elizabeth, who was still suffering from her fall, her forced voyage, and, above all, from her anxiety; besides, I confess that I felt a little fatigue, and should have reluctantly set out to cross the wood a third time; but, in addition to this, I was assured that it was the promptest mode of reaching our friends, and this alone would have decided me. The pinnace was then loosened, the sail set, and we entered with thankfulness. Dreading the agitation of my wife if she saw us suddenly, I entreated our new friend to precede us, and prepare her. He consented; but, as he was coming on board, he was [pg 340] suddenly stopped by the natives, and one of them addressed him for some time. The missionary listened till he had concluded, with calmness and dignity; then, turning to me, he said--

"You must answer for me, brother, the request which Parabéry makes: he wishes me, in the name of the whole, to wait a few moments for their chief, to whom they give the title of king. Bara-ourou, as he is called, has assembled them here for a ceremony, at which all his warriors must assist. I have been anxious to attend, fearing it might be a sacrifice to their idols, which I have always strongly opposed, and wishing to seize this occasion to declare to them the one true God. Bara-ourou is not wicked, and I hope to succeed in touching his heart, enlightening his mind, and converting him to Christianity; his example would certainly be followed by the greatest part of his subjects, who are much attached to him. Your presence, and the name of God uttered by you, with the fervour and in the attitude of profound veneration and devotion, may aid this work of charity and love. Have you sufficient self-command to delay, for perhaps a few hours, the meeting with your family? Your wife and children, not expecting you, will not suffer from suspense. If you do not agree to this, I will conduct you to them, and return, I hope in time, to fulfil my duty. I wait your decision to reply to Parabéry, who is already sufficiently acquainted with the truth, to desire that his king and his brethren should know it also."

Such were the words of this true servant of God; but I cannot do justice to the expression of his heavenly countenance. Mr. Willis, for such [pg 341] was his name, was forty-five or fifty years of age, tall and thin; the labours and fatigues of his divine vocation had, more than years, left their traces on his noble figure and countenance; he stooped a little, his open and elevated forehead was slightly wrinkled, and his thin hair was prematurely grey; his clear blue eyes were full of intelligence and kindness, reading your thoughts, and showing you all his own. He usually kept his arms folded over his breast, and was very calm in speaking; but when his extended hand pointed to heaven, the effect was irresistible; one might have thought he saw the very glory he spoke of. His simple words to me seemed a message from God, and it would have been impossible to resist him. It was indeed a sacrifice; but I made it without hesitation. I glanced at my sons, who had their eyes cast down; but I saw Fritz knitting his brows. "I shall stay with you, father," said I, "happy if I can assist you in fulfilling your sacred duties."

"And you, young people," said he, "are you of the same opinion?"

Fritz came forward, and frankly said, "Sir, it was, unfortunately, I who wounded my brother Jack; he has been generous enough to conceal this; you extracted the ball which I discharged into his shoulder; I owe his life to you, and mine is at your disposal; I can refuse you nothing; and, however impatient, I must remain with you."

"I repeat the same," said Ernest; "you protected our mother and brothers, and, by God's permission, you restore them to us. We will all remain with you; you shall fix the time of our meeting, which will not, I trust, be long delayed."

[pg 342]
I signified my approbation, and the missionary gave them his hand, assuring them that their joy on meeting their friends would be greatly increased by the consciousness of this virtuous self-denial.

We soon experienced this. Mr. Willis learned from Parabéry, that they were going to fetch their king in our pretty canoe when we saw it pass. The royal habitation was situated on the other side of the promontory, and we soon heard a joyful cry, that they saw the canoe coming. While the savages were engaged in preparing to meet their chief, I entered the pinnace, and descending beneath the deck, I took from the chest what I judged most fitting to present to his majesty. I chose an axe, a saw, a pretty, small, ornamented sabre, which could not do much harm, a packet of nails, and one of glass-beads. I had scarcely put aside these articles, when my sons rushed to me in great excitement.

"Oh! father," cried they, at once, "look! look! summon all your fortitude; see! there is Francis himself in the canoe; oh! how curiously he is dressed!"

Two savages took Francis on their shoulders,
and two others took the king in the same way.
"Two savages took Francis on their shoulders, and two others took the king in the same way."

201

I looked, and saw, at some distance, our canoe ascending the strait; it was decorated with green branches, which the savages, who formed the king's guard, held in their hand; others were rowing vigorously; and the chief, wearing a red and yellow handkerchief, which had belonged to my wife, as a turban, was seated at the stern, and a pretty, little, blooming, flaxen-haired boy was placed on his right shoulder. With what delight did I recognize my child. He was naked above the waist, and wore a little tunic of woven leaves, which reached to his knees, a necklace and bracelets [pg 343] of shells, and a variety of coloured feathers mingled with his bright curls; one of these fell over his face, and doubtless prevented him from seeing us. The chief seemed much engaged with him, and continually took some ornament from his own dress to decorate him. "It is my child!" said I, in great terror, to Mr. Willis, "my dearest and youngest! They have taken him from his mother. What must be her grief! He is her Benjamin--the child of her love. Why have they taken him? Why have they adorned him in this manner? Why have they brought him here?"

"Have no fear," said the missionary; "they will do him no harm. I promise you they shall restore him, and you shall take him back to his mother. Place yourselves at my side, with these branches in your hands."

He took some from Parabéry, who held a bundle of them, and gave us each one; each of the savages took one also. They were from a tree which had slender, elegant leaves, and rich scarlet flowers--species of mimosa; the Indians call it the tree of peace. They carry a branch of it when they have no hostile intentions; in all their assemblies, when war is proclaimed, they make a fire of these branches, and if all are consumed, it is considered an omen of victory.

While Mr. Willis was explaining this to us, the canoe approached. Two savages took Francis on their shoulders, two others took the king in the same way, and advanced gravely towards us. What difficulty I had to restrain myself from snatching my child from his bearers, and embracing him! My sons were equally agitated; Fritz was darting forward, but the missionary restrained [pg 344] him. Francis, somewhat alarmed at his position, had his eyes cast down, and had not yet seen us. When the king was within twenty yards of us, they stopped, and all the savages prostrated themselves before him; we alone remained standing. Then Francis saw us, and uttered a piercing cry, calling out, "Papa! dear brothers!" He struggled to quit the shoulders of his bearers, but they held him too firmly. It was impossible to restrain ourselves longer; we all cried out, and mingled our tears and lamentations. I said to the good missionary,--a little too harshly, perhaps,--"Ah! if you were a father!"

"I am," said he, "the father of all this flock, and your children are mine; I am answerable for all. Command your sons to be silent; request the child to be composed, and leave the rest to me."

I immediately took advantage of the permission to speak. "Dear Francis," said I, holding out my arms, "we are come to seek you and your mother; after all our dangers, we shall soon meet again, to part no more. But be composed, my child, and do not risk the happiness of that moment by any impatience. Trust in God, and in this good friend that He has given us, and who has restored to me the treasures without which I could not live." We then waved our hands to him, and he remained still, but wept quietly, murmuring our names: "Papa, Fritz, Ernest,--tell me about mamma," said he, at last, in an inquiring tone.

"She does not know we are so near her," said I. "How did you leave her?"

[pg 345]
"Very much grieved," said he, "that they brought me away; but they have not done me any harm,--they are so kind; and we shall soon all go back to her. Oh! what joy for her and our friends!"

"One word about Jack," said Fritz; "how does his wound go on?"

"Oh, pretty well," answered he; "he has no pain now, and Sophia nurses him and amuses him. How little Matilda would weep when the savages carried me off! If you knew, papa, how kind and good she is!"

I had no time to ask who Sophia and Matilda were. They had allowed me to speak to my son to tranquillize him, but the king now commanded silence, and, still elevated on the shoulders of his people, began to harangue the assembly. He was a middle-aged man, with striking features; his thick lips, his hair tinged with red paint, his dark brown face, which, as well as his body, was tattooed with white, gave him a formidable aspect; yet his countenance was not unpleasant, and announced no ferocity. In general, these savages have enormous mouths, with long white teeth; they wear a tunic of reeds or leaves from the waist to the knees. My wife's handkerchief, which I had recognized at first, was gracefully twisted round the head of the king; his hair was fastened up high, and ornamented with feathers, but he had nearly removed them all to deck my boy. He placed him at his side, and frequently pointed him out during his speech. I was on thorns. As soon as he had concluded, the savages shouted, clapped their hands, and surrounded my [pg 346] child, dancing, and presenting him fruit, flowers, and shells, crying out, Ouraki! a cry in which the king, who was now standing, joined also.

"What does the word Ouraki mean?" said I to the missionary.

"It is the new name of your son," answered he; "or rather of the son of Bara-ourou, who has just adopted him."

"Never!" cried I, darting forward. "Boys, let us rescue your brother from these barbarians!" We all three rushed towards Francis, who, weeping, extended his arms to us. The savages attempted to repulse us; but at that moment the missionary pronounced some words in a loud voice; they immediately prostrated themselves on their faces, and we had no difficulty in securing the child. We brought him to our protector, who still remained in the same attitude in which he had spoken, with his eyes and his right hand raised towards heaven. He made a sign for the savages to rise, and afterwards spoke for some time to them. What would I have given to have understood him! But I formed some idea from the effect of his words. He frequently pointed to us, pronouncing the word éroué, and particularly addressed the king, who listened motionless to him. At the conclusion of his speech, Bara-ourou approached, and attempted to take hold of Francis, who threw himself into my arms, where I firmly held him.

"Let him now go," said Mr. Willis, "and fear nothing."

I released the child; the king lifted him up, pressed his own nose to his; then, placing him on [pg 347] the ground, took away the feathers and necklace with which he had decked him, and replaced him in my arms, rubbing my nose also, and repeating several words. In my first emotion, I threw myself on my knees, and was imitated by my two sons.

"It is well!" cried the missionary, again raising his eyes and hands. "Thus should you offer thanks to heaven. The king, convinced it is the will of God, restores your child, and wishes to become your friend: he is worthy to be so, for he adores and fears your God. May he soon learn to know and believe all the truths of Christianity! Let us pray together that the time may come when, on these shores, where paternal love has triumphed, I may see a temple rise to the Father of all,-- the God of peace and love."

He kneeled down, and the king and all his people followed his example. Without understanding the words of his prayer, I joined in the spirit of it with all my heart and soul.

I then presented my offerings to the king, increasing them considerably. I would willingly have given all my treasures in exchange for him he had restored to me. My sons also gave something to each of the savages, who incessantly cried tayo, tayo. I begged Mr. Willis to tell the king I gave him my canoe, and hoped he would use it to visit us in our island, to which we were returning. He appeared pleased, and wished to accompany us in our pinnace, which he seemed greatly to admire; some of his people followed him on board to row, the rest placed themselves in the canoes. We soon entered the sea again, [pg 348] and, doubling the second point, we came to an arm of the sea much wider, and deep enough for our pinnace, and which conducted us to the object of our dearest hopes.

CHAPTER LIII.

We were never weary with caressing our dear Francis. We were very anxious to learn from him all the particulars of the arrival of the savages in our island, the seizure of his mother and himself, their voyage, and their residence here, and who were the friends they had met with: but it was impossible, his tawny majesty never left us for a moment, and played with the boy as if he had been a child himself. Francis showed him all the toys from our chest; he was extremely amused with the small mirrors, and the dolls. A painted carriage, driven by a coachman who raised his whip when the wheels turned, appeared miraculous to him. He uttered screams of delight as he pointed it out to his followers. The ticking of my watch also charmed him; and as I had several more, I gave him it, showing him how to wind it up. But the first time he tried to do it, he broke the spring, and when it was silent he cared no longer for it, but threw it on one side. However, as the gold was very glittering, he took it up again, and suspending it from the handkerchief that was wound round his head, it hung over his nose, and formed a striking ornament. Francis showed him his face in a mirror, which royal amusement made him laugh heartily. He asked [pg 349] the missionary if it was the invisible and Almighty God who had made all these wonderful things. Mr. Willis replied, that it was he who gave men the power to make them. I do not know whether Bara-ourou comprehended this, but he remained for some time in deep thought. I profited by this to ask the missionary what were the words which had terrified them so when they wished to keep my son from me, and which had compelled them to surrender him?

"I told them," answered he, "that the Almighty and unseen God, of whom I spoke to them daily, ordered them, by my voice, to restore a son to his father; I threatened them with his anger if they refused, and promised them his mercy if they obeyed; and they did obey. The first step is gained, they know the duty of adoring and obeying God; every other truth proceeds from this, and I have no doubt that my savages will one day become good Christians. My method of instruction is suited to their limited capacity. I prove to them that their wooden idols, made by their own hands, could neither create, hear them, nor protect them. I have shown them God in his works, have declared him to be as good as he is powerful, hating evil, cruelty, murder, and cannibalism, and they have renounced all these. In their late wars they have either released or adopted their prisoners. If they carried off your wife and son, they intended it for a good action, as you will soon understand."

I could not ask Francis any questions, as Bara-ourou continued playing with him, so turning to Ernest, I asked him what passed when the savages joined him?

"When you left me," said he, "I amused myself by searching for shells, plants, and zoophytes, with which the rocks abound, and I have added a good deal to my collection. I was at some distance from the pinnace, when I heard a confused sound of voices, and concluded that the savages were coming; in fact, ten or a dozen issued from the road you had entered, and I cannot comprehend how you missed meeting them. Fearing they would attempt to take possession of my pinnace, I returned speedily, and seized a loaded musket, though I determined to use it only to defend my own life, or the pinnace. I stood on the deck in an attitude as bold and imposing as I could command; but I did not succeed in intimidating them. They leaped, one after the other, on deck, and surrounded me, uttering loud cries. I could not discover whether they were cries of joy or of fury; but I showed no fear, and addressed them in a friendly tone, in some words from Capt. Cook's vocabulary; but they did not seem to comprehend me, neither could I understand any of theirs except écroué (father), which they frequently repeated, and tara-tauo (woman). One of them had Fritz's gun, from which I concluded they were of the party that had carried off Jack. I took it, and showing him mine, endeavoured to make him understand that it also belonged to me. He thought I wished to exchange, and readily offered to return it, and take mine. This would not have suited me; Fritz's gun was discharged, and I could not let them have mine loaded. To prevent accident, surrounded as I was, I decided to give them a fright, and seeing a bird flying above us, I took aim so correctly, that my [pg 351] shot brought down the bird, a blue pigeon. They were for a moment stupified with terror; then immediately all left the pinnace, except Parabéry; he seemed to be pleased with me, often pointing to the sky, saying mété, which means good, I believe. His comrades were examining the dead bird. Some touched their own shoulders, to try if they were wounded as well as the bird and Jack had been, which convinced me they had carried him off. I tried to make Parabéry understand my suspicion, and I think I succeeded, for he made me an affirmative sign, pointing to the interior of the island, and touching his shoulder with an air of pity. I took several things from the chest, and gave them to him, making signs that he should show them to the others, and induce them to return to me. He comprehended me very well, and complied with my wishes. I was soon surrounded by the whole party, begging of me. I was busy distributing beads, mirrors, and small knives when you came, and we are now excellent friends. Two or three of them returned to the wood, and brought me cocoa-nuts and bananas. But we must be careful to hide our guns, of which they have a holy horror. And now, dear father, I think we ought not to call these people savages. They have the simplicity of childhood; a trifle irritates them, a trifle appeases them; they are grateful and affectionate. I find them neither cruel nor barbarous. They have done me no harm, when they might easily have killed me, thrown me into the sea, or carried me away."

"We must not," said I, "judge of all savage people by these, who have had the benefit of a [pg 352] virtuous teacher. Mr. Willis has already cast into their hearts the seeds of that divine religion, which commands us to do unto others as we would they should do unto us, and to pardon and love our enemies."

While we were discoursing, we arrived at a spot where the canoes had already landed; we were about to do the same, but the king did not seem inclined to quit the pinnace, but continued speaking to the missionary. I was still fearful that he wished to keep Francis, to whom he seemed to be more and more attached, holding him constantly on his knee; but at last, to my great joy, he placed him in my arms.

"He keeps his word with you," said Mr. Willis. "You may carry him to his mother; but, in return, he wishes you to permit him to go in your pinnace to his abode on the other side of the strait, that he may show it to the women, and he promises to bring it back; perhaps there would be danger in refusing him."

I agreed with him; but still there was a difficulty in granting this request. If he chose to keep it, how should we return? Besides, it contained our only barrel of powder, and all our articles of traffic, and how could we expect it would escape pillage?

Mr. Willis confessed he had not yet been able to cure their fondness for theft, and suggested, as the only means of security, that I should accompany the king, and bring the pinnace back, which was then to be committed to the charge of Parabéry, for whose honesty he would be responsible.

Here was another delay; the day was so far advanced, that I might not, perhaps, be able to [pg 353] return before night. Besides, though my wife did not know we were so near her, she knew they had carried away Francis, and she would certainly be very uneasy about him. Bara-ourou looked very impatient, and as it was necessary to answer him, I decided at once; I resigned Francis to the missionary, entreating him to take him to his mother, to prepare her for our approach, and to relate the cause of our delay. I told my sons, it was my desire they should accompany me. Fritz agreed rather indignantly, and Ernest with calmness. Mr. Willis told the king, that in gratitude to him, and to do him honour, I and my sons wished to accompany him. He appeared much flattered at this, made my sons seat themselves on each side of him, endeavoured to pronounce their names, and finished by exchanging names as a token of friendship, calling Fritz, Bara; Ernest, Ourou; and himself, Fritz-Ernest. Mr. Willis and Francis left us; our hearts were sad to see them go where all our wishes centred; but the die was cast. The king gave the signal to depart; the canoes took the lead, and we followed. In an hour we saw the royal palace. It was a tolerably large hut, constructed of bamboos and palm-leaves, very neatly. Several women were seated before it, busily employed in making the short petticoats of reeds which they all wore. Their hair was very carefully braided in tufts on the crown of the head; none were good-looking, except two daughters of the king, about ten and twelve years old, who, though very dark, were graceful: these, no doubt, he intended for wives for my Francis. We disembarked about a hundred yards from the hut. The women came to meet us, carrying a branch [pg 354] of the mimosa in each hand; they then performed a singular kind of dance, entwining their arms and shaking their feet, but never moving from the spot; this they accompanied with a wild chant, which was anything but musical. The king seemed pleased with it; and, calling his wives and daughters, he showed them his tayo, Bara and Ourou, calling himself Fritz-Ernest; he then joined in the dance, dragging my sons with him, who managed it pretty well. As for me, he treated me with great respect, always calling me écroué-- father, and made me sit down on a large trunk of a tree before his house; which was, doubtless, his throne, for he placed me there with great ceremony, rubbing his royal nose against mine. After the dance was concluded, the women retired to the hut, and returned to offer us a collation, served up in the shells of cocoa-nuts. It was a sort of paste, composed, I believe, of different sorts of fruit, mixed up with a kind of flour and the milk of the cocoa-nut. This mixture was detestable to me; but I made up for it with some kernel of cocoa-nuts and the bread-fruit. Perceiving that I liked these, Bara-ourou ordered some of them to be gathered, and carried to the pinnace.

The hut was backed by a wood of palms and other trees, so that our provision was readily made. Still there was time for my sons to run to the pinnace, attended by Parabéry, and bring from the chest some beads, mirrors, scissors, needles and pins, to distribute to the ladies. When they brought the fruit they had gathered, I made a sign to Bara-ourou to take them to see the pinnace; [pg 355] he called them, and they followed him timidly, and submitting to his wishes in everything, They carried the fruit two and two, in a sort of baskets, very skilfully woven in rushes, which appeared to have a European form. They had no furniture in their dwelling but mats, which were doubtless their beds, and some trunks of trees, serving for seats and tables. Several baskets were suspended to the bamboo which formed the walls, and also lances, slings, clubs, and other similar weapons; from which I concluded they were a nation of warriors. I did not observe much, however, for my thoughts were in the future, and I was very impatient for our departure. I hastened to the pinnace, and my sons distributed their gifts to the females, who did not dare to express their delight; but it was evident in their countenances. They immediately began to adorn themselves with their presents, and appeared to value the mirrors much more than their husbands had done. They soon understood their use, and employed them to arrange with taste the strings of beads round their necks, heads, and arms.

At last the signal was given for our departure; I rubbed my nose against that of the king. I added to my presents a packet of nails, and one of gilt buttons, which he seemed to covet. I went on board my pinnace, and, conducted by the good Parabéry, we took our way to that part of the coast where the dear ones resided whom I so anxiously desired to see. Some of the savages accompanied us in their own canoe; we should have preferred having only our friend Parabéry, but we were not the masters.

[pg 356]
Favoured by the wind, we soon reached the shore we had formerly quitted, and found our excellent missionary waiting for us.

"Come," said he, "you are now going to receive your reward. Your wife and children impatiently expect you; they would have come to meet you, but your wife is still weak, and Jack suffering--your presence will soon cure them."

I was too much affected to answer. Fritz gave me his arm, as much to support me as to restrain himself from rushing on before. Ernest did the same with Mr. Willis; his mildness pleased the good man, who also saw his taste for study, and tried to encourage it. After half an hour's walk, the missionary told us we were now near our good friends. I saw no sign of a habitation, nothing but trees and rocks; at last I saw a light smoke among the trees, and at that moment Francis, who had been watching, ran to meet us.

"Mamma is expecting you," said he, showing us the way through a grove of shrubs, thick enough to hide entirely the entrance into a kind of grotto; we had to stoop to pass into it. It resembled much the entrance of the bear's den, which we found in the remote part of our island. A mat of rushes covered the opening, yet permitted the light to penetrate it. Francis removed the matting, calling--

"Mamma, here we are!"

A lady, apparently about twenty-even years of age, of mild and pleasing appearance, came forward to meet me. She a clothed in a rob mad of palm-leaves tied together, which reached from her throat to her feet, leaving her beautiful [pg 357] arms uncovered. Her light hair was braided and fastened up round her head.

"You are welcome," said she, taking my hand; "you will be my poor friend's best physician."

We entered, and saw my dear wife seated on a bed of moss and leaves; she wept abundantly, pointing out to me our dear boy by her side. A little nymph of eleven or twelve years old was endeavouring to raise him.

"Here are your papa and brothers, Jack," said she; "you are very happy in having what I have not: but your papa will be mine, and you shall be my brother."

Jack thanked her affectionately. Fritz and Ernest, kneeling beside the couch, embraced their mother. Fritz begged her to forgive him for hurting his brother; and then tenderly inquired of Jack after his wound. For me, I cannot describe my gratitude and agitation; I could scarce utter a word to my dear wife, who, on her part, sunk down quite overcome on her bed. The lady, who was, I understood, named Madame Hirtel, approached to assist her. When she recovered, she presented to me Madame Hirtel and her two daughters. The eldest, Sophia, was attending on Jack; Matilda, who was about ten or eleven years of age, was playing with Francis; while the good missionary, on his knees, thanked God for having re-united us.

"And for life," cried my dear wife. "My dear husband, I well knew you would set out to seek me; but how could I anticipate that you would ever succeed in finding me? We will now separate no more; this beloved friend has agreed to accompany [pg 358] us to the Happy Island, as I intend to call it, if I ever have the happiness to reach it again with all I love in the world. How graciously God permits us to derive blessings from our sorrows. See what my trial has produced me: a friend and two dear daughters, for henceforward we are only one family,"

We were mutually delighted with this arrangement, and entreated Mr. Willis to visit us often, and to come and live in the Happy Island when his mission was completed.

"I will consent," said he, "if you will come and assist me in my duties; for which purpose you and your sons must acquire the language of these islanders. We are much nearer your island than you think, for you took a very circuitous course, and Parabéry, who knows it, declares it is only a day's voyage with a fair wind. And, moreover, he tells me, that he is so much delighted with you and your sons, that he cannot part with you, and wishes me to obtain your permission to accompany you, and remain with you. He will be exceedingly useful to you: will teach the language to you all, and will be a ready means of communication between us."

I gladly agreed to take Parabéry with us as a friend; but it was no time yet to think of departing, as Mr. Willis wished to have Jack some days longer under his care; we therefore arranged that I and my two sons should become his guests, as his hut was but a short distance off. We had many things to hear; but, as my wife was yet too weak to relate her adventures, we resolved first to have the history of Madame Hirtel. Night coming [pg 359] on, the missionary lighted a gourd lamp, and, after a light collation of bread-fruit, Madame Hirtel began her story.

CHAPTER LIV.

"My life," she began, "passed without any remarkable events, till the misfortune occurred which brought me to this island. I was married, when very young, to Mr. Hirtel, a merchant at Hamburg, an excellent man, whose loss I have deeply felt. I was very happy in this union, arranged by my parents, and sanctioned by reason. We had three children, a son and two daughters, in the first three years of our marriage; and M. Hirtel, seeing his family increase so rapidly, wished to increase his income. An advantageous establishment was offered him in the Canary Islands; he accepted it, and prevailed on me to settle there, with my family, for some years. My parents were dead, I had no tie to detain me in Europe. I was going to see new regions, those fortunate isles I had heard so much of, and I set out joyfully with my husband and children, little foreseeing the misfortunes before me.

"Our voyage was favourable; the children, like myself, were delighted with the novelties of it. I was then twenty-three years old; Sophia, seven; Matilda, six; and Alfred, our pretty, gentle boy, not yet five. Poor child! he was the darling and the plaything of all the crew."

[pg 360]
She wept bitterly for a few moments, and then resumed her narration.

"He was as fair as your own Francis, and greatly resembled him. We proceeded first to Bourdeaux, where my husband had a correspondent, with whom he had large dealings; by his means my husband was enabled to raise large sums for his new undertaking. We carried with us, in fact, nearly his whole fortune. We re-embarked under the most favourable auspices--the weather delightful, and the wind fair; but we very soon had a change; we were met by a terrible storm and hurricane, such as the sailors had never witnessed. For a week our ship was tossed about by contrary winds, driven into unknown seas, lost all its rigging, and was at last so broken, that the water poured in on all sides. All was lost, apparently; but, in this extremity, my husband made a last attempt to save us. He tied my daughters and myself firmly to a plank, taking the charge of my boy himself, as he feared the additional weight would be too much for our raft. His intention was to tie himself to another plank, to fasten this to ours, and, taking his son in his arms, to give us a chance of being carried to the shore, which did not appear far off. Whilst he was occupied in placing us, he gave Alfred to the care of a sailor who was particularly attached to him. I heard the man say, 'Leave him with me, I will take care to save him.' On this, M. Hirtel insisted on his restoring him, and I cried out that he should be given to me. At that moment the ship, which was already fallen on its side, filled rapidly with water, plunged, and disappeared [pg 361] with all on board. The plank on which I and my daughters were fixed alone floated, and I saw nothing but death and desolation round me."

Madame Hirtel paused, almost suffocated by the remembrance of that awful moment.

"Poor woman!" said my wife, weeping, "it is five years since this misfortune. It was at the same time as our shipwreck, and was doubtless caused by the same storm. But how much more fortunate was I! I lost none that were dear to me, and we even had the vessel left for our use. But, my dear, unfortunate friend, by what miracle were you saved?"

"It was He who only can work miracles," said the missionary, "who cares for the widow and the orphan, and without whose word not a hair of the head can perish, who at that moment gave courage to the Christian mother."

"My strength," continued she, "was nearly exhausted, when, after being tossed about by the furious waves, I found myself thrown upon what I supposed to be a sand-bank with my two children. I envied the state of my husband and son. If I had not been a mother, I should have wished to have followed them; but my two girls lay senseless at my side, and I was anxious, as I perceived they still breathed, to recover them. At the moment M. Hirtel pushed the raft into the water, he threw upon it a box bound with iron, which I grasped mechanically, and still held, when we were left on shore. It was not locked, yet it was with some difficulty, in my confined position, that I succeeded in opening it. It contained a quantity of gold [pg 362] and bank-notes, which I looked upon with contempt, and regret. But there was something useful in the box. In the morocco portfolio which contained the bank-notes, there were the usual little instruments--a knife, scissors, pencils, stiletto, and also a small bottle of Eau de Cologne, which was particularly serviceable in restoring my children. I began by cutting the cords that tied us. I then rubbed my dear children with the Eau de Cologne, made them inhale it, and even swallow a little. The wind was still blowing, but the clouds began to break, and the sun appeared, which dried and warmed us. My poor children opened their eyes, and knew me, and I felt I was not utterly comfortless; but their first words were to ask for their father and brother. I could not tell them they were no more. I tried to deceive myself, to support my strength, by a feeble and delusive hope. M. Hirtel swam well, the sailor still better; and the last words I had heard still rung in my ears--'Do not be uneasy, I will save the child.' If I saw anything floating at a distance, my heart began to beat, and I ran towards the water; but I saw it was only wreck, which I could not even reach. Some pieces were, however, thrown on shore, and with these and our own raft I was enabled to make a sort of shelter, by resting them against a rock. My poor children, by crouching under this, sheltered themselves from the rain, or from the rays of the sun. I had the good fortune to preserve a large beaver hat, which I wore at the time, and this protected me; but these resources gave me little consolation; my children were complaining of hunger, and I felt only how much we were in want of. I had seen a shell-fish on the shore, resembling the [pg 363] oyster, or muscle. I collected some, and, opening them with my knife, we made a repast on them, which sufficed for the first day. Night came--my children offered up their evening prayer, and I earnestly besought the succour of the Almighty. I then lay down beside my babes on our raft, as conveniently as we could, and they soon slept. The fearful thoughts of the past, and dreadful anticipations of the future, prevented me from sleeping. My situation was indeed melancholy; but I felt, as a mother, I ought not to wish for death.

"As soon as day broke, I went close to the shore, to seek some shell-fish for our breakfast. In crossing the sand, I nearly plunged my foot into a hole, and fancied I heard a crash. I stooped, and putting my hand into the opening, found it was full of eggs; I had broken two or three, which I tasted, and thought very good. From the colour, form, and taste, I knew them to be turtle's eggs; there were at least sixty, so I had no more care about food. I carried away in my apron as many as I could preserve from the rays of the sun: this I endeavoured to effect by burying them in the sand, and covering them with one end of our plank, and succeeded very well. Besides these, there were as many to be found on the shore as we required; I have sometimes found as many as ninety together. These were our sole support while we remained there: my children liked them very much. I forgot to add, that I was fortunate enough to discover a stream of fresh water, running into the sea; it was the same which runs past this house, and which conducted me here. The first day we suffered greatly from [pg 364] thirst, but on the second we met with the stream which saved us. I will not tire you by relating day by day our sad life; every one was the same, and took away by degrees every hope from me. As long as I dared to indulge any, I could not bear to leave the shore; but at last it became insupportable to me. I was worn out with gazing continually on that boundless horizon, and that moving crystal which had swallowed up my hopes. I pined for the verdure and shade of trees. Although I had contrived to make for my daughters little hats of a marine rush, they suffered much from the extreme heat,-- the burning rays of a tropical sun. I decided at last to abandon that sandy shore; to penetrate, at all risks, into the country, in order to seek a shady and cooler abode, and to escape from the view of that sea which was so painful to me. I resolved not to quit the stream which was so precious to us, for, not having any vessel to contain water, I could not carry it with us. Sophia, who is naturally quick, formed, from a large leaf, a sort of goblet, which served us to drink from; and I filled my pockets with turtles' eggs, as provision for a few days. I then set off with my two children, after praying the God of all mercy to watch over us; and, taking leave of the vast tomb which held my husband and my son, I never lost sight of the stream; if any obstacle obliged me to turn a little way from it, I soon recovered my path. My eldest daughter, who was very strong and robust, followed me stoutly, as I took care not to walk too far without resting; but I was often compelled to carry my little Matilda on my shoulders. Both were delighted with the shade of the woods, and [pg 365] were so amused with the delightful birds that inhabited them, and a pretty little sportive green monkey, that they became as playful as ever. They sang and prattled; but often asked me if papa and Alfred would not soon return to see these pretty creatures, and if we were going to seek them. These words rent my heart, and I thought it best then to tell them they would meet no more on earth, and that they were both gone to heaven, to that good God to whom they prayed morning and evening. Sophia was very thoughtful, and the tears ran down her cheeks: 'I will pray to God more than ever,' said she, 'that he may make them happy, and send them back to us,' 'Mamma,' said Matilda, 'have we left the sea to go to heaven? Shall we soon be there? And shall we see beautiful birds like these?' We walked on very slowly, making frequent rests, till night drew on, and it was necessary to find a place for repose. I fixed on a sort of thick grove, which I could only enter by stooping; it was formed of one tree, whose branches, reaching the ground, take root there, and soon produce other stems, which follow the same course, and become, in time, an almost impenetrable thicket. Here I found a place for us to lie down, which appeared sheltered from wild beasts or savages, whom I equally dreaded. We had still some eggs, which we ate; but I saw with fear that the time approached when we must have more food, which I knew not where to find. I saw, indeed, some fruits on the trees, but I did not know them, and feared to give them to my children, who wished to have them. I saw also cocoa-nuts, but quite out of my reach; and even if I could have got them, [pg 366] I did not know how to open them. The tree under whose branches we had found protection was, I conjectured, an American fig-tree; it bore a quantity of fruit, very small and red, and like the European fig. I ventured to taste them, and found them inferior to ours,--insipid and soft,--but, I thought, quite harmless. I remarked that the little green monkeys ate them greedily, so I had no more fear, and allowed my children to regale themselves. I was much more afraid of wild beasts during the night; however, I had seen nothing worse than some little quadrupeds resembling the rabbit or squirrel, which came in numbers to shelter themselves during the night under our tree. The children wished to catch one, but I could not undertake to increase my charge. We had a quiet night, and were early awaked by the songs of the birds. How delighted I was to have escaped the noise of the waves, and to feel the freshness of the woods, and the perfume of the flowers, with which my children made garlands, to decorate my head and their own! These ornaments, during this time of mourning and bereavement, affected me painfully, and I was weak enough to forbid them this innocent pleasure; I tore away my garland, and threw it into the rivulet. 'Gather flowers,' said I, 'but do not dress yourselves in them; they are no fitting ornaments for us; your father and Alfred cannot see them.' They were silent and sad, and threw their garlands into the water, as I had done.

"We followed the stream, and passed two more nights under the trees. We had the good fortune to find more figs; but they did not satisfy us, and our eggs were exhausted. In my distress I almost [pg 367] decided to return to the shore, where we might at least meet with that nourishment. As I sat by the stream, reflecting mournfully on our situation, the children, who had been throwing stones into the water, cried out, 'Look, mamma, what pretty fishes!' I saw, indeed, a quantity of small salmon-trout in the river; but how could I take them? I tried to seize them with my hands, but could not catch them; necessity, however, is the mother of invention. I cut a number of branches with my knife, and wove them together to make a kind of light hurdle, the breadth of the stream, which was very narrow just here. I made two of these; my daughters assisted me, and were soon very skilful.

214

We then undressed ourselves, and took a bath, which refreshed us much. I placed one of my hurdles upright across the rivulet, and the second a little lower. The fishes who remained between attempted to pass, but the hurdles were woven too close. We watched for them attempting the other passage; many escaped us, but we captured sufficient for our dinner. We threw them out upon the grass, at a distance from the stream, so that they could not leap back. My daughters had taken more than I; but the sensible Sophia threw back those we did not require, to give them pleasure, she said, and Matilda did the same, to see them leap. We then removed our hurdles, dressed ourselves, and I began to consider how I should cook my fish; for I had no fire, and had never kindled one myself. However, I had often seen Mr. Hirtel, who was a smoker, light his pipe by means of the flint and steel; they were in the precious morocco case, together with tinder and matches. I tried to strike a light, and after [pg 368] some difficulty succeeded. I collected the fragments of the branches used for the hurdles, the children gathered some dry leaves, and I had soon a bright, lively fire, which I was delighted to see, notwithstanding the heat of the climate. I scraped the scales from the fish with my knife, washed them in the rivulet, and then placed them on the fire to broil; this was my apprenticeship in the art of cookery. I thought how useful it would be to give young ladies some knowledge of the useful arts; for who can foresee what they may need? Our European dinner delighted us as much as the bath and the fishing which had preceded it. I decided to fix our residence at the side of the rivulet, and beneath the fig-trees; my only objection being the fear of missing some passing vessel which might carry us back to Europe. But can you understand my feelings, when I confess to you that, although overcome by sorrow and desolation, having lost husband, son, and fortune, knowing that in order to support myself and bring up my children I must depend upon my friends, and to attain this having to hazard again the dangers of the sea, the very thought of which made me shudder, I should prefer to remain where Providence had brought me, and live calmly without obligation to any one? I might certainly have some difficulty in procuring the means of supporting a life which was dear to me for the sake of my children; but even this was an employment and an amusement. My children would early learn to bear privations, to content themselves with a simple and frugal life, and to labour for their own support. I might teach them all that I knew would be useful to them in future, and above all, [pg 369] impress upon their young minds the great truths of our holy religion. By bringing this constantly before their unsophisticated understanding, I might hope they would draw from it the necessary virtues of resignation and contentment. I was only twenty-three years of age, and might hope, by God's mercy, to be spared to them some time, and in the course of years who knew what might happen? Besides we were not so far from the sea but that I might visit it sometimes, if it were only to seek for turtles' eggs. I remained then under our fig-tree at night, and by day on the borders of the stream."

"It was under a fig-tree, also," said my wife, "that I have spent four happy years of my life. Unknown to each other, our fate has been similar; but henceforward I hope we shall not be separated."

Madame Hirtel embraced her kind friend, and observing that the evening was advanced, and that my wife, after such agitation, needed repose, we agreed to defer till next day the conclusion of the interesting narrative. My elder sons and myself followed the missionary to his hut, which resembled the king's palace, though it was smaller; it was constructed of bamboos, bound together, and the intervals filled with moss and clay; it was covered in the same way, and was tolerably solid. A mat in one corner, without any covering, formed his bed; but he brought out a bear's skin, which he used in winter, and which he now spread on the ground for us. I had observed a similar one in the grotto, and he told us we should hear the history of these skins next day, in the continuation of the story of Emily, or Mimi, as she was affectionately called by all. We retired to [pg 370] our couch, after a prayer from Mr. Willis; and for the first time since my dear wife was taken from me, I slept in peace.

CHAPTER LV.

We went to the grotto early in the morning, and found our two invalids much improved: my wife had slept better, and Mr. Willis found Jack's wound going on well. Madame Mimi told her daughters to prepare breakfast: they went out and soon returned, with a native woman and a boy of four or five years old, carrying newly-made rush baskets filled with all sorts of fruit: figs, guavas, strawberries, cocoa-nuts, and the bread-fruit.

"I must introduce you," said Emily, "to the rest of my family: this is Canda, the wife of your friend Parabéry, and this is their son, Minou-minou, whom I regard as my own. Your Elizabeth is already attached to them, and bespeaks your friendship for them. They will follow us to the Happy Island."

"Oh, if you knew," said Francis, "hat a well-behaved boy Minou is! He can climb trees, run, and leap, though he is less than I am. He must be my friend."

"And Canda," said Elizabeth, "shall be our assistant and friend."

She gave her hand to Canda, I did the same, and caressed the boy, who seemed delighted with me, and, to my great surprise, spoke to me in very good German-- the mother, too, knew several words of the language. They busied themselves [pg 371] with our breakfast: opened the cocoa-nuts, and poured the milk into the shells, after separating the kernel; they arranged the fruits on the trunk of a tree, which served for a table, and did great credit to the talent of their instructress.

"I should have liked to have offered you coffee," said Madame Hirtel, "which grows in this island, but having no utensils for roasting, grinding, or preparing it, it has been useless to me, and I have not even gathered it."

"Do you think, my dear, that it would grow in our island?" said my wife to me, in some anxiety.

I then recollected, for the first time, how fond my wife was of coffee, which, in Europe, had always been her favourite breakfast. There would certainly be in the ship some bags, which I might have brought away; but I had never thought of it, and my unselfish wife, not seeing it, had never named it, except once wishing we had some to plant in the garden. Now that there was a probability of obtaining it, she confessed that coffee and bread were the only luxuries she regretted. I promised to try and cultivate it in our island; foreseeing, however, that it would probably not be of the best quality, I told her she must not expect Mocha; but her long privation from this delicious beverage had made her less fastidious, and she assured me it would be a treat to her. After breakfast, we begged Madame Hirtel to resume her interesting narrative. She continued:

"After the reflections on my situation, which I told you of last night, I determined only to return to the sea-shore, when our food failed us in the woods; but I acquired other means of procuring [pg 372] it. Encouraged by the success of my fishing, I made a sort of net from the filaments of the bark of a tree and a plant resembling hemp. With these I succeeded in catching some birds: one, resembling our thrush, was very fat, and of delicious flavour. I had the greatest difficulty in overcoming my repugnance to taking away their life; nothing but the obligation of preserving our own could have reconciled me to it. My children plucked them; I then spitted them on a slender branch and roasted them before the fire. I also found some nests of eggs, which I concluded were those of the wild ducks which frequented our stream. I made myself acquainted with all the fruits which the monkeys and parroquets eat, and which were not out of my reach. I found a sort of acorn which had the flavour of a nut. The children also discovered plenty of large strawberries, a delicious repast; and I found a quantity of honeycomb in the hollow of a tree, which I obtained by stupifying the bees with a smoking brand.

"I took care to mark down every day on the blank leaves of my pocket-book. I had now marked thirty days of my wandering life on the border of the river, for I never strayed beyond the sound of its waters. Still I kept continually advancing towards the interior of the island. I had yet met with nothing alarming, and the weather had been most favourable; but we were not long to enjoy this comfort. The rainy season came on: and one night, to my great distress, I heard it descend in torrents. We were no longer under our fig-tree, which would have sheltered us for a [pg 373] considerable time. The tree under which we now were had tempted me by

217

having several cavities between the roots, filled with soft moss, which formed natural couches, but the foliage was very thin, and we were soon drenched completely. I crept near my poor children to protect them a little, but in vain; our little bed was soon filled with water, and we were compelled to leave it. Our clothes were so heavy with the rain that we could scarcely stand; and the night was so dark that we could see no road, and ran the risk of falling, or striking against some tree, if we moved. My children wept, and I trembled for their health, and for my own, which was so necessary to them. This was one of the most terrible nights of my pilgrimage. My children and I knelt down, and I prayed to our Heavenly Father for strength to bear this trial, if it was his will to continue it. I felt consolation and strength from my prayers, and rose with courage and confidence; and though the rain continued unabated, I waited with resignation the pleasure of the Almighty. I reconciled my children to our situation; and Sophia told me she had asked her father, who was near the gracious God, to entreat Him to send no more rain, but let the sun come back. I assured them God would not forget them; they began to be accustomed to the rain, only Sophia begged they might take off their clothes, and then it would be like a bath in the brook. I consented to this, thinking they would be less liable to suffer than by wearing their wet garments.

"The day began to break, and I determined to walk on without stopping, in order to warm [pg 374] ourselves by the motion; and to try to find some cave, some hollow tree, or some tree with thick foliage, to shelter us the next night.

"I undressed the children, and made a bundle of their clothes, which I would have carried myself, but I found they would not be too heavy for them, and I judged it best to accustom them early to the difficulties, fatigue, and labour, which would be their lot; and to attend entirely on themselves; I, therefore, divided the clothes into two unequal bundles, proportioned to their strength, and having made a knot in each, I passed a slender branch through it, and showed them how to carry it on their shoulders.

"When I saw them walking before me in this savage fashion, with their little white bodies exposed to the storm, I could not refrain from tears. I blamed myself for condemning them to such an existence, and thought of returning to the shore, where some vessel might rescue us; but we were now too far off to set about it. I continued to proceed with much more difficulty than my children, who had nothing on but their shoes and large hats. I carried the valuable box, in which I had placed the remains of our last night's supper, an act of necessary prudence, as there was neither fishing nor hunting now.

"As the day advanced, the rain diminished, and even the sun appeared above the horizon.

"'Look, my darlings,' said I, 'God has heard us, and sent his sun to warm and cheer us. Let us thank him,'

"'Papa has begged it of him!' said Matilda. 'Oh! mamma, let us pray him to send Alfred back!'

[pg 375]
"My poor little girl bitterly regretted the loss of her brother. Even now she can scarcely hear his name without tears. When the savages brought Francis to us, she at first took him for her brother. 'Oh, how you have grown in heaven!' cried she; and, after she discovered he was not her brother, she often said to him, 'How I wish your name was Alfred!'

"Forgive me for dwelling so long on the details of my wretched journey, which was not without its comforts, in the pleasure I took in the development of my children's minds, and in forming plans for their future education. Though anything relating to science, or the usual accomplishments, would be useless to them, I did not wish to bring them up like young savages; I hoped to be able to communicate much useful knowledge to them, and to give them juster ideas of this world and that to come.

"As soon as the sun had dried them, I made them put on their dresses, and we continued our walk by the brook, till we arrived at the grove which is before this rock. I removed the branches to pass through it, and saw beyond them the entrance to this grotto. It was very low and narrow; but I could not help uttering a cry of joy, for this was the only sort of retreat that could securely shelter us. I was going to enter it without thought, not reflecting there might be in it some ferocious animal, when I was arrested by a plaintive cry, more like that of a child than a wild beast; I advanced with more caution, and tried to find out what sort of an inhabitant the cave contained. It was indeed a human being!--an infant, whose age I could not discover; but it seemed too young to [pg 376] walk, and was, besides, tied up in leaves and moss, enclosed in a piece of bark, which was much torn and rent. The poor infant uttered the most piteous cries, and I did not hesitate a moment to enter the cave, and to take the innocent little creature in my arms; it ceased its cries as soon as it felt the warmth of my cheek; but it was evidently in want of food, and I had nothing to give it but some figs, of which I pressed the juice into its mouth; this seemed to satisfy it, and, rocking it in my arms, it soon went to sleep. I had then time to examine it, and to look round the cave. From the size and form of the face, I concluded it might be older than I had first thought; and I recollected to have read that the savages carried their children swaddled up in this way, even till they could walk. The complexion of the child was a pale olive, which I have since discovered is the natural complexion of the natives, before the exposure to the heat of the sun gives them the bronze hue you have seen; the features were good, except that the lips were thicker and the mouth larger than those of the Europeans. My two girls were charmed with it, and caressed it with great joy. I left them to rock it gently in its cradle of bark, till I

219

went round this cave, which I intended for my palace, and which I have never quitted. You see it--the form is not changed; but, since Heaven has sent me a friend," looking at the missionary, "it is adorned with furniture and utensils which have completed my comforts. But to return.

"The grotto was spacious, and irregular in form. In a hollow I found, with surprise, a sort of bed, carefully arranged with moss, dry leaves, and small [pg 377] twigs. I was alarmed. Was this grotto inhabited by men or by wild beasts? In either case, it was dangerous to remain here. I encouraged a hope, however, that, from the infant being here, the mother must be the inhabitant, and that, on her return, finding me nursing her child, she might be induced to share her asylum with us. I could not, however, reconcile this hope with the circumstance of the child being abandoned in this open cave.

"As I was considering whether I ought to remain, or leave the cave, I heard strange cries at a distance, mingled with the screams of my children, who came running to me for protection, bringing with them the young savage, who fortunately was only half awaked, and soon went to sleep again, sucking a fig. I laid him gently on the bed of leaves, and told my daughters to remain near him in a dark corner; then, stepping cautiously, I ventured to look out to discover what was passing, without being seen. The noise approached nearer, to my great alarm, and I could perceive, through the trees, a crowd of men armed with long pointed lances, clubs, and stones; they appeared furious, and the idea that they might enter the cave froze me with terror. I had an idea of taking the little native babe, and holding it in my arms, as my best shield; but this time my fears were groundless. The whole troop passed outside the wood, without even looking on the same side as the grotto; they appeared to follow some traces they were looking out for on the ground. I heard their shouts for some time, but they died away, and I recovered from my fears. Still, the dread of meeting them overcame even [pg 378] hunger. I had nothing left in my box but some figs, which I kept for the infant, who was satisfied with them, and I told my daughters we must go to bed without supper. The sleeping infant amused them so much, that they readily consented to give up the figs. He awoke smiling, and they gave him the figs to suck. In the mean time, I prepared to release him from his bondage to make him more comfortable; and I then saw that the outer covering of bark was torn by the teeth of some animal, and even the skin of the child slightly grazed. I ventured to carry him to the brook, into which I plunged him two or three times, which seemed to give him great pleasure.

"I ran back to the cave, which is, you see, not more than twenty yards distant, and found Sophia and Matilda very much delighted at a treasure they had found under the dry leaves in a corner. This was a great quantity of fruits of various kinds, roots of some unknown plant, and a good supply of beautiful honey, on which the little gluttons were already feasting. They came directly to give some on their fingers to their little doll, as they called the babe. This discovery made me very thoughtful. Was it possible that we were in a bear's den! I had read that they sometimes carried off infants and that they were very fond of fruits and of honey, of which they generally had a hoard. I remarked on the earth, and especially at the entrance, where the rain had made it soft, the impression of large paws which left me no doubt. The animal would certainly return to his den, and we were in the greatest danger; but where could we go? The sky, dark with clouds, threatened a return of the storm; [pg 379] and the troop of savages might still be wandering about the island. I had not courage, just as night set in, to depart with my children; nor could I leave the poor infant, who was now sleeping peacefully, after his honey and figs. His two nurses soon followed his example; but for me there was no rest; the noise of the wind among the trees, and of the rain pattering on the leaves,--the murmur of the brook,--the light bounds of the kangaroo,--all made my heart beat with fear and terror; I fancied it was the bear returning to devour us. I had cut and broken some branches to place before the entrance; but these were but a weak defence against a furious and probably famished animal; and if he even did no other harm to my children, I was sure their terror at the sight of him would kill them. I paced backwards and forwards, from the entrance to the bed, in the darkness, envying the dear sleepers their calm and fearless rest; the dark-skinned baby slept soundly, nestled warmly between my daughters, till day broke at last, without anything terrible occurring. Then my little people awoke, and cried out with hunger. We ate of the fruits and honey brought us by our unknown friend, feeding, also, our little charge, to whom my daughters gave the pet name of Minou, which he still keeps.

"I busied myself with his toilette. There was no need to go to the brook for a bath, for the rain came down incessantly. I then folded Matilda's apron round him, which pleased her greatly. The rain ceased for a while, and they set off for flowers to amuse him. They were scarcely gone when I heard the cries of the savages again; but this time they seemed rather [pg 380] shouts of joy and triumph; they sung and chaunted a sort of chorus; but were still at such distance that I had time to recal my daughters, and withdrew them out of sight. I took Minou with me as a mediator, and placed myself in an angle of the rock, where I could see without being seen. They passed, as before, beyond the wood, armed, and two of them bore at the end of their lances something very large and dark, which I could not distinguish, but thought might be some wild beast they had destroyed; afterwards, I flattered myself it might be the bear, whose return I so greatly dreaded. Following the train was a woman, naked, with her hair hanging down, uttering loud cries, and tearing her face and breast. No one attempted to soothe her; but occasionally one of the bearers of the black mass pointed it out to her; she then became furious, threw herself on it, and tried to tear it with her teeth and nails. I was quite overcome with horror and pity.

"That woman, my friends, was Canda, whom you have just seen. Canda, usually so mild and gentle, was rendered frantic by the loss of her child,--her first-born,-- whom she believed was devoured by the bear. Parabéry, her husband, tried to console her, but was himself in great sorrow. These bears, as I have since learnt, for there were two of them, had come from a mountain, at the foot of which was Parabéry's hut. They had only this son, and Canda, according to the custom of the country, tying it in a piece of bark, carried it on her back. One morning, after having bathed him in the stream, which has its source near their abode, she placed him on the [pg 381] turf a few moments, while she was employed in some household duties. She soon heard his cries, mingled with a sort of growl; she ran to the spot, and saw a frightful beast holding her child in its mouth, and running off with it. It was then more than twenty yards off; her cries brought her husband; she pointed to the horrible animal, and darted after it, determined to save her child or perish. Her husband only stopped to seize his javelin, and followed her, but did not overtake her till fatigue and the heat of the day made her fall, almost senseless, on the ground. Stopping for a moment to raise and encourage her, he lost sight of the bear, and could not recover the track. All the night,--that dreadful night of rain, when I was weeping and murmuring, thinking myself the most unfortunate of women,--was Canda exposed, without clothes, to that frightful storm, hopelessly seeking her only child, and not even feeling that it did rain. Parabéry, not less afflicted, but more composed, went to relate his misfortune to his neighbours, who, arming themselves, set out, with Parabéry at their head, following the track of the animal over the wet ground. They discovered it next morning with another bear, so busy devouring a swarm of bees and their honey, that the savages were able to draw near them. Parabéry pierced one with his spear, and despatched him with a blow of his club; one of his comrades killed the other, and Parabéry tasted the truly savage joy of vengeance. But the poor mother could not be so comforted. After wandering through the rain all night, she reached the party as they were skinning the bear and dividing the flesh. Parabéry [pg 382] only asked and obtained the skins, to recompense him for the loss of his son. They returned home in triumph, Canda following them with bitter cries, tearing her face with a shark's tooth. From observation of these circumstances, I concluded that Canda must be the mother of my little protégé. My heart sympathized with her, and I even made some steps forward to restore him; but the sight of the savage crowd, with their tattooed bodies, filled me with such terror, that I retreated involuntarily to the grotto, where my children, alarmed by the noise, were hiding themselves.

"'Why do the people cry out so?' said Sophia, 'they frighten me. Don't let them come here, mamma, or they may carry Minou away,'

"'Certainly,' said I; 'and I should have no right to forbid them. I think they are his friends who are distressed at losing him; I wish I could restore him to them.'

"'Oh, no! mamma,' said Matilda. 'Pray don't give him back; we like him so much, and we will be his little mammas. He will be far happier with us than with those ugly savages, who tied him up like a parcel in the bark, with the moss which pricked him so much; he is much more comfortable in my apron. How he moves his legs as if he wanted to walk; Sophia and I will teach him. Do let us keep him, mimi.'

"Even if I had decided, it was now too late; the savages had passed on to some distance. I, however, explained to Matilda the beauty of the divine precept, 'Do unto others as you would they should do unto you,' asking her how she would have liked to be detained by the savages, and [pg 383] what, then, would be the suffering of her own mamma? She was thoughtful for a moment, and then, embracing Minou and me, 'You are right, mamma mimi; but if she loves her baby, let her come and seek him,' said the little rebel. In the mean time, Sophia had been out, and returned with some brilliant flowers, fresh after the rain, with which they made garlands to dress up the infant. 'Oh! if his mamma saw him, she would be glad to let us have him,' said Matilda. She then explained to her sister who this mamma was, and Sophia shed tears to think of the sorrow of the poor mother. 'But how do you know, mamma, that she was Minou's mother?' demanded she. This question proved that her judgment was forming, and I took the opportunity of teaching her what information one may derive from observation. She understood me very well; and when I told her on what I had founded my idea, she trembled to think he had been brought here by a bear, and asked me if the bear would have eaten him.

"'I cannot answer for it,' said I, 'if it had been pressed by hunger; they tell us, that the bear does no harm to man unless attacked, and is especially fond of children. But, notwithstanding this, I should not like to trust it. At all events, the poor babe would have died, if we had not found him.'

"'Poor babe, he shall not die of hunger now,' said she. 'Let us give him some figs; but these are not good; we must go and seek some more.'

"The rain having ceased, I consented, passing through the grove, where there are no fig-trees, to search farther. My daughters had fed the [pg 384] child with honey and water; it appeared quite reconciled to us, and had ceased to cry. I judged it might be about eight months old. We soon found some trees covered with the violet-coloured figs. Whilst I gathered them, the girls made a pretty bed of moss, adorned with flowers, for their little favourite, and fed him with the fresh fruit, which he enjoyed much; and with their fair hair and rosy faces, and the little negro between them, with his arch, dark countenance, they formed a charming picture, which affected me greatly.

CHAPTER LVI.

"We had been more than an hour under the tree, when I heard cries again; but this time I was not alarmed, for I distinguished the voice of the disconsolate mother, and I knew that I could comfort her. Her grief brought her back to the spot where she thought her child had been devoured; she wished, as she afterwards told us, when we could understand her, to search for some remains of him,--his hair, his bones, or even a piece of the bark that bound him; and here he was, full of life and health. She advanced slowly, sobbing, and her eyes turned to the ground. She was so absorbed in her search, that she did not see us when we were but twenty yards from her. Suddenly, Sophia darted like an arrow to her, took her hand, and said, 'Come, Minou is here.'

"Canda neither knew what she saw nor what she heard; she took my daughter for something supernatural, and made no resistance, but followed her [pg 385] to the fig-tree. Even then she did not recognize the little creature, released from his bonds, half-clothed, covered with flowers, and surrounded by three divinities, for she took us for such, and wished to prostrate herself before us. She was still more convinced of it when I took up her son, and placed him in her arms: she recognized him, and the poor little infant held out his arms to her. I can never express to you the transport of the mother; she screamed, clasped her child till he was half-suffocated, rapidly repeating words which we could not understand, wept, laughed, and was in a delirium of delight that terrified Minou. He began to cry, and held out his arms to Sophia, who, as well as Matilda, was weeping at the sight. Canda looked at them with astonishment; she soothed the child, and put him to her breast, which he rejected at first, but finally seized it, and his mother was happy. I took the opportunity to try and make her comprehend, that the great animal had brought him here; that we had found him, and taken care of him; and I made signs for her to follow me, which she did without hesitation, till we reached the grotto, when, without entering, she fled away with her infant with such rapidity, that it was impossible to overtake her, and was soon out of sight.

"I had some difficulty in consoling my daughters for the loss of Minou; they thought they should see him no more, and that his mother was very ungrateful to carry him off, without even letting them take leave of him. They were still weeping and complaining, when we saw the objects of our anxiety approaching; but Canda was now accompanied by a man, who was carrying the [pg 386] child. They entered the grotto, and prostrated themselves before us. You know Parabéry; his countenance pleased and tranquillized us. As a relation of the king, he was distinguished by wearing a short tunic of leaves; his body was tattooed and stained with various colours; but not his face, which expressed kindness and gratitude, united with great intelligence. He comprehended most of my signs. I did not succeed so well in understanding him; but saw he meant kindly. In the mean time my daughters had a more intelligible conversation with Canda and Minou; they half-devoured the latter with caresses, fed him with figs and honey, and amused him so much, that he would scarcely leave them. Canda was not jealous of this preference, but seemed delighted with it; she, in her turn, caressed my daughters, admired their glossy hair and fair skin, and pointed them out to her husband; she repeated Minou after them, but always added another Minou, and appeared to think this name beautiful. After some words with Parabéry, she placed Minou-Minou in Sophia's arms, and they both departed, making signs that they would return; but we did not see them for some time after. Sophia and Matilda had their full enjoyment of their favourite; they wished to teach him to walk and to speak, and they assured me he was making great progress. They were beginning to hope his parents had left him entirely, when they came in sight, Parabéry bending under the weight of two bear-skins, and a beautiful piece of matting to close the entrance to my grotto; Canda carried a basket on her head filled with fine fruit; the cocoa, the bread-fruit (which they call rima), [pg 387] pine-apples, figs, and, finally, a piece of bear's flesh, roasted at the fire, which I did not like; but I enjoyed the fruits and the milk of the cocoa-nut, of which Minou-Minou had a good share. They spread the bear-skins in the midst of the grotto; Parabéry, Canda, and the infant, between them, took possession of one without ceremony, and motioned to us to make our bed of the other. But the bears having only been killed the evening before, these skins had an intolerable smell. I made them comprehend this, and Parabéry immediately carried them off and placed them in the brook, secured by stones. He brought us in exchange a heap of moss and leaves, on which we slept very well.

"From this moment we became one family. Canda remained with us, and repaid to my daughters all the care and affection they bestowed on Minou-Minou. There never was a child had more indulgence; but he deserved it, for his quickness and docility. At the end of a few months he began to lisp a few words of German, as well as his mother, of whom I was the teacher, and who made rapid progress. Parabéry was very little with us, but he undertook to be our purveyor, and furnished us abundantly with everything necessary for our subsistence. Canda taught my daughter to make beautiful baskets,--some, of a flat form, served for our plates and dishes. Parabéry made us knives from sharp stones. My daughters, in return, taught Canda to sew. At the time of our shipwreck we had, each of us, in her pocket, a morocco housewife, with a store of needles and thread. By means of these we had mended our linen, and we now [pg 388] made dresses of palm-leaves. The bear-skins, washed in the stream, and thoroughly dried in the burning sun, have been very useful to us in the cold and rainy season. Now that we had guides, we made, in the fine season, excursions to different parts of the island. Minou-Minou soon learned to walk, and being strong, like all these islanders, would always accompany us. We went one day to the sea-shore. I shuddered at the sight, and Canda, who knew that my husband and child had perished in the sea, wept with me. We now spoke each other's language well enough to converse. She told me that a black friend (Emily bowed to Mr. Willis) had arrived in a neighbouring island, to announce to them that there was a Being, almighty and all-merciful, who lived in Heaven, and heard all they said. Her comprehension of this truth was very confused, and I endeavoured to make it more clear and positive.

"'I see very well,' said she, 'that you know him. Is it to Him that you speak every morning and evening, kneeling as we do before our king Bara-ourou?'

"'Yes, Canda,' said I, 'it is before Him who is the King of Kings, who gave us our life, who preserves it, and bestows on us all good, and who promises us still more when this life is past.'

"'Was it he who charged you to take care of Minou-Minou, and to restore him to me?' asked she.

"'Yes, Canda; all that you or I do that is good, is put into our hearts by Him.'

"I thus tried to prepare the simple mind of Canda for the great truths that Mr. Willis was to teach her."

[pg 389]
"You left me little to do," said Mr. Willis. "I found Parabéry and Canda prepared to believe, with sincere faith, the holy religion I came to teach--the God of the white people was the only one they adored. I knew Parabéry, he had come to hunt seals in the island where I was established, and I was struck by his appearance. What was my astonishment to find, that when I spoke to him of the one true God, he was no stranger to the subject. He had even some ideas of a Saviour, and of future rewards and punishments.

"'It was the white lady,' said he, 'who taught me this; she teaches Canda and Minou-minou, whose life she saved, and whom she is bringing up to be good like herself.'

"I had a great desire," continued Mr. Willis, "to become acquainted with my powerful assistant in the great work of my mission. I told Parabéry this, who offered to bring me here in his canoe; I came and found, in a miserable cave, or rather in a bear's den, all the virtues of mature age united to the charms of youth; a resigned and pious mother, bringing up her children, as women should be brought up, in simplicity, forbearance, and love of industry; teaching them, as the best knowledge, to love God with all their heart, and their neighbour as themselves. Under the inspection of their mother, they were educating the son of Parabéry. This child, then four years and a half old, spoke German well, and knew his alphabet, which Madame Hirtel traced on the floor of the grotto; in this way she taught her daughters to read; they taught Minou-minou, who, in his turn, teaches his parents. Parabéry often brings his friends to the grotto, and Madame [pg 390] Hirtel, having acquired the language, casts into their hearts the good seed, which I venture to hope will not be unfruitful.

"Finding these people in such a good state, and wishing to enjoy the society of a family, like myself, banished to a remote region, I decided to take up my abode in this island.

226

"Parabéry soon built me a hut in the neighbourhood of the grotto; Madame Hirtel compelled me to take one of her bear-skins. I have by degrees formed my establishment, dividing with my worthy neighbour the few useful articles I brought from Europe, and we live a tranquil and happy life.

"And now comes the time that brought about our meeting. Some of our islanders, in a fishing expedition, were driven by the wind on your island. At the entrance of a large bay, they found a small canoe of bark, carefully moored to a tree. Either their innate propensity for theft, or the notion that it had no owner, prevailed over them, and they brought it away. I was informed of this, and was curious to see it; I recognized at once that it was made by Europeans: the careful finish, the neat form, the oars, rudder, mast, and triangular sail, all showed that it had not been made by savages. The seats of the rowers were made of planks, and were painted, and what further convinced me was, that I found in it a capital gun, loaded, and a horn of powder in a hole under one of the seats. I then made particular inquiries about the island from whence they had brought the canoe; and all their answers confirmed my idea that it must be inhabited by a [pg 391] European, from whom they had perhaps taken his only means of leaving it.

"Restless about this fancy, I tried to persuade them to return and discover if the island was inhabited. I could not prevail on them to restore the canoe; but, seeing me much agitated, they resolved secretly to procure me a great pleasure as they thought, by returning to the island and bringing away any one they could meet with, whether he would or not. Parabéry, always the leader in perilous enterprises, and who was so attached to me, would not be left out in one which was to produce me such pleasure. They set out, and you know the result of their expedition. I leave it to your wife to tell you how she was brought away, and pass on to the time of their arrival. My people brought them to me in triumph, and were vexed that they had only found one woman and a child, whom I might give to the white lady. This I did promptly. Your wife was ill and distressed, and I carried her immediately to the grotto. There she found a companion who welcomed her with joy; Francis replaced her own lost Alfred, and the two good mothers were soon intimate friends. But, notwithstanding this solace, your Elizabeth was inconsolable at the separation from her husband and children, and terrified at the danger to which you would expose yourself in searching for her. We were even afraid she would lose her reason, when the king came to take away Francis. He had seen him on his arrival, and was much taken with his appearance; he came again to see him, and resolved to adopt him as his son. You know [pg 392] what passed on this subject; and now you are once more united to all those who are dear to you.

"Bless God, brother, who knows how to produce good from what we think evil, and acknowledge the wisdom of his ways. You must return all together to your island; I am too much interested in the happiness of Emily to wish to detain her; and if God permits me, when my missions are completed, I will come to end my days with you, and to bless your rising colony."

I suppress all our reflections on this interesting history, and our gratitude for the termination of our trials, and hasten to the recital, which, at my particular entreaty, my wife proceeded to give us.

CHAPTER LVII.

"My story," she began, "will not be long. I might make it in two words,--you have lost me, and you have found me. I have every reason to thank Heaven for a circumstance, which has proved to me how dear I am to you, and has given me the happiness of gaining a friend and two dear daughters. Can one complain of an event which has produced such consequences, even though it was attended with some violence? But I ought to do the savages justice,--this violence was as gentle as it could be. I need only tell you Parabéry was there, to convince you I was well treated, and it was solely the sorrow of being parted from you that affected my health. I shall be well now, [pg 393] and as soon as Jack can walk, I shall be ready to embark for our happy island. I will now tell you how I was brought away.

"When you and our three sons left, to make the tour of the island, I was very comfortable; you had told me you might return late, or probably not till next day, and when the evening passed away without seeing you, I was not uneasy. Francis was constantly with me; we went together to water the garden, and rested in the Grotto Ernestine; then I returned to the house, took my wheel, and placed myself in my favourite colonnade, where I should be the first to see your return. Francis, seeing me at work, asked if he might go as far as the bridge to meet you; to which I readily consented. He set out, and I was sitting, thinking of the pleasure I should have in seeing you again, and hearing you relate your voyage, when I saw Francis running, crying out, 'Mamma! mamma! there is a canoe on the sea; I know it is ours; it is full of men, perhaps savages.'

"'Silly little fellow!' said I, 'it is your father and brothers; if they are in the canoe, there can be no doubt of it. Your father told me he would bring it, and they would return by water; I had forgotten this when I let you go. Now you can go and meet them on the shore; give me your arm, and I will go too,' and we set off very joyfully to meet our captors. I soon, alas! saw my error; it was, indeed, our canoe, but, instead of my dear ones, there were in it six half-naked savages, with terrible countenances, who landed and surrounded us. My blood froze with fright, and if I had wished to flee, I was unable. I fell on the shore, nearly insensible; still, I heard the cries [pg 394] of my dear Francis, who clung to me, and held me with all his

228

strength; at last my senses quite failed me, and I only recovered to find myself lying at the bottom of the canoe. My son, weeping over me, was trying to recover me, assisted by one of the savages, of less repulsive appearance than his companions, and who seemed the chief; this was Parabéry. He made me swallow a few drops of a detestable fermented liquor, which, however, restored me. I felt, as I recovered, the extent of my disaster, and your grief, my dears, when you should find me missing. I should have been wholly disconsolate, but that Francis was left to me, and he was continually praying me to live for his sake. I received some comfort from a vague notion that as this was our canoe, the savages had already carried you off, and were taking us to you.

"I was confirmed in this hope, when I saw that the savages, instead of making to sea, continued to coast the island, till they came to the Great Bay. I had then no doubt but that we should meet with you; but this hope was soon destroyed. Two or three more of the savages were waiting there on the shore; they spoke to their friends in the canoe; and I understood from their gestures, that they were saying they could not find anybody there. I have since learnt from Canda, that part of them landed at the Great Bay, with instructions to search that side of the island for inhabitants, whilst the rest proceeded with the canoe to examine the other side, and had succeeded but too well. The night came on, and they were anxious to return, which, doubtless, prevented them pillaging our house. I believe, moreover, that none of them could have reached Tent [pg 395] House, defended by our strong palisade, and hidden by the rocks amidst which it is built; and the other party, finding us on the shore, would not penetrate further.

 Six savages with terrible countenances, landed and
surrounded us.
"Six savages with terrible countenances, landed and surrounded us."

"When all had entered the canoe, they pushed off, by the light of the stars, into the open sea. I think I must have sunk under my sorrow, but for Francis, and, I must confess it, my dear dog Flora, who had never left me. Francis told me, that she had tried to defend me, and flew at the savages; but one of them took my apron, tore it, and tied it over her mouth like a muzzle, bound her legs, and then threw her into the canoe, where the poor creature lay at my feet, moaning piteously. She arrived with us in this island, but I have not seen her since; I have often inquired of Parabéry, but he could not tell me what had become of her."

"But I know," said Fritz, "and have seen her. We brought Turk with us, and the savages had carried Flora to that desert part of the island, from whence Jack was carried off; so the two dogs met. When I had the misfortune to wound Jack, I quite forgot them; they were rambling off, in chase of kangaroos; we left them, and no doubt they are there still. But we must not abandon the poor beasts; if my father will permit me, I will go and seek them in Parabéry's canoe."

229

As we were obliged to wait a few days for Jack's recovery, I consented, on condition that Parabéry accompanied them, and the next day was fixed for the expedition. Ernest begged to be of the party, that he might see the beautiful trees and flowers they had described. I then requested the narration might be continued, which had been interrupted [pg 396] by this episode of the two dogs. Francis resumed it where his mother had left off.

"We had a favourable passage--the sea was calm, and the boat went so smoothly, that both mamma and I went to sleep. You must have come a much longer round than necessary, papa, as your voyage lasted three days, and we arrived here the day after our departure. Mamma was then awake, and wept constantly, believing she should never more see you or my brothers. Parabéry seemed very sorry for her, and tried to console her; at last, he addressed to her two or three words of German, pointing to heaven. His words were very plain--Almighty God, good; and then black friend, and white lady; adding the words Canda, bear, and Minou-minou. We did not understand what he meant; but he seemed so pleased at speaking these words, that we could not but be pleased too; and to hear him name God in German gave us confidence, though we could, not comprehend where or how he had learnt the words. 'Perhaps,' said mamma, 'he has seen your papa and brothers,' I thought so too; still, it appeared strange that, in so short a time, he could acquire and remember these words. However it might be, mamma was delighted to have him near her, and taught him to pronounce the words father, mother, and son, which did not seem strange to him, and he soon knew them. She pointed to me and to herself, as she pronounced the words, and he readily comprehended them, and said to us, with bursts of laughter, showing his large ivory teeth, Canda, mother; Minou-minou, son; Parabéry, father; white lady, mother. Mamma thought he referred to her, but it was to Madame Emily. He tried [pg 397] to pronounce this name and two others, but could not succeed; at last, he said, girls, girls, and almost convinced us he must know some Europeans, which was a great comfort to us.

"When I saw mamma more composed, I took out my flageolet to amuse her, and played the air to Ernest's verses. This made her weep again very much, and she begged me to desist; the savages, however, wished me to continue, and I did not know whom to obey. I changed the air, playing the merriest I knew. They were in ecstasies; they took me in their arms one after the other, saying, Bara-ourou, Bara-ourou. I repeated the word after them, and they were still more delighted. But mamma was so uneasy to see me in their arms, that I broke from them, and returned to her.

"At last we landed. They carried mamma, who was too weak to walk. About a hundred yards from the shore, we saw a large building of wood and reeds, before which there was a crowd of savages. One who was very tall came to receive us. He was dressed in a short tunic, much ornamented, and wore a necklace of pierced shells. He was a little disfigured by a white bone passed through his nostrils. But you saw him, papa, when he wanted to adopt me; it was Bara-ourou, the king of the island. I was presented to him, and he was pleased with me, touched the end of my nose with his, and admired my hair very much. My conductors ordered me to play on the flageolet. I played some lively German airs, which made them dance and leap, till the king fell down with fatigue, and made a sign for me to desist. He then spoke for some time to the savages, who [pg 398] stood in a circle round him. He looked at mamma, who was seated in a corner, near her protector Parabéry. He called the latter, who obliged mamma to rise, and presented her to the king. Bara-ourou looked only at the red and yellow India handkerchief which she wore on her head; he took it off, very unceremoniously, and put it on his own head, saying, miti, which means beautiful. He then made us re-embark in the canoe with him, amusing himself with me and my flageolet, which he attempted to play by blowing it through his nose, but did not succeed. After turning round a point which seemed to divide the island into two, we landed on a sandy beach. Parabéry and another savage proceeded into the interior, carrying my mother, and we followed. We arrived at a hut similar to the king's, but not so large. There we were received by Mr. Willis, whom we judged to be the black friend, and from that time we had no more fears. He took us under his protection, first speaking to the king and to Parabéry in their own language. He then addressed mamma in German, mixed with a few English words, which we understood very well. He knew nothing of you and my brothers; but, from what mamma told him, he promised to have you sought for, and brought as soon as possible to the island. In the mean time, he offered to lead us to a friend who would take care of us, and nurse poor mamma, who looked very ill. She was obliged to be carried to the grotto; but, after that, her cares were over, and her pleasure without alloy; for the black friend had promised to seek you. The white lady received us like old friends, and Sophia and Matilda took me at first for their own [pg 399] brother, and still love me as if I was. We only wished for you all. Madame Mimi made mamma lie down on the bear-skin, and prepared her a pleasant beverage from the milk of the cocoa-nut. Sophia and Matilda took me to gather strawberries, and figs, and beautiful flowers; and we caught fish in the brook, between two osier hurdles. We amused ourselves very well with Minou-minou, while Canda and Madame Emily amused mamma.

"The king came the next day to see his little favourite; he wished me to go with him to another part of the island, where he often went to hunt; but I would not leave mamma and my new friends. I was wrong, papa; for you were there, and my brothers; it was there Jack was wounded and brought away. I might have prevented all that, and you would then have returned to us. How sorry I have been for my obstinacy! It was I, more than Fritz, who was the cause of his being wounded.

"Bara-ourou returned in the evening to the grotto; and think, papa, of our surprise, our delight, and our distress, when he brought us poor Jack, wounded and in great

231

pain, but still all joy at finding us again! The king told Mr. Willis he was sure Jack was my brother, and he made us a present of him, adding, that he gave him in exchange for mamma's handkerchief. Mamma thanked him earnestly, and placed Jack beside her. From him she learned all you had done to discover us. He informed Mr. Willis where he had left you, and he promised to seek and bring you to us. He then examined the wound, which Jack wished him to think he had himself caused with Fritz's gun; but this was not probable, [pg 400] as the ball had entered behind, and lodged in the shoulder. Mr. Willis extracted it with some difficulty, and poor Jack suffered a good deal; but all is now going on well. What a large party we shall be, papa, when we are all settled in our island; Sophia and Matilda, Minou-Minou, Canda, Parabéry, you, papa, and two mammas, and Mr. Willis!"

My wife smiled as the little orator concluded. Mr. Willis then dressed Jack's wound, and thought he might be removed in five or six days.

"Now, my dear Jack," said I, "it is your turn to relate your history. Your brother left off where you were entertaining the savages with your buffooneries; and certainly they were never better introduced. But how did they suddenly think of carrying you away?"

"Parabéry told me," said Jack, "that they were struck with my resemblance to Francis as soon as I took my flageolet. After I had played a minute or two, the savage who wore mamma's handkerchief, whom I now know to be the king, interrupted me by crying out and clapping his hands. He spoke earnestly to the others, pointing to my face, and to my flageolet, which he had taken; he looked also at my jacket of blue cotton, which one of them had tied round his shoulders like a mantle; and doubtless he then gave orders for me to be carried to the canoe. They seized upon me; I screamed like a madman, kicked them and scratched them; but what could I do against seven or eight great savages? They tied my legs together, and my hands behind me, and carried me like a parcel. I could then do nothing but cry out for Fritz; and the knight of the gun came rather too [pg 401] soon. In attempting to defend me, some way or other, off went his gun, and the ball took up its abode in my shoulder. I can assure you an unpleasant visitor is that same ball; but here he is, the scoundrel! Father Willis pulled him out by the same door as that by which he went in; and since his departure, all goes on well.

"Now for my story. When poor Fritz saw that I was wounded, he fell down as if he had been shot at the same time. The savages, thinking he was dead, took away his gun, and carried me into the canoe. I was in despair more for the death of my brother than from my wound, which I almost forgot, and was wishing they would throw me into the sea, when I saw Fritz running at full speed to the shore; but we pushed off, and I could only call out some words of consolation. The savages were very kind to me, and one of them held me up seated on the out-rigger; they washed my wound with sea-water, sucked it, tore my pocket-handkerchief to make a bandage, and as soon as we landed, squeezed the juice of some herb into it. We sailed very quickly, and passed the place where we had landed in the morning. I knew it again, and could see Ernest standing on a sand-bank; he was watching us, and I held out my arms to him. I thought I also saw you, papa, and heard you call; but the savages yelled, and though I cried with all my strength, it was in vain. I little thought they were taking me to mamma. As soon as we had disembarked, they brought me to this grotto; and I thought I must have died of surprise and joy when I was met by mamma and Francis, and then by Sophia, Matilda, mamma Emily, and Mr. Willis, who is [pg 402] a second father to me. This is the end of my story. And a very pretty end it is, that brings us all together. What matters it to have had a little vexation for all this pleasure? I owe it all to you, Fritz; if you had let me sink to the bottom of the sea, instead of dragging me out by the hair, I should not have been here so happy as I am; I am obliged to the gun, too; thanks to it, I was the first to reach mamma, and see our new friends."

The next day, Fritz and Ernest set out on their expedition with Parabéry, in his canoe, to seek our two valued dogs. The good islander carried his canoe on his back to the shore. I saw them set off, but not without some dread, in such a frail bark, into which the water leaked through every seam. But my boys could swim well; and the kind, skilful, and bold Parabéry undertook to answer for their safety. I therefore recommended them to God, and returned to the grotto, to tranquillize my wife's fears. Jack was inconsolable that he could not form one of the party; but Sophia scolded him for wishing to leave them, to go upon the sea, which had swallowed up poor Alfred.

In the evening we had the pleasure of seeing our brave dogs enter the grotto. They leaped on us in a way that terrified the poor little girls at first, who took them for bears; but they were soon reconciled to them when they saw them fawn round us, lick our hands, and pass from one to the other to be caressed. My sons had had no difficulty in finding them; they had run to them at the first call, and seemed delighted to see their masters again.

[pg 403]
The poor animals had subsisted on the remains of the kangaroos, but apparently had met with no fresh water, for they seemed dying with thirst, and rushed to the brook as soon as they discovered it, and returned again and again. Then they followed us to the hut of the good missionary, who had been engaged all day in visiting the dwellings of the natives, and teaching them the truths of religion. I had accompanied him, but, from ignorance of the language, could not aid him. I was, however, delighted with the simple and earnest manner in which he spoke, and the eagerness with which they heard him. He finished by a prayer, kneeling, and they all imitated him, lifting up their hands and eyes to heaven. He told me he was trying to make them celebrate the Sunday. He assembled them in his tent, which he wished to make a temple for the worship of the true God. He intended to consecrate it for this purpose, and to live in the grotto, after our departure.

"The day arrived at last. Jack's shoulder was nearly healed, and my wife, along with her happiness, recovered her strength. The pinnace had been so well guarded by Parabéry and his friends that it suffered no injury. I distributed among the islanders everything I had that could please them, and made Parabéry invite them to come and see us in our island, requesting we might live on friendly terms. Mr. Willis wished much to see it, and to complete our happiness he promised to accompany and spend some days with us; and Parabéry said he would take him back when he wished it.

We embarked, then, after taking leave of Bara-ourou, [pg 404] who was very liberal in his presents, giving us, besides fruits of every kind, a whole hog roasted, which was excellent.

We were fourteen in number; sixteen, reckoning the two dogs. The missionary accompanied us, and a young islander, whom Parabéry had procured to be his servant, as he was too old and too much occupied with his mission to attend to his own wants. This youth was of a good disposition and much attached to him. Parabéry took him to assist in rowing when he returned.

Emily could not but feel rather affected at leaving the grotto, where she had passed four tranquil, if not happy years, fulfilling the duties of a mother. Neither could she avoid a painful sensation when she once more saw the sea that had been so fatal to her husband and son; she could scarcely subdue the fear she had of trusting all she had left to that treacherous element. She held her daughters in her arms, and prayed for the protection of Heaven. Mr. Willis and I spoke to her of the goodness of God, and pointed out to her the calmness of the water, the security of the pinnace, and the favourable state of the wind. My wife described to her our establishment, and promised her a far more beautiful grotto than the one she had left, and at last she became more reconciled.

After seven or eight hours' voyage, we arrived at Cape Disappointment, and we agreed the bay should henceforth be called the Bay of the Happy Return.

The distance to Tent House from hence was much too great for the ladies and children to go on foot. My intention was to take them by water to the other end of the island near our house; but [pg 405] my elder sons had begged to be landed at the bay, to seek their live stock, and take them home. I left them there with Parabéry; Jack recommended his buffalo to them, and Francis his bull, and all were found. We coasted the island, arrived at Safety Bay, and were soon at Tent House, where we found all, as we had left it, in good condition.

Notwithstanding the description my wife had given them, our new guests found our establishment far beyond their expectation. With what delight Jack and Francis ran up and down the colonnade with their young friends! What stories they had to tell of all the surprises they had prepared for their mother! They showed them Fritzia, Jackia, the Franciade, and gave their friends water from their beautiful fountain. Absence seemed to have improved everything; and I must confess I had some difficulty to refrain from demonstrating my joy as wildly as my children. Minou-minou, Parabéry, and Canda, were lost in admiration, calling out continually, miti! beautiful! My "wife was busied in arranging a temporary lodging for our guests. The work-room was given up to Mr. Willis; my wife and Madame Emily had our apartment, the two little girls being with them, to whom the hammocks of the elder boys were appropriated. Canda, who knew nothing about beds, was wonderfully, comfortable on the carpet. Fritz, Ernest, and the two natives, stowed themselves wherever they wished, in the colonnade, or in the kitchen; all was alike to them. I slept on moss and cotton in Mr. Willis's room, with my two younger sons. Every one was content, waiting till our ulterior arrangements were completed.

[pg 406]

CONCLUSION.

I must conclude my journal here. We can scarcely be more happy than we are, and I feel no cares about my children. Fritz is so fond of the chase and of mechanics, and Ernest of study, that they will not wish to marry; but I please myself by hoping at some time to see my dear Jack and Francis happily united to Sophia and Matilda. What remains for me to tell? The details of happiness, however sweet in enjoyment, are often tedious in recital.

I will only add, that after passing a few days with us, Mr. Willis returned to his charge, promising to visit us, and eventually to join us. The Grotto Ernestine, fitted up by Fritz and Parabéry, made a pretty abode for Madame Hirtel and her daughters, and the two islanders. Minou-minou did not leave his young mammas, and was very useful to them. I must state, also, that my son Ernest, without abandoning the study of natural history, applied himself to astronomy, and mounted the large telescope belonging to the ship; he acquired considerable knowledge of this sublime science, which his mother, however, considered somewhat useless. The course of the other planets did not interest her, so long as all went on well in that which she inhabited; and nothing now was wanting to her happiness, surrounded as she was by friends.

The following year we had a visit from a Russian vessel, the Neva, commanded by Captain Krusenstern, a countryman and distant relation [pg 407] of mine. The celebrated Horner, of Zurich, accompanied him as astronomer. Having read the first part of our journal, sent into Europe by Captain Johnson, he had come purposely to see us. Delighted with our establishment, he did not advise us to quit it. Captain Krusenstern invited us to take a passage in his vessel; we declined his offer; but my wife, though she renounced her country for ever, was glad of the opportunity of making inquiries about her relations and friends. As she had concluded, her good mother had died some years before, blessing her absent children. My wife shed some tears, but was consoled by the certainty of her mother's eternal felicity, and the hope of their meeting in futurity.

One of her brothers was also dead; he had left a daughter, to whom my wife had always been attached, though she was very young when we left. Henrietta Bodmer was now sixteen, and, Mr. Horner assured us, a most amiable girl. My wife wished much to have her with us.

Ernest would not leave Mr. Horner a moment, he was so delighted to meet with one so eminently skilful in his favourite science. Astronomy made them such friends, that Mr. Horner petitioned me to allow him to take my son to Europe, promising to bring him back himself in a few years. This was a great trial to us, but I felt that his taste for science required a larger field than our island. His mother was reluctant to part with him, but consoled herself with a notion, that he might bring his cousin Henrietta back with him.

Many tears were shed at our parting; indeed, the grief of his mother was so intense, that my son seemed almost inclined to give up his inclination; [pg 408] but Mr. Horner made some observations about the transit of Venus, so interesting that Ernest could not resist. He left us, promising to bring us back everything we wished for. In the mean time Captain Krusenstern left us a good supply of powder, provisions, seeds, and some capital tools, to the great delight of Fritz and Jack. They regretted their brother greatly, but diverted their minds from sorrow by application to mechanics, assisted by the intelligent Parabéry. They have already succeeded in constructing, near the cascade, a corn-mill and a saw-mill, and have built a very good oven.

We miss Ernest very much. Though his taste for study withdrew him a good deal from us, and he was not so useful as his brothers, we found his calm and considerate advice often of value, and his mildness always spread a charm over our circle, in joy or in trouble.

Except this little affliction, we are very happy. Our labours are divided regularly. Fritz and Jack manage the Board of Works. They have opened a passage through the rock which divided us from the other side of the island; thus doubling our domain and our riches. At the same time, they formed a dwelling for Madame Hirtel near our own, from the same excavation in the rock. Fritz took great pains with it; the windows are made of oiled paper instead of glass; but we usually assemble in our large work-room, which is very well lighted.

Francis has the charge of our flocks and of the poultry, all greatly increased. For me, I preside over the grand work of agriculture. The two mothers, their two daughters, and Canda, manage [pg 409] the garden, spin, weave, take care of our clothes, and attend to household matters. Thus we all work, and everything prospers. Several families of the natives, pupils of Mr. Willis, have obtained leave, through him, to join us, and are settled at Falcon's Nest, and at the Farm. These people assist us in the cultivation of our ground, and our dear missionary in the cultivation of our souls. Nothing is wanting to complete our happiness but the return of dear Ernest.

POSTSCRIPT TWO YEARS AFTER.

We are now as happy as we can desire,--our son is returned. According to my wishes, he had made out Captain Johnson and Lieutenant Bell, our first visitors, whom the storm had driven from us, but who were still determined to see us again. My son found them preparing for another voyage to the South Seas. He at once seized the opportunity of accompanying them, impatiently desirous to revisit the island, and to bring to us Henrietta Bodmer, now become his wife. She is a simple, amiable Swiss girl, who suits us well, and who is delighted to see once more her kind aunt, now become her mother.

My wife is overjoyed; this is her first daughter-in-law, but Jack and Francis, as well as Sophia and Matilda, are growing up; and moreover, my dear wife, who has great ideas of married happiness, hopes to induce Emily to consent to be united to Fritz at the same time as her daughters are married. Fritz would feel all the value of this [pg 410] change; his character is already softened by her society, and though she is a few years older than he is, she is blessed with all the vivacity of youth. Mr. Willis approves of this union, and we hope he will live to solemnize the three marriages. Ernest and Henrietta inhabit the Grotto Ernestine, which his brothers fitted up as a very tasteful dwelling. They had even, to gratify their brother, raised on the rock above the grotto a sort of observatory, where the telescope is mounted, to enable him to make his astronomical observations. Yet I perceive his passion for exploring distant planets is less strong, since he has so much to attach him to this.

I give this conclusion of my journal to Captain Johnson, to take into Europe, to be added to the former part. If any one of my readers be anxious for further particulars respecting our colony and our mode of life, let him set out for the Happy Island; he will be warmly welcomed, and may join with us in Ernest's chorus, which we now sing with additional pleasure,--

All we love around us smile,
Joyful is our Desert Isle.

Disclaimer and Terms of Use: The Author and Publisher have strived to be as accurate and complete as possible in the creation of this book, notwithstanding the fact that he does not warrant or represent at any time that the contents within are accurate due to the rapidly changing nature of the Internet. While all attempts have been made to verify information provided in this publication, the Author and Publisher assume no responsibility for errors, omissions, or contrary interpretation of the subject matter herein. Any perceived slights of specific persons, people, or organizations are unintentional. In practical advice books, like anything else in life, there are no guarantees of results. Readers are cautioned to rely on their own judgment about their individual circumstances and act accordingly. This book is not intended for use as a source of legal, medical, business, accounting or financial advice. All readers are advised to seek the services of competent professionals in the legal, medical, business, accounting, and finance fields.

Made in the USA
Coppell, TX
24 November 2020